PURGATORY

Angry Cat Publishing

Printed in Australia
First Printing: November 2022
Second Edition: October 2024

Cover design by Jess Chaplin
Typeset by Jess Chaplin

Paperback ISBN 978-7637549-0-4
Hardback ISBN: 978-1-7637549-2-8
eBook ISBN 978-1-7637549-1-1

Angry Cat designed by Freepik.com

A catalogue record for this work is available from the National Library of Australia

PURGATORY

ROBERT M. SMITH

DEDICATIONS:

For Judi, Reid, Shannyn, Kortnye, Cameron and Ashleyn.

ACKNOWLEDGEMENTS:

While some of the peripheral characters and incidental events are based on real people and occurrences, the main storyline and central characters are entirely fictional. The location and warmth of the community where the novel is set are authentic.

PROLOGUE

If Ferret Igoe had a real first name, nobody knew what it was. He'd arrived in the district fifteen years earlier with his skinny wife, Joan – or Bones, as locals referred to her in private. Ferret scratched out a living as a roustabout at shearing time and helped a handful of farmers sow their crops when the weather broke in autumn. His only permanent employment came over the harvest period when he supervised the receival of grain at Cocamba, a railway siding ten kilometres south of the Mallee township of Manangatang.

With instructions from the Grain Elevators Board to have Cocamba operational by the next Monday, Ferret arrived at the silos on a blistering hot and dusty Wednesday morning. The wind howled through the gap between the steel giants and screamed in the superstructure overhead. Ferret slotted his key into the control room door, instinctively pushing against the corrugated iron to allow the lock to move freely. Once unlatched, the wind caught the door, flinging it back violently against the wall and catching Ferret on the back of a hand already smarting from contact with the hot iron. He entered the metal-clad furnace and activated the mains power. Above him, a fluorescent light flickered to life. Ferret closed his eyes and breathed a sigh of relief that last year's power outage wasn't being repeated. Before commencing a test run of the elevators and augers, he undertook a visual inspection of the facility's exterior, hunting for sticks, branches, dead possums – anything which could foul its operation. Everything was clear.

In the lee of the grain shed, the smell hit him. Somewhere in close proximity was a dead animal, almost certainly a kangaroo, but possibly a stray sheep hit by a vehicle whilst chasing the green pick by the side of the Sea Lake Road. Ferret searched near the highway, looking for roadkill, but found no carcass. With cockies set to deliver grain after the weekend, he was desperate to avoid the criticism and disparagement that would certainly come if the foetor remained. Finding and burying the decaying creature now became his priority. Three laps of the silo area left him bereft of ideas.

It was his kelpie bitch that finally solved the mystery. The human body, or what was left of it, lay on the concrete floor of the giant grain shed, visible only when a sheet of iron was forced open by the ever-strengthening northerly. Ferret shied away and vomited violently into the red dust.

CHAPTER 1

Bowker's road map also told him to turn left at Piangil, to head due west and away from the Murray. The old Peugeot's air conditioner was on full bore and, if not for the roar of its fan, could easily have been declared missing in action. He suspected that had already occurred until he stopped at Nyah for a cold drink fifteen minutes earlier. When he opened the door, he struggled to breathe. The heat was stifling and his car a virtual fridge by comparison. His shoes stuck in the melting bitumen and he immediately stepped back inside the vehicle.

'Don't get out, Rach. I'll leave the motor running. In two minutes, it'll be an oven in here without the air con.'

'Don't be too long. Feels like the wind will flip us over,' Rachael said, her eyes locked on the shimmering mirage cloaking the highway and the journey in front of her.

'Won't be a minute. Coke or a milkshake?'

'What I feel like is cold water. Pity you can't buy a bottle of that. I'll settle for a Coke. One of those medium ones.'

Bowker strode quickly to the café, hoping for cool air inside. Except for the shade, he was disappointed. The shop was hot and stuffy, the air thick with the cloying smell of bananas turning black in a cardboard box by the door. Bowker waved his way through a miasma of tiny flying insects and made his way to the shop counter. An elderly man in torn work pants and a sweat-stained white singlet came through from a residence at the rear. A half-smoked roll-your-own hung from the left confluence of his blistered lips. His body odour rendered the bananas almost pleasant.

'It's the 1980s, mate. Don't you believe in air conditioning?' Bowker quipped.

The shopkeeper smiled, exposing stubby, nicotine stained teeth. 'Got one going in the house. Bloody nice it is too.'

'Why don't you put one in your shop?'

'Do have one in the shop.' He pointed to a unit above the door. 'Just not turned on.'

Bowker sighed loudly. 'It has to be fifty-something degrees out there in the sun! How hot does it have to get before you run the bloody thing?'

The old man remained straight-faced. 'I generally turn it on when it gets to around thirty-five, thirty-six.'

'So why isn't it on now?'

'Because I didn't expect there'd be a dickhead driving around in this heat. Nearly didn't open the shop at all. Most people have enough brains to stay indoors until it cools off a bit.' The shopkeeper suppressed a smile, tapping half an inch of ash from his rollie into a coffee jar lid on the counter.

Bowker knew that at any other time there was truth in what the old man was saying, but not today. 'Yeah, well I'm out there through no choice of my own. I'm chasing bottles of Coke.'

'In the fridge behind you. Bottom shelf.'

Bowker turned and opened the fridge, feeling the cold air roll out on his legs. 'Glad to see you left the fridges on.'

'Bit of a smart arse as well as a dickhead, eh? Where you headed?'

Bowker lingered in the cool air as he gathered the Cokes. 'Manangatang,' he replied as he placed the drinks on the counter.

The old man took a long draw on his cigarette and blew smoke up towards the ceiling. 'Manang, eh? Shit, it'll be hot out there.'

'Unlike here.'

'Always hotter there. We've got trees and the river. All they've got is sand.'

Bowker retrieved his wallet from his back pocket. 'What's the quickest way to get there?'

The shopkeeper paused for a moment as if mentally calculating distances and road surfaces. 'Probably by car,' he said finally.

'Shit, you're a comedian.'

'You could have gone to Chillingollah then turned north and up through Chinkapook to Manang. But the turn off was back towards Tyntynder, so you've missed it.'

'You're just making those places up. Taking the piss.'

The shopkeeper shook his head. 'They're real, mate. But not as thrivin' as they once were. Ghost towns now, really — just a couple of tennis courts, a hall, silos and a handful of houses. Used to have banks, shops, footy teams, the lot. Gollah had the Railway Hotel — a big fancy brick joint. Burnt down in '61, five weeks after the Manang pub went up in flames. Didn't rebuild it. The writing was already on the wall there.'

'What about the Manangatang pub? That get rebuilt?'

The old man laughed out loud. 'Shit yeah! Never missed a beat. Sold grog from trestles in the street while they were puttin' up the new building. That pub sells more beer than any hotel in the state, just about.' He perused a pricelist sticky-taped to the counter and then opened the old-fashioned till with a clang.

Bowker unzipped his wallet. 'So they fancy a drink is what you're saying?'

The shopkeeper smiled. 'Are the Kennedys gun-shy? Manang pub was the first one opened in the entire bloody Mallee. Anyway, that's $1.60 you owe me. Too hot in here to be gas-baggin'. Need to get back under the cooler.'

Bowker handed over a pair of dollar notes. 'Keep the forty cents.'

'Thanks, mate.' The old man's attitude visibly mellowed as he closed the till. 'Look, the best way to get to Manang from here is to go up the highway and turn left at Piangil. There's a big sign that points to Adelaide. You head west towards Ouyen.' He shook his head and exhaled in a low whistle. 'Ouyen; shit, *there* is a hot place!'

'It's always on the news when they do the weather. Top temperature in the state, usually,' Bowker said as he put away his wallet.

'Only in summer, mate. During winter, Mildura always comes out on top. All to do with tourism.' The shopkeeper chuckled. 'Truth be known, Manang would be hotter than both of them. Just don't have a weather station to measure.'

'Great.' Bowker turned to leave.

The shopkeeper butted his cigarette. 'Hey, before you go. Can I interest you in a couple of pound of bananas? I've got 'em on special today. Half price.'

Bowker walked back to the car and felt the cool air hit his sweaty skin when he opened the door. He handed a Coke to Rachael and they both downed half a bottle without saying a word.

***

Bowker made the turn onto the Mallee Highway at Piangil – a one-horse town if ever he'd seen one. A general store, a small post office, a servo, and a cluster of houses was about all it had going for it. But at least it was green.

That changed as they headed west. River red gums and irrigation were almost immediately replaced by stunted Mallee scrub. Paddocks were brown and dry, a roaring northerly tearing at the topsoil, lifting dust in swirling billows. It had been a bad year in the Mallee, but the stubble in the odd paddock was evidence that a few blokes had a crop worth firing up the header.

'I thought it would be flatter than this,' Rachael said as she searched for the horizon behind the shroud of dust.

'Me too,' Bowker nodded. 'But it's just sand hill after bloody sand hill.'

'And scrub. Not a decent tree in sight. How do people live out here, Greg? Especially on days like today.'

Bowker shrugged, his eyes fixed on the debris-covered black serpent leading him ever westward. 'I guess you adapt,' he said hopefully.

Nothing was said for the next ten minutes. Rachel stared through her side window, the savage desolation on the other side of the glass sapping her natural optimism. She was a city girl born and bred but had adapted well to country life in Ballarat. But that was Ballarat – a large, leafy regional centre surrounded by green hills and clear blue lakes. This was a different planet. All she could see was a broiling cauldron of heat and isolation with a ribbon of melting tar disappearing into a wall of swirling dust. This was the road to perdition, she felt sure. Finally, she broke the silence.

'What have we got ourselves into, Greg? Surely we could have found another option. In spite of all the other shit, I loved Ballarat.'

'We couldn't stay there after what happened.'

'But Manangatang! Look out your window, Greg. Bloody hell! Literally!'

His eyes never left the road. 'I was in no position to pick and choose. You know that, Rach. They said I needed a fresh start. Away from Ballarat. Anywhere but Ballarat. They said there's a vacancy at Manangatang. Take it or look for another career.'

'Yeah, I know,' she said in resignation. 'I've been a policeman's wife long enough to understand how the system works.' She was quiet for a few moments then started to chuckle.

Bowker flashed her a glance and smiled. 'What's so funny all of a sudden?'

'When you said you'd been posted to Manangatang I was really happy. I was sure I'd heard of the place. A little town just off the Hume Highway near Seymour, same distance to Melbourne as Ballarat. But when I checked on the map, I realised I was thinking of Mangalore!'

'There's no police station at Mangalore.'

'I know that now! I scanned the map looking for Manangatang, getting further away from Melbourne as I went. Then I found it! God!'

Bowker smiled. 'Look on the bright side: at least I'll be my own boss.'

She affectionately patted his thigh. 'Boss of yourself,' she said with a sarcastic laugh, 'Don't get too carried away with the power.'

'Probably be bored shitless, I'd say. The odd drunk, the occasional driving offence, maybe someone pinching a few sheep. Not exactly Russell Street or even Ballarat Central.'

'A quieter life may be good for you. Take the edge off that ambitious streak that's always rubbed people the wrong way.'

He shrugged. 'Perhaps. Also means I can forget about making detective or the Homicide Squad.'

Things again went quiet as the mile posts slipped by, the occasional roly-poly arriving on the wind and bouncing off the windscreen and over the car. Sticks and bark were lifted from the scrub and flung across the shimmering road. The dust became ever thicker. The temperature outside continued to rise.

Bowker read a sign through the dusty haze. 'Only four hundred and fifty kilometres to Adelaide. I'm glad we don't have to go that far.'

'How long before we're there, you reckon?'

'Twenty minutes should pull us up.'

'I hope so.' Rachael put her bare feet up on the dash in front of her. Bowker stole a glance out of the corner of his eye. Shit she looks good in shorts, he thought. Rachael was in her mid-twenties, a couple of years younger than Bowker. With a background in sport and dance, she was tall and athletic with long tanned legs. She wore her long brown hair tied back in a ponytail. She had beautiful eyes and a smile you'd die for. Bowker grinned. She was a keeper.

Rachael caught his look. 'What are you smiling at?'

'Nothin'.'

'Come on, big boy, fess up.'

'I was just thinkin' that you're a bit of alright, that's all. Willing to stick by me when I was transferred out here.'

'Somebody has to look after you. Besides, I kinda like you. And it wasn't your fault that…'

There was a loud bang.

Rachael's feet came down off the dash. 'What the hell was that?'

'Must have run over a big stick or something. The car is still running okay.'

She frowned and shook her head. 'God, I hope it's not a blown radiator. Not out here. Please no.'

Bowker scanned the old car's primitive instrument panel. 'Temperature gauge is steady. And it's not a tyre, the old girl is steering straight. Perhaps I better stop and look under the bonnet.'

Rachael shook her head vehemently. 'No way! While it's still going, let's just get there.'

'Yeah, probably the best option.' Bowker forced a laugh. 'If I stop and lift the bonnet, I'd die of heat stroke anyway.'

Five or six kilometres passed.

'Greg, I think the air con is blowing hot air,' Rachael said warily. 'It's getting uncomfortably hot.'

Bowker put his palm against a vent. 'Shit!' He reached down and rotated the AC switch.

'How far to go?'

'I keep expecting to see the town over the next rise. But there's so much bloody dust I'm battling to see the front of the car.'

The interior temperature continued to rise. Rachel fanned herself with a magazine and Bowker pulled up the waist of his polo shirt and wiped the sweat from his face.

'I'll have to wind down my window, Rach. I've got the sun on this side and I'm about to cook.' Bowker wound down his window and was immediately mugged by the hot dusty air. 'Shit! Dunno which is worse.'

They drove the next ten minutes with the front windows down and sweat soaking their clothes. Finally, they topped one last rise and there it was, shimmering in the heat and dust. To Rachael it came straight from the pages of *Wake in Fright*.

CHAPTER 2

The signs told them everything they needed to know. Manangatang, population 419, speed restriction 60, rail crossing, stop sign ahead, caution school crossing. Left turn to Sea Lake, right turn to Robinvale, straight ahead to Ouyen and Adelaide. Leaving a school set in spacious but bone-dry grounds to their left, they crossed the railway line and came to a halt at the stop sign. A row of shops headed off to the north, with the odd business straight ahead.

'Centre of the known universe, eh Rach?'

Rachael scanned the main street in disappointment. It was the antithesis of the majestic tree-lined boulevard that was Sturt Street in Ballarat. Except for a couple of recently built small banks, it was a hotchpotch of timber and fibro buildings where design involved little more than a box with a front window, and a bespoke veranda shading the footpath. Maybe there were more substantial structures further up the street, but it was too dusty to see.

In his rear-view mirror Bowker watched a late-model yellow Holden ute exit the school driveway and close in behind him. Bowker scanned both ways checking for traffic before the driver of the ute delivered a long, sustained blast on his horn.

'What's the hurry, dickhead,' Bowker said to himself. As he prepared to cross the Sea Lake–Robinvale road, the yellow ute thundered past him on the wrong side of the road, turned right with an ear-piercing screech and accelerated loudly up past the shops to the north. As the ute sped past, a green-haired, nose-ringed teenage girl in school uniform hung out the passenger-side window, giving Bowker the finger. Bowker looked at Rachael and shook his head in disbelief. He had no way of knowing at the time, but this girl, this same green-haired schoolkid with the nose ring and the errant middle finger, would haunt him for the rest of his days.

'I'll keep those two in mind for when I get settled in and have a decent pursuit vehicle,' Bowker said as he drove slowly past a moisture-starved park separating the two lanes of the highway as it passed through the town.

Rachael pointed ahead. 'That looks like a garage further down the road, Greg. The sooner we get this air con sorted out, the better.'

'Can't it wait till we've moved in? The police car will have air con.'

'Yeah, well I can't drive the police car, can I?'

Central Mallee Motors was a ramshackle affair set four hundred yards up the Ouyen road. Bowker drove the old Peugeot into the shade beside the bowsers, shocked by the 52 cents a litre price for super. As he climbed from the car, a skinny bearded man came out the garage door wiping his greasy hands on an equally greasy towel.

'After some juice, mate?' the garage man said moving towards the bowser. 'It's a fair way to the nearest fuel, so it's best to be sure.'

'Nah, petrol's fine. The air conditioner gave up the ghost halfway from Piangil.'

Garageman chuckled. 'Picked a good day. Still, coulda been worse if you believe the forecast for tomorra. S'posed to warm up a bit. Flick the bonnet and I'll take a look.'

Bowker reached into the car and released the bonnet. Garageman unclipped the hood and lifted it up. He waved away the heat with his towel and poked his head into the engine compartment, feeling belts and hoses. 'You've lost your air con drive belt, mate.' He stood up straight and looked at Bowker. 'It's a wonder you didn't hear it go. Sometimes when they give way, they hit the underside of the hood with a hell of a bang.'

Bowker chuckled. 'Don't worry, we heard it.' He placed his left elbow on the car roof, then quickly pulled it away as his skin burnt. 'So, I'm guessing it won't need re-gassing or any of that specialist stuff?'

Garageman wiped his hands on his towel. 'Wouldn't think so. If she was pumpin' cool air when the belt broke, then I'd say your compressor's workin' fine. Only a fifteen-minute job to get you goin' again. Loosen off the pulley, fit the belt and then tension everything up again.'

'Have you got time to do it now?'

'I have.'

'Great.'

''Cept I haven't got a belt that'll fit.' He slammed down the bonnet. 'Have to order it from Swan Hill. It should be over tomorra or the day after. That's if they've got one. For these older models, it might have to come from Adelaide.'

Bowker frowned. 'Don't you carry spares?'

'If you had a Holden or a Ford, or certain models of Jap crap I could help you. But these frogmobiles are pretty thin on the ground out this way.' He smiled as he wiped the bonnet with his towel, leaving grease smears on the duco.

Rachael climbed out of the car, legs first.

Garageman was taken aback. 'Whoa! No wonder it was hot in the car.'

Bowker was not in the mood. 'Hot in the car because the air con broke down? Is that what you're saying, mate? I'm Senior Constable Bowker, by the way. I'm the new copper in town. And this is Rachael.'

Garageman was flustered for a moment, then put out an oily hand to shake. 'Ray Gregson. Everybody calls me Greasy. You know, always covered in grease and oil.'

Rachael was keen to keep moving. 'So, what's the bottom line, Greg?'

'Bring it back in few days when Mr Gregson gets the right part.'

Gregson ogled Rachael as she climbed back into the car, then wolf-whistled to himself as they drove away.

***

The police station and residence was on the main drag, on the corner of Wattle and Coghill Streets, a block north of the main shopping area. The house was a recent build, a comfortable brick veneer with a police station and cell attached. Bowker found the fuse box and turned on the power. He removed the keys from a brown envelope in his pocket and threw them to Rachael.

'Want me to carry you over the threshold?'

'Too hot. I'll walk thanks.'

Rachael led the way through the front door. The temperature inside was stifling. 'Brick veneer. Good choice for summers like this,' she said sarcastically.

'But think about the wintertime. It'll be nice and cosy.' Bowker closed the door behind him then put his arm around her shoulders. 'I bet after a week or two, we won't even feel the heat.'

Rachael mellowed. 'A likely story, senior constable.'

Inside the house, they quickly went their own way, Bowker heading straight through to the police station. He smiled to himself as he surveyed his new domain. A spacious area behind a front counter, a large glass-topped office desk, two filing cabinets at the rear, and most importantly, a modern refrigerated air conditioner. A door at the side led to a toilet and a secure lock-up. He flicked on the air con and scanned the notices on a pinboard as they fluttered in the cooling breeze. He tore down a wanted notice for an Ararat prison escapee he knew had been apprehended a week earlier in Albury. In the centre of the board was a large poster warning farmers to lock their houses and sheds when they were away. Obviously not a regular practice in the sticks, he thought to himself. The corner of the board displayed a list of emergency phone numbers, along with contacts for neighbouring police stations. He sat down and read a note left on his desk by his predecessor, Senior Constable Roy Pace.

Welcome to Manangatang. The climate is brutal, but if you embrace all the district has to offer then you'll enjoy your time here. You will have received my official handover brief, but I've jotted down a few personal observations to give you a heads-up.

- *There is very little criminal activity within the district.*
- *Touch wood, but so far I have seen little evidence of illicit drug use, although there are rumours that marijuana is being brought south from Robinvale or Mildura. (I guess no community is immune forever.)*
- *Alcohol causes the biggest headaches in the area, especially the tolerance of underage drinking in some quarters.*
- *Every now and again a few of the local lads behave like dickheads, especially with hoon driving. If you reckon a couple of blokes need a good kick up the arse, do a swap with Robinvale one Saturday night. Let them do the dirty work so you stay sweet with the natives.*
- *Occasionally trouble comes from outside of town like some blow-in running away from something, or a drug addict driving through and trying to knock over the chemist shop looking for a hit. Very rare, but it has happened.*
- *Keep an eye on Greasy Gregson at the garage. Some of the women won't go there for fuel because he's such a sleaze. He hasn't broken any laws, but I don't trust the bastard as far as I can throw him. Have spoken to him a couple of times, but he says he's just being friendly! Only a matter of time before one of the local blokes decks the prick.*
- *I've had words with a new kid at the school who's moved up from Melbourne. If there's anything suss happening in town, she's up to her armpits in it. Her name's Yvonne Bryant, and I'll wager you'll come across her before your first week is up.*
- *Keep your eyes open for bloody snakes!*

Pace signed off at the bottom, wished his replacement luck and left a Portland phone number where he could be contacted if needed. Bowker reread the list. He smiled to himself as he folded the paper, acknowledging he'd felt like decking Ray Gregson himself and he'd been in town less than ten minutes.

Rachael quickly completed her inspection tour of the house. She'd heard tales of primitive police housing in remote areas, some dating back to the early 1900s. Bowker had promised her that the Manangatang residence was virtually brand new, but given the bullshit surrounding Bowker's transfer to the town, who could believe anything they were told? The house was no mansion, but it looked comfortable enough. A switch on the passage wall labelled *A/C* was good news as well. She flicked the switch and a unit above her head roared into action. She slid up a window in the living area and one above the sink in the kitchen. The curtains blew hard against the fly-wire screens and within moments a cooling breeze made everything seem a smidgeon better.

Bowker found her in the kitchen. 'How about we leave unloading the car until it cools off a bit outside?'

'Let's hope it does.' She paused for a moment, looking up at the policeman. 'I knew we were going bush, Greg, but I didn't realise this place was so isolated.'

'Out of sight, out of mind. Their problem solved, I guess.' Bowker shrugged. 'Then again, we're unlikely to run into the bastard way out here, so there's a positive.'

Rachael nodded. 'Yeah.' She looked back into the empty house. 'What time is the furniture due tomorrow?'

'Mid-afternoon, they reckon. I won't care if it's closer to evening. Forecast is for another hot one, apparently.'

She closed her eyes. 'Oh, great.'

'But less wind,' he added.

'S'pose that's something.' She rested her head on Bowker's shoulder.

***

The couple celebrated the first day of their new life with soggy sandwiches and warm orange juice brought from Ballarat in an Esky originally stacked with ice but now quarter-filled with water. As the sun went down it became marginally cooler and Bowker unloaded the car, not that much had fitted into the old Pug anyway. Just a pair of suitcases, a couple of pillows, two rubber camping mats, and making Bowker smile, two sleeping bags.

By the time they'd finished tea, washed up and set up makeshift sleeping arrangements it was nearly dark. Bowker went to the bathroom, stripped off and stood under the shower, allowing cool water to cascade over his head and down his body, feeling the day's heat leech from his very core. Through the glass he saw Rachael enter the bathroom and throw off her clothes.

'Is there room in there for two?' she asked.

'Absolutely,' he answered quickly.

As Rachael entered the shower, Bowker forgot about the horrific weather, the car troubles and the isolation of his posting. All things considered, this had the makings of a good day.

CHAPTER 3

The furniture truck arrived earlier than expected, the driver and his offsider keen to be out of the Mallee before the worst of the heat. Both men wore shorts, steel-capped boots and singlets printed with the company name and logo. Both were tanned and heavily muscled, their job as effective as a gym membership. The truck driver looked in his mid-thirties with a tattooed sleeve on his right arm and some artistic ink work on his back and legs. His offsider was younger and sported prison tatts, indistinct patterns and lettering up his arm. The truck was unloaded by one o'clock and the removalists, hot and sweaty, were keen to hit the road. The driver pointed at two wardrobes on the ground in the back yard. 'Do you want those inside before we go?'

'The house has built-in robes so we don't really need them,' Bowker replied. 'I'll figure out where to put them when we get the house set up.'

'Then we'll head off, mate,' the offsider said. 'Sooner we leave, the sooner we'll be back to bloody civilisation.'

The driver shook his head as he climbed up into the cabin of the Isuzu. 'Dunno how people live up here,' he said. 'Shouldn't be hard being a copper though. Too hot to get up to anything dodgy.'

Bowker laughed. 'I hope you're right. You blokes drive carefully, okay? Don't want a truck accident on my second day in town.'

The driver looked down at the policeman. 'Don't worry about us, mate. We do this for a livin'. These local yokels are the ones you need to watch. Fire up their trucks once a year for harvest. Bloody menace.'

The truck left for parts down south, its big diesel engine roaring with each gear change. Bowker watched it turn into Wattle Street then, just as he was about to retreat to the cool of the house, he saw its passenger side indicators come on and the truck shuddered to a halt under a line of sugar gums opposite the pub. The driver and his mate crossed the street and disappeared into the town's most lucrative business house.

Rachael was storing sheets and pillowcases in a linen closet when Bowker wandered up the passage, mopping his brow with a handkerchief. 'The furniture boys only got as far as the pub,' he said as he gathered a pile of pillowcases from a cardboard box and handed them to his better half.

'Does that worry you?' she asked as she stretched to put the linen on the top shelf.

'They're not breaking any laws as long as the driver sticks to a lemon squash. Truck drivers have a double zero limit if they're in charge of vehicles rated above fifteen tonne Gross Weight.'

'Are you goin' down to check?'

'Well, I have to, really. Just because they delivered our stuff shouldn't change things. If I saw them moving somebody in next door and they went to the pub, I'd be onto them in a flash.'

'Nothin' much for a copper to do in a small town, everybody said. Piece of cake, they reckon.' She laughed and touched him on the end of the nose with her finger.

'Yeah, I know. Been here for a day and I've already got a tricky one. Not even officially on duty yet.'

Bowker, dressed in civvies, drove slowly to the pub, pondering the best way to handle this. If the driver had consumed just the one beer and was heading straight back to Ballarat, then Bowker knew he'd be labelled a prick if he booked him. Then again, maybe if he came down hard it would show the locals he wasn't taking any crap. What did new teachers say? Don't smile till Easter?

Bowker parked in the shade behind the truck and crossed the road to the hotel. From the murmur of voices, he judged there were more patrons inside than just the two furniture blokes, but it didn't sound like a big crowd. He pushed open the door and the bar immediately fell silent, the noise vanishing with the escaping cool air. The truck driver and his mate were sitting on bar stools, each cradling a pot containing the dregs of a beer. A group of locals was sitting at a round table in the centre of the room taking in the unusual spectacle of three strangers in the pub at the same time.

The driver broke the silence. 'So, you need a cool one as well, Sarg?'

There was a murmur from the locals' table as the town's new policeman was identified. A couple of patrons shot a look towards the barman.

'Wish it was that easy. And at this stage I'm still only a senior constable. You know what the law says about drinking alcohol and driving trucks. Or at least you should know.'

'Only having the one,' the driver said brightly. 'Just opening up the throat. We've got an esky full of ice water in the truck. That's all we'll be drinking until we get back to Ballarat.' He put his hand on his heart. 'I promise.'

Bowker was having none of it. 'The limit is double zero for driving a truck that size, and I'm afraid you're both over that already.'

The driver held up his glass. 'Come on, mate. It's one beer,' he said.

'Then you'll be one beer over the limit,' Bowker replied quickly.

'I'll lose my job if I get done for drinkin' on the job.'

'Well the good news is that right now you haven't broken any laws,' Bowker said. 'But the moment you slip behind the wheel of that truck, I'll put the breathalyser on you.' Bowker turned to the barman. 'Are they drinking heavy or light?'

'Heavy. Carlton Draft, this bloke,' the barman reluctantly replied as he pointed to the driver, 'and VB the other fella.'

'At the moment, you'll both probably blow about .02,' Bowker told the men.

The driver slid off his stool. 'We've got to get the truck back to Ballarat to reload. We're going to Canberra tomorrow,' he said.

'Don't have any more to drink and you can leave here in about two hours.' Bowker looked at his watch. 'Should get you home in plenty of time.'

'What do we do for two fuckin' hours?' the offsider asked heatedly.

'I suggest you stay here in the cool,' Bowker replied without expression.

'What? Sit in a bar and not have a drink? That'd be torture in this weather,' the driver said.

'I didn't say you couldn't drink. I said you couldn't drink alcohol. The pub will have plenty of lemon squash or Coke or soda water, I'm sure.' Bowker smiled. 'Can I see your licences, please.'

The driver irately opened his wallet and removed his licence. 'You'll find everything is spot on.' He shook his head. 'Fuck me.'

Bowker took the licence and studied it closely, turning it over to read the back. 'All good. Got all the correct heavy endorsements. Thanks, Sean.' He handed it back. 'Now what about you mate?'

'I'm not the driver,' said Sean's offsider.

'Maybe not. But I'll still check your licence in case Sean here gets a bit tired on the way home and needs a break.'

'I'm disqualified for twelve months. Had a few too many, a few too many times.'

'Well that makes it easy, doesn't it? You can have a beer if you want, but don't even think about driving that truck.'

The offsider exhaled loudly. 'I'm not a fuckin' idiot.'

'I hope not.' Bowker turned back to the driver. 'Now, Sean, I'm going to be watching that truck until three thirty. If it leaves before then, I'll be straight down the road after you.'

'You've made your bloody point,' the driver said as he turned to the barman and theatrically ordered a lemon squash.

'I might even wander up later and put the breatho on you just to make sure you haven't downed a sly one.'

Bowker turned to leave. One of the locals had some advice. 'Bit hard on the lads, mate. I often sneak a beer when I bring a load into the silo. Last copper didn't say anything.'

'Probably to do with the size of your rig,' Bowker replied.

'Everybody knows you've got a small one, Thumper,' one of the other locals joked. All his mates laughed.

Thumper continued. 'My point is, that out in these areas you gotta give a little, if you know what I mean.'

'I'm willing to give whatever I can. But one thing I won't give is the green light to break the law.'

The driver yelled across the room. 'Hey, officer. Sorry I called you Sarg before. If I'd known you were a constable I could have come up with a more appropriate abbreviation.'

'Three thirty at the earliest. I'll be watching,' Bowker said, as he turned and left.

The locals sniggered. 'He's got a lot to learn, Wombat,' Bowker heard one of them say.

***

Rachael walked out of the kitchen when she heard the front door open. 'How'd it go? Were they sneaking a drink?'

'Yeah, already downed a pot by the time I got there.' Bowker threw his keys on the hall table. 'The house is nice and cool, Rach.'

'Yeah, it's beautiful inside. Helps put things into perspective. So, what happened when you sprung them?'

'The driver is the only one with a current licence. His mate is disqualified. I told the driver not to consume any more alcohol and not to drive the truck before three thirty.' Bowker walked into the kitchen and took a jug of water from the fridge.

'Won't be cold yet,' Rachael said. 'Fridge's only been on for an hour or so.'

'Better than out of the tap.'

'Do you reckon they'll wait till three thirty?'

'I told them I'd be watching.' Bowker poured two glasses of water and passed one to Rachael.

'He'll probably sneak the odd beer while he's waiting,' she said.

'Warned him that I might breatho him before he leaves.'

'And will you?' She took a sip of water.

'Don't think I'll need to. My gut feeling is he'll do the right thing. He's on a warning from his boss, I reckon.' Bowker downed the water in one go and put the glass on the sink.

'Any locals in the pub?'

'Half a dozen. One of them was called Thumper. Bit of a mouth. They called another one Wombat.'

Rachael laughed. 'Wombat? Thumper? Greasy? Has everyone around here got a nickname?'

'I think I was given one at the pub.'

'Yeah. What?'

'A name that shouldn't be used in front of a lady.'

Rachael put her arms around his neck. 'So I'm presuming it wasn't Hunk or Spunk or Stud?'

'Cut it out, you're embarrassing me.'

She reached up on her toes and kissed him on the cheek, then released her arms. 'What do you feel like for tea?'

'What about we hit the pub for a counter meal? We can test the water. See if word has spread that the new copper is a prick.'

'What do I wear to impress?'

'Whatever you wear will impress. I'm sure they'd be impressed even if you wore nothing.'

Rachael pushed an index finger against his chest. 'I think you're biased.'

'You could strip off so I can check.'

'Too cold in here for that!'

'I could turn off the air con.'

'Don't you dare!'

The doorbell rang. Bowker looked quizzically at Rachael, walked to the front entrance and opened the screen door. Standing on the doorstep was a short, rotund man in his forties with a weathered friendly face and wearing brown-rimmed glasses. With a big smile, he thrust out his hand. 'Ian Lyon's the name. Everyone calls me Prong. Welcome to Manang.'

Rachael smiled at yet another nickname as they ushered their visitor into the kitchen. With no furniture arranged, Prong lifted himself backwards onto the bench beside the sink. 'Been drafting lambs at Bullpup Graham's place out near Annuello. Saw your car here and thought I'd drop in and say g'day. I'm a livestock agent, by the way.'

Bowker leant against the fridge. 'Pretty hot day to be working with sheep,' he said.

Prong laughed. 'If I waited for a cool day, the lambs would be mutton by the time I saw them. So where are you from?'

'Ballarat,' Rachael said. 'Bit cooler down there.'

'Been there twice,' Prong said. 'Froze me nuts off both times.' He laughed again. 'Bet you couldn't believe your luck when you were posted to Manang?'

Rachael smiled. 'You're right there. Couldn't believe our luck.'

'New house, plus all the town has to offer. Pretty sought-after place apparently. My brother's a copper at Wangaratta over in the north-east. Keep asking him when he's coming back home, but he reckons the competition's pretty hot for these one-man stations in the bush.'

Bowker looked at Rachael who had dragged in a kitchen chair from the hall. 'I told you we'd lucked-in, Rach.'

'I realised this wouldn't be another Ballarat, but the town's a lot smaller than I expected,' Rachael said brightly, disguising her disappointment in the town's appearance.

'Not as big as a couple decades ago,' Prong explained, 'and a few businesses have closed down. But still, it's doing better than a lot of places. The town was a regional centre at one stage, believe it or not. You should see the old photos. The place was buzzing with activity.

Do you know the history of the area?'

'Only that the original farmers were soldier settlers after the first world war,' Bowker replied.

'Yeah. The government gave them a square mile block of uncleared scrub. That's only six hundred and forty acres, so it's not very much in Mallee terms. A lot of blokes couldn't make a go of it. But others with the better ground did. In the early days, a decent block fed a family, plus its workers and their families.'

'But not today, obviously?' Bowker surmised.

'Nah. One family on ten or fifteen thousand acres nowadays, and the families are much smaller as well. One cocky buys out the blokes around him and with modern machinery needs bugger-all help with the cropping. Used to be a whole football league centred around Manang. Now it's just Manang, and one day we'll need to merge with someone else.'

'Sad really,' Rachael said.

'That's progress, they say.' Prong paused, then rubbed his hands together. 'Now, down to the important stuff. You play sport? Tennis, cricket, footy, netball?'

Rachael looked at Bowker and was first to respond. 'I play netball and we both love tennis. Greg played A Pennant in Ballarat, but I haven't seen him play footy.'

Prong looked up at Bowker towering above him. 'Built like a football player. Have to be six-four?'

'About that,' Bowker said. He was not only tall but broad shouldered as well. A good cut of a bloke, his father had once said. Sandy hair, with brown eyes and a strong jaw line. And he was in good physical nick. Hadn't let himself go like some coppers did once they'd graduated. 'I haven't played footy since juniors, Prong. So not likely to take it up again at the ripe old age of twenty-seven.'

'We'll see,' Prong said with a grin. 'Everybody plays some sort of sport in this town, regardless of ability. Involvement's the name of the game, out here.' Prong dropped the volume of his voice and spoke in covert tones. 'My tennis team's always on the lookout for new players. Been premiers the last four years in a row.'

Rachael frowned. 'You wouldn't play in this heat though, surely?'

'Got a rule. If 3SH announces it's over 38 at eleven o'clock on Saturday morning, then tennis is supposed to be called off.' Prong chuckled. 'But usually, the two captains agree to play regardless. Amazing what a wet towel around your shoulders and a quick trip to the pub between sets can do.' Prong slapped himself on the thighs and slipped down off the bench. 'Anyway, can't stay here all-day gasbagging. A big Manang welcome to you both. Yell out if you need anything.' He shook their hands then waved over his shoulder as he walked to his car. As he opened the door, he turned and called back. 'Don't let the old bastard in the chemist shop feed you any bullshit about his tennis team. They're a bloody rabble.'

***

After lunch, Bowker braved the heat to store the plywood wardrobes left baking out of shape in the back yard. Cluttering up the new garage wasn't a practical option, and to Bowker putting indoor furniture on a veranda wasn't aesthetically pleasing. That was despite its popularity among a few households he'd noticed coming in. Behind the garage was an old, corrugated iron shed. With some effort, he heaved the door open, breaking the top hinge and jamming a bottom corner into the dirt. It was dark but hot inside, with tiny shafts of light streaming through nail holes in the iron. A pair of long horizontal rods covered in white droppings, and a row of decaying laying boxes lining the back wall, told Bowker the structure had once been a chook shed. How the hell could poultry survive in here in this weather, he thought. Instant roast chicken on days like today.

The chooks were long gone, and the shed was now piled with junk. A couple of decaying tea chests sat beside the door, the final resting place of yellowed and tattered chronicles of yesterday's news.

In the opposite corner were the skeletons of at least three old mowers, some derelict fishing gear, a pile of rabbit traps and an assortment of rotting bags filled with who-knew-what. Bowker shook his head and reluctantly accepted he'd eventually need to clean out this old fire trap, or alternatively just pull the damn thing down. But, for now it could house the wardrobes, providing he could rearrange all the junk to fit them in.

As he dragged the first three-ply tea chest out through the door, a fountain of mice erupted from the box, scampering in all directions. Bowker recoiled in surprise. He sheepishly checked his surrounds, relieved to find no-one watching. He smiled to himself. *Hey, everybody, the new cop just shat himself over a few mice. How long will he last in the Mallee?* He re-entered the shed and hauled out the second chest, this time thumping its side with the palm of his hand, provoking the immediate evacuation of another dozen tiny rodents. At the top of the box were tattered newspapers with a *Manangatang Courier* masthead. *This town has a newspaper? There's bugger-all people here*, he thought. He straightened a fold and read the date of publication. May 27, 1928. Inside the paper he found cricket scores, advertisements for shops and products that no longer existed, and articles about the district. He drove his hand into the box to retrieve more editions when the pile stirred of its own accord and the unmistakable head of a brown snake pushed aside the papers as it made its way over the edge of the box and down to the ground.

'Fuck!' Bowker jumped backwards. A brilliant shiny bronze colour and perfectly patterned, the snake seemed to go on forever. In the paralysed policeman's mind, it conjured images of an endless train passing through a rail crossing when you're in a hurry. Bowker didn't move until the snake had disappeared into the dry grass behind the shed. He then sprinted inside, returning thirty seconds later with his service revolver in hand. Rachael followed him out. 'Aren't snakes protected?' she said.

'I'll look up the regulations after I shred the bastard.'

Rachael progressed no further than the veranda. 'Be careful. He could be anywhere in that long grass.'

Bowker tentatively crossed the yard. 'There could be a hundred of them, for all I know.'

'Remember, he's probably more scared of you, than you are of him.'

Bowker looked back at her. 'You reckon? I bet *he* doesn't need to change his pants!'

Bowker picked up a disused tomato stake from the abandoned vegetable garden and began probing the knee-length grass in front of him. After ten minutes, he was satisfied the snake was gone for the time being, the bottom rail off the back fence leaving plenty of room for its escape. And plenty of room for its return.

***

Bowker elected to give the removalists the benefit of the doubt when he watched their truck depart the town at precisely three thirty. Well done, boys. Have a safe journey. He spent the rest of the afternoon studying the Country Fire Authority's detailed maps to help orient himself with the area's roads and farming properties. Tomorrow's mission would be a tour to inspect the district with a naked eye. Tonight, the plan was a quiet counter tea with the girl of his dreams. A few hours to relax and get a feel for the place and its people. That's what he thought anyway.

CHAPTER 4

The sun was still a flaming ball, but the temperature was slowly falling and the shadows lengthening as Bowker and Rachael made the short stroll towards the pub. This was their first public appearance together and first impressions were important in a small community such as this. Those not in town this evening would receive a briefing about the new copper and his missus via the bush telegraph. Thus, many in the district would have their minds made up before they'd even laid eyes on the couple, their views focussed through the lens of others. Bowker wore jeans with a neat grey and navy-blue polo shirt although he craved to be in shorts and thongs. Rachael sported a pair of denim cut-offs, a silky pink blouse and a pair of flat shoes. Fashionable, but not over-the-top.

Manangatang's main shopping area was concentrated on the western side of Wattle Street and stretched two blocks from Ouyen Road to the police station on the Coghill Street corner. Most businesses at the northern end of the street were service providers, Red Cameron's stock and station agency, Tuppence Pengilly the plumber's workshop, a new Westpac bank on the corner across from the pub. Opposite were enormous grain silos, two older concrete monoliths and several others constructed of heavy steel.

Dominating in this block was the Manangatang Hall, an uninspiring timber and cement sheet construction where, in less than twelve months, this small community's world would begin its spiral into darkness.

At the Westpac bank, the couple crossed Rainbow Street and stood on the pub corner. A few cars were parked on the other side of the road outside the only three shops on that side of the street. Next to the silos was Trimble's hardware-and-anything-else-you-might-want store, further up Prong's stock agency and then Billy Carroll's butcher shop. A few cars dotted the main side of the street. Bowker and Rachael ambled along the footpath prior to their counter tea taking in the shops, a second bank, a supermarket, a newsagency, a café, a bakery, and a pharmacy. Another dozen shopfronts stretched further to the south.

The sound of the pharmacy door sliding closed halted their stroll. Pharmacist Terry Rivers turned the key in the lock and walked over. Terry was about fifty, was rapidly balding with grey hair on the sides of his round head Friar Tuck style. Physically, he was in good nick for his age. He wore wire-rimmed glasses, long grey walk socks and a white chemist's coat concealing a pair of shorts.

He thrust out a hand. 'Terry Rivers. And you must be the new copper.'

'Greg Bowker,' the policeman said shaking hands and feeling his fingers being crushed. 'And this is my better half, Rachael.'

'I'm so glad there's a chemist in the town,' Rachael said as the pharmacist gently shook her hand.

'How'd you end up in this dump, Greg? Shoot the chief commissioner's dog and get sent off to Purgatory?'

'Something like that,' Bowker replied with a guilty chuckle. 'Just looking for a change of scenery, actually. Thought I'd slow down and be my own boss.'

'I bet this place is a shock to the system, Rachael?' Terry said with a chuckle.

'I'm pretty adaptable. I'll get used to it,' she said cheerily, disguising her doubts with a wide smile.

'You been here long, Terry?' Bowker asked.

'A few years now. I worked in Swan Hill before I bought this shop to run my own business. Last bloke abandoned it decades ago. It doesn't really pay its way. I can't purchase in bulk, because my turnover is so low. I can buy things cheaper from a Swan Hill pharmacy than I can get them wholesale, so my profit is bugger-all. Luckily, I'm subsidised by the hospital to keep the shop open as a community service. Same with the doctors. They're on a retainer to practice here, plus they get a house and the new clinic thrown in. Whatever they make from patients is a bonus. Young South Australian husband and wife team here now. In a few years, they'll be cashed up enough to buy into a practice in the city somewhere.'

Rachael swatted away a fly. 'You here for good?'

'I'll stay until I'm sick of the joint and then the shop will be shut for good. Nobody in their right mind will buy me out, so I'll finish up on the aged pension.' Terry smiled broadly. 'Actually, I could have retired when I first took possession of the shop. Amongst the old stock was a giant jar filled to the brim with pure heroin. Like a fool I washed it down the sink!'

Bowker shook his head in disbelief that quantities like that were kept and left lying around. Then again, earlier in the century, heroin was regarded as just another pain killer. 'You did the right thing getting rid of it,' he said. 'That stuff makes you a target.'

'I only carry enough opiates to make up prescriptions. They're kept in a pissy little wall safe that any kid could open. Prefer to be burgled than woken up by some crazed addict in the middle of the night. Happened once. A bloke from Adelaide had a knife and everything. I've also had the safe stolen. Ripped right off the wall. Found out the Ouyen road with the door jimmied off it.'

Bowker took Rachael by the hand and started to move off. 'Be sure to give me a call if you notice anything suspicious or a stranger hanging around for no reason.'

Terry raised a hand. 'Hey, before you go. I heard you play tennis. I've got a team called Renegades. Got a couple of vacancies in the A grade.'

Bowker smiled. 'We've already been asked.'

'By a little fat bastard called Prong, I bet. His team is already loaded with talent, doesn't need any more.'

'Decisions, decisions,' Rachael said with a laugh.

'Don't stress too much. It's all just a bit of fun,' Terry said. 'If you're gonna survive in a dump like this, you have to see the funny side of things.'

If only he knew what was ahead.

***

All eyes locked onto the new couple when they walked into the pub lounge. Bowker smiled and said g'day to people as he led Rachael by the hand to a vacant table at the back of the room. 'I'll just grab us a drink.'

Bowker strolled to a small counter which opened onto the main bar next door and was quickly attended by the same barman who had served the removalists in the afternoon. He was shortish in stature, wore a beard and was in terrific physical condition.

'Can't keep away from the place, mate?' the barman asked with a smile.

'Social visit this time. Rachael and I thought we'd sample one of your counter teas.'

'Best in the Mallee. What are you drinking?'

'Lemon, lime and bitters and a pot of Tab, thanks.'

The barman constructed Rachael's drink then poured the Tab from a half empty bottle. That'll be as flat as possum piss, Bowker thought, but said nothing.

The barman offered his hand across the counter. 'Anyway, I'm Rick Brennan. Father-in-law owns this place.' They shook hands.

Bowker studied Brennan's face for a moment. 'You're not Rick Brennan, the league footballer? Melbourne footy club?'

'That's me. Fifty-three games for the Mighty Dees.'

'Pretty young to be giving it away.'

'Knees are shot, but I'm not hanging up the boots just yet. I'm captain-coach of the local team. Manangatang Saints. What do they say? There's no fool like an old fool.'

'VFL to a bush league. Bit of a drop down in standard in one hit.'

'I planned to play in Mildura, but the locals made it clear that if Manang was good enough to support our business, then its footy team was good enough for me to coach.' He chuckled. 'Probably turned out for the good. Don't have to make the two-hundred-mile round trip to Mildura three times a week. Don't have to dodge a thousand bloody roos at the Hattah lakes in the evening.' He smiled and said quietly 'Plus, they pay me more to coach here than I was offered to play up there. You play?'

'Not since junior days.'

'Come down and have a run with us when training starts. Haven't got a lot of blokes your size.'

'I'll see how the job pans out before I make any commitments.' Bowker felt for his wallet. 'How much do I owe you?'

'Dollar fifty'll do.'

Bowker put a two dollar note on the counter. 'Near enough. Thanks mate.' He picked up the drinks and turned towards his table where Rachael was reading the menu.

Rick called after him. 'Before you go, Greg, those two blokes in the furniture truck.'

Bowker returned to the counter. 'Yeah?'

'As they were leaving, the VB drinker bought two six-packs of stubbies.'

'No law against him having a few travellers. He's not the driver.'

'One of the packs was Carlton Draught.'

Bowker was immediately fired up. 'The bastards! Thanks mate.' Bowker returned the drinks to his table. 'Sorry, Rach. Got to leave you on your own for ten minutes. Explain when I get back.' Bowker left in a hurry, leaving Rachael to contemplate her drink and feign another perusal of the menu. Twenty pairs of eyes watched her every move.

A tall, attractive woman in her late twenties with her hair tied back in a ponytail and wearing shorts and a light singlet top wandered over. 'Hi, I'm Judi,' she said as she sat down. 'I gather the new police officer has arrived. You must be Rachael.'

Word spreads quickly, Rachael thought. 'Came up yesterday. Just settling in.'

Judi laughed. 'You picked the right weather for it.'

Rachael leant forward. 'Is it always like this?'

'Most of the time it's fantastic,' Judi replied with a don't-worry wave of her hand. 'But this heat can be scary when you first arrive. My husband and I are teachers and we first saw Manang on a day like yesterday. We came up to check out accommodation and meet the principal and staff. The place was a furnace with a wall of dust rolling in from the west. When we found the school, the staff and kids were running around having a big water fight. Some of the males were in their jocks – and that included the teachers!' They both laughed.

'It's a wonder you didn't turn around and get out of the place. To be honest, that's what I felt like doing yesterday.'

Judi smiled. 'Don't worry, that's happened. A female graduate came up and left on the first day. Didn't even see the kids. Must admit, I've never seen a dust storm like it. Black as night. All the streetlights came on in the middle of the day.'

'Obviously you've toughed it out.'

'We love it. Town's like one big family. We've had two children in Manang and there's no better place to raise kids. You won't regret coming here, I guarantee it.' Judi put both palms on the table and spoke more seriously. 'Now, down to business. I coach the A grade netball. The team hasn't won a premiership since 1960 and I intend to change that. I've got some super talented kids, just need a few older heads. You look like the sporty type.'

Rachael shrugged. 'I guess so. I've played a lot of things. Tennis, basketball, netball, plus a bit of aths.'

Judi slapped her palms together. 'Great. I'll let you know when training starts.' She glanced across the room. 'I'd better get back to my table. The littlies are becoming a bit restless.'

Rachael resumed her faux menu analysis until Bowker returned after a couple of minutes. 'Sorry to leave you in the lurch, Rach, but I reckon the furniture truck driver had a few beers after he'd safely exited the town. I calculate he'd be three quarters of the way back to Ballarat. I've contacted the boys at St Arnaud and asked them to pull him over and run a breatho if he goes home that way.'

Rachael raised her eyebrows and smiled. 'Less than two days here and you're already controlling half the state. So much for a bludge job.'

'Let's order. I'm hungry enough to eat a horse.'

'You're in luck. It's on the menu.'

'You're joking! Tell me you're joking.'

'Of course I'm joking.'

***

After a terrific home-style meal and some social chit-chat with the locals, Bowker and Rachael left the hotel, hand in hand. It was now totally dark and, without the dust of the night before, the sky was virtually white, a lacework of stars.

'Every person on earth should see this,' Bowker said as he stared into the heavens. 'Puts everything else into perspective, don't you reckon?'

'Certainly better than yesterday,' Rachael replied, gazing at the gossamer firmament.

Passing the vacant block adjoining the hotel, they heard adolescent voices beneath a large peppercorn tree, the drooping canopy of which roofed much of the grassless area and brushed the ground to form a natural hiding place. Bowker thought nothing of it until he heard the clinking of bottles.

'Who's under the tree there? This is Senior Constable Bowker.'

'We're just under here waiting for our parents to come out of the bar,' said a disembodied voice.

'Come out here where I can see you, please,' Bowker ordered.

Two boys gingerly edged forward into the half-light cast by one of the pub windows. The younger-looking lad had sandy hair, was short in stature and was wearing shorts, a green tee shirt with yellow trim, and a pair of rubber thongs. His face was moon-shaped and Bowker could imagine him at thirty-five, his blond hair gone and his head mimicking a bowling ball. The other boy sported a dark mane of hair, had a longer face and a hint of dark bum-fluff on his top lip. He was taller by comparison and wore jeans, a black polo shirt and bare feet.

'How old are you, lads?' Bowker asked.

'Fifteen,' the sandy haired boy replied.

'Seventeen' said the other.

'What have you been drinking?'

'Coke,' one said quickly. 'Solo,' the other said.

There was a giggle from under the tree.

'Alright. You, under the tree. Come out here now.'

There was no movement.

Bowker put his hands on his hips. 'I said now! Before I have to come in and get you.'

A teenage girl emerged and walked onto the footpath. The first thing Bowker noticed was the green hair and the ring through her nose. The girl in the yellow ute. Up close he could see she had half a dozen studs in each ear and black ink marks scratched into the back of each hand. She was dressed in a loosely fitting black top teamed with jeans that were ripped off at the knee. She wore pink sneakers covered in graffiti with no socks. She had a pretty face which she tried to disguise with a constant scowl. A city kid trying to shock the locals was Bowker's assessment.

'How old are you, young lady?' he asked.

'Sixteen,' she answered in an irritated tone.

'Okay, so what were you drinking under there? And I don't want any lies.'

'Just soft drink,' the girl answered too quickly.

'So, if I fish around under that tree, I'm going to find nice cold soft drink bottles, am I?'

The dark-haired boy cracked. 'We had a stubby each. Just one.'

'Yeah. Just one while I was waiting for my dad to finish his session in there,' the other boy said, pointing to the pub.

Bowker turned to the girl. 'A stubby for you too, was it?'

'A UDL can. Rum and Coke. Big deal.'

'What are your names? And I don't want any bullshit. I'm the policeman here for at least two years and I'm sure I'll get to know everyone so well I'll be able to send out birthday cards.'

'Yeah, well don't save too many cards for me,' the girl snarled. 'I'm pissing off back to Melbourne as soon as I turn eighteen. I'm sick of this fuckin' hole already.'

'What's your name, young lady? And go easy on the language, okay?'

'Yvonne Bryant,' she snapped back. 'But the last copper probably told you about me already, I bet. The silly old bastard had it in for me the moment I came to this dump.'

'Town seems like a nice friendly place to me.'

The girl sniggered. 'Don't lie. You're counting down the days until you leave. Just like me.'

Bowker grinned to himself and turned to the boys. 'Names, please, lads.'

'My name's James Brodie,' the sandy haired boy said nervously.

'I'm Paul Donovan,' the other boy said.

'James Brodie, Paul Donovan, Yvonne Bryant,' Bowker recounted sternly. 'Right. I'm going to let the three of you off with a warning. But this is it, understand? If I find you drinking alcohol again before you turn eighteen, you will be charged. Are you totally clear on this?'

'Yes, sir,' the boys said together quickly.

'What about you, Yvonne? You clear on that?'

'S'pose I am,' she muttered.

'Right, the three of you wait here. I'll go in and get your fathers and they can take you home.'

'My father's not in there,' Yvonne said sourly. 'Don't even know who my father is.'

'Do you live in town?' Bowker asked.

'Live out at Winnambool.'

'How were you getting home then?'

'My boyfriend. He's in the pub.'

'How old's your boyfriend?'

'Twenty-three,' she said proudly.

'Shit,' Bowker said under his breath as he looked at Rachael in exasperation. 'What's your boyfriend's name?'

'Skeeta Allender. That's his car over there. The hotted-up yellow Holden ute.'

'I guessed as much. And that was you giving me the finger at the stop sign yesterday.'

'Didn't know you were a cop, did I?'

Bowker exhaled loudly. 'Shouldn't matter. Any driver obeying the law deserves respect.'

'Skeeta thought you were some old fart who couldn't find first gear in that shit-heap you were driving.'

That'd be right, thought Bowker. When he entered the main bar, it fell instantly quiet. 'I've just bailed up three kids drinking booze under the peppercorn tree next door. Waiting for my father to finish up his grog so he can take me home, one said. Mr Donovan and Mr Brodie: would you like to do the honours with your boys.'

'Bloody little bastard,' Brodie said loudly with his bowling ball shaped head glistening with sweat under the lights of the bar. 'Where does he get the idea he can drink grog at his age? I'll give him what-for when I get him home!'

'We all drank at his age,' Donovan said. 'Didn't do us any harm.'

'I can see that,' Bowker said sarcastically. 'Is there a Skeeta Allender in here?'

'That's me, mate,' said a skinny sunburnt young man with longish blonde hair, ripped jeans and a sleeveless shirt. 'What can I do for you?'

'There's a child outside called Yvonne Bryant who claims you're giving her a ride home to Winnambool. Is that right?'

'Yeah, I said I would. Her family don't come to town much, so I help out occasionally. I live out that way. I'm sorta like a big brother.'

A few of the locals sniggered.

'No bus to get her home from school today?' Bowker asked, the question dripping with cynicism.

Skeeta shrugged. 'Must have missed it,' he replied.

'And she just happened to have spare clothes so she could change out of her school uniform?'

'Fucked if I know. I just take her home if she needs a lift, mate.'

'And pick her up from school. I was in front of you yesterday when you pulled that dickhead move at the rail crossing.'

Skeeta inhaled audibly through his teeth. 'Sorry about that. I thought you were some old city bastard on his way to Adelaide whose frog-shit car had packed up in the heat. Had to get around you somehow.'

'Yeah? Do it again and I'll take your licence.' Bowker turned to the barman. 'How much has Skeeta had to drink, Rick?'

'Couple of glasses of light with his mixed grill.'

'On your way, Skeeta. Get that girl home. Its past her bedtime.'

Bowker left the bar and stood hands on hips as the three kids departed in different directions.

CHAPTER 5

The next day marked the official start of Bowker's stint as Manangatang's sole police presence. He alone was now charged with maintaining law and order over approximately three thousand square kilometres, a geographic area triple the size of Greater Melbourne. By eight o'clock he was in full uniform, and the police station was open for business.

'What's on the agenda today, senior constable,' Rachael asked as she followed him into the station.

Bowker dropped the keys on his desk. 'A bit of paperwork, then I'll go for a drive to get a feel for the place.' He put his hands on her shoulders. 'So far, so good, eh, Rach?'

She held his wrists. 'So far, so good, Greg. Except for this weather. Another scorcher. But at least there's no wind. It's the wind and the dust that does my head in.'

She released his wrists and Bowker sat down at his desk. 'Right, those kids from last night.' He opened a note pad and scribbled down the names. 'I have a feeling this won't be the last time I tangle with young Yvonne. Roy Pace said she'd come to my attention in the first week. How about before we even entered the town!'

Rachael pulled up a chair and sat with her forearms resting on the desk. 'And this boyfriend-with-the-ute business gives me the heebie jeebies, as well. She's just a kid, Greg.'

'Skeeta said he's a friend of the family who gives her a lift home, sometimes. Not sure about that, but she *is* sixteen years old.

That's the age of consent.'

'And he's how old? Twenty-three, didn't she say?' Rachael leant back in her chair. 'S'pose he hasn't broken any laws. And when I was her age, I went out with a bloke who was nineteen. But twenty-three would have seemed ancient.'

'Not if he's got a hotted-up ute.'

Rachael threw out her arms. 'What is it with you men and hotted-up cars? I haven't met one female who's ever been attracted by one. Check it out next time you see a bloke in a car that's been lowered, with the big loud muffler, half a dozen aerials, and a sexual innuendo painted on the back. You know what you won't see?'

Bowker chuckled. 'I'm sure you'll tell me.'

'A female. It'll be a bloke on his own for sure. In most cases some weedy little runt whose feet hardly reach the pedals and he'll be wearing a wide-brimmed Akubra that makes him look like an oversized roofing nail!'

Bowker burst out laughing. 'I'll keep my eyes open to test your theory.'

'I'm right, you can count on it. In this case, I think young Yvonne sees Skeeta as the status symbol, not his car.' She stood and leant over the desk and kissed him gently. 'See you at dinner time. What do they say on *Hill Street Blues*? Be careful out there.'

As she left, Bowker marvelled at how nice her bum looked in jeans, before picking up the phone and calling the St Arnaud police station. The sergeant there had good news. 'Yeah, the van pulled over the truck in the main street up near the gardens. They breatho-ed the driver and he blew .04.'

'The stupid bastard. He'll probably do his job,' Bowker replied.

'The officers took his keys. His mate was unlicenced, but he was half-cut anyway. They got a room at the top pub. This trip will cost them a few bob.'

'Serves them right. They can't say they weren't warned. Pass on my thanks to your boys for a job well done. If you're ever up this way, drop in and I'll shout you a coffee.'

'Not much chance of that, mate. This joint is far enough north for most of us.' He chortled. 'Manangatang! Shit mate! You shag the chief commissioner's daughter or something?'

'Beautiful place, Brian. At the moment, it's a balmy fifteen degrees. Out the window I can see green lawns with fountains spraying a fine rainbow mist and birds fluttering in the rose gardens.'

'Turn on your air conditioner, mate. The heat is causing hallucinations.'

Bowker laughed. 'I'll have to leave you to it, Brian. I need to find a jumper.'

'Good luck up there. I suppose somebody has to do it.'

Bowker smiled as he put down the phone. The temperature inside was already thirty-plus according to the mercury on the wall, but there was no point firing up the air con until he got back at dinnertime. He paused for a moment, reflecting on the St Arnaud sting with a self-satisfied smirk. Senior Constable Bowker one, smart arses nil.

***

It didn't take long for the car's air con to cool the interior. Bowker drove down Wattle Street spotting activity inside a couple of the shops, but it was still too early for most of them to open. He noted the businesses he hadn't reached on the previous evening's stroll, a post office with its black wall of letter boxes, an agricultural chemical distributor, what looked like a dress shop in an ancient-looking fibro building, a store with 'Pengillys' painted faintly above its roughly built veranda, a closed-up car dealership with a rusted steel roller door, a solicitors' office with the sign 'Herbert and Herbert', and finally Arenz's farm supplies on the corner.

He turned right onto the highway then took the next right into Pioneer Street, one of the two major residential streets in the town. The Manangatang Bowling Club was on his left, a mechanics workshop on the right, then it was all houses until he passed the hospital, a modern building with the doctors' surgery at the front. He drove on past a couple of churches, more houses of varied age and condition, an infant welfare centre in need of a paint, then more houses. He turned left again into Sackville Street, then left again onto a dirt lane which ran at the back of the Pioneer Street houses and bordered open paddocks on the opposite side. Fifty metres along the lane, a harness horse, with jogging cart and driver, crossed from a training track in the paddock opposite. The driver turned the horse to face up the lane and waited for Bowker to bring the police car up beside him. Bowker wound down his window.

'G'day, mate. Getting work into her before it gets too hot?'

The filly snorted and threw her head up and down against the bit, sending a hundred flies into the air. 'Usually work them a bit earlier than this, actually,' the driver said. 'Get it out of the way before I go to work.'

'What do you do for a quid?'

'I'm a stock agent.'

'One of Prong's mob?'

'Yeah, my main opposition. Red Cameron's the name.'

'Pleased to meet you, Red. I'm Greg Bowker, the new policeman.'

'Yeah, the uniform and the car probably gave that one away.' The filly spun sideways in a circle, an equine clock hand sweeping around the dial. Red straightened her again and she pawed the ground with her near front hoof. There wasn't much doubt about how Red gained his moniker with his ginger hair and ruddy complexion. He'd spent a lot of time outdoors, the elements crafting a weathered face, his spotted hands and arms evidence of the sun doing its best to destroy his pale skin.

Bowker nodded towards the horse. 'Any good, this one?' he asked.

'Shows a bit of promise but she belts her off knee when she goes around bends. Tends to skip and break. That's why I've got the knee boots on her.'

'Have you tried spreaders?'

'You know a bit about this game, do you?'

The filly lunged forward and now had her head over the police car's bonnet, depositing strings of saliva onto the vehicle. 'Had stock horses on the farm growing up, but I used to work trotters for a bloke when I was going to school,' Bowker replied.

'No money in them. But they're a bit of fun.'

'Ever had a good one?'

'Won the Mildura Cup a few years ago. Horse was called Manang. Bet you can't work out where the name came from.' He laughed.

'It's one of the things I really miss. Used to love mucking around with the buggers.'

'If you're interested in working a horse, give me a yell. I've got another bloke in the shed that I jogged before this one. Wouldn't hurt to work them together if you can make time one morning'

'I'd enjoy that, Red. I'll get back to you.'

Red slapped the reins on the filly's rump, and she paced slowly up the lane in front of Bowker's car. When Red turned into a backyard full of old sheds and horse boxes, Bowker stopped the car, leaned over the passenger side and wound down the window. He put two fingers in his mouth and whistled. 'She puts that near foreleg down on an angle. Might help if you build up the inside of the shoe to balance her up. Just a suggestion.' Red gave the policemen the thumbs up.

Bowker drove off with a smile on his face. The smell of a horse in his nostrils brought back memories of happy times. Times when he was young, without a worry in the world, just the rhythm of the horse's feet pounding the ground, the rustle of the leaves, and the warm sun on his back. Ah, life was a lot simpler then. A lot simpler than it was now, that's for sure. What happened in Ballarat wasn't right, no matter how far away they sent him.

He doglegged to the right into Church Street, a gravel road lined with houses all the way back to the Ouyen road. Over the highway was the town's swimming pool with its blue water already beckoning in the fierce morning sun. He turned left back onto the highway, passed through the main intersection, and fifty metres later crossed the railway line. A stream of school kids from the town were crossing the rails, not one bothering to look for trains. Practically on top of the railway line was the main school crossing over the highway. The red crossing flags were out but there was no supervision. To Bowker, this whole pedestrian set-up was a death trap, with a myriad of signs to distract the driver as they approached. He pulled up at the crossing as a big semi roared in from Piangil way, dropping down through the gears as it approached the chiacking kids crossing the road. The massive truck shuddered to a halt and its driver looked down at Bowker and tapped his temple as he pointed to the kids. Bowker nodded in agreement, making a mental note to visit the school and talk about road safety.

The policeman checked his rear vision mirror before moving off and there was Skeeta Allender's golden Holden ute again, shaking laterally as its big V8 struggled to idle under low revs. And there was Yvonne Bryant in the passenger seat, complete with a self-satisfied grin. A few seconds later, the Winnambool school bus rolled to a stop behind Skeeta. Why doesn't she take the bus like the other kids? Bowker thought with irritation.

Bowker proceeded over the crossing, turned left towards the recreation reserve and watched in his side mirror as Skeeta planted his foot and fishtailed through the school gate. The ute accelerated up the track to the school car park where Yvonne would no doubt alight in front of her peers as if arriving at the Academy Awards. Sooner or later that lad's going in the book, Bowker thought as he continued on, passing through a heavily vegetated area that quickly gave way to the recreation reserve. He drove slowly past the golf course which enclosed the famous racecourse. 'They're racing at Manangatang!' he said to himself out loud. Inside the racetrack was the footy ground, the home of the mighty Saints. What was it legendary football writer, Lou Richards, claimed in the *Melbourne Sun*? So-and-so VFL team couldn't beat the Manangatang Thirds? Bowker smiled and headed out via the netball and tennis courts and past a small paddock half-filled with rusted-out cars dumped amongst the mallee scrub. A portly old man, with a walking stick in one hand and a Jack Russell terrier on a leash in the other, limped along beside the road. Bowker pulled up beside him and wound down the car window. 'G'day, mate. I'm the new copper. Greg Bowker.'

The old bloke leant the stick against his hip, extended an arm and shook hands. 'Tub Keller. Pleased to meet ya.'

Bowker pointed towards the automotive carcasses. 'Who owns all those rust buckets?'

'Nobody now. It's crown land and whenever somebody wants to get rid of an old bomb, they just dump it there. No wreckers in the district, so they're better left there in the scrub than scattered in people's yards around the town.'

'Fair enough.' Bowker looked up at the sun. 'Getting a bit warm for a walk, don't you reckon?'

'If I waited for cooler weather, I wouldn't get much exercise.' The Jack Russell cocked his leg on the car's front wheel.

'Do this walk every day?'

'Most days, if I'm feelin' alright. The dog doesn't let me take too many mornings off.' He pulled the dog away from the wheel.

'Well, I'll leave you to it, Tub. Look after yourself.'

'Good onya, mate.'

Tub shuffled off, growling at the dog. Bowker crossed back over the railway line north of the silos and turned onto the road to Robinvale. This might work out alright, he thought. Me and Rach living in our own little Mallee universe, light years away from anyone who knows us. People seem friendly; good house; plenty of sport to play; maybe muck around with some horses. Could be just what the doctor ordered.

CHAPTER 6

Back in town, Rachael went shopping. Her first stop was Wraith's supermarket. There was no one at the checkout, so she grabbed an aging trolley and moved from section to section, accumulating the articles on her list. Prices were a bit steep by Ballarat standards, but that was understandable given the remoteness of the town. The instant she ticked off the last item, Liz Wraith materialised as if by magic and headed to the front. She was a short, friendly-faced woman, her ginger hair set in rollers. 'By the looks of what's in your trolley, you're not just passing through. So, I'm guessing you must be the Rachael that Terry met yesterday. Rachael Bowker. From the police station.'

Rachael smiled at the speed of the bush telegraph and the assumptions people made. 'Actually, I go by my maiden name. So it's Rachael Stow.'

Liz hesitated for a split second. 'Right. Okay. Pleased to meet you, Rachael,' she said, keying the price of each item into the register. 'I'm Liz. Liz Wraith. My husband, Col, and I own this business.'

'Glad you're here. Be a hell of a trip to get things otherwise.'

Liz stopped her keying. Rachael had hit a raw nerve. 'Tell that to some of the locals. They spend two hours travelling to a supermarket in Swan Hill. False economy, if you ask me. Prices might be a tad lower, but they forget how much they spend on petrol. Plus, there's wear and tear on their car. Plus their time.' She resumed her keying and finally hit the total button with a flourish. 'That's $18.19.'

Rachael retrieved cash from her purse as Liz loaded the groceries into a pair of cardboard boxes. After accepting her change, Rachael picked up the larger of the cartons. 'Nice to meet you, Liz. I'm sure we'll see lots of each other.'

Liz picked up the second box and followed her to the car. 'Go by your maiden name, eh? Things tend to stay pretty traditional here in the Mallee. This young female teacher arrived over at Murrayville and convinced a lot of the women that they were basically the slaves of their husbands. Nothing more than unpaid cooks and housekeepers kept in isolation on their farms to breed the next generation. Blokes were ready to run her out of town.'

Rachael placed the box on the Peugeot's bonnet as she fumbled for the car keys buried somewhere in her handbag. 'Well, you can tell everybody that I'm not here to stir up trouble. I just prefer to go by the name I was born with, that's all. No disrespect meant to anyone else.' Rachael unlocked her car.

'Nobody ever locks their car in Manang,' Liz said as she placed the second box on the back seat. 'If you walk along the street now, you'll find most have the keys hanging in the ignition.'

'Not sure what Greg will feel about that.'

'Tell him there's more chance of locking your keys in your car than having it pinched. See you next time.' Liz returned to the shop without looking back.

Rachael relocked the car and collected the papers from the newsagency. There she underwent the same introductions and gentle grilling. Still, everyone was friendly, and she came to accept that new residents were a novelty in this community.

***

Bowker was ten kilometres out of town when he first spotted Skeeta Allender's ute looming ever larger in his mirrors. He looked at his speedo and did the calculations. No problems. He had a head start on Skeeta but was travelling well below the speed limit as he took in the countryside. Two semis had even passed him. The moment they came to a straight stretch, Skeeta flicked on his indicator and overtook the police car, offering a cheeky wave as he passed. Bowker accelerated slowly and tracked the ute for a couple of kilometres, confirming Skeeta was observing the 100 km limit. Smart boy. When they reached the Bolton turn off, Skeeta turned left down Webster Road leaving contrails of dust billowing in his wake. Bowker stayed on the Robinvale Road, its bitumen surface a placid lake twinkling in the heat, the roadside trees reflecting in the mirage. He slowed to 80 km as he entered Annuello, expecting to see a small settlement of some kind. Save for an old hall and a CFA shed, there was nothing besides a quartet of silos and a long grain shed adjacent to the railway siding.

The police car left Annuello along the unsealed Winnambool Road and followed it all the way to the Winnambool reserve where Bowker quickly concluded that if a township ever existed, there was absolutely no evidence of it now. He drove south, still following Winnambool Road until he came to its intersection with Webster Road, little corner-cutting tracks creating a diamond pattern if viewed from the air. He stopped in the shade at the centre of the maze. A homemade sign said Piccadilly Corner. Finger boards went off in different directions, displaying the names of local families. Barnes, Dawes, Storer, Legg, Cullen, Mowatville. Mowatville? He consulted the open fire map on his passenger seat, noting that this very spot was actually called Piccadilly Corner. He laughed to himself as he found Mowatville, a small collection of farmhouses off to the north-west. The name that caught his eye however, was Bryant. He turned and headed in the direction indicated by the map.

He drove in the dust for ten minutes without a sign of human habitation before spotting a Toyota one-tonner inside the fence line. A worker close by was twitching wire to a fence post. The man looked up for a moment then returned to his work. Bowker pulled his vehicle to the roadside and got out, the blistering heat instantly attacking him. He wandered over to the fencer, a tall man in his forties with strong arms and wide shoulders. He wore a battered leather hat, a torn navy-blue polo shirt with a Tooleybuc Club logo, dirty jeans with the knees worn out, and cracked elastic-sided leather boots. Like all farmers, he sported the obligatory weathered face and arms. His head was oblong in shape, his lips cracked and chaffed, his eyes a piercing blue.

'G'day, mate. I'm Greg Bowker, the new copper in Manangatang.'

'Is that right,' the fencer said, barely looking up from his work.

'Hot enough for you?'

'Not too bad today. No dust until you ploughed the road up.'

'Sorry.'

The fencer attached a wire strainer to the second top wire. 'What are you doin' out here? Haven't seen a police car out this way for years.'

'Just looking around the district. Getting an idea where everything is so I know what the locals are talking about.' He took a step backwards as the fencer strained the wire tighter and tighter.

The fencer was satisfied he had the right tension. 'The middle of nowhere is where you're at right now.'

'You couldn't point me in the direction of the Bryant's place, could you?'

The fencer stopped work and looked up. 'You're looking at it. Takes up most of this block.'

'Right.'

The conversation evaporated momentarily as the fencer tied off the opposing strands of wire. Bowker admired the man's skill. 'That knot makes a lovely number eight shape,' he said.

The fencer looked at him with a faint smirk. 'Called a figure 8, believe it or not. Thread the wires the wrong way and you get what we call a dog's balls. Both loops on the same side.' The fencer snipped off the excess wire. 'So, you've met Yvonne already, I presume?'

'Why would you presume that?'

The fencer put one hand on the small of his back as he straightened. 'Because that little bitch is the only reason you'd see a copper way out here. What's she done? Pinched something from the shops? Rooted some underage kid?'

'No. Nothing like that. Are you related to her?'

'Sorta.' The fencer grabbed his canvas water bag from a hook on the Toyota's bullbar. 'If you want to get technical, she's my step-niece. Her grandfather, Percy Bryant, is married to my mother. Percy lost his first wife, Shirley, to cancer, and my father died when a slasher dropped on him while he was underneath fixing it.' The fencer unscrewed the cap of the water bag and took a long draw. He motioned for Bowker to take a swig.

Bowker took the bag from over the fence, put it to his mouth and felt the cool water cut away the grime in his throat. 'Thanks, mate.' He handed it back. 'You wouldn't reckon those things could keep the water so cool. Just a canvas bag really.'

'Evaporation. Same principle as a Coolgardie safe. Or the human body sweatin' on a hot day.'

Bowker nodded. 'Sorry to hear about your dad. What was his name?'

'Keith. But everyone called him Crayfish. Crayfish Harris. Red hair, bright red face, especially after a day in the sun, or a few beers, or both.'

Bowker chuckled as the fencer continued. 'Mum and Percy went to school together at the old Winnambool primary school and were pretty close then, apparently. Seemed a natural thing to team up when they both lost their spouse.' He hooked the water bag back on the bullbar. 'Got married a dozen or so years ago. Doubled the holdings, made both farms more profitable. Economies of scale, they call it. Everybody was as happy as Larry, until Percy brought Yvonne back from Melbourne when her mother died.' He shook his head. 'Should have left the bitch down there to fend for herself. She's as cunning as a shithouse rat and thinks she knows everything. She'd have coped one way or another.'

Bowker leaned against the strainer post. 'I suspected Yvonne was brought up in the city,' he said.

'Dragged up, more like it. And the whole bloody Lynette saga raises more questions than it answers.'

'Who's Lynette?'

'Lynette Bryant. Percy's daughter. Yvonne's mother. Died last year.'

'Okay.'

Bowker watched the fencer take a Tupperware container from the seat of the Toyota and unwrap a round of sandwiches. The fencer took a bite, then continued. 'Lynette was a quiet, solitary sort of kid when she was growing up. Used to come over to our place to help with some housework when Mum was down the paddock helping my old man. Earned herself a bit of pocket money at the same time. Then, out of the blue, she pisses off to the city and gets herself knocked up by some bloody no-hoper who shoots through once he realises she's up the duff.' He offered a sandwich to Bowker.

The policeman shook his head. 'No thanks, mate. The missus will have dinner waiting when I get back to town. Anybody know why Lynette left? There'd have to be a reason, surely.'

'The wife and I were overseas on holidays, so I don't know the intricate details. But it appears she just shot through and told nobody.'

'She have friends in Melbourne to stay with?'

'No. Just became a street addict in St Kilda somewhere. Percy went to Melbourne a dozen times trying to do something. Even paid for Yvonne to go to a decent school down there, but she only attended when she felt like it, apparently. In the end, Lynette overdosed and died while a couple of other dead shits were beltin' into the ambos who were there trying to save her life. So, Perce brought Yvonne back here and now she's wrecking our lives as well.' The fencer waved a fly off his face and started a new sandwich. 'The little bitch takes everything and shits in your face. And laughs while she's doin' it. We had the happiest home in the district, you know. Perce and I get on like a house on fire, and Mum and my wife, Marlene, are like sisters. Now Yvonne's ruined everything.'

'You have to cut her a bit of slack, I s'pose. Pretty ordinary start to life.'

'We've all cut her some slack – miles and miles of bloody slack. Especially Percy.' He threw the remains of the sandwich into a salt bush further up the fence. 'Maybe he thinks he was too hard on Lynette, and that caused her to run away and everything else that happened. He treats Yvonne with kid gloves just trying to make up for Lynette, I reckon. In his mind, his granddaughter's become the daughter he lost, and he won't risk losing her as well.'

'So how old is Percy?'

'Just turned sixty. Bit old to be raising an out-of-control teenager. And what's Mum done to deserve this?'

'Is Percy home at present? I'd like a quick word about an incident in town last night.'

The fencer threw the lunchbox on the front seat of his vehicle. 'Him and Mum have gone to Patchewollock to pick up a kelpie pup.'

'How far to Patchewollock from here?'

The fencer thought for a moment. 'Patchy's about a hundred k's if you go through Ouyen. But Perce will take a shortcut using the back roads.'

'Hope he's a careful driver. Some of these dirt roads look a bit tricky.'

The fencer put his hands on the top plain wire of the fence and leant forward. 'That's another thing. If something happens to Perce and Mum, there's only two people left in the family to inherit this place. Me and bloody Yvonne. Beautiful thought, eh?'

Bowker wiped his brow with his shirt sleeve. 'Who moved in with who when your mother and Perce married?'

'Perce moved across to Mum's. His joint is a dump. Fills with sand in a dust storm, and the garden died with old Shirl. It's just been rented out to a new family. Fly-by-nighters, I'd say. Get a lot of them up this way. Cheap housing and nobody asks too many questions. This one's a single mother, no job, got a useless son about the same age as Yvonne. Our taxes at work, eh?' He waved away another fly.

'At least they've got a roof over their heads, I s'pose.'

The fencer chuckled. 'Assumin' the old dump didn't blow over in the wind we've had recently.'

Bowker stood up straight. 'Can you let Percy know I called in? He might like to give me a ring at the station and save me another trip.'

'Will do.'

'Don't think I got your name.'

'It's Kevin Harris. But everybody calls me Yabby. You know, little crayfish. Pretty imaginative people around here.'

Bowker smiled as he shook hands.

'Mum's name is Cath, if she rings.'

'Thanks, Kevin. See you soon.'

'Doubt it. Don't go into Manang much. Marlene and I like to keep to ourselves.'

'To each their own, as the saying goes. Good luck with Yvonne.'

Yabby didn't answer as he dragged a roll of barbed wire off the tray of his vehicle. Bowker walked across the road towards his car, then stopped and went back. 'I assume you know Skeeta Allender?'

Yabby dropped the wire on the ground and moved back to the fence. 'Everybody in the district knows that useless piece of shit.'

'Does he live somewhere around here? He passed me on the Robinvale Road and turned down in this direction.'

'Only son of Peter and Dawn Allender next door. Old Pete's strugglin' to keep the farm going, and if Skeeta puts in more than a couple of hours a day over there I'd be surprised. Spends most of his time showboatin' around in that bloody ute. Dunno where he got the money to buy the thing. The Allenders haven't got two bob to rub together.'

'What's his relationship with Yvonne? He says he's like a big brother.'

'Brothers root their sisters, do they?'

'You reckon that's what's going on?'

'Soon as Yvonne arrived, he started coming over here to talk about cropping. Hardly been here before, plus everyone knows he has zero interest in farming. People talk about dogs travellin' miles to sniff out a bitch on heat. Skeeta was here the morning after she arrived.'

'No law against sexual relations with a female over the age of sixteen, even if the other party is twenty-three. Or sixty-three, for that matter.'

'Mightn't be a law against it, but it's still not bloody right.' Yabby pulled his work gloves from his back pocket.

'What's Percy think?'

'Doesn't want to upset the apple cart. While she's fuckin' around with Skeeta, she's less likely to piss off back to Melbourne.'

'What's Skeeta's real name?'

Yabby shook his head. 'Wouldn't have a clue. He's been Skeeta ever since he could walk. Buzzin' around and annoyin' the shit out of everyone. And nothin's changed.' Yabby pulled on his gloves.

Bowker returned to his car, started the engine, and cranked the air con up to flat out.

CHAPTER 7

Rachael opened the fridge and put away the last of her food shopping, leaving the frozen chook on the bench to thaw. Should put it outside on the veranda, she thought. Just add a few vegies! She dropped the newspapers on the table, *The Age*, *The Sun* and *The Swan Hill Guardian*. On top was the latest edition of *Connexions*, a Manangatang community newspaper produced by the local school. In twenty minutes, she'd read it front to back, absorbing not only the news, but the community's character and spirit as well. What really caught her eye was a situation vacant listing:

Integration Aide Wanted

20 hours per week

In-class student support role

Applications to the Principal

Manangatang Consolidated School

c/o Manangatang Post Office 3546

Rachael was a trained kindergarten teacher but hadn't worked in that field since moving to Ballarat to be married. Twenty hours a week would suit her. It would leave time for social engagement with the local women, plus add a few extra dollars to the household income. Her reverie was broken by the phone ringing in the police station. After fifteen seconds, the new-fangled answering machine cut in.

'This is Senior Constable Bowker of the Manangatang Police. I'm away from the office at the moment, so please leave a message with your phone number, and I will call you back as soon as possible. In cases of emergency, phone the Robinvale police on 5005 3002.' The machine beeped.

A hostile voice answered, the words dripping with sarcasm. 'Oh, sorry. I thought I'd rung the Ballarat police station. But of course, you're not there anymore are you, Senior fuckin' Constable fuckin' Bowker? Even the backwoods is too good for a bastard like you! At least in a one-cop shithole no other officer has to rely on your loyalty. And you want me to leave a message? Well here's the fuckin' message. Don't you or that little slut come anywhere near Ballarat again if you know what's good for you. I won't leave my number. You know where I can be contacted.' The line went dead.

Rachael stood in the doorway unable to move. This wasn't going away.

***

Bowker drove a hundred metres to where he could turn around in one of the wide gateways built to allow giant machinery entry to the paddocks. He drove back past Yabby Harris who didn't bother to look up from his work but threw up an arm in half-hearted acknowledgement of Bowker tooting his horn. A kilometre or so from Piccadilly Corner, he noticed a layer of dust floating above Winnambool Road to the north. As he approached the intersection, he made out Skeeta Allender's ute parked under the shade in the middle of the diamond. Skeeta was leaning against the bullbar, drinking from a stubby. Bowker pulled up under a tree and wandered across.

'Car troubles, Skeeta?'

'Nah, just stopping in the shade for a cold one before I get home and the old man starts ordering me around like he's in the bloody army.'

Bowker folded his arms and leant his backside against the bullbar next to Skeeta. 'Where do you get a cold one at this hour of the day?'

Skeeta stared straight ahead. 'It's not cold, actually. It's one left

over from a six pack I bought last night. Better than nothin', though.'
He took another pull on his beer.

'And you delivered Yvonne home last night?'

'Yeah. I said I would.'

'You're not supplying her with grog, are you? That's against the law.
But I suppose you know that already.'

'Of course I do.' He stood up straight. 'Took her straight home
then had a few quiet ones in the shed after I parked the ute. The oldies
don't approve of alcohol in the house. Bloody wowsers. Go to church
in Robinvale every Sunday, without fail.'

Bowker looked him in the eye. 'Did Yvonne miss the bus again
this morning?'

Skeeta looked away. 'Yeah. Lucky I was driving past to give her a
lift.'

'How come the Winnambool bus was behind you when you hit
town?'

'I passed it out the road. It only does about eighty. Plus, it stops to
pick up kids along the way. That's its bloody job.' He sat against his
car again and took another sip.

Bowker stood up, turned and put both hands on the bullbar.
'Could have saved coming all the way in if you'd dropped her off at a
stop ahead of the bus.'

'Never thought of it.' Skeeta paused and stared across the paddock.
'Do you think I'm on with Yvonne or something?'

'None of my business if you are. She's sixteen. No laws being
broken.'

'Then why do you keep asking me about her?'

'She's just a kid. My job is to keep the community safe.'

Skeeta finally looked straight at Bowker. 'And you don't think she's
safe with me?'

'Not if you drive like I've noticed in the last couple of days. Not if
you're drinking stubbies on the side of the road in the middle of the
day.'

'Only having the one. Told you that.'

'Somebody pass through here a few minutes ago? Saw dust up Winnambool Road.'

Skeeta looked away. 'Probably mine just driftin' across. Only been here five minutes or so. Bugger-all wind today. Dust hangs around for ages.' Skeeta finished his stubby and threw it into the scrub where it clinked amongst a few other empties. 'The old man'll be lookin' for me so I better get going.'

Bowker stood up. 'Not before you pick up those bottles and put them in the ute. Littering's an offence.'

Skeeta took a step back with arms outstretched. 'You're bloody joking. If you're gonna book everyone in the district for that, it'll be a full-time job.'

'Maybe so, but at least we'll have a more attractive place to live.'

'Take more than cleanin' up rubbish to make this place attractive, mate. Have a look around you,' Skeeta said with a theatrical sweep of his arm.

'All part of the natural landscape. Not like those bottles you dumped there.'

Skeeta picked up more than a dozen empty stubbies and dropped them noisily into a toolbox on the tray of his ute. 'Satisfied?'

'I am. Don't you feel a warm glow inside knowing you have helped save our environment.'

'Nuh.' He pointed at Bowker. 'You keep going this way mate, and you'll be as popular around here as a tiger snake in a lucky dip.'

'Just doin' my job.'

Skeeta got into his car and drove off at a sensible speed.

***

Bowker spent the rest of the morning driving the backroads of the cropping country to the north of Manangatang, getting his head around the local roads and whatever landmarks he could find — typically a silo or a bush reserve. The landscape was predominantly mile after mile of sandy rises and Bowker pondered how easy it would be to become lost or disoriented, especially on a windy dusty day, or worse, on a windy dusty night. Thank God for the CFA maps.

'How'd the senior constable survive his first morning on the job?' Rachael asked as she pecked him on the cheek.

'Good. Had a couple of interesting conversations on my travels. I'm gradually working out the lay of the land, but when people casually drop these place names, there's nothing to mark where they actually are. Often, it's just a crossroad where there used to be a school or a hall, or a bush reserve that looks just like all the other bush reserves, or the name of a property that doesn't have a name displayed anywhere.' Bowker put his hands on her shoulders. 'What about you, Rach? Have a good morning here on your lonesome?'

'Yes and no.'

'No?' Bowker frowned. 'That bloody snake's not back?'

'Of a type, yes.' She took him by the hand and led him through into the police station. She replayed the message on the answering machine.

Bowker was livid. 'Bloody bastard. He just won't let things go. I was the one who was transferred to the back of Bourke. He had a win. Why can't the prick just move on?'

'Because he doesn't think that way, Greg. We both know that.'

Bowker took a deep breath to compose himself. 'Okay. Let's forget about him. He's two hundred miles away.' He put his arm around her shoulders, and they strolled back to the kitchen. 'Tell me about the good part of your morning.'

Rachael showed him the copy of *Connexions*. She pointed at the ad for the school job. 'What do you think?'

He read the advertisement and smiled. 'Not sure I can fit in the twenty hours on top of my duty roster.'

Rachael slapped him with the newspaper. 'For me, you dipstick!'

'If you want to do it, then apply. You'd be great.'

'I think I might give it a go. Probably won't be successful. Probably got someone already lined up. But you never know if you don't try. Right?'

'Right.' Bowker rubbed his hands together. 'Now, what feast have you prepared for dinner? I'm so hungry I could eat a horse.'

'Funny you should say that...' The phone in the station rang. 'Surely not again.'

'I hope it is. I'll give him both barrels.'

Bowker went into the station and picked up the receiver. 'Senior Constable Bowker, Manangatang police.' There was a pause. 'G'day, Tom.'

Rachael breathed a sigh of relief, and after a brief conversation, Bowker hung up and returned to the kitchen. 'Tom McColl. A cocky out the Sea Lake Road, worried he's had some sheep pinched. I'll drive out there after dinner. I was heading down that way to have a look around anyway.'

***

At the four-kilometre post, Bowker spotted the McColl mailbox. He turned left, crossed the railway line then followed a track to a farm ute parked outside a long machinery shed. He climbed from his car, sucked in the heat and walked towards two men chatting beside an enormous Versatile tractor.

'Hope I've got the right place. One of you blokes Tom McColl?'

'That's me,' said a slim man wearing jeans, an old tee shirt and a Versatile cap above a ruddy and perpetually sunburnt face. 'This is my brother, Prickles'. Prickles had dark hair, a bushy beard and a friendly smile. He was dressed similarly to Tom except for a wide brimmed hat which protected the top of his forehead, leaving it pale compared to the rest of his face.

'So, when did you notice the sheep were missing?' the policeman asked.

Tom's face flushed. 'This is pretty embarrassing. I was about to walk up to the house to ring you. Prickles has been up the paddock and there's a panel of fencing on its side next to the railway line. Looks like an old post broke off in the wind and the sheep have walked over the top of it looking for fresh tucker in the railway reserve.'

Bowker laughed. 'This is alright. I've taken less than five minutes to solve my first case. Hope the trend continues.'

'All we have to do now is find the bloody sheep,' Prickles said. 'They'll be somewhere along the railway line unless they left the reserve at one of the road crossings. In which case, they could finish up anywhere.'

'I'm gonna fly around the roads and see if I can find the bastards,' Tom said. He looked at Bowker. 'Want to come for a ride? Get a feel for the area?'

Bowker nodded. 'Why not. This arvo's plan was to drive out this way anyway.'

'Jump in the ute,' Tom said. He looked back at Prickles. 'I'll call you on the CB if we find them, and you can bring the dogs out.'

Pondering why they weren't taking the dogs themselves, Bowker swept some drenching gear from the seat of the ute and onto the floor. He climbed in and donned his seat belt.

'Probably won't need that, Greg. We're only going a couple of hundred yards.'

'I thought we were checking the roads.'

'We are. In that.' Tom pointed ahead.

Bowker was flabbergasted. In the shade of one of the bigger trees was a Cessna single engine plane. 'You know how to fly one of those?'

'Nuh. But we'll work it out between us,' Tom said with a broad laugh. 'You can relax. Haven't had a crash, yet. Always try to match the number of landings with the number of take offs.'

Bowker had flown a few times before, but always in a large passenger jet where the sense of altitude was tempered by the stability and the size of the cabin. Things were very different in this little plane where he felt every vibration and rumble of turbulence. As they climbed, he could see the patterns of roads and lanes, and for the first time had a true appreciation of the size of the paddocks and the uncleared areas of bush.

'We'll follow the railway line as far as Chinky,' Tom said.

'Would they have got that far?'

'Probably not, but they're big first-cross wethers and they'll keep walking until they find a green pick somewhere. If we get as far as Chinky and there's no sign of them, we can assume that they've left the railway line at one of the crossings. Then it'll be a process of elimination to find which road they're on.'

They dropped in altitude and followed the railway line southwards. In less than five minutes they were over Chinkapook.

'Looks like they must have gone bush somewhere along the way.'

'Aren't we going to Chinkapook?'

Tom pointed towards the floor of the plane. 'That's Chinky down there, mate.'

Bowker stared out his window, amazed. 'What? A handful of houses and a couple of tennis courts? And two silos?'

'You missed the hall beside the tennis courts. But that's it, Greg.'

'I imagined it as a bit like Manangatang.'

'It probably was at one stage. Banks in the main street, shops; the lot. Oldies talk about Raphael's general store. Big joint. Timber and steel merchants, and massive inside. Sold everything. Had walls of dress materials, knitting wools, haberdashery, manchester, ladies' hats, groceries – you name it.'

'You're jokin'.'

Tom shook his head. 'Not joking, mate. Chillingollah is few miles further down the railway line and it's just as sad. Probably worse. It was once a really thriving, well-known town. Even had a big brick pub. Now it's the same as Chinky. Tennis courts, a hall, silos, but even less houses.'

Bowker looked across at Tom. 'Depressing.'

'What you're seeing down there is what Manang will look like in thirty years. Maybe more houses, but bugger-all else. The population is dropping by the year, businesses are closing. Have a look at what's happening in the main street already. A few empty shops starting to appear. I'm predicting that eventually there'll be a milk bar, the pub maybe, and perhaps a couple of stock agents. A lot of cockies are getting out of sheep, so even the agents might find it hard going.'

'No police station?' Bowker asked seriously.

'Yeah, probably. If they keep the pub, they'll need a cop.' Tom laughed. 'I'll swing back to the north and see if the sheep are on a side road. There are a couple of places where the Sea Lake Road leaves the railway. Better check they're not there before we go bush.'

The little plane was now several kilometres beyond Chinkapook. It banked steeply to the right and picked up the highway where it headed south-west towards Sea Lake and away from the railway line which continued due south towards Chillingollah.

Bowker pushed his face hard against his window. 'Is that sheep down there?'

Tom brought the nose of the Cessna around for a clearer view. 'About the right number.' He dropped in altitude as he turned the plane in a wide circle. 'That's them. Not very smart, walking up the middle of a highway. Then again, sheep aren't renowned for their intellect.'

'What's that in amongst them. It's a vehicle of some sort,' Bowker asked, now becoming more confident that he may live to tell the tale.

Tom looked down to the ground. 'Yeah, some dickhead in a car pushing his way through the mob instead of moving to the side and letting the sheep get out of the way themselves. Finish up running over one, the stupid prick.'

'That's Skeeta Allender's Holden ute, I reckon,' Bowker said.

'Explains why he's driving straight through the mob. He's a fuckwit.'

'Gets around. Saw him out near Winnambool this morning.'

'I often pass him on this road. Must have a sheila down this way somewhere. Occasionally see him parked at the Cocamba silos. He'll be knockin' down a stubby or two, knowin' Skeeta.'

'That's what he was doing at Piccadilly Corner,' Bowker replied.

Tom took the radio handpiece from the plane's instrument panel. 'I'll give Prickles a call. He'll bring the dogs out and walk these silly bastards home.' He looked at Bowker. 'You can tell your mates down south you've joined the flying squad.'

They both laughed.

CHAPTER 8

With his feet now on terra firma, Bowker abandoned his planned visits to Chinkapook and Chillingollah, instead heading west to visit a remote primary school at Mittyack. After half an hour, he spotted the Mittyack silos. Dwarfed below was the tiny school, the location's only other structure. He parked on the road out the front where several youngsters were pouring water on the ground under the shade of a mallee gum. Wandering over to say hello, he was stopped in his tracks by the largest spider he had ever seen emerging from a watery hole in the earth. The creature's blue body was the size of a mandarin, and attached was a bright red head and massive black legs. Bowker stared open-mouthed at the spider. The kids stared at him.

A female voice bellowed from behind him. 'Didn't I tell you to leave the spiders alone? You keep doing that and a female will come out. You know how scary they are.'

Bowker turned around to see a young woman with dark wavy hair, dressed in a pretty pink dress and matching runners.

'Hello, officer. I'm Breanna Dawkins, the principal here.' she said. 'As well as its only teacher,' she added with a grin. 'I hope there's not a problem.'

Bowker took a wary step away from the arachnid. 'No problem. I'm the new policeman over at Manangatang. Senior Constable Greg Bowker.'

'You're a long way from home, constable,' the teacher said brightly. 'Say hello to Constable Bowker, girls and boys.'

The kids chanted 'Hello, Constable Bowker,' in unison.

'G'day, kids,' Bowker replied. He turned back to the teacher. 'I'm just driving around, getting a feel for the area. I didn't know they made spiders that big.'

'Yeah. Bit scary the first time you see a mallee mouse spider, but they're pretty docile unless you stir them up.' She glared at the children. 'Like when you pour water down their holes.'

Parents started arriving one after the other and within a few minutes all the students had been collected. Bowker watched the last of the cars depart. 'Left here on your own now?'

'Yeah, for a while. I'll do another hour's work then head home.'

'Where's home?' He looked around. 'Can't see a teacher house.'

'I'm married to a farmer up at Winnambool. Hopefully I'll transfer to Manang when a vacancy comes up. But then I'd have to give up my principal position here.' She laughed.

Bowker wondered if the whole Mallee centred around Winnambool. 'Ever get nervous working out here in the middle of nowhere?'

She shrugged. 'It's on the Calder Highway, so there's always a bit of Mildura traffic going up and back. But like any teacher in a little rural school, Faraday is never far from your mind. We've set a few processes in place if a stranger's wandering around, but you don't know whether they'll work in a real crisis.'

Bowker nodded, then after a pause asked, 'Do you know a character called Skeeta Allender. Lives out your way?'

The teacher smiled. 'Everybody knows Skeeta. The bane of his poor parents' life. Drink driving fines, getting into fights up in Robinvale, rumours about smoking dope. You name it, Skeeta is probably into it.'

'What do you know about Yvonne Bryant?'

'Not a lot. Hasn't been in the district long. Her mother left the area years before I arrived. From what little I've heard, the poor kid hasn't had a chance. Started life behind the eight ball. Born a month premature, according to her grandfather.'

'How long after her mother ran off was Yvonne born?'

'Less than nine months. So some bugger moved in on her pretty quickly once she got down to the city.'

Bowker rubbed his chin. 'Yeah.'

***

Bowker rolled back into town mid-afternoon having toured the districts of Leitpar and Daytrap. Well, that's what his maps said; there was nothing physical to indicate that these places even existed. He parked outside the post office, hoping he'd remembered the correct number for the police station's mailbox. He slid the key into the lock and it turned. His memory was accurate. As he began clearing the contents, a feather duster shot out and he jumped backwards. 'The rest of your mail's inside with a couple of parcels,' a voice from the mailbox said.

Bowker entered the post office and introduced himself to the postmaster, a jovial Mr Tim Turner. 'You scared the life out of me,' he said with a grin.

'Probably only work the once. Although there's a couple of people I get every time. You'd think they'd be ready for it.' Tim slid the police mail across the counter.

Tim was a middle-aged man of medium stature, dark hair with a tinge of ginger, Bowker surmising he probably had red hair as a kid. He had a kind face with lines attesting that he'd spent most of his life smiling. A few tiny scars showed above his eyebrows, Bowker later discovering Tim had been a handy boxer in his day and could fire up if pushed hard enough. After the usual introductory chit-chat, Tim addressed what appeared to be the town's obsession. 'Who are you gonna play tennis for? Heard Prong and Terry are both in your ear.'

Bowker sat on the stool beside the counter. 'Haven't really thought about it, to be honest. Been trying to get my head around what the job involves.'

Tim slapped the countertop. 'I'll make it easy for you. You're playing for Renegades. Pronga's got enough good players, so he doesn't need any more. At Renegades, we're on the cusp of something special. Got the core of a premiership. Throw in yourself and your missus and I reckon a flag is in the wind.'

'Prong and Terry are pretty keen. Are they any good?'

'Pronga doesn't look much of an athlete but he's an absolute gun. Not that we'd ever tell him that. He was coached by Harry Hopman in Melbourne. Could have played in the big time except he was a Mallee boy at heart and just wanted to come home. And believe it or not, the big T was a terrific all-round sportsman. Played centre half back in the Bendigo Football League when he was just a kid. On the tennis court, he's got a big topspin forehand and a vicious kick serve. Used to kick it straight into the side fence when he first came to Manang.'

'Rachael and I are just happy to fit in. We don't want to ruffle any feathers over a game of tennis.'

Tom leant on the counter. 'Nobody will give a shit. This rivalry stuff is just for entertainment. Pronga, Terry, and me all play night tennis together against teams from around the region. Some places take over an hour to get there. Makes for a pretty late night after you hang around for a few stubbies, or stop to light a few twigs and have a drink on the way home.'

'Hope there's a designated driver.'

'Yeah, we always work something out. Now, can I tell Terry you're in?'

'Why not. We're in. The mighty Renegades, eh?'

'The mighty Renegades.'

***

It was an enthusiastic Rachael who greeted Bowker when he arrived home. She'd rung the principal about the job advertisement and he'd encouraged her to apply. Bowker sat down at the kitchen table and Rachael pulled her chair round close to him. 'They have a boy in form

4 with an intellectual disability. Jimmy Cobb is his name. He needs support in some of his classes, and that would be my main role.'

'Job's made for you, Rach. You're a shoo-in, I reckon.'

'I hope so.' Rachael leaned over and pecked him on the lips. 'Now, how'd you go cracking the great sheep heist?'

'It was solved before I arrived. The wethers got out through a broken fence and we found them up the road.'

'Ooh. The *wethers* did, did they?' she asked playfully, moving her chair closer and putting her arm on his shoulder. 'Talking like a local already.'

'Do you know how we found them, Rach? In an aeroplane.'

She grinned and shook her head. 'Bullshit.'

'No bullshit, I promise.'

'What? You've been up in a plane this afternoon?'

'Yep. Tom McColl owns a Cessna. We found the sheep down near Chinky.'

'And it's Chinky now is it? So, you left *Manang* and flew down to *Chinky* looking for *wethers*?'

'We were halfway to Gollah before we found them,' he said with a smile and she punched him on the arm. 'Any police business back here?'

'No visitors, but Percy Bryant rang a few minutes ago and left a message to call him. Said you asked his stepson to give him the message.'

'I'll do that now. He must be back from Patchewollock. He was buying a new sheep dog.'

She laughed. 'Was that Patchewollock, or Patchy?'

Bowker went through into the station, replayed the message on the machine and wrote down Percy's number. He dialled and after thirty seconds a female voice answered.

'Hello, Cath Bryant.'

'Hello, Cath. Senior Constable Greg Bowker from the Manangatang police.'

'What's she done now? She's supposed to be on the bus coming home.'

'I'm just returning a call from your husband.'

She hesitated. 'He's just going out the back door. I'll grab him and put him on.' In the background Bowker could hear Cath's muffled explanation to Percy.

'Senior constable, this is Percy Bryant. Kevin said you wanted a word with me?'

'Yeah. Last night I found Yvonne consuming alcohol with a couple of boys in the street outside the hotel.'

'Is that all?' Percy said with relief.

'Well, I probably don't have to remind you, Mr Bryant, that she's only sixteen and that it's against the law to consume alcohol in a public place while under the age of eighteen.'

'Sorry. That came out the wrong way. I'm certainly annoyed that she was drinking, but I half expected that it would be something much worse.'

'Like what, Mr Bryant?'

'I dunno. Taking drugs or something.'

'Alcohol is a drug, Mr Bryant. A very dangerous one.'

'Yes, I know that. But I was thinking about the illicit ones. There's lots of it up in Robinvale. And they grow marijuana up there too.'

'Well, I've only seen her with alcohol. I've given her a warning, but next time I'll charge her. You understand that?'

'Yes, constable. Thanks for letting me know.'

'You realise she gets transported around by Skeeta Allender, I presume?'

'Unfortunately, yes. I'd prefer someone else if she needs male company, but I'm prepared to overlook Skeeta's obvious shortcomings if he means the difference between her staying up here or heading back to the city where who-knows-what will become of her.'

'Well, we'll leave it there for now, Mr Bryant. But just out of interest, how did your Patchewollock trip go? Productive?'

'Very. Bought a lovely kelpie bitch. She's a beautiful dog. As a matter of fact, I was on my way to feed her when you rang.'

'That's terrific. Thanks for your time, Mr Bryant. If you need support on what we've discussed, just give me a yell.'

'Appreciate that, constable. Good day.'

Bowker hung up. He opened his diary and recorded the details of his conversation and his other activities for the day. He was about to leave the office when the phone rang.

'Cath Bryant here, constable. Percy's gone outside to feed the dogs. I need a private word about Yvonne before he comes back.'

'Okay. Shoot.'

'Percy thinks that unless we treat her with kid gloves, she'll run away to Melbourne.'

'He mentioned that.'

Cath's tone became impatient. 'Well, I say good riddance! I don't want her here! I married Percy, not that little tramp. If she nicks off to the city, then so be it!'

'Isn't that a bit harsh, given what's she's been through?'

'My advice to you, senior constable, is don't let her get away with anything. She's a cancer in this family and probably in the whole district as well. I've heard where she leads some of the young people, and maybe older ones too if you believe the rumours. I'm just making sure that you don't let her put anything over you like she has with a lot of people.'

'Everything is not always as black and white as you might think.'

'Well, it should be. The law is the law. Apply without fear or favour. I hear Percy on the back veranda. I must go. Good day, officer.'

The phone went dead before Bowker could reply. He walked back into the kitchen where Rachael was sitting with head in hands. On the table were a few opened envelopes with accompanying correspondence and a low pile of unopened mail addressed directly to the Manangatang police. Bowker slowly sat down beside her.

'Oh, Rachael.'

In front of her on the table, still partly in its package, was a toy uniformed policeman with a toy knife sticking out of its back. Bowker picked up the packaging and looked at the postmark. 'Ballarat,' he said.

CHAPTER 9

A month passed in the blink of an eye, with the weather finally showing signs of moderating. The last few weeks had been kind to the couple. They were settling into the community without hassle, and there'd been no further vile contacts from Ballarat. Rachael landed the job at the school, working the equivalent of three days a week. Wednesday was her only full day off and she planned to try golf after the fairways turned green and the course was open for play. At present, its red dirt fairways were barely distinguishable from surrounding paddocks and its eighteen oiled sand scrapes were ringed with straggly dry weeds.

Rachael found the school staff supportive, friendly and welcoming. It comprised a mixture of graduates keen to make their mark on the kids' development, and more experienced teachers with families. Malcolm Swindon, the principal, was the oldest on staff with a significant age gap to senior teachers Peter Hindmarsh, Bob Wikman and primary campus leader Dwayne Jones. Several of the older women on staff had arrived as first year teachers themselves and married district farmers. This tradition was continuing with two or three current female graduates dating locals and destined to spend their lives in the district. Locals joked of the old days when the new teachers arrived by train and potential gallants hid in the scrub and selected their quarry as they disembarked. Very few among the current staff had experience in other schools unless moving to Manang for promotion. Still, there were a few. Among them was the agricultural science teacher, Adrian Weston, who had transferred to Manangatang with his wife and two daughters, the younger of whom was afflicted with a heart condition requiring regular testing at the Royal Children's Hospital in Melbourne. Prickle McColl's wife, Karly, had transferred from Ouyen to be closer to home, and Alan Henderson had taken up a position at the school to help out his aging parents who were struggling to keep the family farm running.

Rachael's role mainly involved the support of Jimmy Cobb, an integration student with an intellectual disability and a slight speech impediment. Jimmy struggled with formal learning, but was popular with the other kids. Rachael found him a likable lad who would give everything a try, even when success was probably beyond him. He was part of the form 4 cohort, the same group that contained Yvonne Bryant and the other new student, Travis Urdevic. Their coordinator was the Ag teacher, Adrian Weston, who Rachael found pleasant enough, but had a testy disposition around his students. She suspected that he didn't really like kids, despite having two of his own. During her own schooling, Rachael had seen teachers she suspected were similar. Teaching was a job – often one they excelled at – but there was little emotional attachment to their charges. Weston seemed particularly hard on Jimmy and made little allowance for his disability, expecting the same from him as he did from more able students. When annoyed, Weston became demonstratively angry and this scared Jimmy, even when he was not directly affected. But in the main, Jimmy coped well with school, particularly in classes such as Woodwork, Home Economics and surprisingly, Ag Science. He struggled in English, maths, science, and other subjects where he was required to complete written work. This was where Rachael was of most help to him, and they quickly developed a strong, happy relationship.

On Wednesday, and as if on cue with the cooling weather, Ray Gregson from Central Mallee Motors rang to report that the air conditioner drive belt had arrived and was ready to be fitted. Bowker was out and about, so Rachael delivered the old Peugeot to the garage.

Gregson came out in his oily overalls and motioned to Rachael to drive the car into the workshop. It was darker inside, taking Rachael's eyes a moment to adjust. What she saw disgusted her. The walls were adorned with calendars picturing women in various states of undress. When the car was parked in position, Gregson came across and opened the driver's door. Aware that he was looking down the front of her top, Rachael heaved the door wide open, hitting Gregson in the groin and forcing him to step back.

'The part had to come from Adelaide,' Gregson said. 'Only take fifteen minutes to fit, if you want to wait around.'

'I've got a few errands to run up the street.'

'Suit yourself.'

Rachael walked across the highway to the main street, happy to be away from Mr Greasy, even if it meant telling lies about running errands. Pengilly's shop was the only one she hadn't visited in the month they'd been in the town, and it was a good place to kill a few minutes while she waited for the car. It was difficult to assign a genre to Pengilly's store. Maybe hotchpotch or potpourri described it best. Plumbing fittings, building supplies, dog food, flour, and sugar, were all interspersed with hundreds of packets of knitting wool, rolls of sewing fabrics, toys, dolls and lollies. A bell tinkled as Rachael entered the shop. A late-middle-aged woman with grey hair and wearing an apron over a long cotton dress approached from the back.

'Hello. I've seen you around. The police lady,' the woman said, tightening her apron. 'I'm Maureen Pengilly.'

'Glad to meet you, Maureen. My name is Rachael Stow. I'm just having a quick squiz while my car's getting fixed. You certainly carry a variety of stock.'

'Just try to fill the gaps of what's not available elsewhere in the town. My husband is the local plumber, so we specialise a bit in that area.'

A partly bald man wearing work gear entered the shop and walked to the lolly counter.

'Excuse me,' Maureen said quietly. 'Better serve this bloke. I know what he's after and he won't be happy.' She tightened her apron again, probably more through habit than need.

Rachael continued to browse, amazed at what this place had in stock. Maureen moved to her customer. 'What can I get for you today, Barry?'

Barry leant forward with both hands on the counter. 'Those bloody ball taps I ordered. I've got the troughs built and all the pipe laid. I'm ready to turn on the pump.'

Maureen put her hands in her apron pockets. 'Haven't come in yet.'

'Shit, Maureen! You said they'd be here a fortnight ago!'

'They'll be on the next train for sure.'

Barry threw his hands in the air as he turned to leave. 'That train will need four diesels to pull the bloody thing it's carrying so much of your stuff!'

'Tomorrow probably.'

'I'll be back in town again Friday. They better be here by then.'

'Doin' our best.'

Barry looked back as he stormed through the shop door. 'And you wonder why blokes are goin' to Swan Hill.'

Maureen shrugged her shoulders and moved back to Rachael who was admiring a pretty doll in a blue lacy dress. Designed to sit on a little girl's bed, it had a wide, round skirt spread over the weighted cushion at the base. Rachael looked at the price and was pleasantly surprised. 'I think I'll take this. I've got a blue bedspread at home and this will look lovely sitting on top.'

Maureen rifled around under cardboard and plastic sheeting. 'There's a pink one somewhere here as well if you've got another bed.'

'I'm tempted. But I think I'll just go with the one.' Rachael felt for her bag. 'I've left my purse in the car. I'll go and get it. Won't be a minute.'

'Don't be silly. I'll book it out to you,' Maureen said as she touched

Rachael on the arm. 'Now you're a local you'll need an account here anyway.' Maureen pushed the doll into a second-hand plastic bag. 'There you go, Rachael. Come again, there's always a bargain.' She leant closer and lowered her voice. 'Before you go, a word of warning, woman to woman. Watch out for Greasy Gregson over there at the garage. I don't normally talk about other people, but you're the new woman in town and I don't want to see you harassed. He's a sleaze of the highest order. A lot of the women won't even buy petrol there. He makes these crude little jokes about checking your grease nipples or polishing your headlights. Yuck.'

Rachael already had Gregson tabbed as a slime-ball, but played a straight bat. 'Thanks for the heads-up.'

Rachael crossed the road to the garage where Gregson was tightening the last of the bolts. He leant in the driver's side and started the car. He checked that the belt was spinning correctly, then slammed down the bonnet and put his head in the car door and turned on the air conditioner. He stood up straight. 'All spot on.'

'Thanks for that. I presume you'll send out a bill?'

'Yep, at the end of the month.' Gregson hesitated for a moment. 'Could be a way to forget about the bill, if you know what I mean?'

'Goodbye, Mr Gregson,' Rachael said sharply as she climbed into the car. Then she backed out, and roared up the road, her foot flat to the floor.

***

Three weeks of tennis confirmed the chase for the services of Bowker and Rachael was not ill-conceived. From the first ball he hit, it was clear the new policeman could really play. Big serve, great ground shots, crisp volleys and a devastating overhead quickly had him ranked amongst the competition's top players. His first few sets also confirmed that Prong Lyon's reputation was not undeserved. No great power, but exquisite control and placement which manoeuvred opponents around the court until an opening was created for the easy put-away. Bowker's partner, Terry the chemist, was also an accomplished player. He hit with vicious top spin, his metal Wilson racquet flashing in the ever-present blinding sun.

Rachael likewise made her mark. Partnered with Judi Wikman, they made a powerful combination. Both tall and athletic, they dominated the net, and in doubles that's what counted most.

But the Saturday competition was more than just four sets of tennis. It was a time to sit in the shade and chat, an opportunity to catch up on the week's events whilst sharing an ice-cold lemon-flavoured drink from one of the ubiquitous foam-covered coolers. It was a time for the little kids to run wild in the environs of the courts and the surrounding bush. And it was a time to enjoy a cuppa at afternoon tea time and hopefully secure a square of Nyree Templeton's famous jelly slice or Nola Grant's passionfruit-iced sponge before the kids descended on the shed like an army of sugar ants. In spite of the heat and the isolation, Bowker and his better half were developing a soft spot for this little slice of serenity, far from the madding crowd.

On this Saturday, a new duo arrived for afternoon tea. Yvonne Bryant was accompanied by a scruffy, scrawny-built kid who looked in need of a decent feed, a drench for worms, or both. He wore his mousy brown hair in a rat-tail halfway down his back, and a good dose of acne reddened his cheeks. An earring in each lobe completed the picture of another dragged-up city kid out of his natural habitat. He and Yvonne plonked themselves down at one of the long tables, immediately tucking into sandwiches and cupcakes. A pair of older women looked at each other before one finally spoke. 'This afternoon tea is for the tennis players only.'

'I've seen kids from school having some,' Yvonne snapped back.

'They're either playing tennis, or their parents are playing,' the woman explained.

'So? I haven't got parents, have I?' Yvonne replied.

'Neither have I,' her companion added.

'You can't stop us anyway,' Yvonne warned, as she defiantly

shovelled two sandwiches into her mouth. Suddenly she caught sight of Bowker standing in the doorway, wiping sweat from his brow with a hand towel. He was staring directly at her and her friend. She looked away and grabbed another sandwich.

'Here's the policeman. He'll arrest you for stealing food if you don't leave,' the woman said. By now, the whole shed had gone quiet. Bowker was again on show.

'What's the problem, Yvonne,' Bowker asked.

'We're just having a sandwich,' she replied.

'This afternoon tea was brought by the tennis players. Unfortunately, it's not open to the public.'

Yvonne sprung to her feet. 'Well, you can shove your afternoon tea up your arse, then.' She grabbed another sandwich and stormed out, followed closely by the new lad.

'Yeah, up your arse sideways,' the boy said as he kicked a chair out of the way.

Bowker followed them outside. 'Yvonne. Back here, please.'

Yvonne came back defiantly, the boy trailing behind. 'Yeah, what?'

'Well, I don't like your attitude for a start.'

'Yeah, well I don't like theirs,' Yvonne said, hands on hips. 'A couple of sandwiches wouldn't send anyone broke.'

'If you'd asked first, they may have let you share. But obviously you went in there like a bull in a china shop.'

'If you don't take what you want, you get nothing in this world.'

'Spot on,' the boy added without looking at Bowker.

Bowker towered over the lad. 'What's your name, son?'

'Don't have to tell you if I don't want to,' the boy said looking at the ground.

'Afraid you do,' Bowker replied.

'You're not wearing a uniform, so you're not on duty. So technically you're not a cop at the moment,' Yvonne said smugly.

'I'm always on duty. You can depend on it. So, what's your name, lad?'

The boy looked at Bowker for a moment then relented. 'Travis Urdevic.'

'You live out in Percy Bryant's old farmhouse?'

Yvonne jumped in first. 'It's not a house. It's a dump. Wouldn't let pigs live in there.'

'Yeah. Fuckin' shit hole.' Travis added.

'How'd you get into town, Travis? It's Saturday, so no school buses.'

'Me mother brought me in. She needed more grog, so I came in with her.' He looked at the ground again.

'Thought you didn't have parents.'

'Got no father. Just a mother.'

'What's her name?'

'Wendy.'

'Wendy Urdevic?'

'Wendy Blake. Urdevic is my old man's name.'

'You said you didn't have a father. Is he deceased?'

Travis again looked up at Bowker. 'May as well be. Hardly ever see him. Last I heard he was in jail.'

'Sorry to hear that, Travis.'

'Best place for him, according to me mum.'

'What car does your mum drive?'

'An old grey Falcon shit-heap with a maroon quarter panel on the passenger side.'

Bowker turned to Yvonne. 'You come in with Travis's mum as well, Yvonne?'

'Nuh,' she said disinterestedly.

'Did Skeeta bring you in?'

Yvonne immediately fired up. 'So what if he did? There's no law against it.'

'Where's Skeeta now? At the pub?'

'Prob'ly. Said to meet him later and he'll buy me something for tea at the fish shop. Then he'll give me a lift home. Not that it's any of your business.'

'He know you're with Travis?'

'Don't think he'd care.'

'How are you getting home, Travis?'

'Probably just hitch.'

'Hitch to Winnambool? You might be waiting a while.'

'Might climb in with Skeeta, then.' Travis glanced hopefully at Yvonne, then looked at the ground.

'Where you heading to now?' Bowker asked.

'Up the street, probably,' Travis replied.

'Not that it's any of the police's business where we're goin',' Yvonne said. 'We ain't broke no laws.'

'Haven't been smoking anything you shouldn't, have you?' Bowker asked.

'Don't believe in that bullshit,' Yvonne said as she folded her arms across her chest. 'My mother died of that.' She stared out into the distance.

'Empty out your pockets, please. Both of you,' Bowker said

'You're joking,' Yvonne said.

'No, I'm not, Yvonne. Empty them out, please.'

They turned out their pockets. There was little of interest except for a half-full packet of Escort cigarettes.

'You buy these, Travis?' Bowker asked.

'Mum gave them to me so she wouldn't be tempted. She's trying to give up.'

Bowker smiled as he put the cigarettes in his pocket. 'Tell her I've taken them for safe keeping.'

'You finished with us now?' Yvonne asked in annoyance.

'I have. As long as you keep out of trouble.'

The two teenagers wandered off mumbling and giggling. Bowker was sure he could still smell a sweet aroma in the air. He kept an eye on them as they left the tennis courts and walked by the rear of horse boxes used only on race days. As they passed under the biggest eucalypt in the area, they stopped abruptly, dropped to their haunches and examined something on the ground. They both looked up into the tree before Yvonne carefully picked up what Bowker now assumed to be a baby bird. Travis helped her scramble onto the roof of the stables, and on tiptoes she carefully placed the bird in a hollow in the trunk of the tree. As she clambered down, a kookaburra fluttered in from a higher branch and nestled into the hollow. There's hope for those kids yet, Bowker thought as wandered back to the afternoon tea shed even more eager for a cuppa and some of those home cooked delicacies.

'Hey, Greg, you're wanted on Court 2. Pay attention, you dopey bastard,' Prong yelled.

Dopey Bastard, thought Greg with a smile. He was quickly being accepted as one of them.

CHAPTER 10

Bowker and Rachael joined most of the players after tennis for a few drinks and a counter tea at the hotel. Two hundred metres away in the main street, Skeeta was buying food at Hackle's milk bar. 'I'm havin' a hamburger with the lot. What do you want?' he asked Yvonne.

'The same, but with no egg. Couple of potato cakes as well.' Yvonne replied with her arm through his.

'Just a plain hamburger will do me,' Travis said, not game to look at Skeeta.

'Couldn't give a shit what you have, mate,' Skeeta said. 'You're payin' for it.'

'Got no money, have I?'

Skeeta shrugged. 'Your problem, not mine.'

'Don't be so nasty, Skeeta,' Yvonne said quietly. 'A plain hamburger won't break you.'

'Well, you buy it for him, then.'

'You know Percy won't give me money. He's shit-scared I'll buy grog or something.' Yvonne removed her arm from Skeeta's and looked at Travis. 'You can have one of my potato cakes, Trav,' she said.

Skeeta reacted nastily. 'So, you only feel like one potato cake, do you Yvonne? Is that what you're saying?'

'Yeah, Travis can have the other one,' she said defiantly.

Skeeta turned to Hackle. 'I'll have two hamburgers with the lot, but one without egg, thanks Hack.' He looked at Yvonne. 'Oh, yeah. And *one* potato cake.'

Yvonne protested, pushing Skeeta in the side. 'I said I wanted two potato cakes.'

'Yeah, but you were gonna give one to this useless dickhead. Let him get his own.' He turned back to Hackle. 'Just one potato cake, Hack.'

When their food was cooked, they adjourned to a bench on the footpath outside the shop. When Skeeta trotted to his ute to fetch his grog, Yvonne slipped the potato cake to Travis who wolfed it down in three quick bites. Skeeta returned with two cans of rum and Coke, handing one to Yvonne. He looked at Travis. 'If you need something to wash down that fuckin' potato cake, there's a tap outside the chemists.'

No-one said a word while Skeeta and Yvonne finished their burgers. Skeeta stood up and brushed crumbs off his shirt. 'Think it's time to hit the track, Yvonne. You ready?'

'Yeah. What about you, Travis?'

Before he could answer, Skeeta jumped in. 'He can make up his own mind. Nothin' to do with us.'

'Can't he get a ride home with us, Skeeta? He lives just across the paddock.'

'I'm not a fuckin' taxi service for dead-shit kids,' Skeeta said as he strode off towards his ute.

'We can't leave him in town,' Yvonne said as she stood up. 'If you won't take him, I'll go to the phone box and get old Perce to come in and pick us both up.'

'This is bullshit, Yvonne,' Skeeta said, angrily stabbing a finger towards her as he retraced his steps. Yvonne was unmoved and after a moment her boyfriend relented. 'Alright, I'll take him. But this is the one and only time. He's not my responsibility and he's not yours.' They walked to the ute. 'You can ride in the back, mate.'

Travis stepped up onto the tow bar and climbed into the tray. 'Better than walking, I s'pose.'

Yvonne opened the passenger door. 'He'll choke in the dust, Skeeta.'

'Well, he's not getting' in the front if that's what you're thinkin'.' Skeeta climbed behind the wheel and slammed his door. He dropped a squealing U turn in the main street before they headed out of town, Skeeta using the dustiest and most corrugated parts of the unsealed Winnambool Road. At Piccadilly Corner, he stopped and wound down his window. 'This is as far as you go, mate.'

Yvonne instantly protested. 'It's miles from where he lives.'

'He's got two legs, hasn't he? It'll only take him an hour or so to walk home.'

Yvonne crossed her arms and stared angrily towards him. 'You're just being nasty, Skeeta. Travis hasn't done nothing to hurt you.'

'He came up here to live.' Skeeta stuck his head out his window. 'Get out, mate.'

Travis jumped out, and even in the moonlight Yvonne could see he was layered in red dust. 'See you at school Monday,' she said as Skeeta floored the accelerator and the big V8 blasted a bonus cloud of thick dust back in Travis's direction.

For thirty seconds there was silence in the ute. 'You can be really nasty at times, Skeeta,' Yvonne said, her arms still crossed.

'Not as nasty as I'll get if you start hanging around with that loser.' He angrily pushed her shoulder with the heel of his palm. 'Get my drift?'

Yvonne didn't answer, just turned away and stared out her side window.

***

At six the next morning, Bowker walked to Red Cameron's stables where two horses were tied to the rail. The filly was already in her full racing harness, so Bowker knew today would be fast work on the track rather than jogging for miles along the dirt roads to the west of the town.

Red emerged from a small shed carrying the colt's harness and heaved it atop a wooden rail. 'Thought we might let 'em slip along for a mile or two this morning.'

Bowker smiled. He grabbed the bridle from a nail on the post, opened the horse's mouth, pushed the bit between the horse's teeth, slipped the bridle over his ears and fastened the cheek strap. There was a dull jingling sound as the horse rolled the bit on his tongue, then a loud vibrating snort as the colt blew air between his lips. Bowker grinned. These were the sounds of his adolescence. He grabbed the harness off the rail and threw the saddle over the colt's wither. He buckled the girth, crupper and breastplate then threw the hopples over the colt's back, put the horse's legs through each loop and did up the carrier straps. He brought up the cart and threaded the shafts into the saddle, tied them down and ran the traces back to the lugs on the cart. As he buckled up the reins, he realised he had just harnessed the horse without a conscious thought. Years working with harness horses made it automatic. Like swimming or riding a bike.

'What year did you win the Mildura Cup?' Bowker asked.

'1959. Peter Carr drove him. Came off thirty-six yards behind. Rated two minutes thirteen, which was pretty good for then.'

'Win a fortune?'

'The race was worth a hundred and fifty quid. Winner got a hundred. But it's better than losing.'

The two men swung into the carts and crossed the lane and onto the track. Soon they melded into a cloud of dust, zipping along to a rhythm of hoof beats. Bowker had come home to his boyhood.

***

Monday morning broke warm and clear, and by eight thirty the sky was a cobalt blue. Rachael left for work and Bowker strolled to his office. He had a call to make. To IBR, the section of the force which handled criminal records.

'I'm checking if you've got anything on an Yvonne Bryant. She's a juvenile, sixteen years old.'

There was a short delay, then a response from the female voice. 'There's a Yvonne Lynette Bryant of that age.'

'That's her. What's on her sheet?'

'No time in detention, but several charges of minor shoplifting and a couple for assaults at her school.'

'What about her mother? A Lynette Bryant?'

Another delay. 'We've got a Lynette Karen Bryant and a Lynette Shirley Bryant.'

'Lynette Shirley sounds right. Mother's name was Shirley.'

'She's deceased.'

'Yeah, I know. What's on her record?'

'Mostly drug related. Couple of cases of petty theft from cars and houses. Sound familiar?'

'Yeah. Financing the habit. Can I run a couple more past you?'

'You got a crime syndicate running out of Manangatang or something?'

'Pretty quiet up here actually. But I've got a feeling there could be something in the wind.'

'Well, if it's in the wind I wouldn't worry about it. By tomorrow it'll be on the other side of the state and won't be your problem.'

'So, you've been up here?'

'Hubby and I camped on the Murray at Boundary Bend a couple of years ago. Bloody wind nearly blew the caravan into the river. And the dust – shit! Had to clean out my ears with a shovel.'

Bowker laughed out loud. 'Bit like that at times. Just a zephyr outside now.'

'Is that the breeze or a car?'

'Ha ha. Very funny. Can you run a Wendy Blake, please?'

Another pause. 'I've got a Wendy Dianne Blake. By her date of birth, she'd now be twenty-nine years old.'

'No, she's too young. The one I'm after has a sixteen year-old son. Got any others?'

'Not by that name.'

'Maybe she hasn't got a record. What's on the history of the twenty-nine year-old?'

'Petty stuff. Underage drinking, drug possession, drunk in a public place a few times, minor assault, breaking and entering. Lots of bonds, but never been to jail.'

'Does a Travis Urdevic appear? U-R-D-E-V-I-C, I think it's spelt.'

Another delay. 'Got two Urdevics. Yeah. One's a Travis. Just a kid. Sixteen.'

'That's him.'

'Been in juvenile detention. Possession of marijuana, breaking and entering, common assault. Threats to kill. Only came out of Turana a month ago.'

'The other Urdevic you've got will be his father. Still inside, according to his son.'

'Joseph Francis Urdevic. Currently serving a ten-year sentence at Ararat for armed robbery. But he's got a record as long as your arm. Petty theft, drug possession, extortion, belting up his family. His first beef was sex with a thirteen year-old girl, would you believe?'

Bowker stared out the station window. 'I believe alright. It's starting to make sense.'

'One last thing about your Joseph Urdevic. He's eligible for parole.'

***

That evening Bowker and Rachael strolled around the town debriefing their day, the sun now an orange disc slipping below the western horizon, a few scattered red and purple clouds escorting its descent. The breeze barely moved the leaves in the trees. The town seemed eerily quiet.

A well-dressed octogenarian man walked slowly towards them. Rachael recognised him as Blair Herbert, a man of enormous intellect who had practised law in the town since his graduation from university in the 1920s. She had met him at a book club meeting the previous week and was astounded at his insights into *The Grapes of Wrath*. She could have listened for hours as he related stories from the early days of the town. Like about how the Mallee scrub was cleared with twin Bulldog tractors pulling a chain stretched between them. About a football train that took the whole of Manangatang to Chillingollah for the grand final of the district league. About a drought when two horses died of thirst when they failed to step over a knee-high wire fence to access the nearby dam. 'It just never occurred to them,' he lamented. As Mr Herbert passed, he tipped his hat and continued his walk, reciting French poetry to himself.

'I rang Melbourne today and chased down a few criminal records,' Bowker said after a minute or two.

Rachael took his hand as they walked. 'Yeah? Like whose?'

'Yvonne Bryant and her new friend out at Winnambool.'

'And?'

'Pretty much what I expected.' They waited to cross Rainbow Street as a local woman passed in an old black Valiant, giving them a friendly wave as she went by. 'Yvonne's had a few minor run-ins with the police. Travis's record is a bit more serious. Some violence and threats to kill. Not long out of Turana.'

'Any drug use with Travis?'

'Yeah. Possession of marijuana.'

Rachael hesitated before continuing. 'Today he was sprung sharing a joint with another kid down the back of the school.'

Bowker stopped walking, turned and looked at Rachael. 'What's the other kid's name? Yvonne Bryant, I bet.'

'No. A boy named Leigh Davidson.'

Bowker released Rachael's hand. 'How come I wasn't called in?'

The principal had asked that the issue be kept in-house, but Rachael knew she should have informed Bowker when she first arrived home from work. 'The boss was worried about Leigh. Good kid, first mistake. Parents are fantastic supporters of the school. Kept Leigh in Manang when half his classmates were sent away to private school.'

'It's not Travis's first mistake. He hasn't earnt any favours.'

'If the principal had called you about Travis, he'd have to do the same with Leigh.'

'So, what did he do? Give them a slap on the wrist and say, "naughty boys, don't use drugs"?'

'Suspended them both for a week with the threat of expulsion if they do it again. Mr and Mrs Davidson are distraught. Malcolm couldn't get hold of Travis's mother. No phone out there, so he sent home a letter to be signed and brought back.'

'Where'd they get the weed? If someone in the area's dealing, then they're going to jail if I have anything to do with it. The last thing I want is Manang kids being exposed to that shit. Or something worse. Alcohol is a big enough problem here already.'

'Neither kid would say where it came from, but I'll bet a thousand dollars Travis brought it to school. Probably came with him from Melbourne.'

'I feel like visiting the school tomorrow and putting the heat on Travis and his mate.'

'What's Leigh Davidson going to tell you? What you know already. Travis supplied it. And Travis is an old pro at this game. He'll give you nothing. Why don't you give it a few days to settle down, then ring Malcolm and ask to come up and talk to the senior kids about substance abuse?'

Bowker stared into space for a few moments. 'It shits me that these kids get a week off school for using drugs.'

Rachael took his hand. 'You've always got the heavy option up your sleeve if you need it.'

'That's true, I s'pose.'

They walked hand-in-hand down to the end of Pioneer Street and returned home via the main drag. By now it was dark, and the moon was rising out of the east, yellow and full.

Bowker smiled. 'A full moon, a balmy night; only one thing for it.'

'I'll race you home,' Rachael said as the couple sprinted the last hundred yards like a pair of school kids.

CHAPTER 11

A week passed with little on the policeman's agenda except helping an Annuello farmer move sheep across the highway to his shearing shed. Sitting in the police car with the reds and blues flashing was usually sufficient to slow drivers to a sensible speed, but today it was difficult to see any distance through the dust being thrown up by the sheep. As the mob crossed an intersection with a dirt road, Bowker spotted Wendy Blake's old grey Falcon cross the bitumen highway at a senseless speed, sending ewes and lambs bolting in all directions. He couldn't make out Wendy for the dust but could imagine her crouched behind the wheel like an old lady. During his short time in the force, he'd seen far too many drug and violence affected women who had aged beyond their years and faced their future with little hope and even less joy. At twenty-nine years of age, he imagined Wendy Blake would probably look more like a woman of fifty.

A day later he set up a breath-testing station on the highway just inside the town limits. Much to his satisfaction, of the fifty or so car drivers he tested, only three registered any alcohol in their blood, and none were over the limit. Semi-trailers delivered less clear-cut success. Seventeen drivers were tested, all of whom were alcohol free. Bowker suspected a couple may have taken pep pills to stay awake, but had no equipment to conduct testing, and none of the drivers exhibited sufficient symptoms to justify taking them off the road. Of greater concern was compliance with logbook regulations, with several drivers having uncompleted books. He felt some sympathy for their situation, but none for their failure to follow the law. He knew they had tight schedules, often under orders to have their load delivered within an impossible timeframe. With fierce competition within the trucking industry, many drivers, particularly owner-operators, could not afford to refuse assignments, even those requiring them to stretch the law. Many just gambled they wouldn't be pulled up and could fudge their records when safely at their destination. Since Manangatang fell somewhere near the halfway point on a major route between Sydney and Adelaide, Bowker knew most drivers had been on the road for an extended period and legislated rest breaks couldn't be avoided. He issued half a dozen infringement notices that would automatically trigger fines and licence demerit points.

He was just about to pack the gear into his vehicle, when a car-carrying semi-trailer dropped down through the gears as it entered the town. One last one, he thought, as he stepped onto the bitumen to flag down the big green rig. The driver ignored him and accelerated across the main intersection and headed for Piangil. Bowker hurriedly threw everything into the boot, leapt in the front seat and sped off in pursuit, lights flashing and siren wailing. To his amazement, the truck was around the first bend pulled up on the side of the road. Its doors flew open just as Bowker pulled alongside and he jumped out in time to see an attempted driver-swap. 'Stay where you are mate.'

'Didn't realise you were pulling us over until we got through the town. That's why we stopped now,' the driver said, leaning with hands against the truck and his back to Bowker.

'Yeah, sorry about that,' said the bloke on the passenger side.

'Show me your licence, please,' Bowker said to the driver.

The driver turned around angrily. 'It's bloody suspended, thanks to you.'

'Shit, mate,' was all Bowker could think to say as he stared at the tattooed driver who had delivered his furniture.

'You dobbed me in to your bastard mates at St Arnaud, didn't ya? They were sitting there waiting for us. Bloody entrapment, if you ask me.'

'Only one person to blame, Sean,' Bowker said. 'It is Sean, isn't it? Sean Doherty? What are you doin' up here again, mate?'

'Lost me job, didn't I? This is my brother's rig. Just givin' Brian a breather.' He looked into the sky and then slammed his fist into the truck door in exasperation. 'Fuck!'

'Didn't think you'd be stupid enough to drive without a licence,' Bowker said.

'Out here in the middle of bloody nowhere? Never seen a traffic cop.' Sean said.

'Thought Manangatang would be the last place you'd risk your luck,' Bowker replied, resisting the urge to declare 'Bowker two, arsehole nil'.

Brian walked around the front of the truck to the driver's side. 'I've been travellin' this way for fifteen years and I've never been pulled over between Tailem Bend and Narrandera. That's four hundred and fifty fuckin' miles mate. What are the fuckin' chances?'

'Can I see your licence, please, sir?' Bowker said.

'It's all in fuckin' order,' Brian replied as he dragged his wallet from his back pocket.

Bowker pointed into the cab of the truck. 'I'll have your logbook too, please.'

Sean grabbed the book from the dashboard and practically threw it at Bowker. 'Why don't you leave us to do our job and spend a bit of time pullin' the locals into line. I nearly skittled half a dozen school kids fart-arsing around on the crossing when I was leavin' in the furniture truck'

'Yeah, gotta talk to them about the crossing,' Bowker said absently as he flipped through the logbook.

'Have a special talk to that sexy little piece with the green hair and the nose ring. Lifted up her dress and mooned me when I blasted the horn.'

Bloody Yvonne, Bowker thought to himself, but said nothing as he flipped through the last few pages of the book. 'Been a long time between rest stops, Bryan. Which means your logbook's either filled out wrongly, or Sean here's been doing a fair bit of unlicenced drivin'. Either way, you've been breaking the law.' Bowker went back to his car and completed the relevant paperwork on the bonnet.

On his return, Bowker handed Brian his logbook and his licence, plus the appropriate infringement notices. 'Okay. On your way boys,' he ordered. 'Nobody drives except Brian. And all the proper rest breaks need to be taken. Might ask my interstate colleagues to keep an eye on you.'

'You don't give a bloody inch, do you mate?' Sean said nastily.

'I could have done you both for trying to swap seats before I caught up with you. I could also have charged you with failing to stop when ordered to do so by a police officer. So count your lucky stars I'm in a good mood.'

'Bloody Manangatang!' Sean said as he climbed into the passenger side of the truck. 'Arse end of the earth!'

'And you're just passing through,' Bowker said with a huge grin. Bowker three, arseholes nil.

Brian shoved the big semi into gear and it slowly headed up the highway in a northerly direction. Bowker counted eight gear changes before it went out of sight around the next corner.

***

Thursday was one of Bowker's days off this week and, with Rachael at work, he spent a leisurely time at home on his own. His latest project was a vegetable garden in the back yard. The soil was light and sandy, but likely to grow something if given enough water. The irrigated blocks along the river, rich with citrus fruit and grapes, were evidence of this. Bowker thought tomatoes and zucchinis might be the go.

If he couldn't grow zucchinis, then forget about trying anything else! At four in the afternoon, as he stood admiring his rowed-up cultivated masterpiece, his office phone rang. So much for my day off, he thought. He was within his rights to let the call go to the answering machine, but that wasn't how Bowker wanted to run his patch. He went inside and answered.

'Tim from the post office here, Greg. Might need to come down the main street. There's about twenty bikies at Hackle's café, and they're givin' the school kids a hard time.'

Bowker washed his hands, locked the house and drove the two blocks to the shops, thinking it more impressive to arrive in the police car than just strolling down in his civvies. He parked in front of Hackle's, squeezing between a pair of slung-back Harleys. The motorcycles were parked in formation, backed in against the curb one beside the other. Like a row of dominoes, Bowker thought. Kick one over and they'd all go down in a pretty spectacular display. A group of leather-clad men, most with bushy beards and tattoos, stood around the café entrance laughing and swearing. Two were eating Chiko rolls, three or four others scoffing down hamburgers. Bowker walked across to a group of the older school kids.

'They won't let us in the shop,' a form 6 boy said nervously. 'Told us to go fuck ourselves.'

'One of them asked me for a root,' a red-faced schoolgirl added with the faintest of smiles.

'Is that right?' Bowker said. He walked to the bikies closest to the shop door. 'Move out of the doorway, please. Some of the kids want to use the shop.'

The biggest of the men, with a long red beard, put his arm across the doorway. 'Yeah? Well they can wait their bloody turn.'

'I'm not going to ask again. Please move out of the doorway,' Bowker ordered.

'And who the fuck are you to be givin' us orders, mate?' red beard replied.

'Manangatang Police. But I bet seeing me arrive in the police car probably gave you a clue.'

'You could be a mechanic or somethin'. Just servicin' the car,' another rough head chimed in.

Bowker flashed his Freddy. 'Senior Constable Greg Bowker.'

Red beard looked at the badge. 'Pretty badge. Pretty fuckin' useless out here in the middle of nowhere.' The other men laughed.

'Excuse me,' Bowker said as he pushed through the group and into Hackle's shop. Five bikies were inside. Cindy, Hackle's wife, was wrapping up burgers. 'Any problems in here, Cindy?'

'Not if you ignore the filthy comments, senior constable,' she replied, emphasising the police reference. 'Made them pay before I cooked anything.' Cindy was a petite girl with brown hair in a ponytail. Petite, but not one to be messed with.

'I just asked her for one with the lot. She took it the wrong way. Dirty bitch,' said one of the customers leaning against the counter.

'Watch your mouth, pal,' Bowker snarled. 'Soon as you get your food move outside so the kids can use the shop.'

'Yes, sir, senior constable,' one of the men said sarcastically as he offered a mock salute.

Bowker left the shop and spoke loudly. 'Okay, boys. Soon as you've finished your food, I'd like you to mount up and be on your way. I don't appreciate the way you've treated people here and how you've spoken to the kids – especially the girls.'

'They've heard it before,' said red beard with his foot up on a bench seat at the edge of the footpath. 'Make out they're little innocents, but I bet they screw 'emselves silly at the weekend. Or wish they could. Isn't that right, girls?' None of the students responded. 'Come on, tell the truth. Deep down you're all like that green-headed bitch with the nose ring.'

Bowker turned to the school kids. 'Was Yvonne here?'

'She rode off on the back of one of their bikes,' one of the boys replied.

'Did she get on the bike herself?' Bowker asked.

'It was her own fuckin' decision, officer, so don't try and make out it's a bloody abduction or somethin',' red beard said. 'Rooster asked her if she wanted something big, hot and throbbing between her legs and she was on the back of his Harley in two seconds flat.' The bikies all laughed.

'Where'd they go?' Bowker demanded.

'Out the road for a spin. It'll be a quickie, I'd say. We want to be in Balranald before dark,' rough head said.

'You never know, the horny little bitch might want to come to New South with us,' red beard said with a chuckle. 'Entertain us on the way. Bet she's up for it too.'

'Your friend has five minutes to bring her back before I go looking,' Bowker said. He turned to the kids. 'Which way did they go?' They all pointed south. Down the Sea Lake Road.

Half a dozen leather-clad men joined the group from the direction of the pub, all carrying bottles of spirits. 'Hope you blokes aren't intending to drink that on your way to Balranald. Point oh five, over the river as well,' Bowker said.

'And who are you, dickhead?' A short fat hairy man of about thirty said.

'That dickhead is the local police, Fat Guts,' red beard said with a chuckle. 'So watch your language.'

'Sorry, officer, I didn't know you were a policeman, otherwise I wouldn't have called you a dickhead,' Fat Guts said with mock regret. 'Had I known, I would have called you a fuckin' arsehole!' He looked at the others, chortling at his own attempted humour.

'You're getting pretty close to spendin' the night in the lock up,' Bowker said, moving towards him. 'So I'd show a little respect.' It was becoming too much for three of the kids who hurried down the street towards the pub corner.

The tension was broken by the rumble of a Harley as it came down the main street, a man with a long blond beard on the front and

Yvonne behind, holding him around the waist. Rooster backed the bike into the curb and the two dismounted.

'Get in the police car, Yvonne,' Bowker ordered immediately.

'What?' Yvonne exclaimed. 'You can't make me. I ain't done nothin' wrong.'

'Get in the car now,' Bowker repeated.

'Who the fuck are you, mate?' Rooster said. 'I've a good mind to belt you into next week.'

'And if I wasn't a policeman, I'd have great pleasure in seeing you try.' Bowker turned again to Yvonne and pointed to the police car. 'Get in the car. You're under arrest for riding a motorcycle without a helmet.' Yvonne stormed to the car, got in the back seat and slammed the door closed.

'You can't arrest someone for that,' Rooster said, chesting Bowker.

'I just did, arsehole. Now get out of my face or you'll be next,' Bowker said.

Rooster took a step backwards. 'Did you fuckin' hear that, fellas? The sheriff of this one-horse shithole is threatenin' to run me in. Have to give you full marks for guts, officer.'

'Or fuckin' stupidity,' red beard added.

'Piss off, the lot of you!' came a voice behind them. Bowker glanced across and saw Tim from the post office, his face glowing red and his eyes standing out like ball-bearings. From the direction of the pub, a dozen or so of the local colts led by Basher Duncan moved towards the group. 'Yeah, get the fuck out of the district and don't come back,' said Heifer Delahunty, a colossus of a man.

'Hope this shit hole has a hospital, dickhead?' Fat Guts said.

'Even got a morgue that'll fit a garden gnome like you,' Heifer shot back.

'Okay, let's all settle down,' Bowker said holding up both hands, realising that things were becoming explosive and that he was close to the edge himself. 'You blokes dropped in to get something to eat, and you've done that. Things have got a bit heated, but nobody's been hurt, so how about we keep it that way. Get on your way to Balranald and everyone's happy.'

There were a few moments of tense silence.

'You can get fucked, the lot of you,' Rooster said as he climbed on his bike and kick-started it with a theatrical flourish. The others followed and soon there was a cacophony of rumbling Harley Davidsons. Rooster led off, and as a final display of false bravado, each rider roared from the curb in sequence, like a squadron of spitfires peeling away from their World War 2 formation. The column reached the main intersection, turned east, and roared away towards the border at Piangil.

Heifer gave an almost imperceptible nod to Bowker and turned back towards to pub. 'I feel like we've earnt a beer,' he said. The group walked back up the street laughing and chiacking.

Bowker turned to Tim. 'Thanks, mate.'

'Renegades have to stick together, mate. See ya Saturday.' Tim returned to the post office as Bowker walked to his car to confront the teenage tirade he knew was coming.

CHAPTER 12

'This is bullshit,' Yvonne babbled immediately as Bowker climbed in the police car. 'You can't arrest me for not wearin' a helmet and put me in jail for that. I thought it was just a fine or somethin' if you got caught.'

'I'm not arresting you and you're not going to jail. I'm driving you home. I need to talk to your grandfather.'

She leaned over the back of the front seat. 'Skeeta's taking me home when he gets back from Sea Lake.'

'Not today, he's not.'

'This is kidnapping!'

'Tell that to the local copper. Put on your seat belt.'

Yvonne connected her seatbelt, but she hadn't finished saying her piece. 'I could get you into trouble, you know. I could say you tried to shag me in the car on the way home.'

Bowker looked over his shoulder as he backed out of his park. 'You could. But you won't.'

Yvonne folded her arms across her chest. 'Why won't I?'

'Because deep down you're not a bad kid. You've just had a rotten upbringing.' Bowker slowly headed north up Wattle Street. 'And secondly, I'm picking up a friend to take her sight-seeing at Winnambool, just to cover my back.'

Yvonne unfolded her arms and leaned forward. 'The one you live with. Rachael Stow from school?'

Bowker glanced at Yvonne in the rearview mirror. 'Yeah. You like her?'

'She's alright. Better than some of the others. She doesn't treat me like shit like some of 'em do. And she's really good with Jimmy.'

'So I've heard.'

'He likes her too. Helps him with his work. Helps me sometimes as well.' She paused. 'She's too nice to be hangin' around with a dumb copper.'

'That's what I think sometimes.'

'I s'pose you're not as bad as some of the Melbourne police. At least you talk to me like I'm a person.'

Bowker smiled as he glanced again in the mirror. Poor bloody kid. Who knows what she's been through?

Luckily Rachael had just arrived home from work and Bowker explained the situation as Yvonne waited in the backseat of his car. The trip out to Winnambool was relatively quiet until they reached Piccadilly Corner.

'Gonna buy a Harley when I get my licence,' Yvonne said, looking out her side window. 'It was fun beltin' down the road with Rooster. We got up to over a hundred and twenty.'

'Kilometres?' Bowker asked, already knowing the answer he'd receive.

'No, miles an hour, derr,' Yvonne said. 'Made me eyes sting.'

'Do you think you'd be able to handle a big bike like that?' Rachael asked.

'Been practising with the motor bikes on the farm. Old Perce doesn't know, but.'

Bowker looked at her in the rear vision mirror. 'Wear a helmet?'

'Don't need to. It's on private property.' She again crossed her arms.

'Your brain doesn't care whether it's private or public ground when it smashes into it,' Bowker said.

'My brain's fucked anyway, just like my life. Best to have fun while you can. People like me don't seem to make it into old people's homes.' Yvonne paused before unfolding her arms and asking, 'You going to come to my funeral, Bowker?'

Bowker and Rachael exchanged glances. 'I'll be dead twenty years before you need a funeral,' Bowker answered.

'I'll bet ya twenty dollars I die before you,' Yvonne said, leaning forward.

'Pretty hard to collect if that happens,' Rachael replied.

'Oh, yeah. Never thought of that.' Yvonne leant back in her seat.

There was silence for a few minutes as the dust boiled up on each side of the police car leaving a mile-long red cloud suspended above the road behind.

Eventually, Yvonne spoke. 'You got any brothers, Bowker?'

'One.'

'Older or younger?'

'Younger,' Bowker replied.

Rachael smiled to herself.

'How old?' Yvonne asked.

'Twenty-two. Bit old for you, Yvonne,' Bowker said.

'Age is just a number, Bowker.'

Bowker smiled. 'He's engaged. So he's unavailable, I'm afraid.'

'Everybody's available except your own family. A couple of my friends in Melbourne were shagged by their old man. Now that's wrong, don't you think?'

'It's also against the law,' Bowker said.

'Good. Most laws are stupid, but that one makes sense.'

Bowker chuckled. 'Glad you approve of some parts of our legal system.'

'Should get the electric chair if you root your kids.' Yvonne then resumed her focus on the horizon outside her window.

Bowker slowed down as three kangaroos jumped effortlessly over an adjoining wire fence and bounded through the dirt in front of the car. A kilometre or so passed in silence before Yvonne resumed the conversation.

'Hope I do make it through to next year so I can do my deb.'

Again, Bowker and Rachael glanced at each other. The contradictions within this girl were mind blowing.

'Might ask Jimmy if he'll be my partner, 'cos nobody else will probably ask him. That'd be sad if nobody did, wouldn't it? You do your deb, Ms Stow?'

Rachael was struggling to keep it together. Who was this girl? So capable of outrageously shameful, delinquent behaviour and yet able to empathise with the feelings of a mentally disabled kid like Jimmy. 'Yes, Yvonne. Made my debut in Melbourne.'

'You do it with Bowker, or some good-looking kid?'

Rachael smiled. 'Didn't know him then. Did it with another guy who also went on to become a policeman.'

'Coincidence, eh?' Yvonne said.

'Yeah,' Rachael replied quietly.

Yvonne leant forward again. 'Did your family all come and see you do your deb?'

'Whole table of the Stow family,' Rachael replied.

'Won't need a big table to hold my family,' Yvonne said. 'Old Perce'd be the only one who'd want to come, probably. Do you and Bowker want to be on my table?'

Bowker stared straight ahead, and Rachael wiped a sniffle. 'Yeah, we'll come, won't we Greg?'

Bowker nodded.

They were now passing the edge of the Bryant property, but the front gate was another couple of miles up the road.

'What are you gonna tell old Percy? Gonna tell him to ground me or something? 'Cos it won't work.'

'I just want to discuss some of the dangerous situations you seem to get yourself into,' Bowker said.

'What situations?' Yvonne snapped back, her arms refolding defensively.

'Jumping onto the back of some stranger's motorbike, smoking dope with Travis next door, hanging around with a loser like Skeeta

Allender, drinking alcohol when you're underage. That's a pretty good start.'

The defiant Yvonne was returning. 'I was just having a bit of fun on the motorbike. Ever heard of fun? And you've got no proof I was smokin' weed. And I'm sixteen so I can shag anyone I like. So lay off me. You're not my bloody father. Nobody is.'

Nothing more was said until they reached the Bryant farmhouse. It was an old home but well-kept, boasting wide verandas and high gables. A large air conditioning unit protruded from the green corrugated iron roof. The garden was minimalist, but green and tidy, with a perimeter of fully-grown sugar gums shading the house for most of the day. A large patch of kikuyu grass served as lawn and today was being watered by a row of permanent sprays, generating rainbows that danced in the mist. Half a dozen magpies jumped in and out of the sprays, shaking their feathers and pecking at tiny targets in the grass. Bordering the lawn were thick clumps of agapanthus, and ivy climbed its way up the eastern wall of the house. North of the residence was a row of sheds housing farm machinery. The closest bay contained a workshop where Cath's son Yabby was working in an access pit under his one tonner ute. Two sheepdogs tied up beneath a tall Murray Pine were straining at their chains, barking loudly as Bowker drove in.

Yvonne got out and walked straight inside, pushing her way past Perce and Cath who'd seen the police car arrive through their kitchen window. Bowker climbed out of the vehicle. 'Won't be too long, Rach.'

'I'll wander down and talk to the dogs,' she replied. 'Too hot to sit in the car.' Yabby looked up from the pit as Rachael approached. The suddenly friendly canines wagged their tails enthusiastically.

Cath was in no mood for pleasantries as she confronted the policeman. 'What's the little trollop done now?' she asked, lips pursed.

'Take it easy, Cath,' Percy said quickly. 'Let's not jump to conclusions.'

'A police car out here with Yvonne? What other conclusion is there?'

Bowker waved away a fly. 'Manang had a visit from a motorcycle gang this afternoon and Yvonne went for a ride with one of the men.'

Cath sniggered. 'I bet he got a ride as well.'

Perce closed his eyes wearily. 'Give it a break. Please, Cath.'

'Fair dinkum, Percy, it's getting close to being either me or her. I can't take much more of this.'

'Go on, officer,' Percy said quietly.

'I also suspect she's smoking marijuana with the boy from your old house next door. This on top of consuming alcohol and keeping company with Skeeta, makes me worry she'll end up doing herself some serious harm.'

'Sooner the better,' Cath said nastily.

Percy was clearly annoyed. 'Go back inside, Cath, you're not helping,' he said, his troubled face betraying his irritation. This weeping sore within the Bryant household was showing no signs of healing.

Cath threw her hands in the air as she stormed off to the house. 'Suit yourself. I'll be in the kitchen if you need any sane advice.'

Percy took a deep breath. 'I'm caught between a rock and a hard place here, Greg. I know she's trouble, but I'm the only family the girl's got and I can't just tell her to leave. Where would she go? She's sixteen. Back to the streets in the city? If you've got an answer, I'd love to hear it.' He put his forearms on the roof of the police car and dropped his head to look at the ground.

Bowker mirrored Percy's posture as he turned and leant on the car's roof. 'While she's at school she's fine, apparently. But when she doesn't go home on the bus, she hangs around town and that's where she finds trouble. I know you tolerate Skeeta in preference to her running away, but it's not helping. She doesn't catch the bus because she knows she can always get a lift home.'

Percy stood up straight and looked at him. 'At least she comes home. I thought that new lad moving in next door might be a blessing for us, but if he's taking drugs then he's probably worse than Skeeta.' He shook his head. 'I'm at my wits end. I don't want her ending up like her mother.'

Bowker turned and leant his backside against the car, arms folded. 'Yabby told me about what happened with Lynette. How do you ever get over something like that?'

Percy put his forearms back on the roof with his face lowered. 'It hit me hard. But I wasn't surprised when I heard she died of an overdose. Fifteen years living from room to room, from street to street, from one drug to another. Then add in trying to drag up Yvonne as best she could.'

Bowker couldn't see Percy's face, but he suspected he was tearing up. 'Before she ran away, was she behaving like Yvonne is now?'

Percy's gaze remained fixed on the dirt below him. 'No. Just the opposite. She was the quietest little thing. Teachers used to say she needed to be more confident, to have more to say, not to be so reserved.'

'Did she have a boyfriend?'

Percy lifted his head and took out a folded hanky from his trouser pocket and blew his nose. 'There were no boyfriends to my knowledge. I'd be very surprised if she had one. There were a couple of lads around her age on the Winnambool bus, but none she talked about, except if they were teasing her or doing something silly. You know, stupid boy things like putting spiders on the girls, or trying to light their farts with a cigarette lighter.'

'Yabby said she did some housework over here.'

'Yeah. Cath often helped Crayfish down the paddock, so at times the housework was neglected. She paid Lynette a few dollars to come over and change the beds, do some vacuuming, washing and ironing, that sort of thing. Lynette was good at those type of jobs. She was a big help to my first wife, Shirl, while she was fighting the cancer.'

'And one day she just packed up and left?' Bowker snapped a thumb and middle finger. 'Just like that?'

Percy turned and leant his backside against the car. 'Yep. Just like that. Shirl and I visited the Peter McCullum Clinic in East Melbourne as part of her cancer treatment and when we arrived home, Lyn was gone. She took a few clothes and a few other bits and pieces, and that was it.'

'She leave a note?'

'No. But we got a letter in the mail about a fortnight later. One sentence. Love you both, but not going back, ever.' Percy again blew his nose. 'I found her in Melbourne half a dozen times but couldn't convince her to come home. She wasn't my little girl any longer. She was a totally different person. I gave her money to find a place to live, but I think she spent it all on drugs. When she died, I was determined to give her daughter a better life.'

Bowker touched him lightly on the shoulder. 'Good on you.'

'Cath doesn't see it that way. She loved Lynette like her own daughter when she worked here, but she just can't take to Yvonne.' Percy shook his head. 'Dunno what it is. Yvonne is very much like her mother to look at, a bit taller maybe and much more assertive as you've found out.' He smiled weakly.

'And obviously Cath wants her gone?'

'Can't blame her. She hasn't had an easy life herself. An old slasher dropped on Crayfish while he was underneath welding a crack in one of the blades.'

Bowker exhaled loudly. 'Bloody hell.'

'I was there on the day. Told him to replace the bloody thing, but he was a stingy old bastard. Why spend a quid on replacement parts when a machine could be jury-rigged to make it work? That was his attitude. Should have learned his lesson years ago. He welded two old header drive chains together when he should have just bought a bloody new part. Of course, on the third day of harvest, the weld broke and the chain smashed a cast iron sprocket on the front of the machine. Had to wait a fortnight for a replacement, and in the meantime a big storm came through and flattened the crop and halved his yield. If he'd fitted a new chain in the first place, the crop would have been off a week before the storm.'

'You see the slasher fall on him?'

Perce shook his head. 'Nah. Left after he started welding. Couldn't have done anything anyway. He was dead as soon as it hit him.' He looked up at Bowker. 'So that was tragedy number two for Cath. She'd lost Lobster three years earlier.'

'Lobster? Another son, I'd assume by the name.'

'Yeah, their oldest. Bernard was his real name. Eighteen months older than Yabby.' He pointed to further down the yard. 'Hanged himself at the back of that shed down there. No note, no nothin'.'

Bowker stood up straight. 'How old?'

'Twenty-four. Worked on the farm. All he ever wanted to do. They sent him away to St Paul's in Ballarat as a boarder in form 1. At the end of form 3 he said he wasn't going back. Just wanted to stay home and work on the property. Married, twin daughters. Hell of a shock to everyone.' He picked up a stone from the ground. 'Nearly killed Cath.' He under-armed the stone into a nest of rusty machinery parts piled under a mallee tree a few metres away.

'Where's his family now?'

'Geelong. Wife remarried. New husband used to be a teacher in Manang years ago. Terrific footballer. Centre half forward. Kicked seven in the grand final. Cath has the grandkids up here occasionally.'

'Yabby go to St Paul's as well?'

'Nah. Stayed in Manang. Left after form 5. Married a lovely young nurse named Marlene.'

'Mallee girl?'

'Yeah. Her family's from Tooleybuc on the other side of the river from Piangil. They can't have kids which is a pity.'

Bowker looked down towards the sheds. Rachael had moved from the dogs to the machinery shed where she was leaning on the workbench, chatting with Yabby.

Bowker slapped the roof of the car. 'Well, Percy, I don't envy your family situation and my only advice is to try and hang in there. I'll keep an eye on Yvonne in town and let you know how she's doing.'

'Thanks, Greg, I appreciate your concern.' He shook Bowker's hand. 'I'm hoping she might mature a bit and create a little less angst. I'm not sure how much more Cath is willing to put up with.'

Bowker pointed towards the sheds. 'I better go and round up Rachael.' He patted Percy on the back. 'Talk to you soon.'

'Thanks, mate. Time to smooth the waters with the wife. Again!'

Percy walked slowly to the back door as Bowker strolled down to the workshop. He leaned on the ute. 'Moved from a dog to a Yabby, Rach,' he said with a grin.

Rachael looked puzzled.

'My nickname is Yabby,' the farmer said. 'I think the police officer was attempting a little humour.'

Bowker shook Yabby's hand. 'How are you, mate?'

'Alright, I s'pose. Our resident bitch in more hot water today, I hear.'

'Not as bad as it could have been, but she certainly has a talent for finding trouble, that's for sure.' Bowker looked in the next bay of the shed. It was filled with stacked-up household goods. 'Having a garage sale?'

'Perce brought a fair bit of stuff from his place when he moved over. Some of it was better than Mum's so her old crap ended up down here. Probably put it on a bonfire at some stage.'

Bowker moved closer to the junk pile and slid a framed picture from the top. 'What's the artwork?'

'Some old paintings and prints of the Mallee in the early days. Won't burn them. There are three or four framed photos of the old man there as well. Apparently Mum didn't want him looking down at her and Perce in their married bliss. One's a wedding photo she had in the bedroom. Guess they don't want old Crayfish eyeballing them while they're going at it! But old people don't do that, do they? Yuck!'

'Crayfish?' Rachael wondered aloud.

'Yabby's father.' Bowker grinned as he returned the picture to the pile. Then asked seriously. 'You had an older brother, Bernard?'

'Yeah. Lobster. Topped himself,' Yabby said sadly. 'Crushed Mum.'

Bowker waved another fly from his face. 'You didn't go to boarding school?'

'Wasn't leavin' Manang. Lobster wasn't the same after he went away. All me mates were here anyway.'

Bowker nodded. 'Makes sense.' He put his arm around Rachael's shoulders. 'We'd better keep going, got another visit to make.'

As Bowker and Rachael moved towards the car, Yabby tugged the policeman's arm. 'Got a private minute, mate?'

'I'll meet you at the car, Rach.' Rachael nodded and kept walking. Bowker turned to the farmer. 'What's the worry?'

'You've got to do something about bloody Yvonne. It's getting worse, mate. She's tearing our family apart. Mum and Perce are constantly at each other's throats about the bitch. Marlene and I don't go across to their place anymore because we're sick of the arguments. Before she came, we'd spend half our life over there.'

Bowker shrugged his shoulders. 'Not a lot I can do except keep an eye on her. I can check if there's family counselling services in Swan Hill or Mildura.'

'Family counselling! Shit, mate, we don't need counselling, we just need to get rid of the bitch.'

Bowker put his hands in his pockets. 'That's not going to satisfy Percy, is it? You'll be replacing one problem with another.'

'Can't you recommend she goes into juvenile detention or something? She seems to be breaking the law left, right and centre.'

'Nothing that warrants detention, even if I charged her.'

'Well, something's gonna break soon. Mark my words.' Yabby turned and walked back to the workshop.

Once out on the road, Rachael's curiosity got the better of her. 'It's none of my business, I know, but what was that all about?'

'Yabby reckons the whole family will splinter if Yvonne keeps behaving the way she is. Wants me to send her to juvenile detention.'

'Is that possible?'

'No. Only a court can order that, and she'd have to do something pretty serious for a magistrate to even consider it.'

'Hopefully her behaviour will improve as she matures and finds closer friends at school.'

'I'm not sure that will appease Yabby, or more particularly Cath. There's more to all this than meets the eye. I just can't put my finger on what it is.'

CHAPTER 13

Bowker flicked on his left blinker and turned into a gateway flanked by a pair of rusted cast iron tractor wheels.

'Where are we going?' Rachael asked as the police car rumbled over a stock grid.

'To see Wendy Blake. Travis's mother.'

'About the marijuana?'

'Yeah. Plus, I'd just like to meet her.' Bowker paused for a moment. 'How's Travis behave at school? Generally, I mean; not when he's smoking dope.'

Rachael recognised the thinly veiled criticism of the school, but let it go. 'He's lazy. Not super bright. Hasn't acted up in class, just doesn't do the work. Probably can't. When I get Jimmy settled in, I'll try and give him a bit of help, if he'll accept it.'

They drove into the yard adjoining the house. When Yvonne described it as a shithole, she'd been generous. Since the days when Percy and Shirley had lived here it had been allowed to run down to a state of total dereliction. There remained the wind-blown skeleton of an extensive garden with paved paths overgrown with dry grass and covered in places by drift sand blown in from the paddocks. A half-broken lattice arch spanned the front walkway with a struggling, stunted rose bush intertwining the rusting wrought iron. The gutters overflowed with leaves and the dry remnants of grass that had flourished in the winter. A couple of loose sheets of iron flapped on the veranda roof and Rachael counted three broken windows along her side of the house. It was obvious that Perce had lost interest in maintaining the place when Shirley died, and it had deteriorated further in the years since he'd moved over with Cath. For all intents and purposes, the house was unliveable, except it was being lived in.

Bowker walked to the locked-up rear entrance, its fly-wire door laying on its side in the grass. A blue tongue lizard scurried out of his way as he banged on the door. 'Is anybody home?' No reply. He banged again. 'Anybody home?' Still no reply. He walked around to the front door, stepping over broken pieces of ancient furniture and the remains of venetian blinds. He banged on a faded timber door with a cracked glass panel in the top section. 'Hello. Is anybody home?' Again, there was no reply. He continued circumnavigating the house, ducking under a sagging tank stand supporting a rusted-out corrugated iron tank. A rusty Southern Cross windmill freewheeled above him, two of its blades missing and its pumping rod disconnected at the bottom and clanging against the corroded steel superstructure. A pile of empty beer and wine bottles blocked his way as he turned another corner. The old grey and maroon Falcon was parked under a tree, bird shit dyeing its roof white. Bowker was now at the back door again. 'Hello. Is anybody home? This is the police.' After a moment or two, Travis, still dressed in his school uniform, slipped the pad bolt and pulled the door inwards scraping it across the dirt covered floor.

'G'day, Travis. Why'd it take you so long to answer the door?'

'Didn't know it was you. Thought it might be the old man lookin' for us. He's due out about now.'

'Does he know you live out here?'

'Nuh. But he'll find us. Mum said he always does.'

'Is your mum home?'

'In the lounge room. She's half pissed.'

'I just need a quick word with her.'

Travis turned and led Bowker into the house. It took a minute for his eyes to adjust from the glare outside. He wished they hadn't. The kitchen made the exterior of the house look immaculate by comparison. Most of the cupboards had no doors, the floor was an inch deep in red dirt, the benches smeared with sticky, greasy grime. On the sink were opened packets of biscuits, empty stubbies, a stale loaf of bread with a half-liquefied tub of margarine, and an opened jar of Vegemite with a dirty knife protruding from the top. The smell of the place was overpowering, Bowker forcing himself not to retch. He followed Travis down the passage. An open door to the side revealed a decaying bathroom containing a shower with a torn plastic curtain over the tin bath and a basin mounted on a decrepit vanity unit where a cheap veneer had long ago started to peel away. The bath and basin were both filthy and pitted with large coins of rust. The towels – if that's what they were – lay on the floor with a heap of dirty washing which probably would never get done. Further down the hall were bedrooms opposite each other. Both had torn mattresses on the floor with a filthy assortment of blankets and sheets strewn over them. The remaining floor space in both rooms was the Blake version of cupboards and drawers. Bowker struggled to accept that human beings could live here. The next open door led to the lounge room. It was another rancid space complete with ancient armchairs where the mice had pulled out much of the horsehair stuffing. A shaft of light from the sinking sun pushed through a three-cornered tear in a blind and thrust a sparkling sabre through the smoke in the room. On an old couch, where the supporting springs had long since rusted and given way, sat a fifty year-old woman who Bowker knew hadn't yet turned thirty. Wendy Blake had the sunken eyes of an alcoholic and the facial skin of a sunburnt lizard. She wore tattered dirty jeans and a soiled white top with nothing underneath. She held a roll-your-own in one hand that, judging by what Bowker could smell, contained at least some marijuana.

'Mum. This is the policeman from Manangatang,' Travis said loudly, shaking his mother out of her stupor.

'G'day, Wendy,' Bowker said, making no attempt to find a seat.

'What do you want?' Wendy muttered without looking up.

'Just a quick word.'

'Bullshit. Never met a copper yet that only wanted to talk,' she said wearily.

'Travis has been smoking marijuana at school. Did you know that, Wendy?'

She looked up at her son then dropped her head. 'Didn't tell me about it, if he was,' she said.

Travis dropped onto his haunches beside her chair. 'It was in the letter I gave you, Mum,' he said quietly.

'Didn't read the fuckin' thing, did I? Thought they were after fees or something.'

'You must have read some of it when you signed it,' Bowker said.

'Didn't sign nothin'. My old man always said to sign nothin'.' She took a long drag on her rollie.

'I signed it,' Travis said reluctantly. 'I had to take it back, otherwise I woulda got into more trouble.'

'Wendy, I've got to warn you that possession of marijuana or any other illicit drug is against the law. That applies to both of you.'

'Illegal, is it? Who woulda thought.' She coughed out a sarcastic laugh.

'Where do you get you supplies from?' Bowker asked, knowing he wouldn't get a straight answer.

'We don't get supplies. It's illegal. That's right, isn't it Trav?'

'That's right, Mum,' he mumbled quietly.

'Consider this your official warning,' Bowker said, fully aware he was merely going through the motions.

'If you're finished now, you can piss off,' Wendy said, staring at the smoke in her nicotine-stained fingers.

Bowker looked at her son. 'What do you eat for meals, Travis?'

Travis shrugged. 'Barbecue Shapes, frozen pizzas when I can get the stove to work. Toast and Vegemite sometimes. Fridge doesn't get cold when the weather's real hot, so we can't keep meat or anything in there.'

'Have you asked Percy for another fridge? He might have a better one in a shed somewhere.'

Wendy looked up, then back down. She was more than half-pissed. 'He lets us have this dump for ten dollars a week providin' we keep an eye on the sheds and stuff. And providin' we don't ask for nothing to be fixed in the house.'

Travis looked up at Bowker. 'He said it'll never be rented again after we leave, so he's not puttin' any money into it.'

Bowker put his hands in his pockets. 'What about I have a look around town and see if there's anything for rent? Has to be somewhere better than this place.'

'Don't want to live in town,' Wendy said, coughing out a lungful of smoke which whorled in the shaft of sunlight above her. 'Easier to find in a town. And we don't want the bastard to find us. Sick of being bashed up. So, thanks, but no thanks.'

'Okay,' Bowker said. 'But if you're going stay out here, you'll need to be a bit more careful when you're driving on these dirt roads. You were going way too fast when you went through that mob of sheep the other day.'

Wendy didn't look up. 'What mob of sheep?'

Travis answered quickly. 'On the highway near the crossroads — you remember, Mum. You didn't see them till the last moment.'

'Oh, that mob.'

'Probably the dust, eh, Mum?' Travis added.

'Yeah. Lots of dust,' Wendy muttered.

'Where do you get your groceries? Haven't seen you in Manang,' Bowker asked.

'Piangil. At the general store,' Travis said.

'Bit further to go, isn't it?'

'Don't have to see as many people. That's what you said, wasn't it, Mum?'

'Whatever you say, Trav. You're the brains of this outfit.'

When Bowker returned outside, Rachael was sitting on the bonnet of the car leaning back with her arms behind her. The setting sun was shining through her hair giving it the appearance of spun gold. At any other time, Bowker would have been entranced, but his only thought now was to get away from this place before its pall of despair fully engulfed him.

On the way home Bowker described the inside of the house and the train wreck that was Travis's mother. 'Some kids haven't got a bloody chance, Rach. Travis – and Yvonne for that matter – both had their papers stamped before they were born.'

It was quiet in the car for a few minutes as they both watched the sun slip out of sight in a blaze of different colours. On a road to their left, Prong Lyon's Commodore came to a stop and gave way as they passed through a dirt crossroad. Both drivers acknowledged each other with the lift of a steering wheel finger.

A mile or so further down the road, Rachael brought up the topic of the day. 'Do you think it was a smart move to confront that motorcycle gang on your own, Greg? Especially when you were off duty.'

'I have to be flexible out here, Rach. You know that. It's easy enough to organise my time-off around when I'm needed.'

'You could have let Tim's call go through to Robinvale. They could have sent a car with three or four officers.'

'By the time they got organised, it would've been the best part of an hour before they arrived in Manang. God knows what could have happened by then.'

'You were lucky this time. It could have gotten really nasty.'

There was silence for a couple of minutes. Two emus sprinted across the road in the distance.

'I heard about this copper in a one-man station down in western Victoria, Bowker finally said. 'He was dropping off his own kids outside the school, when there was a road accident twenty metres away. He told the bystanders to call the police in the next big town because he was off duty! Went up like a lead balloon, and the coppers from the next town were super-shitty as well.'

Rachael put her hand on his knee. 'I just don't want anything to happen to you, that's all, Greg.'

'I don't want anything to happen to me either. But if I'm going to ask the people around here to do the right thing, then I have to make sure I'm holding up my end of the bargain.'

There was quiet for a few seconds.

'I love you, Greg.'

'I love you too, Rach.'

CHAPTER 14

Bowker sat at the post office counter rehashing the weekend's tennis. After analysing the Renegade's rise to the top of the ladder, Bowker slapped both palms on the counter as he changed the topic. 'Anyway, Tim, the reason I came in was to ask if anybody in town fixes air conditioners.'

Tim leant on the counter. 'Tuppence Pengilly does, but you'll need to keep tabs on him,' he said. 'Tuppence takes short cuts to save you money, but it ends up costing you a shitload more in the long run. He installed a wash trough in Merle Kennedy's new laundry. To save on materials he ran the pipes diagonally across the window.'

'Bullshit,' Bowker replied with a wide grin. 'I didn't come down in the last shower.'

'It's dinkum,' Tim said. 'Merle nearly had kittens. And at Wik and Judi's place, he replaced all the guttering. When it rained, the water flowed everywhere except in their tank!' They both laughed. 'But if it's just an air con, then Tuppence'll probably be alright. If it's not working now, then there's not a lot to lose by giving him a go.'

'The actual unit's working fine,' Bowker replied, 'but there's water running back into the house. It's forming a big puddle on the floor.'

'Probably just needs re-levelling,' Tim said. 'Tuppence should handle that, no problems.'

***

The next day, Tuppence Pengilly arrived bright and early to attack the air conditioner. He made a cursory examination of the problem and assured Bowker the job would be finished by lunchtime.

After a meeting of the local Recreation Reserve Committee of which the policeman was a permanent member, Bowker drove to Robinvale for an orientation briefing at the riverside town. Rachael had a shorter drive to the school.

She was on yard duty for the first half of dinnertime and after completing a lap of the school grounds, sat at a table under a shady tree beside the basketball court to eat her homemade sandwiches. The weather was exquisite with a clear blue autumn sky and the gentlest of breezes. A pair of pink galahs screeched overhead as they dipped and dived around the many trees in the playground. God was in his heaven and everything was perfect. Travis Urdevic was on the asphalt court shooting hoops with a group of younger kids. The first shot Rachael saw was all net, not that there was any physical net. Even Travis was capable of the odd fluky shot, but good for his self-esteem, she thought. His second shot also went through the hoop cleanly, then the third. She started to take particular notice. He kept shooting the ball and each time it went through the ring without touching the rim. With each successive shot, the cheers from the other kids became louder. He began taking shots from more difficult positions. The result was always the same. Swish! Rachael put down her lunchbox and wandered over. 'Travis. Your shooting is unbelievable.'

'Get plenty of time to practise in Turana.'

'It's a real talent,' she said genuinely.

'Thanks, Miss.' He struggled to suppress a smile.

'Have you had any dinner?'

'On a diet. See ya.'

He wandered away and Rachael doubted he'd brought any lunch. Something she'd have to chase up, she thought as she checked her watch. Her duty stint was finished, and she could see Kay Noble moving into the yard to replace her. In the staffroom, the Phys. Ed. Teacher, Steve Linton, who everyone called Pixie, was at the hot water urn making his coffee.

Rachael collected her cup from a pegboard. 'Have you seen that new kid play basketball, Pixie?'

'Nuh. But he'd be useless. He's useless at everything except smoking dope.'

'I just watched him shoot twenty baskets in a row. He never misses.'

Pixie loaded a generous spoonful of sugar into his coffee, stirring it vigorously. 'Get your eyes tested, Rachael. That kid wouldn't have touched a basketball in his life unless he was pinching it from a shop.'

Rachael placed a tea bag in her cup and filled it with hot water from the urn. 'Haven't you got a sports day in Mildura next month? Get him into the basketball team. It'd be good for him.'

'As if I'd take him to Mildura, the marijuana growing capital of Victoria.'

'He'd be supervised. Give the kid a chance.'

'Look, I'll see what the boss says. Right now, I've got aths training on the oval.' Pixie threw his dirty spoon into the empty sink and left.

As Rachael joined others at the lunch table, Kay called through the staffroom door. 'Got a minute, Rachael? Jimmy Cobb's hurt himself.'

Rachael descended a small set of steps to where Jimmy was standing with a wet sickbay towel held to the side of his face. 'Thanks, Kay. I'll look after him.' As her colleague walked away, Rachael removed the towel and bent down to survey Jimmy's injuries. He had a red mark around his left cheek bone with bruising starting to appear. He'd certainly have a black eye by the morning. 'Did someone punch you, mate?'

'No no no nobody punched me. I runned into the tank stand. The tank stand hitted me in the face,' Jimmy said, looking at the ground.

'Which tank stand, Jimmy?'

'The one neared the tractor place. Where there's the shovels and the chooks.'

'Near the ag science shed?'

'Yeah, yeah yes. Near the aggle sines.'

Rachael dabbed the wet towel on his cheek. 'How'd you crash into it?'

'I runned around the corner and forgotted the tank. Hurted my face.'

'You've got to be more careful, mate,' Rachael said as she stood up. 'Let's get you to the sickbay and I'll put some ice on your cheek. There are no cuts, but it will swell up and you'll have a big bruise on your face.'

'I'm frighted, Rachwell.'

Rachael put her arm around his shoulder. 'No need to be scared, mate. We'll have that face back to normal in no time.' They slowly walked to the sickbay with Jimmy holding the towel against his face. Travis jogged over with a peeled orange in his hand. 'Do you want a bit of my orange, Jimmy?' he said. 'Make you feel better.'

'Nooo no. They stinged my mouth, owangers do.'

Rachael smiled. 'Nice of you to offer, though, Travis. Thought you were on a diet.'

'Simon Blakey gave it to me. Won't hurt to have a bit of fruit.'

'I'm sure it won't,' Rachael said with a smile.

***

Bowker arrived in Robinvale ahead of time and explored the town, getting a feel for the area. A community of around two and a half thousand people, Robinvale is situated on the banks of the Murray, opposite Bumbang Island, and across the river from the small New South Wales village of Euston. Spacious sporting grounds are set on the river flats, Bowker's interest especially piqued by a complex of grass tennis courts, so green and cool compared to the heat and glare of the Manang gypsum. The Robinvale caravan park has river frontage and a community arts centre stands in spacious grounds. All this combined with a decent retail precinct make the town a little oasis in the semi-desert that surrounds it. Bowker purchased a salad roll and a carton of ice coffee at a local milk bar and found a spot by the river to eat lunch. Ah, the serenity.

At precisely one o'clock, Bowker pulled the car into one of the reserved spots outside the police station and was met inside by Senior Sergeant Graham Webster, the officer in charge. They shook hands. 'Thanks for coming up. My apologies for not getting down to Manang to introduce myself.'

'Thanks for the invitation. Robinvale's a pretty little town.'

'Got its problems, like every other place, but it could be worse. As you're finding out, no doubt.'

'I'm enjoying it so far,' Bowker answered honestly.

Webster chuckled as he led Bowker into his office. 'When was your last psych assessment?' he joked.

'No. I'm genuinely loving it. My own boss. Playing lots of sport. Never been fitter, actually.'

'To each his own, I guess. I need to be close to water.' Webster slid a spare chair to Bowker and he took a seat across the desk from the sergeant. 'The last time I was down in Manang it was hot as buggery. The day after Roy Pace transferred out, some dickhead smashed in the door of the station. Bloody blow-in. We get them all through the Mallee. Useless bastards running away from something.'

Bowker thought of Wendy Blake and nodded. 'It's my understanding that every now and then I'll spend a day up here and your blokes will cover me in Manang.'

'Yeah. Mainly for your benefit. We have thirteen coppers stationed here so we can share the angst. But in a one-copper town where you're trying to make a life for yourself, it gets hard if you want to give someone a kick up the arse. Especially tricky if you play footy with him, or your missus is trying to fit in. Just give us a heads-up if you think someone needs a licence check or a breatho, or just a lecture on pullin' their head in. We'll do the dirty work, and they'll think you're a terrific bloke by comparison. And it won't hurt some of our local dickheads to know you're around, anyway.' Webster grinned and leant back in his chair with his hands behind his head. 'They won't take on a copper who singlehandedly arse-holed a bikie gang out of town.'

Bowker gave a sheepish chuckle. 'Wasn't just me. A few of the locals backed me up.'

'Still, you took them on. A mob of bikie shitheads nearly destroyed Kooloonong. The local cop saw them in town and decided it was time to patrol the bush. Pissed off and left the bastards to it. By an amazing coincidence he arrived back in town just after they'd left. Radioed Horsham, and the boys down there pulled them up and charged them. As you can imagine, he was about as popular as a Polly Waffle in a public pool with the good folk of Kooloonong after that.'

Bowker was embarrassed and tried to move the conversation along. 'Anything specific I should look out for when I'm up here?'

'Bit of racial conflict. There's ongoing trouble between some of the local indigenous lads and a number of pacific islanders who work on the fruit blocks here.'

'What about drugs?'

'Yeah, like most country towns, unfortunately. And there's a lot of marijuana grown in irrigation districts like this one. Check out some of the fancy homes along the river, particularly in Mildura. Grass houses, people call them.' Bowker laughed. Webster leaned forward and spoke furtively. 'Keep this under your hat, okay? The Melbourne drug squad is organizing a big sweep of the river area between Swan Hill and Mildura on Monday. Light planes, police helicopters, over a hundred officers, the lot. The operation is being run out of Mildura, but Swan Hill and Robinvale will look after this end of the show and we'll need all hands on deck. Manang might have to go without a policeman for the day.'

'I'm sure they'll cope.'

'Whole thing relies on surprise. Officers from Melbourne won't fly in until dawn on Monday.'

'Doesn't the air wing check these areas all the time? A marijuana crop should stick out like dogs' balls from the air.'

'Not as much as you think. Often the marijuana is planted between rows of other crops like corn or grapes, or between lines of fruit trees. From the road, you see fuck-all, and even from the air with shadows and undulations, it just looks like a green patchwork quilt. That's the reason for the choppers, to get down close to anything suspicious.'

'What time do you want me up here?'

'In Robinvale and ready to go by dawn. Could be a long day, so let your missus know you probably won't be home for tea. And don't wear your dress uniform!'

'I'll be here,' Bowker said enthusiastically. 'I hate bloody drugs. Except for a new kid at school, I haven't picked up any sign of them in Manang yet, touch wood. But maybe I'm naïve.'

'May not have hit the town, but we're pretty sure there's somebody distributing weed further south on a small-scale basis. Maybe even down as far as Sea Lake.'

'Any ideas who?'

Webster shook his head. 'Not at this stage, no.'

'Ever see a late model yellow V8 Holden ute up here?'

'Who drives it?

'A twenty-three year-old bloke by the name of Allender. Everybody in Manang calls him Skeeta.'

Webster rolled his eyes. 'That dickhead! Comes from out Winnambool way.'

Bowker nodded. 'That's him.'

'Been fined a few times for doing donuts in the main street. Searched his car once or twice but found nothing but a few bottles of piss. Don't think he's bright enough to organize a drug network.'

'He might be just the delivery boy. Might collect his supply up here after he does his lairising'

'Hold on a minute.' Webster called over his shoulder. 'Benny, you got a minute?'

A young constable walked in from an office up the passage. Webster introduced Bowker and they shook hands. 'Benny, you pulled over that Allender fuckwit in the yellow Holden ute halfway to Annuello, didn't you?'

'Yeah, followed him out of Robinvale near midnight. Pulled him over when he planted the foot and got up to near one-forty. Booked him for exceeding the speed limit and dangerous driving. Searched the cab and the tray for anything suspicious, but he came up clean. Couple of stubbies on the front seat, that was all. Judging by his demeanour, I don't reckon he was hiding anything.'

The constable returned to his office. Webster stood up from his chair. 'Come on, Greg, I'll give you a tour of the town.'

'I had a quick drive around before I came here.'

'Not where I'm taking you.'

CHAPTER 15

Rachael was home when Bowker walked into the kitchen. Before he could utter a word, Rachael grabbed him by the hand and led him into the hall. 'This seems promising,' he said with a wide grin.

She ignored his comment and pointed at the floor. 'No more problems with the air conditioner leaving puddles.'

Right below the air con, Manangatang's cost-cutting plumber had drilled a rough drainage hole straight through the floor. Problem fixed. Bowker was caught between outrage and uncontrolled laughter. 'He has to be joking, surely?'

Rachael put her hands on her hips. 'Nobody drills a hole through the floor of a house as a joke, Greg.'

'Has he even looked at the air conditioner?'

'I turned it on and it still leaks water on the floor, so I suspect not.'

Bowker shrugged his shoulders. 'Well, my instructions were to stop the air con leaving puddles on the floor. Technically, he's done that I s'pose,' he said, before bursting into laughter when he saw the expression on Rachael's face. He threw his arms around her. 'I'll call him tonight. He'll need to come back and fix the hole as well as the air con.'

That evening, Bowker recounted his day in Robinvale, including the upcoming drug operation. If he couldn't trust Rachael, then who could he confide in? As it turned out, the operation didn't go ahead anyway. Webster rang him from Robinvale on Sunday night.

'Forget about tomorrow, Greg. I've just had a call from Melbourne.

The whole shebang has been cancelled. Since we spoke last week, there have been tractors and earthmovers running twenty-four hours a day all the way from Swan Hill to Mildura ploughing crops into the ground and getting rid of any evidence. Obviously, there's been a whopping big leak somewhere.'

Yeah. A whopping big leak that's destroyed the season's marijuana crop, Bowker thought. A pretty good outcome for an operation that was probably never designed to happen in the first place.

***

On the next Tuesday night, Bowker played his first game of men's night tennis for the combined Manangatang team. With the team captained by Prong, Bowker also joined Saturday teammates Terry and Tim to journey the 120 kilometres to Watchupga to the south. Prong volunteered to take his car on the proviso that someone else drive home. A few stubbies after tennis was apparently his unbreakable tradition. Terry had neither car nor licence, so it was left to Bowker or Tim. Bowker was happy to oblige.

The journey was uneventful and packed with good natured conversation and tongue-in-cheek banter. As darkness fell over the Mallee, the only moment of concern were the lights of a semi-trailer coming over the rise towards them and Prong dropping the line, 'Watch me split these two motorbikes!'

Watchupga is not a town or a village or even a silo. As far as Bowker could discern in the darkness, it was a pair of floodlit tennis courts with a tin shelter to the side. The Watchupga team comprised four local farmers who provided fantastic company but little competition, finally going down to the Manangatang combination 48 games to 3 across six one-sided sets. This wasn't an unexpected result and except for a couple of teams such as Sea Lake and Nandaly, Manangatang normally cruised to victory. But the night wasn't just about tennis, and Bowker quickly realised that the spirit of bonhomie flowed as much from social connectedness as it did from sport. Take sport from rural areas and the community disappeared with it. It explained why small towns fought so hard to keep their football clubs alive even if it meant importing most of their players. For an hour or so following the match, the eight men sat around with drinks in hand chatting about a myriad of topics before Bowker and his crew began the long trip home.

Halfway between Sea Lake and Manangatang with the policeman at the wheel, Prong suggested they pull over into a small roadside reserve. Bowker was intrigued.

'We're making pretty good time,' Prong said. 'Pull over and we'll light a twig and have a chat. It's a tradition.'

Who am I, the debutant, to break with tradition? Bowker thought as he pulled off the road. On a patch of bare ground, Prong lit a little fire of sticks and half-rotted bark. It was an experience Bowker would never forget. The stars blazed in the jet black Mallee sky, the little fire crackled, and the four men just stood around discussing the state of the world. After fifteen minutes, a big semi appeared in the distance with its driving lights turning night into day. It slowly dropped down through the gears as it approached the tiny orange glow in the bush. Finally, it pulled over, air brakes exhaling. The driver slid down from the cabin and walked across to the group.

'Where you headed, mate?' Prong asked.

'New South. Wouldn't have a spare stubby? Dry as a pommy's shower mat.'

Prong looked at Bowker with a smirk. 'Perhaps Senior Constable Bowker might have something to quench your thirst.'

'Got a cold Coke, if that's any help,' Bowker said, straight faced.

'Coke is really what I'd prefer,' the driver said quickly. 'Only mentioned a stubby 'cos I didn't think you'd have something non-alcoholic. Would've only been able to have a sip anyway.'

The truck driver stayed for half an hour, chatting and slowly downing his Coca Cola, licking his lips subconsciously every time one of the others took a swig of beer. He finally headed off and the group had a chuckle about the look on his face when he discovered Bowker was a copper.

'Saw you out on the Winnambool Road the other day, Prong,' Bowker said. 'Chasing sheep?'

'Yeah, Stan Barnes' place. Checking if his lambs are ready to take into Swan Hill.' Prong threw a few more sticks on the fire and a shower of sparks lit up the area. 'You out visiting Perce Bryant I presume?'

'Among other places, yeah.'

'Been a fair bit of tragedy out that way, over the years,' Tim said, his face illuminated by the lengthening flames.

'Yeah. Cath Bryant must have walked under a ladder chasing a black cat reflected in a broken mirror. To lose a husband and a son.' Bowker took a sip of his drink.

'Lobster toppin' himself was bloody awful,' Prong said. 'Shouldn't have sent him away. Country boy. Should have left him in Manang like Tim's and my kids. Something happened to him in Ballarat I reckon. Occurs more than you think.'

The four men sipped their drinks and stared into the fire.

'Crayfish's death seems suss to me,' Prong said.

'Why so?' Bowker asked, eyes locked on the fire. 'Slasher fell on him while he was underneath welding. Farming accident. These things happen all too often.'

'The slasher was up on the three-point linkage. I've never heard of an implement just dropping like that,' Prong said. 'Not unless a hydraulic hose blew off. And there's no evidence that happened. And the dog business sounds like bullshit.'

Bowker looked up from the fire. 'What dog business?'

Prong wiped his mouth with the back of his hand before answering. 'Crayfish had a kelpie bitch. Went everywhere with him, even on the tractor. His old Massie Ferguson had no cab, so he would chain her to the seat to stop her jumping off and ending up under the bloody tractor or the implement he was towing. Percy Bryant was there just before the accident and he said she was still chained up on the tractor when he left to go home.'

'So?' Bowker asked.

'The story goes that the dog tried to get down and got her chain hooked around the linkage control lever and brought the whole shebang down on top of Crayfish.'

'The police investigated it, I presume,' Bowker replied. 'Must have ticked it off as an accident. There would have been a coronial enquiry as well.'

'The story makes sense to me, Prong,' Tim added. 'Cath said the chain was wound around the linkage lever when she found Crayfish under the slasher. The dog was still on the tractor, barking her head off. That's what brought Cath down to the shed.'

Prong kicked a few half-burnt sticks into the fire, sending another fountain of sparks into the black sky. 'Just got a funny feeling in my guts, that's all.'

'Plenty of room for it,' Terry said laconically as he took another sip of his beer.

Bowker was keen to hear Prong expand on his theory. 'So, Prong, you're suggesting that somebody purposely dropped the slasher on Crayfish? Who'd want to do that?'

Prong twisted the top off another stubby. 'Perce was a lonely widower and he and Cath go back a long way. He was with Crayfish that day and says when he left, Crayfish was welding under the slasher. What do you coppers say? Means, motive, opportunity. They're all there, Greg.'

Bowker frowned. 'What about the dog chain on the lever?'

'Perce could have wound the chain around the lever before he left so the dog would get the blame. Sillier things have happened,' Prong said.

'Yeah, like my stubby being empty. Pass me another one, Timmy boy,' Terry said. They all laughed.

Nothing more was said about Crayfish's death, and after another fifteen minutes, the four men extinguished the fire and continued their journey home. Bowker arrived at his front door at 1.45 am, snuck into the house and down to the bedroom.

'How'd you go?' Rachael asked drowsily.

'Easy win, and the strangest trip home.'

'How come you're so late?'

'I'll explain it all in the morning.'

Bowker threw off his tennis clothes and slid into bed. 'I'm stuffed.'

'Hope you're not too stuffed,' Rachael said as she pushed her naked body against him. 'I've been waiting for hours.'

CHAPTER 16

Bowker searched the Manangatang police files the next morning, seeking information relating to the death of Keith Crayfish Harris. The archives were not stored in alphabetical order but ran backwards in time. He finally located a folder labelled simply "Crayfish". Inside was Senior Constable Roger Alexander's notes with timelines, witness statements, medical reports, photos of the scene and a coroner's report.

He read the policeman's notes first. At 5.36 pm, Alexander received an hysterical phone call from Cath Harris reporting a slasher falling and crushing her husband. She was certain he'd died in the accident but was hoping for a miracle. Alexander immediately phoned the hospital, requesting the ambulance and the local doctor attend the Harris property at Winnambool. Alexander arrived at the accident scene at 6.20 pm. where he was ushered to the machinery shed by Mrs Harris. There he found the body of Keith Harris pinned under a slasher with the implement still connected by three-point linkage to an older model Massie Ferguson tractor. After a quick examination of the body, Alexander agreed that Crayfish was deceased. He noted that Harris had major gashes to his head, caused almost certainly by the impact of the falling implement, and that the full weight of the slasher was resting on the farmer's chest. Alexander also reported that a sheep dog was still on the tractor with its chain tangled around the three-point linkage control lever. The officer theorised that the entanglement of the chain and the dog's movements had caused the lever to shift and the implement to fall.

According to the report, the ambulance with Dr Marshall on board arrived approximately ten minutes later. Dr Marshall examined the body and officially proclaimed the farmer's death. Alexander took photos of the gruesome scene, including the tractor and slasher. He released the distraught dog, which immediately jumped off the tractor and laid whimpering beside her master's body.

Bowker looked up from the report and stared out the window. Not man's best friend on this occasion, he thought. He resumed reading. Percy Bryant arrived shortly afterward, having seen the police car and ambulance speeding down the road. According to Alexander's report, he was upset when he saw the accident scene and walked away on his own for a few minutes before returning to the others. Dr Marshall requested the implement be lifted so the body could be removed and transported back to the Manangatang hospital. There it would remain in the morgue awaiting an autopsy. Percy Bryant started the tractor, lifted the slasher, then drove fifty metres before turning the machine off. Alexander noted that the slasher remained elevated, even with the tractor engine not running. Harris' body was lifted onto a stretcher and then slid into the back of the ambulance. The ambulance left the property at 8.15 pm.

Bowker turned to witness statements taken by the senior constable. The first was from Cath Harris. She stated that Percy Bryant had been helping her husband service machinery during the afternoon and she assumed the two men were still in the workshop. At around 5.30 pm she heard a dog barking incessantly in one of the sheds. Worried that something was amiss when neither her husband nor Perce silenced the animal, she went to investigate. She first noticed that Percy's ute was gone and in the machinery workshop she found Keith trapped under the slasher. She felt for his pulse several times but failed to detect a heartbeat. Fearing the worst, she rushed back to the house and phoned for help. Alexander asked if she had considered starting the tractor and lifting the implement off her husband. She replied that she was worried that moving the slasher might cause more injury if Keith was somehow still alive. Alexander asked if she had heard Percy Bryant leave in his ute. She had no recollection of hearing his vehicle but pointed out that their farms adjoined each other and he may have gone home via a track through the paddocks. Asked about the whereabouts of her son Yabby and his wife Marlene, Cath explained that they were holidaying overseas and not due home for two weeks.

Nothing in Cath's account caught Bowker's eye, so he moved onto Percy Bryant's statement. Percy had been at the Harris property earlier in the afternoon but left shortly before the accident. He told Alexander that the dog was always tied to a strut under the seat when Crayfish used this tractor. It had no cab and Crayfish worried the kelpie might end up under the wheels if she fell or jumped off. Percy also stated that the dog was still tied up on the tractor when Harris was working under the slasher. Crayfish worried she would annoy him while he was on the floor welding if let loose. Alexander asked Percy if he thought this method of repair was the safest option. Percy replied that if it had been him working under the slasher, he would have chocked the linkage arms just to make sure the implement couldn't drop if a hydraulic hose split or came off. He added, however, that he had never heard of an implement dropping on its own, so he wasn't overly concerned when he left Crayfish to his repairs and headed home. Alexander asked if he had noticed the dog chain twisted around the linkage control lever before he left. Absolutely not, Percy stated, because had he seen it, he would have immediately realised there was a danger of the lever being displaced. He would have removed the dog from the tractor and tied her up somewhere safe in the shed.

Means, motive, opportunity, Bowker thought. But faced with a choice between a criminal act and a tragic stuff-up, you pick a stuff-up every time. He moved to the medical report. It read pretty much as expected. Cause of death was a crushed chest, creating incapacity to breathe. The report also referred to severe lacerations and lesions in the skull. The coroner concluded the death was accidental. She also made common sense recommendations relating to the carrying and tethering of animals on farm machinery but noted that later model tractors had control devices designed to better safety standards. The coroner also condemned the practice of working under farm implements when supported solely by three-point linkage and hydraulic systems. She recommended the use of mechanical lock-out hydraulic devices, solid non-timber supports or the use of garage pits.

Bowker then turned to the photos of the incident, taking each picture, perusing it, then building a neat little pile in front of him. The first few showed Crayfish's body under the slasher, all taken from different angles. Other photos detailed the slasher connections, and one showed the kelpie dog on the tractor beside the control lever with its knot of wound-around chain. Bowker put the last one on top of the pile in front of him and continued to stare at it. There was something about this photo that bothered him. He picked it up again. The detail of the chain on the lever was difficult to discern with the naked eye. But something wasn't right about how the chain was looped around the lever. He found a magnifying glass in the bottom drawer. If the dog's antics had wound the chain around the control lever, then the collar-end of the chain should have been on the outermost part of the kinked coil it created. But with the magnifying glass, he could see that this wasn't the case. The dog's end of the chain was on the inner part of the tangle, with chain nearest the anchor point wound over the top of it. To Bowker, that could only have happened if the dog was pulled towards the lever and the slack chain wound tight starting near the collar. He leant back in his chair, searching to explain why the anomaly had been missed. Admittedly the way the chain was twisted and coiled made it difficult to identify exactly where each end exited the crumpled gnarl, but surely somebody must have looked closely at it. Especially Constable Alexander or the coroner. But they were investigating a farm accident, he reminded himself. Not a suspected homicide. They weren't looking for evidence of foul play, and in this context the causes of the tragedy appeared obvious. If they'd already concluded what had happened, then they looked for the things that supported that conclusion. And in reality, Bowker had to accept that he was only looking at things from a different standpoint because of what Prong had theorised. Even then he'd nearly missed it.

Bowker stared into space, pondering who had removed the chain from the tractor after the incident. Was it Percy when he moved the lever to lift the slasher off Crayfish, or perhaps the senior constable when he'd earlier freed the dog. Surely, one of them would have noticed the anomaly with the chain. Bowker was certain the file didn't address the chain's removal, but he rescanned the various statements to make sure. His second reading confirmed there was no reference to it. Obviously, at the time it was an extraneous detail not worth recording.

Bowker made detailed notes outlining his thoughts on Crayfish's death and wrote in large red letters at the end of his summary ACCIDENTAL DEATH FINDING PROBLEMATIC. For now, he was at a loss as to where he should take his misgivings. The incident happened sixteen years ago, and everyone had moved on. Case closed. And in reality, besides Prong's means-motive-opportunity theory about Percy, he had nothing to support a non-accidental finding except a blurry photo of tangled chain. This was hardly sufficient to request reopening a case going back a decade and a half. He decided to let things sit until he'd thought through matters more clearly and perhaps asked a few questions of his own. He added his summary to the Crayfish folder and placed it to the side of his desk. It wasn't returning to the archives just yet.

***

The next day, dressed in full uniform for maximum affect. Bowker visited the school to speak at the student assembly on the topic of road safety. Sitting on their backsides down the front with their legs crossed were the preps, wide eyed and awaiting the wise words from this big, strong policeman. With each row back, the kids became progressively older and less enthusiastic, with the form 6 class standing at the rear. A couple of rows from the back, Bowker noticed Yvonne Bryant and Travis Urdevic among the form 4 group. Yvonne was dressed in full uniform and Travis had at least made an effort, with a school jumper and similar coloured pants to the other boys. Given his home situation, Bowker was impressed by his attempt to conform. Also within this group was a smaller, chubby boy standing beside Rachael, who Bowker assumed to be Jimmy Cobb. The teachers stood in a semi-circle around the student group, Bowker recognising a few who played tennis or who he'd met at the pub. In his address, he warned of the dangers of the school crossing, how the main roads were a risk to pedestrians, and the perils of dismounting buses on country roads. The little ones took in every word with great concentration, while the older kids gave the impression that they'd heard it all before. Still, Bowker hoped he had reinforced some important teachings.

At the end of the assembly, forms 4, 5 and 6 assembled in the science room with Rachael and level coordinators Adrian Weston and Anne Ronke. Bowker leant with his backside against the front desk and spoke about the dangers of illicit drugs, finally casting a bait into the sea of faces. 'Luckily no drugs have made it out to Manang as yet, but I can't promise this will always be the case.' The half-muffled sniggers told him what he wanted to know. 'From that reaction, I take it you don't all agree with me?'

'Just heard rumours about a bit of marijuana. Haven't seen any,' one of the older boys said.

'It's everywhere up in Robinvale,' a senior girl in the front row added.

'Travis had some marryjarmers,' Jimmy blurted out. All the kids laughed except Travis and another boy. Jimmy was now on a roll and had everyone's attention. 'And so did Leigh Daveson. They both got suspenc-ed.' This time virtually no-one laughed and a senior boy left the classroom in tears. Bowker assumed it was Leigh Davidson. 'I know who sells the marryjarmers, too,' Jimmy added.

'Don't tell lies, Jimmy,' Yvonne said urgently. 'You're just making stuff up to get attention.'

'I do knowed, Yvonne. And you knowed too,' Jimmy said.

'Don't believe him, Bowker. He tells a lot of lies,' Yvonne said.

'No'd I don't,' Jimmy replied.

'Enough!' roared Adrian Weston. 'The officer hasn't got time to listen to your fairy tales.' Weston looked at Bowker. 'I'm sorry, senior constable, but this happens all the time. Jimmy has a fertile imagination and he makes up things to get the other kids' attention.' He then moved closer to Bowker and spoke more furtively. 'He should be in a special school. We can't meet his needs here.'

Bowker finished his talk with an open invitation to the kids to chat with him at any time and to pass on information, no questions asked. The students gave him a polite round of applause and then filed out of the room, chatting to one another as they left. Bowker stopped Jimmy and waited until the others had gone. Rachael stood beside him.

'Now, Jimmy. Do you really know who is selling marijuana in Manangatang?'

Jimmy stared at the floor. 'No no. I just maded it up. So the other kids would thinked I is smart,' he replied. 'Some kids tease-ed me because I aren't smart.'

Bowker patted him on the head. 'You seem pretty smart to me, Jimmy,' he said. 'Thanks mate. See you around, okay?'

Jimmy smiled. 'Yeah. See ya.' He trotted off.

Rachael started to follow. 'See you after work, officer.'

'Do you reckon he's telling the truth, Rach? You spend your time with him.'

Rachael stopped and shrugged. 'He does make up a lot of stories, Greg. Tries to big-note himself with the other kids. Reckons he killed twenty-five big tiger snakes the other day!'

'But the way Yvonne jumped on him, she might think he knows something.'

There was a tiny shake of her head. 'I've got my doubts. He comes in and out on the bus, so there's not much opportunity to know what happens around town.'

Bowker leant down close to Rachael and whispered. 'I wish I had teachers like you when I was at school.'

'I'm not a teacher, but I appreciate the sentiment. I'll catch you after work.' She checked that the coast was clear then pecked him on the cheek.

***

Tennis finals started the next weekend and the mighty Renegades had an easy win over the fourth-placed Eureka, a team drawn from farming families from the area south-east of the town. Bowker and Rachael won all their sets and the mood among all teams, including the two cricket elevens, was jolly in the pub on the Saturday night. But all that community merriment came to a horrifying end in the early hours of the Sunday morning.

Bowker was woken from a deep sleep at 2.30 am by a panicked phone call reporting an horrendous collision between a car and a semi-trailer on the highway west of the town. Bowker immediately rang the Swan Hill highway patrol, the ambulance, and Dwayne Jones, head of the primary campus and amateur photographer. It would be Dwayne's gruesome duty to record the accident scene.

It was a vision of horror that confronted Bowker and Jones when they reached the collision site. Amongst the flattened roadside scrub was a small, twisted and concertinaed sedan fused to the front of a massive Kenworth prime mover hauling a refrigerated semi-trailer. Given the hour, only two other cars and another truck had encountered the scene. A man in his late fifties was sitting on the ground with his head in his hands being comforted by the bystanders. Truck driver, thought Bowker. Talk to him in a minute.

'All dead. Three of them. Two blokes and a woman,' one of the bystanders said. 'No hope of getting them out. They're twisted up in the metal.'

Jones was already shaking before he looked inside the crushed car, pretty sure he recognised the vehicle – or, what was left of it. Once he shone his torch inside, his worst fears were confirmed. 'Shit, Greg. Three of our teachers.' The image seared his brain and would be reinforced again and again through the lens of his camera. He walked to the side of the bitumen and vomited.

Bowker put his hand on Jones' back. 'Which ones, mate?'

'Brad, Kyle and Susie. All just kids.'

Bowker shook his head. 'Fuck. What were they doing out here?'

'Birthday party out at Barber's place. The younger staff were talking about it on Friday.'

Bowker walked over to the truck driver and knelt down on his haunches. 'You alright, mate?'

'I couldn't miss 'em. They were on the wrong side of the road. I went bush to avoid 'em and they just followed me across. You can see where we collided.'

Bowker put a hand on the man's shoulder. 'Ambulance will be here soon,' he said.

The driver looked up at Bowker. 'This load is due in Sydney tomorrow night.'

'Well, you won't be driving it, mate. Besides, the truck will be impounded until the accident investigation is finished.'

'Are they dead?'

'Yeah, mate. They're dead,' Bowker said quietly.

'Fuck! I tried to miss 'em. They kept following me across into the scrub.'

'I can see that, mate. You'll have to go to hospital. You're in shock.'

The ambulance from Manangatang arrived with a first-aid volunteer driver and the two young doctors from the town. Bowker went to his car and radioed in the details. After forty minutes, police reinforcements arrived with a second ambulance.

It took several hours for Jones to take his photos, the bodies to be removed, and the vehicles taken away. But it would take years for the school and the community to recover. Memorial services, counselling and replacement teachers all helped, but the stain of the tragedy was impossible to wash from the fabric of a small community like this one.

CHAPTER 17

A few weeks on from the accident, life settled back into a routine with tennis and cricket finals resuming. Renegades won their first tennis premiership, in spite of not taking a set off Prong. But keeping the scores close in these matches enabled the rest of the team to carry the Renegades to victory.

In the week following the tennis finals, a group of Manangatang students journeyed to Mildura for a carnival of team sports. Pixie Linton accepted Rachael's recommendation and took Travis Urdevic as part of the basketball team. Despite the Manang boys being trounced by the big Mildura colleges, Travis was a stand-out, hitting jump shot after jump shot. The medal he won for the tournament's highest point scorer was probably the first positive accolade ever bestowed on him. He tried to act nonchalantly in front of the other kids, but his face struggled to repress the smiles that crept up on him. His picture appeared in the *Sunraysia Daily* and an enlargement was pinned on the main noticeboard at school. All his teachers noticed an immediate impact on his attitude and achievement in class. He was never going to be an Einstein, but at least now he was giving his best. With Yvonne gradually settling down, the school's two major discipline problems began to abate.

***

Before daybreak the next morning, Bowker was at Red Cameron's stables yoking up one of his young pacers for jog work along the sandy roads to the west of the town. To Bowker, this was the most relaxing time of his day. It was just him and his horse, the metronomic rhythm of equine hoofbeats, the stars blazing above and just the faintest glow of the sun beneath the horizon in the east.

They were about a mile out past Billy Sutton's place with just the sound of the harness jingling and the occasional snort from one of the horses when Bowker broke a long silence. 'You do any stock work out at Winnambool?'

Their carts were side by side and Red glanced across. 'Got three or four clients out that way. Why?'

'Was Crayfish Harris one of yours?'

'Yeah. But when Cath married Percy Bryant, Prong took over. He's been Percy's agent for twenty-five years.'

'What did you think when you heard how Crayfish died?'

'Shock. Bloody tragedy. That family already had its share of bad luck.' Red's filly slowed a little and he hurried her up with a double click of his tongue.

'Ever heard of an implement dropping on a person like that?' Bowker asked.

'No, but from what I've been told, his bloody dog dropped the slasher down.'

'Yeah. That's what I've heard too.' Bowker swapped the reins from one hand to the other. 'It's hard to imagine how that could happen, don't you think?'

'Anything can happen on a farm. The most dangerous bloody workplace in the world. Five blokes have died in this district in farm accidents. Two were tractor roll-overs. How the hell do you roll a tractor in the Mallee?'

Bowker frowned. 'How *did* they roll them?'

'Bert Duke was on a dam bank, and Dave Raulings had the bucket on the front and was heaping up dirt.'

'Shit. Have to be unlucky.'

'Have to be stupid.'

They came to a sand hill and the horses strained in the traces to pull the heavy jogging carts through the deep sand. Down the other side the traces slackened as the carts, with their heavy motorbike wheels, pushed against the harness.

'How were the other blokes killed?'

'Bluey Parkes was trying to get the tow-ball off his ute. Its tongue was jammed tight, so he hooked high tensile wire onto the ball and pulled it with the tractor. The tongue came loose, flew straight through the tractor cab and killed him stone-dead.'

Bowker whistled softly. 'Shit. Poor bastard.'

Red looked down the side of his horse, assessing the filly's action. 'Darren Bennison was bailing straw out at Daytrap. Those big square bastards. Tried to clear a choke by kicking it loose and got dragged into the machine. Found him pressed in the bail. Dead of course. Wife and two kids.' Red gave his filly a bit more rein. 'Brendan Tanner got his Driza-Bone caught on the power take-off between the tractor and a water pump. Picked him up and spun him headfirst into the ground a few hundred times.'

Bowker grimaced and inhaled loudly. 'Fuck!'

'There are two kids at school right now who are just plain bloody lucky. Ashley Pollock's got a tin leg. Stuck his foot in an auger box when he was a toddler. Took his leg off at the knee. Tina Chamings, in about form 3, always wears a wig. Got her long hair caught in the universal joint of the power take off. Ripped her scalp off.'

Bowker shook his head. 'Poor kid!'

'Bloody lucky kid! It's a miracle she wasn't killed the same way Brendan was.'

There was silence as the horses covered another two hundred metres with the sun just peeping above the horizon.

'Were you surprised when you heard about Crayfish?' Bowker asked.

'Shocked but not surprised. He was always taking risks. Putting belts on his shearing plant without stopping the engine, carrying such heavy loads on the carry-all that the tractor's front wheels were hardly touching the ground. Eventually fate gets its way.'

'Right,' Bowker said quietly.

Red adjusted the hessian bag between his backside and his cart's old metal plough seat. 'He should have propped that slasher so it couldn't fall, and he shouldn't have taken the dog on the tractor in the first place. Lovely bloke, but his negligence finally caught up with him.'

'He and Percy Bryant were mates, I take it?'

'Yeah. Same grade together at school. And the same grade as Cath.'

'What about Perce's first wife? Same group?'

'Shirl? Nah. She was a teacher from down Warrnambool way I think. Everybody expected Perce to marry Cath, but Crayfish beat him to it.'

'And they stayed mates?'

'Bit of tension early around the Cath thing. But once Perce found Shirl, everything was sweet between the four of them. Pretty ironic that Perce and Cath got together again after all these years.'

'Yeah, ironic,' Bowker muttered as his horse broke into a gentle canter. He touched on the reins and brought him back into a trot.

'Are the Allenders your clients?'

'Yeah, been with Dalgety's for decades.'

'How are they travelling, business-wise?'

'Scratching out a living, but a couple of bad years in a row will finish them off I reckon. They work from daylight to dark, and most of their machinery came out of the ark.' Red chuckled. 'Would you believe they haven't got a self-propelled header? Still use this ancient fourteen-foot Horwood Bagshaw machine that they pull behind this old Fordson kero-powered tractor. Pete's pretty good in the workshop, so every time it breaks down he builds a new part for it.'

'How's Skeeta fit in?' Bowker knew the answer, but he thought he'd ask anyway.

'Useless turd is all he is. If you hollowed him out he'd make a decent dog kennel. That's about all he's good for.'

Bowker laughed out loud.

'Helps out occasionally,' Red continued, 'but when I've been out there looking at stock or drafting lambs, he's nowhere to be seen. Poor old Dawn has to come and help out.' Red started to laugh. 'She's a large woman and she wears these long cotton dresses. A big merino wether tried to get past her in the yards and she stepped into the gateway to cut him off. He went straight between her knees and got his head tangled in her dress. She finished up riding him backwards down the paddock. Old Pete and I laughed for an hour.'

Bowker chuckled. 'She break anything?'

'Only the elastic on her dress. Few bruises and scratches, that's all. Shit it was funny.'

'Wish I was there to see it,' Bowker said.

'When you haven't got the money to go anywhere, I s'pose these little incidents are a highlight for Pete. And for Dawn too probably. Once she got over the shock, she'd have a good laugh about it. Good old stick, she is.'

There was silence for a hundred yards before Bowker asked the question on everyone's mind. 'If they're doing it so hard, how come Skeeta drives around in that fancy car? Worth thousands.'

'Got me beat. Course, there's rumours he's dealing drugs.'

Bowker nodded. 'Do you know if Peter pays him a wage?'

'If he was paid by the hour, it'd take him twenty-five years to pay for that car. Every time I go out their way, the useless prick is parked at Piccadilly Corner drinking stubbies with that bloke in the blue Toyota Land Cruiser.'

Bowker's interest was immediately piqued. 'What bloke in the blue Toyota Land Cruiser?'

'No idea. Not a Manang car, not a Manang bloke.'

Bowker was about to push the conversation further when both horses pricked their ears and shied sideways snorting, catching both drivers by surprise. In the trees, a glowing orange ball of light rose, then remained stationary a few metres off the ground.

'Fuck!' Bowker yelled as he brought his horse around and under control. 'What the hell is that?'

'It's a Min Min light,' Red replied as he climbed out of his cart, grabbing his filly by the bridle and patting her neck. 'Haven't seen one for a while, but they still scare the shit out of me.' Red quietened the horse then swung back into the cart. Both animals were now facing up the road and began to trot forward, snorting with ears pricked.

Bowker looked back, searching for the light, but it was gone. 'What did you say it was?'

'Probably a Min Min light. People see them a lot in the outback. They just appear, but you can never get near them. As you approach, they recede at the same pace. As you move along a road, they stay to the side and move with you, then all of a sudden, they might disappear. You often see them above salt pans. The old black fellas talk about them being spirits, so they must have been around for centuries. They call them devil-devils. Scientists reckon they might be glowing pockets of gas or some form of mirage.'

'A mirage in the dark?'

Red shrugged. 'I'm only telling you what they say.'

'I'll take any explanation at this stage.'

'People talk about seeing UFOs up this way, but UFOs are bullshit. I suspect they've seen a Min Min light.'

'People claim there are UFOs up here? Around Manang?'

'Des Birchall's daughter, who by the way is now one of the top physicists in America somewhere, was coming home from uni one Friday night. She normally tooted the horn when she got to the gate to let Des and Pearl know she was home. This night the horn was blasting all the way up the drive, and when she came into the house she was as white as a sheet and had the metal horn rim in her hand. Torn it right off the steering wheel. She said a UFO had followed her the last part of her trip. I'd say it was more likely a Min Min light.'

'I'd say it was more likely bullshit,' Bowker said.

'She's a very smart girl and she was convinced there was something out there.'

'Long trip, tired, reflection of the dash lights.'

'A lot of truckies swear by them. At first they think there's a car behind them, but it turns out there's not.'

'Long trip, tired, reflection of the dash lights.'

'Maybe. But I'll tell you one story that'll make you laugh.'

Bowker grinned. 'I need a laugh right at this moment. At least until the sun's up properly.'

'There was this old cocky down at Gollah. This was years ago, before the Railway Hotel burnt down. In the pub, he told a few blokes that these strange lights often circle him when he's ploughing at night. Thought they were UFOs.'

'Again, reflection of the instruments in the cab.'

'No cabs then. Just sitting up on the seat in the open. Anyway, one pitch black night when he was out ploughing, a couple of the young bucks snuck out into the paddock and laid in a furrow waiting for him to come past on his next round. When his tractor lights passed, they jumped on the plough, then climbed up the drawbar and onto the back of the tractor. The old bloke was gazing up at the sky, obviously on the lookout for UFOs. One of the young blokes placed their hand on his shoulder and they reckoned they could see three foot of clear space between the old bloke's bum and the tractor seat. Bloody funny, eh?'

'It's a wonder he didn't die of a heart attack!'

'He did.'

'Shit.'

'But not until fifteen years later.'

They both laughed.

'So, you're suggesting he was seeing Min Min lights?'

'Buggered if I know what he'd seen,' Red said. 'But it's a great story.'

They reached the turn-around point and began the trek back to the stables. The homeward leg was always quicker since they cantered the horses most of the way. Bowker decided he would put the death of Crayfish – and the Min Min light, for that matter – on hold and just enjoy the ride home. But the blue Toyota Land Cruiser kept gatecrashing his reverie.

***

Later in the week, there was action aplenty over the railway line opposite the police station. A couple of caravans and several portable sleeping huts arrived on low loaders and parked in the grounds of the disused railway station. Bowker drove to the area and found the supervisor busily instructing drivers on where he wanted the various buildings placed.

'What's going on?'

'Setting up the railway gangers camp,' the supervisor replied.

'What are they up here for?'

'Maintenance on the line between Waitchie and Robinvale. This is about the halfway point.' The supervisor put two fingers in his mouth and whistled to the truck driver, pointing to a spot where he wanted the demountable building located.

Bowker waved flies from his face. 'Where'd all this gear come from?'

'Ultima, further south down this line. Been down there twelve weeks.'

'How long are you here for?'

The supervisor finally gave his full attention to the policeman. 'A few months at least. We have to replace nearly every sleeper. Bloody white ants are dynamite up this way.'

'Any wild bastards among your lot? Can do without complications in the town.'

'Two or three of them might go a bit over the top at times, but nothing too serious. One bloke in particular I could do without. During the week, they're usually too buggered to cause any trouble. They'll normally go to the pub and have a beer, or maybe a counter tea, but we start before sparrow fart so they're normally in bed pretty early. A couple of the blokes might head home on the occasional weekend.'

Bowker brushed away another fly. 'When does your crew arrive?'

'After the weekend.' The supervisor slapped his forearm and then flicked a dead fly off his sweaty skin. 'There's twenty of us, all up.'

'I'll come over and say g'day.'

The supervisor grinned. 'I'm sure they'll look forward to it.'

'I bet,' Bowker muttered as he walked to his car. Just what he needed. Twenty blokes camped a hundred yards from the pub.

As he drove back onto the road, he met old Tub Keller and his Jack Russell on their daily stroll. He pulled over and wound down his window.

'See anything on your rounds that I need to worry about, Tub?'

'Nah. Always quiet on this side of the line unless there's races or the footy's on. These railway blokes might keep you on your mettle, though.' The Jack Russell smelt the car's front wheel, then peed on the tyre. 'Last time there was a railway camp in Manang, things got out of control a few times. That was a few years ago, of course.'

Bowker smiled. 'The two of us could handle anything they throw up, don't you reckon?'

'I could fight a bit when I was a young bugger. But that was seventy years ago, mate. I wouldn't be much help to you now. A good root and a green apple would kill me.'

Bowker laughed out loud. 'If I'm as fit as you when I get to your age, I'll be a happy man, Tub.' He tapped him on the arm and drove home.

***

Bowker walked into the kitchen as Rachael was sorting the mail. She eyed him anxiously. 'There's a parcel for you. Postmarked Ballarat.'

'It's been a while, the pricks. Thought maybe we'd been forgotten about.' Bowker tore open the parcel then smiled with relief. He pulled out an engraved tennis trophy and held it up proudly. 'Easts must have won the A Pennant grand final. Didn't think they'd count me in the team when I haven't played since my transfer.'

'I guess anyone who played during the season gets to share the glory. Two tennis premierships in one season. You'll have trouble getting your head through the door if Manang wins the night comp as well.'

They both laughed and embraced, more relieved about the parcel they didn't receive than thrilled in the one they did.

That night, the school staff travelled in one of the school buses to the Oasis Hotel in Swan Hill to watch the world-famous crooners, The Platters, in concert. Bowker boarded the bus dressed casually in black slacks and a pale lemon shirt, but it was Rachael who stole the show. Wearing an olive-green skirt which would have been deemed too short for netball, and teamed with a cream blouse and high heels, she barely made it out of the bedroom, as Bowker suggested giving The Platters a miss. Most of the other staff were also dressed in their finest for this rare excursion to civilisation. Bob and Judi Wikman boarded behind Bowker and Rachael, Bob in a light brown corduroy suit and Judi competing with Rachael for the shortest hemline in her pink satin mini dress with a smocked top. The Wikmans took the seats in front of Bowker and Rachael, and across the aisle from the Westons. Adrian Weston was a short man, trying to look taller with thick-soled shoes. He sported a floral open-necked shirt worn out over cream moleskins. Around his neck was a clunky gold chain. He had a pinched face, a dark moustache starting to grey, and wore wire-rimmed glasses. His wife, Belinda, was a mouse of a woman with short brown hair falling down the sides of a plain pallid face. Her dress was conservative compared to the other women on the bus, wearing flat shoes, a knee-length fawn skirt and a brown knitted twinset. She was one of those individuals who didn't speak without first being spoken to.

Bowker stretched across the aisle. 'Don't think I've met your wife, Adrian.'

'Sorry, Greg. This is Belinda.' He leant back in his seat so Bowker and Belinda could make eye contact.

'Hi, Belinda. I'm Greg. You a fan of The Platters?'

She smiled weakly. 'Not really. But Adrian is.'

'Chance for a night out, though?'

'Yes. Good to get out of the house,' she said quietly.

'Got any kids?' Bowker asked.

Weston answered for her. 'Two girls. Lorraine Parker is looking after them tonight. They live just out the Nyah West road. We sometimes look after her daughter when she and Andy have a night out or go down to the wool sales in Melbourne.'

Bowker shook his head. 'Haven't come across them,' he said.

'They play sport over at Nyah West and tend to socialise there,' Weston replied.

Bowker leant back into his seat and gazed at Rachael who was standing up, leaning over the seat in front, talking to the Wikmans. The Platters better be bloody good, he thought. As they got off the bus Bowker whispered to Rachael. 'Smell it?'

'Smell what?' she whispered back.

'Marijuana. Really faint. Somebody must have smoked a joint before they got on the bus.'

'I've never heard anyone mention weed in the staff room. Might be one of the First Years. Straight out of uni. You know.'

'Possibly,' he said as he took her hand and they followed the others into the hotel.

The Platters *were* bloody good, pounding out their old hits with spine-tingling harmonies. The trip home was a happy one and the bus disgorged its passengers in the main street, well after midnight. Bowker and Rachael walked the two blocks back to the police residence, hand-in-hand. Fifty yards from home, they felt a couple of spits of rain. 'Quick,' Bowker said. 'Let's get you home and out of those wet clothes.'

CHAPTER 18

The next Monday morning, Bowker drove to the school and waited in the bus area. The asphalted turn-around zone adjoined the now disused consolidated school, a collection of ten rural school buildings transported from surrounding areas in 1947 to house the students of fourteen district schools. Bowker strolled the area reading the weathered wooden nameplates displayed on each classroom. Some hailed from places he'd never heard of. Gingimrick, Prooinga, Koimbo, Larundel North. Cupping his hands around his eyes, he peered through the various classroom windows. Several were completely empty; others were filled with ancient equipment left in limbo awaiting its final jettison. He found the old Winnambool school and looked through a dirty twelve-paned window. It was practically empty inside, but Bowker could picture rows of old-fashioned desks with infant versions of Crayfish and Percy and Cath writing with chalk on slate, the dust from the endless paddocks swirling around outside. The Winnambool bus was the last to arrive. Travis Urdevic was one of the first off, but as he expected, there was no Yvonne Bryant.

Bowker drove the hundred metres to the school carpark and waited. The staff arrived in dribs and drabs, Bowker acknowledging each one and reviewing the weekend's excursion to The Platters. Finally, Skeeta's ute arrived at full tilt and Yvonne climbed out as soon as the vehicle stopped.

'What have I done wrong this time,' she snapped as Bowker

approached. 'I'm not in the bloody mood for bullshit.'

'Good morning to you too, Yvonne,' Bowker said with a smirk. 'Actually, it's your chauffeur I want a word with. Is that alright with you, my lady?'

'You can do what you want with the dickhead,' she said as she hauled her schoolbag from the tray of the ute.

Skeeta leaned across the seat and yelled through the passenger window. 'Don't call me a dickhead, you stupid bitch!'

Bowker gestured towards the locker room. 'Just go to class, Yvonne,' he said.

Skeeta ignored Bowker's presence, his eyes locked on the departing Yvonne. 'Hope you're in a better mood when I pick you up,' he yelled.

'Piss off. I'll go home on the bus.'

'What, so you can suck Travis's dick?'

'Fuck off,' Yvonne screamed as she walked towards the school buildings.

'You can fuck off too, bitch,' Skeeta shouted after her.

Bowker walked around to Skeeta's side of the car and leaned a forearm on its roof. 'Problems in paradise, eh, Skeeta?'

Skeeta shook his head. 'Sometimes she acts like a child!' he said.

'That's because she is a child, mate. Ever thought about that?'

Skeeta avoided eye contact. 'She's sixteen. She's legal.'

'Do everything according to the law, do you?'

'Try to.' He looked up at Bowker. 'So what are you on about this time?'

'Somebody is supplying weed down this way, Skeeta. Know anything about that?'

Skeeta's eyes left Bowker's. 'Heard there's a bit around. Not sure how it gets here.'

'Maybe you bring it down from Robinvale. The coppers see you up there a bit.'

Skeeta took his hands off the steering wheel and folded his arms across his chest. 'I socialise up there. Manang is a fuckin' hole.

Besides, the cops have searched the car heaps of times. Found nothin' cos there's nothin' there.'

Bowker tapped his palm on the roof of the ute. 'Where'd you get the money for this baby?'

'Old man pays me a wage.'

'That's bullshit. The farm barely pays its way, and the amount of work you do wouldn't pay for a matchbox toy.'

'Okay, so I've got a bank loan. Not that it's any of your bloody business.'

'Who drives the blue Toyota Land Cruiser?'

Skeeta hesitated. 'Drives the what?'

Bowker crouched down so he was face to face with Skeeta. 'You heard me. The blue Toyota Land Cruiser.'

Skeeta turned his head and looked out the passenger side window. 'Don't know anyone who drives one of those.'

'Bullshit, Skeeta. I've seen you at Piccadilly Corner talking to a bloke in one of them,' Bowker replied, fudging the facts.

Skeeta called his bluff. 'I've only seen you once at Piccadilly Corner, so you're talking bullshit.'

'We'll see.' Bowker walked to his car and drove off. In his rear-view mirror, he saw Skeeta angrily slam his fists on the steering wheel.

Bowker drove down the main street where he spotted Prong's car outside his stock and station office. Maybe he'd seen that blue Toyota Landcruiser. It was worth asking the question. He pulled up a chair in Prong's shambolic office, the pair sitting across from each other at a cluttered old desk. Papers lifted and settled with each pass of an oscillating fan. After small talk around the upcoming night tennis grand final, Bowker got down to business.

'You handle all Percy Bryant's sheep work, right?

Prong leaned back in his creaky office chair, hands behind his head. 'Yep. Since the early sixties.'

'Ever see Skeeta Allender's ute at Piccadilly corner when you're out that way?'

'Sometimes. Bum against the bullbar drinking a stubby usually. Lazy bastard. His parents are working themselves into an early grave, and he's lollin' around, drinkin' piss in the middle of the day.'

Bowker leant forward and put his forearms on the desk. 'Ever see a Toyota Land Cruiser out there with him? Blue one.'

'Twice. Both times on a Thursday morning, about ten o'clock.'

Bowker was amazed. 'How do you remember that?'

'Because Swan Hill sheep sales are on a Thursday and I was picking up Percy to take him across to buy wethers. He used the same bloody joke twice. What's the difference between a Land Cruiser and an echidna? The echidna has the pricks on the outside. An oldie but a goodie, until you've heard it ten times.' Prong chuckled.

'Didn't get the Toyota's rego number?' Bowker asked hopefully.

'Fuck, Greg! Do you think I just drive around memorising people's number plates?'

Bowker raised his palms in a half apology. 'Nah. Just a long shot. You know, strange car on back roads out in the middle of nowhere.'

'All I can give you is the letters. Didn't even look at the numbers. P.A.T. Got a son called Pat. Sorta jumped out at me.'

Bowker returned to the station and rang the motor registration branch in Melbourne seeking a match for any blue Toyota Land Cruisers with the registration number prefix of PAT. As he expected, there was only one. The vehicle was registered to an Ian Rumas of Mildura. It was now starting to make sense.

Bowker phoned his colleagues in Mildura, quoted the vehicle and rego details and explained his suspicions concerning the car. An officer with the CID responded that Ian Rumas was the son of a local fruit grower rumoured to be cultivating Marijuana, but recent raids had revealed nothing of an illegal nature. The officer promised that his colleagues would monitor Rumas junior, paying special attention if he headed out of town. Bowker thanked him and hung up, hoping the phone call didn't ultimately provoke a tip-off to Rumas. But what were his options? His job was impossible without having trust in his fellow officers. Besides, he'd already let the cat out of the bag by quizzing Skeeta about the sightings of the Mildura vehicle.

***

Bowker returned to the school in the afternoon where buses were lined up in their preordained order awaiting the kids' release from class. He parked the police car behind one of the old rural classrooms, then wandered back and climbed aboard the Winnambool bus.

'Lookin' for a ride into the sticks, mate?' the driver said with a grin.

'Nah, Don. Just making sure a couple of your kids get on without any hassle.'

'Those kids would be my new ones? Travis and the Bryant girl?'

'Picked it in two, mate.' Bowker sat down in a seat opposite the driver.

'They usually behave themselves,' the driver said. 'Travis is just one of those poor little bastards. How Percy allows them to live in that hovel's got me beat. And he charges rent! He should be paying *them* to stay in the dump.'

'How do you find Yvonne?'

'She's friendly enough when she's on. Most of the time she travels with Skeeta Allender. Dunno why Percy doesn't put a stop to that. I'd give her a good kick up the arse if she was mine.'

'I s'pose Perce reckons she's had a pretty rough life already. Just cutting her a bit of slack.'

'Bloody Skeeta's the one who needs cuttin'.'

The school bell rang in the distance triggering a stampede of students from the various classrooms. Bowker tapped the chrome rail in front of him as he watched the kids hurry to their lockers. 'Were you around when Lynette Bryant shot through to Melbourne?'

'Yeah. First year driving this bus. Big surprise to everyone. She was as quiet as a church mouse, know what I mean?'

'Happy enough kid?'

The driver nodded. 'Seemed that way. Then out of the blue, she just pissed off to the city and nobody up here's ever seen her again. They say that cancer killed Shirl, but I reckon Lynette running away probably caused the biggest damage.' He swatted away a fly and slid his side window closed.

'I've asked around, and nobody has a clue why she just up and left.'

'Perce kept her on a pretty tight rein, but she wasn't the type of kid who'd cut loose anyway.' The driver shrugged his shoulders. 'Then again, it's hard to know what happens to kids in their adolescence. I've seen quiet young lads turn into bloody dickheads when they get to puberty.'

'Skeeta?'

'Always been a dickhead, mate. Just changed the way he's gone about it.'

By now the kids were filtering onto the bus, each child saying hello to the two men as they walked past.

'You keep track of who's on and who's off each day?'

'Nuh. The bus captain marks the bus roll. Before Yvonne and Travis arrived, she had a pretty easy job. But now with those two? Shit. You'd have to be Sherlock Holmes to work out what they're up to.'

'I can understand that with Yvonne, but why isn't Travis on every day?'

The driver shrugged. 'Dunno, Greg. But if he's not on in the morning, then you can bet he's not on in the arvo either. Happens maybe once a week. It's not as though he takes a day off school, the kids say he's in class.'

Bowker thought for a moment. 'His mother might run him in and do some shopping. Haven't seen her car in town, though.'

'What would she do in Manang all day then?' The driver winked. 'Unless she's getting a bit on the side.'

A mental image of the Wendy Blake he had met, flashed through Bowker's mind and he shook his head. 'I doubt that.'

'Here are your mates now,' the driver said, pointing to Yvonne and

Travis as they approached the bus, school bags over their shoulders. Yvonne was first to board. She looked at Bowker.

'What are you doin' here?'

'Just checking if the bus is roadworthy.'

'Pull the other one, Bowker. It plays *Jingle Bells*.'

Bowker smiled to himself. Travis climbed the steps behind her. 'G'day, Travis. Killed them on the basketball court in Mildura, I hear.'

Travis tried desperately to suppress a smile. 'Did alright I s'pose.'

'You won a medal.'

'Yeah, got a bit lucky.' A couple of kids squeezed past behind him.

'From what I'm told, luck had nothing to do with it. You were a goal scoring machine.'

'A lot of flukes.'

'A fluke is hitting a couple of baskets, not sixty or whatever.'

Travis smirked. 'Maybe.'

He started towards the back of the bus and Bowker could see the medal's ribbon behind his collar across the nape of his neck. The policeman called him back. 'How do you get to school when you're not on the bus, mate?'

Travis looked at the ground. 'Mum brings me in, so she can buy some groceries.'

'And she waits around all day for school to finish?'

Travis hesitated before looking up. 'Nothing else to do. Sleeps in the car and has the occasional smoke, I suppose. May as well be here as at home doing jack-shit.'

'Makes sense,' Bowker said, knowing full well that it made no sense at all. 'Thanks mate.'

Travis shuffled towards the back seat and sat down with Yvonne.

The bus driver looked at Bowker. 'Sounds like bullshit to me.'

'Probably,' Bowker replied. Maybe Wendy Blake travelled somewhere to buy her drugs during these days, he thought. But why come into Manang when Skeeta lived just up the road, assuming of course that Allender did deal drugs? Something didn't add up. He was about to exit the bus when the big yellow V8 burbled up alongside. Skeeta got out and yelled. 'Are you on the fuckin' bus, bitch? Cos if you are, I'm comin' on to get you.'

The kids on the bus fell silent. Yvonne stood up, opened a small sliding window near the back, and poked out as much of her face as would fit. 'Piss off, Skeeta. I'm goin' home on the bus tonight.'

'You'll go home with me, or else,' Skeeta threatened, slapping the side of the bus.

'Or else what?'

'You know exactly, bitch.'

There was a collective inhaling of breath onboard. A couple of little kids were frightened and started to cry.

'You touch me, and I'll dob you in.'

Yvonne pulled her head inside, slid the window closed with a bang, and looked at Bowker. 'You gonna take this, Bowker?'

Bowker shushed her with a finger to his lips.

'Right. I've had enough of this, Yvonne. I'm coming on to get you!' Skeeta roared. 'And I'll flatten pencil-dick as well.'

'Over my dead body,' the driver said quietly.

Bowker stood and patted the driver's shoulder. 'Leave him to me, mate.'

Skeeta stormed up the steps in the door-well and ran straight into Bowker towering over him. 'Get off the bus, and wait beside your car,' Bowker ordered.

'I haven't done nothing wrong. I just want to take Yvonne home like I normally do,' Skeeta said.

'You're scaring the kids and making threats. Right now, I've got a mind to lock you up for the night. Now go and stand beside your car.'

Skeeta backed down the stairs and walked to his ute, taking an exaggerated kick at a stone on the ground. The older kids reacted with a Bronx cheer, riling Skeeta still further.

Don started the bus. 'Give me two minutes with Yvonne, please, mate,' Bowker said.

Yvonne came down the aisle and followed Bowker to the driver's side of the bus and away from straining ears.

'What are these threats he's making, Yvonne?'

She shrugged her shoulders. 'I dunno. Kill me, he reckons. But it's all bullshit. He wouldn't do nothin' like that. He's threatened to whack me, but he's never done nothin' except push me over a couple of times.'

'Well, that's assault. I can charge him.'

'Don't do that. He's alright normally. We just had a fight this morning because I said Travis had won a really cool medal. Skeeta said it was just a pissy little piece of tin. I said it was more than he'd ever won, and he cracked it. I think he's jealous of Travis because I get on pretty well with him.' She looked up at Bowker. 'But I've never had sex with him or nothin'.'

'What did you mean when you said you'd dob him in? Dob him in for what?'

She gave a false chuckle. 'I was just making up bullshit to stir him up.'

'I don't think you were making it up. I reckon you've seen Skeeta dealing drugs.'

Yvonne threw her arms out. 'No way, Bowker. Not Skeeta. He maybe a dickhead sometimes, but he wouldn't do that. No way.'

Me thinks she protesteth too much, thought Bowker. 'Alright, get on the bus. Everyone's keen to get home.'

Yvonne climbed back on board, and roaring like some mythical beast, the bus resumed its endless loop to Winnambool. Skeeta stood leaning against his car's bonnet, drawing circles in the sand with the toe of his shoe.

'What was that all about?' Bowker asked.

Skeeta didn't look up. 'Nothin'. Yvonne and me just had a difference of opinion.'

'You threatened her. You acted like an idiot in front of a busload of kids and scared the hell out of the little ones.'

'I lost my temper, that's all.'

'Time to grow up, Skeeta. Find a girlfriend who's out of nappies and stop sponging off your parents.'

Skeeta looked up at Bowker. 'You're full of shit.'

'Am I? You let your mother traipse around in the dust chasing sheep while you're off doing who-knows-what. You spend the day drinking stubbies while you wait for an adolescent girl to finish school.'

Skeeta rolled his eyes. 'Yeah, yeah, yeah. Lecture finished yet, officer? Can I go now?' He stared into the distance, contrived boredom stretched across his face.

Bowker poked Skeeta's shoulder to gain his full attention. 'You're going to inherit that farm at some stage, Skeeta. And the way you treat your parents, that might be a lot sooner than you think. You're not doing much to learn the ropes.'

'Soon as I own it, I'll sell the fuckin' thing,' Skeeta shot back. 'Do you think I want to spend the rest of my life eating dirt in this shithole? Bet you hate it too. Bet you got sent up here because you stuffed up somewhere else. Nobody volunteers to come to this dump.'

'If you leave the land, what will you do? You've got no skills, absolutely no work history.'

'Once I sell the farm, I'll have cash to burn.'

'Burn is probably exactly what you'll do with it.' This time Bowker poked him a little harder. 'You're dealing drugs, Skeeta. And as soon as I get the evidence I need, I'm going to nail you to the wall. Get my drift?'

'This is police harassment.'

'It sure is.'

'Am I free to leave now, constable?'

'Senior constable to you, mate. And you'll be free to go when I say you're free to go. And if I hear you threatening Yvonne again, I'll charge you.'

'Fancy her yourself, do you?'

Bowker grabbed Skeeta by his lapels and thumped him against the side of his car. 'I'll repeat it so even a pot-head like you can understand. If I hear you threatening Yvonne again, or Travis, or any other kid, I'll charge you. Do I make myself clear?'

'This is police brutality,' Skeeta managed to squeak out.

'Report it to your local police. Or better still, report it to Robinvale or Mildura and they can do a full investigation into both of us.' Bowker let Skeeta go, then straightened his shirt collar. 'There you go, mate. Good as new.'

Skeeta was visibly shaken. 'Can I go now?'

'Yep. You can go. But the speed limit in these grounds is thirty kilometers and out on the road there is sixty. Hate to book you after we've had such a pleasant chat.'

Skeeta climbed into his ute and left the grounds at crawling speed. Bowker watched him go over the railway line and disappear behind the silos up Wattle street before hearing the big V8 thunder to life with a squeal of tyres. Gee, that's a surprise, he thought.

CHAPTER 19

That night over chops and three vegies, Bowker described his altercation with Allender. 'I lost my cool, Rach. It's the one thing a policeman can't afford to do.'

'He provoked you, Greg. And he got more than he was looking for.'

'Shouldn't have happened. You'd think that after Ballarat I'd have learnt to control my temper.'

'Don't be too hard on yourself, Greg.' She put her hand on his. 'You're a good man, never forget that.'

'If you say so.' He paused for a moment, then squeezed her hand. 'Enough about me. How'd your day go?'

'Pretty normal. Had lunch duty. The boys had the footies out, playing kick to kick. Nothing much for the girls to do, though.'

'Don't they throw the netball around? Shoot a few goals?'

'Some of them do. But there's a lot of kids who just sit around, bored to death. I think I'll ask the principal if I can run a dance class at lunch time, perhaps one day a week. What do you think?'

He smiled. 'I think you look great in a leotard.'

She slapped him playfully on the arm. 'No, what do you think about me offering lessons for the kids?'

'I think it's a great idea.' He smiled. 'Now let's find your leotard.'

***

Before class the next morning, Rachael met the principal and floated her idea. Her boss was immediately on board, suggesting she commandeer one of the disused consolidated school buildings where she could permanently set-up for the class. He recommended the old Winnambool classroom. It was bigger, virtually empty, and had more storage than most of the other old buildings. She thanked him and wandered across to inspect her new kingdom. The main door opened onto a porch with hooks for coats and bags. An inner door led into the main classroom with a blackboard up one end, windows to the north and south, and a storeroom to the west. Under the blackboard were cupboards, with a steel cabinet and large deep shelves inside the storeroom. The dusty floor needed a thorough vacuuming and the walls and windows required washing to remove cobwebs and built-up dirt. But it would do the job. Part of the sales pitch to her boss was a dance extravaganza for speech night. Standing in the centre of the space, a theme was already beginning to crystalise. The Parents Club would hopefully finance a portable tape player and she'd need to approach the textiles teacher for help with costumes. She couldn't wait to get started.

The following Thursday morning, Bowker drove his old Peugeot out to Piccadilly Corner. He smiled at the irony of using the old sedan as an unmarked car in the Mallee, when it was likely more conspicuous than a fully badged police vehicle. But it was green, and that was important. He passed through the Piccadilly Corner intersection, drove up Winnambool Road, and turned onto a bush track with the inflated title of Dawes Road. The car's colour melded perfectly with the Mallee scrub, a French icon absorbed seamlessly into desert Australiana. His vantage point was no more than six hundred metres from Piccadilly Corner, and when he saw Wendy Blake's old grey Falcon pass through the intersection in a cloud of dust, he was certain he'd see Skeeta's bright yellow ute when it arrived.

The day was dry, but the temperature pleasant enough. There wasn't a cloud in the endless Mallee sky, and a light northerly mustered scarcely sufficient strength to gently disturb the leaves of the scrub around him. There were worse things to be doing, Bowker thought, as he lounged back in his seat, the wind drifting through the open windows and the honeyeaters flitting about as they scoured the gum blossoms for avian fare.

Without warning, a loud scratching noise roused Bowker from his languid state. He sat bolt upright. 'What the fuck!' A huge reptilian head appeared above the front of his car. Then came a big-clawed leg, then another, a body, two more legs and finally an enormous scaled tail. Bowker rapidly wound up the two front windows as the goanna made its way across the bonnet towards the windscreen. The creature stared at him with beady eyes, its tail waving back and forward and its forked tongue flicking. In the background, Bowker saw the Allender family's battered EK Holden heading south down Winnambool Road. Thursday must be shopping day for Pete and Dawn, Bowker thought. I could use you right now, Pete, he pondered as he watched the car drive past in the dust. The EK continued through the intersection and disappeared on its way to town. In the foreground, the goanna continued to devour grasshoppers pasted to the windscreen before slithering off the car, leaving deep scratch marks on the mudguard. Bowker watched it waddle across the lane and disappear into long grass and broken branches. He waited for a few moments before winding down both windows and letting the breeze flow through the vehicle. He exhaled loudly and returned his eyes to the Piccadilly intersection.

After an hour, he assumed Skeeta wasn't coming. He was annoyed with himself. In his haste to track down the Land Cruiser, he had spooked Skeeta and his Mildura mate. Still, might stop the supply of weed into Manang, he thought, without really believing it.

***

On Tuesday night, Bowker travelled with Terry, Prong and Tim to Sea Lake for the final of the night tennis. Being unbeaten is always a cross to carry into any grand final, but given the total domination of the Manangatang team, the result appeared a forgone conclusion.

Nandaly was the opponent in the season decider, a team that had always given them the most trouble and had even taken the odd set. All the matches were hard fought, but only one set was dropped, that being the last when the result was beyond doubt and Terry had already started to celebrate. The Nandaly team was another collection of great country characters, super-competitive on the court and enjoyable company off it. If a stranger had visited the shed after the match, they would have found difficulty identifying winners from losers. In Bowker's mind, they were all winners.

After an hour of socialising, the Manang quartet set off on the relatively short trip home. They lit a twig at Cocamba, stood around and reminisced about the team's victory. It was mostly bullshit, but Bowker loved the camaraderie. The moon was rising in the east, so full and white against the black treeless horizon that Bowker felt he could reach out and touch it.

'Playing footy, Greg?' Tim asked.

'Yeah. Rick's been in my ear. Training starts this week.'

'Should have a pretty good team,' Prong said. 'Two new teachers straight out of the VFA and one who played for St Kilda seconds last year. Tommy Temp is home from Richmond and Barnesy's back from his round-Australia trip.'

'Skeeta Allender ever play footy?' Bowker asked.

The other three men burst out laughing, Tim spraying a mouthful of beer onto the fire. 'That'd mean he'd have to get off his arse and put some effort into something other than rootin' schoolgirls,' he said.

Prong took a sip of his stubby. 'Good to see his old man out and about a bit more. Spotted his old EK Holden two or three times in the last week.'

Bowker nodded. 'Yeah, saw him heading into town last Thursday morning. Must be shopping day for Dawn.'

'Well, he hasn't been into the post office,' Tim said.

'Or the pharmacy,' Terry added. 'They normally pick up Dawn's tablets when they're in Manang.'

Prong shrugged his shoulders and threw a handful of sticks on the fire, sending a shower of sparks into the starry sky. 'Well, old Pete's definitely been out and about. He's got a sister who lives out this way at Chinky. Thelma. Charlie Palmer's missus. I saw Pete parked here at Cocamba on Friday arvo. I nearly stopped in case he had car trouble, but as I slowed down, he started moving off. Assume he pulled over for a piss.'

The cunning little shit, Bowker thought, he's using his old man's car.

CHAPTER 20

After Rachael left for school the next morning, Bowker took his cup of coffee and sat on his front veranda. It was another magical autumn day, blue sky with the occasional cotton wool cloud casting a migratory shadow over the fallowed paddocks beyond the silos to the north-east. Prong drove up and pulled in parallel to the curb. 'Our taxes at work!' he yelled through the passenger-side window. Bowker gave him the thumbs up. Prong pointed up the road as he moved off. 'Here comes your mate.'

After a moment, Pete Allender's EK Holden with Skeeta driving and Yvonne Bryant hard against him on the bench seat, sped past. Bowker abandoned his coffee and drove to the school carpark, arriving as Yvonne climbed from the old car.

'Patched up your differences, you two?' Bowker said as he approached the Allender car.

'Everything's sweet,' Skeeta said. 'Not that it's got anything to do with you.'

'What's with the old man's car? A yellow ute a bit conspicuous when you're making your deliveries?'

'It's over at Greasy Gregson's garage, if you must know,' Skeeta shot back. 'Been there a few days gettin' lowered and fitted with twin carbies and extractors.'

Bowker whistled. 'Expensive. Another loan, I guess,' he said sarcastically.

'Had enough left over from the car loan.'

'Must have a very generous bank manager. Granting a personal loan to a bloke with your earning power.' Bowker scratched his chin. 'When'd you decide to put the ute in at Gregson's?'

Skeeta revved the car a little, nervously. 'Been on the cards for a fair while,' he said.

'I bet,' Bowker replied with a chuckle. 'Just happened to be the time you needed an excuse to drive the old man's EK. Coincidence, eh?'

Skeeta just scowled. 'See you after school, Yvonne.' He planted the foot and the old Holden stalled. He restarted the engine and drove off in a huff.

Yvonne dropped her schoolbag on the ground. 'Get off his back, Bowker. It's not against the law to drive your father's car.'

'You should have learnt your lesson last week, Yvonne. This bloke is a sleazy piece of work who'll end up hurting you.'

Yvonne pointed to the west. 'If you want a real sleaze, go over and talk to the bloke in the garage. You should have heard some of the things he said about me.'

'I'm sure your knight in shining armour defended your honour.'

'If you're talkin' about Skeeta, he just laughed. And the two of them looked through these nudie girl calendars. The garage bloke said I'd look good in one of them. Old pervert!'

'What did Skeeta say to that?'

'Just agreed with him. Then they started laughing and carrying on about what month I'd be.'

'Birds of a feather.'

'Dunno what that means.'

'It means, be careful with Skeeta.'

Yvonne picked up her bag and started to walk away. Then she turned. 'Hey, Bowker. Your missus is running a dance class. I've put my name down. It'll be cool, don't you reckon?'

'It'll be great,' Bowker said. He watched her walk to the locker room and felt immense sorrow for her. Trapped between a normal kid and a thirty year-old woman.

***

After work, Bowker and Rachael attended the opening training sessions for football and netball. The Manangatang footy ground was inside the famous horse racing track, which itself cut its way through the eighteen-hole golf course. The oval had been watered, daubing a green splotch on a brown, depressing background. Golf season would open when the autumn break brought the fairways to life, and the racetrack wouldn't be watered until spring, in readiness for the famous October cup meeting.

With the first game still weeks away, most of the footy training concentrated on physical conditioning, although given the labour-intensive demands of most local employment, the players already had a strong fitness base. What surprised Bowker was the wide spectrum of talent on display, from Pixie Linton straight out of St Kilda, to blokes who struggled to kick the ball. Only forty-odd players were needed to fill the seniors and reserves, yet at least sixty blokes were training. Getting a game was less important than being part of the group.

They trained hard, with coach Rick Brennan keen to utilise every minute, knowing that once it rained, half his charges would be preoccupied with sowing, and footy training would run a distant second. Bowker trained well and thought himself a good chance to play seniors.

Over at the netball courts, numbers were also strong with enough players to easily fill the three senior grades plus the respective under-age teams. Judi Wikman put the girls through a rigid fitness session before introducing a variety of set-plays. Rachael trained strongly, her eyes firmly set on making the goal defence position her own.

At 8.45 pm, Bowker and Rachael sat down to watch the last half of *Happy Days* when the phone in the police station rang. Bowker reluctantly walked through to the station and answered the call. It came from Rick Brennan. There was a problem at the pub.

'Sorry to bother you at home, mate, but we've got one of those railway blokes causing trouble down here.'

'What sort of trouble?'

'Had a few too many after tea and he's got himself into an altercation with Skeeta Allender. I've tried to sort it out, but he's just telling me to fuck off. Sorry mate.'

Bowker put on his police jacket and cap and walked the couple of hundred metres to the hotel. Rick was waiting outside and pointed to the lounge. A burly railway man had Skeeta Allender by the throat and was forcing him backwards against a table. At the same time, Yvonne Bryant had the assailant by the hair, attempting to drag him away. Bowker shook his head. What the fuck was she doing here at this time of night? he asked himself.

'You ripped me off, you slimy little turd,' grunted the railway man with biceps the size of tree trunks.

Yvonne sunk her teeth into his arm. The railway man howled in pain as he let Skeeta go and cocked his fist. 'You little bitch. You're gonna pay for that.'

'Wouldn't do that, mate,' Bowker said coolly, keen to deescalate matters.

The railway man aggressively presented his arm to Bowker. 'The little slut bit me on the arm!'

'Yeah, I saw that,' Bowker said. 'Saw you gettin' into Skeeta as well. Looks like assaults all around.'

'I didn't do nothin',' Skeeta said, straightening his shirt. 'This dickhead just attacked me.'

'He said you ripped him off,' Bowker said.

Skeeta looked away. 'You must have heard wrong,' he said.

Bowker turned to the railway man. 'How'd he rip you off, mate?'

The rail worker hesitated slightly. 'It was his shout, and he said he was going home. He owes me a drink.'

'That's bullshit,' Bowker said aggressively. 'You buying weed off him?'

'That's illegal, officer,' the railway man said, becoming a little too smart-arsey for the policeman's liking.

Bowker was done with pussyfooting. 'Okay. The three of you: empty your pockets.'

'Do you have a warrant?' the railway man asked smugly.

'Don't need one if we're in a public place and I suspect a drug offence may have been committed. So empty them out.'

The three deposited the contents of their pockets on the table, but there was nothing of interest to Bowker. He checked each man's wallet before handing them back.

'You can't pin this drug stuff on me, Bowker,' Skeeta said as he slid his wallet into the back pocket of his Levi's. 'I don't do that sort of thing.'

Bowker shook his head. 'Only a matter of time before you make a mistake, Skeeta. Or someone dobs you in.' He turned to Yvonne, placing his hands on his hips like a surrogate father. 'And what the hell are you doing here, Yvonne? You should be home in bed.'

'That's where she'd do her best work I reckon. Or on the back seat of a car,' the railway worker said.

'Shut up, shit face,' Yvonne said aggressively.

'I hope you let Percy know you'd be home late. He's probably worried sick by now,' Bowker said.

'Of course I told him,' she said indignantly, 'what do you think I am? I rang him from the phone box and told him we had a careers night at school that I forgot about. Told him Skeeta would bring me home.'

'Well, Skeeta's taking you home now.' Bowker pointed at the door. 'So go!'

The railway man grabbed Bowker by the bicep. 'Aren't you gonna charge her for biting me?' he growled.

Bowker looked down at the man's hand still holding his arm and removed it very deliberately. 'If I do, I'll also charge you with assault, making threats, disturbing the peace and making physical contact with a police officer.'

As Yvonne left with Skeeta she turned to face the railway man, and in the manner of a much younger child, leaned forward and aggressively stuck out her tongue.

The railway man motioned to follow them out. 'I won't forget about this, you bitch! You'll pay!' he yelled.

'You stay here with me, mate,' Bowker ordered.

'You arresting me or something?'

'Not yet. But just a kindly word. Your boss reckons you'll be camped in this town for months. It will be helpful for everybody concerned if I don't have need to speak with you again. If you can't hold your grog, then I'll ban you from the pub. And if you're buying dope, I'd save my money, because when I collar Allender there'll be others who'll go down with him.'

The railway man rolled his eyes. 'Finished the lecture?'

'Just about.' Bowker took a small notebook and a pencil from his jacket pocket. 'What's your name?'

The worker shook his head and exhaled loudly. 'Barry Lowbury.'

'L-O-W-B-E-R-R-Y?'

'U-R-Y. Can I go now?'

'Yep. Thanks for your cooperation, Barry.'

Lowbury left in a huff.

***

Rachael's dance classes started the following week in the newly cleaned Winnambool school building. She was on a high when she came home and found Bowker working at his desk.

'The dance class was fantastic, Greg. The kids are so enthusiastic.'

'That's great, Rach.' Bowker leaned back in his chair. 'Got any stars?'

'You're not going to believe this, but Yvonne Bryant has got so much natural talent.' Rachael sat on the corner of the desk. 'She could be anything, Greg. She's got the athletic build and is so expressive in her movements.'

'Nothing surprises me about that girl.'

'And she'll try anything. No hint of self-consciousness. And the other girls feed off her energy.'

'Any others impress?'

'Sophie Weston, Adrian's daughter, is very good as well. I suspect she did ballet when the family lived in Melbourne. She has that poise and elegance that all good dancers have.'

Bowker smiled. 'Any boys turn up?'

Rachael feigned a laugh. 'Have a guess. They're all into sport and wouldn't be caught dead learning dance. Sad really. A bit of dancing would improve their movement and balance for footy.'

Bowker stood up, took Racheal by the hands, and raised her to her feet. 'So, you're queen of the girls?'

'Not quite. Jimmy Cobb was there.'

'Another John Travolta?' Bowker put his arms around her.

Rachael looked up at him. 'What do you think? Pretty uncoordinated, but he has a good time and the exercise won't go astray. The girls are terrific. They encourage him and include him in everything.'

'How many kids altogether?'

'About thirty-two today. But Judi has volunteered to help me. And you know what else was nice, Greg? Three of the male staff came across to show their support.'

Bowker burst out laughing. 'Came across to perv on you in a leotard more like it! Still, can't blame them.' He kissed her on the nose.

'Adrian Weston dropped in to make sure Jimmy wasn't being a nuisance, and to see how his daughter went as well. He's sure Jimmy will turn the class into an attention-seeking exercise, but Jimmy was terrific today.'

'Maybe just what he needs to give him some self-confidence,' Bowker surmised. 'Be part of the group where they need to rely on each other. Always brings out the best in people, I reckon.'

'And I've been thinking about speech night, Greg. We might do a routine with an ancient Egypt theme. Base it around Cleopatra and her handmaidens.'

'Put on your leotard and I could turn you into a mummy?'

'You are so smooth, Bowker.' She kissed him on the forehead. 'So smooth.'

CHAPTER 21

For the next few months, police work was routine and included a couple of uneventful shifts in Robinvale. Bowker contacted the Parole Board in Melbourne to clarify the status of Travis's father, only to be informed that Urdevic had been granted parole the week before. There were strict conditions on his release, including reporting to his parole officer daily, and making no contact with his former partner or his son. Bowker also checked if Barry Lowbury had a criminal record and was told he'd faced court on a number of occasions for minor assaults. His last appearance was in the Swan Hill Magistrates' Court for offences committed against a woman while the railway gang was camped at Ultima. In his downtime, Bowker reviewed the Crayfish file several times, but remained unsure whether to informally reopen the case, or let sixteen year-old sleeping dogs lie. The file remained on his desk, awaiting his decision.

The season broke on Anzac Day, the whole district receiving two days of steady, consistent rain. Dark cloud rolled in from the north-west bringing walls of raised dust and spectacular lightning displays before the rain finally set in. Most locations reported at least a couple of inches and with the light, sandy Mallee soils, this was ideal for sowing wheat and barley. Enormous high-powered four-wheel drive tractors towing massive air seeders worked twenty-four hours a day to sow down the vast acreages. Numbers at footy training dwindled to a dozen or so non-farmers, but Rick knew the team would be ready to go come the weekend.

The senior netball team performed well in the first months of the season, remaining undefeated. There was no room for overconfidence, however, since they were yet to play Sea Lake, the other powerhouse of the comp. On the football field, Bowker was holding down centre half forward and contributing a couple of goals a match. His football highlights however did not involve goals, or marks, or kicks, or even wins. The first came at Nullawil in his second game, when he was forced to act as goal umpire while the white-coated official killed a snake some kid had bailed up under a car behind the goals. The second incident occurred on his home ground. Bowker was on a long lead towards the wing when he crashed over Terry River's golf buggy. The pharmacist had sliced his tee shot over the cars ringing the oval and marched into the football game to play his ball where it lay. As Bowker gingerly picked himself off the turf, he watched with amusement as Terry's next shot narrowly cleared spectators' cars and lobbed back onto the first fairway. The pharmacist then strode from the ground as if walking up the eighteenth at Augusta National, lifting his club to acknowledge the cheers of the footy crowd.

As Bowker hobbled back to his position, still a little unsteady on his feet, he wiped a trickle of blood from his cheek. The sight of Tadpole O'Keefe, the team's trainer, sprinting out with the infamous towel instantly restored his equilibrium. Older players swore the towel had never been washed and Bowker had seen it used ten minutes earlier on another player's injured groin.

The overweight Tadpole approached Bowker, totally out of breath. 'Are you alright, Greg? 'I'll get rid of that blood off your face.'

Bowker dragged up the front of his jumper and wiped his cheek. 'Thanks, Tad. Don't want to dirty your towel.'

'Don't worry about that, Greg,' Tadpole replied seriously, 'it's got everybody else's blood on it already.'

What a day for stories to tell the grandkids. Earlier in the afternoon he'd strolled out to the three-quarter time huddle during the reserves match. The Manang boys faced a twelve goal deficit and were in dire need of inspiration. Bowker was expecting words of football wisdom or tactical genius in the coach's final address. He heard neither. 'We have to win this one, boys,' the coach roared. 'You know why? Because we've got a barbecue tonight and there's nothing worse than a barbecue when you bloody lose!' Where else but in the Mallee?

***

On Monday, Bowker walked to pick up the police mail and have the obligatory VFL football chat with Terry and Tim. Amongst his mail was a brown papered parcel and Bowker's stomach turned until he saw the Melbourne postmark. He smiled at his own edginess and walked to the supermarket for milk and bread. Col Wraith was his usual smiling self, encouraging Bowker to confide any police information that might constitute news in a town where discussion was dominated by inches of rain and bags to the acre.

'Any police goss?' Wraith asked, as he put Bowker's bread and milk into a brown paper bag.

'Pretty quiet at the moment, Col.'

'The Robinvale coppers booked Sammy Austin and Butch Coleman while you were away on Saturday night. Well over the limit, apparently.'

Bowker played a dead bat. 'So I heard.'

'Warned a couple of railway blokes for having a box-on outside the pub too.'

'Heard that as well.'

Wraith folded over the top of the bag. 'Seems like when you're away for a day, the place falls apart.'

Bowker smiled. 'Coincidence, Col. Pure coincidence.'

'Maybe. That's a dollar seventeen, Greg.'

Bowker fished a two-dollar note from his pocket. Wraith handed him eighty-three cents in change. 'How many times a week does Wendy Blake come in shopping?'

The grocer looked puzzled. 'Who?'

'Wendy Blake. Lives in Percy Bryant's old house at Winnambool.'

Wraith shook his head. 'Don't know the name.'

'She'd be buying things like cigarettes, Barbecue Shapes, Coco Pops, frozen pizzas. You know, mostly shit.'

'We don't sell shit here, officer,' Wraith replied po-faced. 'But about once a week that new kid from school comes in and buys that sort of thing. Plus milk and bread. Don't know what his name is.'

'Mousy brown hair with a rat-tail down the back? Earrings in each ear?'

'That's him.'

'Travis Urdevic. Wendy's son.'

'Always has just enough small change to pay for things. Like he's using his last cent.'

'He probably is. Thanks, Col.' Bowker left the shop and walked home, his mind desperate for answers. Maybe Wendy can't face people, he wondered. Maybe she's incapable of conducting a shopping transaction. If that's the case, she shouldn't be driving her bloody car! he thought. Then again, maybe she wasn't.

Bowker heard his telephone ringing as he entered his house. He went straight to his office, deposited the shopping and mail on his desk and picked up the receiver. It was Rachael ringing from school. She sounded agitated.

'Greg, it's Rachael. I'm worried about Travis Urdevic. I just heard his father took him out of school about an hour ago. I thought his father was in jail.'

Bowker's breathing quickly deepened. 'He's on parole. But he's just broken every condition of it. He'll be heading out to Wendy's place. I'll catch you later, Rach.'

'Be careful, Greg.'

'I will. Love you.' He hung up and contacted the Robinvale station, requesting a couple of officers meet him at Percy Bryant's old house. He took his Smith & Wesson service revolver from the gun safe and ran to his car.

Bowker reached the Blakes' house in under twenty minutes with lights flashing and siren blaring, a ribbon of dust stretching almost all the way back to the town. Parked beside the old falcon was a dust-covered early model orange Datsun. As he climbed from his car, he heard yelling from inside the house. With no time to wait for his Robinvale back-up, Bowker stormed in through the back door with revolver in hand. 'Police. We're coming in.' He found Wendy crying on the couch in the lounge room, her face smeared with blood, and bruising already obvious around her eyes and on her lower lip. There was a hunting knife on the floor beside the window that Bowker assumed probably belonged to Joseph Urdevic. At least he didn't have it with him.

The source of the ruckus was an adjacent bedroom. Bowker pushed the door open with his weapon raised. He peered around the doorframe. To his surprise, he saw Travis holding his father down on a mattress with his knees, landing punch after punch on the older man's face.

'I'm going to kill you, you fuckin' bastard,' Travis screamed over and over.

'Leave him to me, Travis,' Bowker said as he placed his hand on the boy's shoulder.'

'No. I've got to kill him,' Travis cried, still raining blows on his father's face. 'Did you see what he did to Mum? He'll keep doing it unless I kill the fucker.'

'Stand up, mate. He's going back to jail and there'll be no parole this time.'

Travis stopped punching and gradually got to his feet. He started to cry. 'He had a knife and made me show him where we lived.'

'It's alright now, mate. It's all over,' Bowker said quietly.

Travis ran back into the lounge room and hugged his mother.

Once Travis had gone, Bowker showed his anger. 'Alright, you weak prick, get up! And if you try anything, it'll give me the greatest pleasure to knock you into next week.'

Urdevic wiped blood from his mouth. 'Are you going to charge him with assault? He was going to kill me,' he said.

Why do they always play the victim? Bowker thought, then said 'Didn't see any assault. Just a kid protecting himself and his mum.'

'Attempted murder. You saw it. He was going to kill me.' He spat blood on the floor.

'Stand up now, otherwise it's resisting arrest,' Bowker said pointing his revolver. 'And right now, it wouldn't take much for me to pull this trigger. World wouldn't mourn an arsehole who beats up women and kids.'

Urdevic stood up painfully and wiped his bloody face with the front of his tee shirt.

'Turn around and put your hands behind your back,' Bowker ordered. The policeman holstered his revolver and handcuffed Urdevic as forcibly as he could. 'You're under arrest for breach of bail conditions, for assault with a deadly weapon, and for grievous bodily harm.' Bowker then read him his rights. 'Do you understand this?'

Urdevic nodded.

Bowker marched Urdevic outside when he heard the siren of the Robinvale divisional van. Senior Sergeant Webster saw that Bowker had things under control and sent a constable to unlock the back of the van. Bowker pushed Urdevic towards the vehicle and he was quickly locked inside.

Webster was apologetic. 'Took a while to find the place. RMB numbers tell you jack shit out here,' he said. 'Anyway, looks like you handled it okay on your own.'

'Heard a lot of screaming when I arrived. I was worried that if I waited for backup, someone might get killed.' Bowker explained the charges and the circumstances of the arrest. 'I'll fill out a full report and send it up to you. Can you radio for a Robinvale ambulance? The woman is pretty badly knocked around. Best if she goes up your way in case she needs more specialist attention.'

Bowker watched the divi van move towards the gate and for the first time started to shake. He re-entered the house to where Travis was attending his mother. She was sobbing gently. 'Gutsy effort, Travis,' he said, dropping to his haunches beside the boy.

'I just lost my temper and didn't care what happened. I dragged him away from Mum, and as soon as I started hitting him, he tried to pick up his knife. I kicked it across the floor and he just ran away into the other room.'

'Bullies are like that, Travis. Gutless.'

'Once I started punching him, I couldn't stop. If you hadn't come I would have killed him.' Again, the tears welled in the boy's eyes.

'Did he say how he found you and your mum?'

'One of his mates saw my picture in the Mildura paper when I won the basketball medal. It had my name and said underneath that I came from the Manang school.'

Bowker exhaled audibly. 'Of course.'

Travis turned and looked directly at the policeman. 'Will I have to go to jail for trying to kill him?'

Bowker put his hand on the boy's shoulder. 'Nope. You won't even be charged. As far as I'm concerned it all happened in self-defence.' Tears of relief streamed down the boy's face. 'I'll wait with you until the ambulance arrives from Robinvale. I think your mum will need stitches and perhaps spend a night in hospital while they check for concussion. You should go with her. You're both in shock, plus I don't want you here all night on your own.' Bowker considered asking Travis about his supermarket shopping and the mystery surrounding his mother's car, but it wasn't the right time.

It took nearly an hour for Bowker to type up his report in triplicate on the old Olivetti manual typewriter, and at least that long again to debrief with Rachael. She wanted to know every detail, and marvelled, not only at Bowker's courage and common sense, but also the strength and maturity displayed by Travis in the protection of his mother.

Finally, the details of the day were exhausted and so was Bowker.

He walked through to the station and collected the mail he had dumped on his desk prior to Rachael's call earlier. 'Every time I pick up a parcel, I get jumpy,' he said. 'This one worried me until I saw the post mark.' He ripped open the parcel, then threw it down on the table. Inside was a preserved rat, like those used for dissection in biology classes or for feeding pet reptiles. A sticky label on the plastic bag read 'Thought you could do with a friend.'.

CHAPTER 22

Winter passed into spring with the Bowker household feeling increasingly comfortable in their rural surrounds. After the drama of his father's visit and subsequent arrest, Travis Urdevic traversed Bowker's firmament less and less. He dispensed with his rat-tail and Rachael reported that the earrings had also disappeared. Bowker quizzed him about his purchases at Wraiths and the mystery of his mother's activities during the school day. Travis explained that he and his mother were banned from the Piangil store after being caught stealing chocolates, so they now did their shopping in Manang.

'What's your mum do while you're at school?' Bowker asked.

'She visits a friend near Sea Lake, I think. Lives in an old farmhouse like us. Cheap rent and nobody knows who you are.'

Bowker wasn't convinced. The Wendy Blake he'd seen was not the visiting type. Aside from her son, there was only one thing she cared about in life, and it didn't relate to friends. The thought of her behind the wheel sent shivers up his spine, but his gut told him it was Travis who drove the car.

'Sure you're not the one driving into Manang, Travis?'

'Me?' The boy said in mock surprise. 'I haven't got a licence.'

'I know that, Travis. That's what I'm worried about.'

'And where would I leave the car when I was at school?'

That was the missing piece for Bowker. He had searched the town and its surrounds on numerous occasions and failed to find any sign of the old grey Falcon.

The next week, Travis requested a school lunch pass to visit the main street to do some shopping. On his return, he stored the groceries on a staffroom bench and used its fridge for his milk and frozen pizza. When Rachael relayed these new arrangements to Bowker, he was in two minds as to what they implied. Did they confirm his theory about Travis driving the car and now he was scared off? Or was it his mother who'd been spooked, if indeed she'd been buying drugs in Sea Lake? Either way, a hazardous driver was off the road.

***

Football season ended disappointingly. The Manangatang Saints lost by four points to Nullawil in a tight grand final at Berriwillock. Bowker had a good match, kicking five goals and Rick Brennan starred, but in the end a more even performance from the maroon and whites won them the flag.

The netball was a different story. Manangatang finished second behind Sea Lake on the ladder, unable to beat the Lakers in any of their home and away matches or in the second semi-final. But if the Manang girls needed any further motivation, the champagne on ice in the Sea Lake players' area certainly provided it. The Saints prevailed by one goal to claim the first Manangatang A Grade premiership in twenty years.

***

With footballs and netballs now in storage at school, tennis racquets and cricket bats appeared at lunchtime. But the constant was Rachael's dance classes. Now with thirty-seven girls plus Jimmy, the standard had lifted dramatically, and Rachael's only disappointment was Sophie Weston's withdrawal from the class.

'She and Yvonne were the standouts,' Rachael told Bowker. 'But after our session last week, she said she was quitting. Said she's done so much ballet in the past she was sick of dancing.' That sounded strange to Rachael, but she could think of no other reason for the girl's decision. The other kids were in awe of her talent and there appeared no rivalry with Yvonne. The two girls seemed good friends in the class, always encouraging each other. But who knows what might be said behind the scenes?

By now, most of the girls sported colourful leotards and leggings, while Jimmy's favoured outfit combined a pair of purple satin shorts, a bright yellow tee-shirt, and a lime green headband. Yvonne Bryant wore an exact replica of Rachael's attire.

'Love the outfit, Yvonne. Cath and Percy buy it for you?' Rachael asked.

'Nah. Bought it myself in Swan Hill. Went over on the bus last Satny morning. Used all me spare money.' Yvonne smiled. 'Looks a bit like yours, don't you reckon, Miss Stow? Coincidence, eh?'

Rachael's throat caught. 'Yeah.'

Judi Wikman continued to help out with the class and Adrian Weston attended on most occasions to keep an eye on Jimmy's behaviour, but so far the boy had not put a foot wrong. It was now official that their speech night theme would be ancient Egypt and the students were bringing along costumes sewn in their textiles class, or by their mothers. Space was becoming a problem, so Rachael went to work cleaning the old shelves in the storeroom.

As she pushed the vacuum cleaner head deep into an old cupboard, the motor rose in pitch as something obstructed the air flow. She pulled the vacuum head from the cupboard and found an old black and white photo being sucked against the intake tube. She turned off the machine and the photo floated to the floor. She picked it up with her free hand and perused it with a smile. Three rows of children were smiling dutifully at the camera, a stern teacher standing to the side. A small chalkboard held by the little ones sitting at the front read 'Winnambool State School No.4045, 1931.'. She turned the photo over and saw the pupils' names written in ink on the back. Some were familiar from her discussions with Greg: Percival Bryant, Peter Allender, Keith Harris, Catherine Jensen – now Cath Bryant. She turned the photo over and looked at the faces again, musing how all adults were once just little kids. Then one face caught her eye and she flipped the photo over quickly and checked for the name. 'Shit!' she said out loud as she dropped the vacuum cleaner.

Often it takes the confluence of two elements for riddles to be solved. As Rachael was studying the photo, Bowker was perusing the Crayfish file for the umpteenth time. Finally, he resolved to let the old case go before it totally consumed him. He tidied the folder, pulled out the filing cabinet drawer and found the place where the file belonged. He was about to drop it into its chronological slot when he noticed that the file directly behind it related to the abrupt disappearance of Lynette Bryant. Logically, her disappearance and Crayfish's death must have happened roughly around the same time. He retrieved Lynette's file, sat down and began to read. As Bowker expected, it contained very little. He found the record of Senior Constable Alexander's enquiries, along with transcripts of interviews he had conducted with Lynette's father, Percy; her mother, Shirley; and neighbours Keith and Cath Harris at whose house she did part-time work. Alexander had requested a state-wide missing person notice and had spoken to many locals, transport services and even truck drivers stopping for fuel. In Bowker's opinion, the policeman had completed a very thorough job. Bowker checked the date she was reported missing and found it was about a fortnight before the Crayfish fatality. There seemed nothing to connect the two events, so Bowker returned both files to the drawer and vowed to forget them. But he couldn't.

When Rachael arrived home from work, she raced straight through to the station where Bowker was now filling out time sheets. 'Greg. I've got something to show you,' she blurted out.

Bowker stood up with a smile and took her hand. 'Suits me. Let's go,' he said.

'Settle down. I found this old photo in the Winnambool school room where I do my dance class.' She put the photo on the desk. 'Sit down and have a close look.'

Bowker sat down and picked up the photo. 'Winnambool school, 1931, eh? Bet it'll have Percy and his mates in it.'

'Look at each face closely, Greg.' She leaned over his shoulder.

'I am. Lots of little kids.' Then he saw it. 'Shit! Is that Yvonne Bryant with short hair?' He looked up at Rachael. 'It can't be if it's 1931.'

'It's one of the boys, Greg. I'd say about grade five or six.'

'Must be Percy Bryant. Like grandfather, like granddaughter.'

'Look at the names on the back. The Yvonne look-alike is top row, third from the left.'

Bowker turned the photo over and his face went white. 'Fuck! It's Keith Harris. Crayfish!'

'Yep.' She stood up straight.

Bowker looked up at her again. 'Has to be a mistake. They must have got the names in the wrong order.'

'That's what I thought. But then I checked. They've recorded Percy as six from the left, top row. Check out six from the left in the photo.'

Bowker looked closely. 'That's Percy, no doubt. Same little smirk he has now. And that's Cath beside him, I reckon.' He turned the photo over again. 'The Yvonne face definitely belongs to Crayfish.'

'You know what we're saying here, Greg? Like grandfather, like granddaughter. Yabby is Yvonne's father.'

Bowker stared at Rachael before speaking. 'Yabby was overseas when Lynette shot through, Rach. Been there for over a month.'

'Surely you don't think Crayfish...'

'Like father, like daughter.' He leant back in his chair. 'It's all starting to fit together.'

CHAPTER 23

The next weekend saw the social event of the year, the Manangatang Cup. The town's population soared from three or four hundred to around three thousand as visitors rolled in from parts unknown. Some patrons were dressed to the nines, while for others it was shorts and thongs. In a way, the horse racing was irrelevant, just an excuse for a social extravaganza. Race day was a time of reunion for families and former residents and a major assembly point for the current locals. But like the races at outback Birdsville and Oodnadatta, the Manangatang Cup was a magnet for bush track junkies: a festival of fun, fashions, and music with a bit of horse racing thrown in. *They're racing at Manangatang* was one of the long-established catch-cries of Australian sport. For a horse owner, if you couldn't win a Melbourne Cup, why not have another coveted talking point on your mantle-piece?

The day dawned with a cloudless azure sky and the lightest of breezes. The track was a rich green, the smell of cut grass in the air. Unfortunately for Bowker, race day was one of his busiest, on duty from the time the gates opened, to the early hours of the next morning. Today he was dressed in full uniform as he parked in a reserved spot between the ambulance and a fire truck. He opened the passenger door for Rachael who had dressed for the event, complete with an extravagant hat, white lace mini-dress and the highest of stiletto heels.

'You should enter the Fashions on the Field, you'd be an absolute monty to win,' Bowker said, holding Rachael's hand as she swung her long legs out of the car.

'That's for the young chicks, Greg. But I appreciate your confidence.'

'You're a young chick.'

She laughed as she straightened her dress. 'On a day like this, over twenty-one is old.'

The day went smoothly, with good-humoured behaviour among the crowd and keen racing between the equine visitors. A bonus came with the victory of the locally owned Manaroa in the main race. The weather remained perfect, the temperature peaking around twenty-seven degrees, the light breeze cooling the crowded lawn areas.

For many – particularly the ladies – the highlight of the day was Fashions on the Field. A parade of beautifully dressed women crossed a raised dais, their fashion ensembles triaged by a panel of local women chaired by Cath Bryant. The competition ran with military precision until Yvonne Bryant, dressed in cut-off jeans and a tank top, pushed her way into the line of voguish candidates and crossed the stage throwing kisses to the crowd. The spectators erupted in wild applause with a pair of local lads leading an 'Yvonne Yvonne Yvonne' chant that the majority of the bystanders joined. If looks could kill, Cath Bryant executed Yvonne three times over. Despite her popular appeal, Yvonne did not triumph. The Fashions on the Field winner was a leggy blonde from South Yarra wearing a designer outfit from an exclusive boutique in Toorak. This was her first trip to the dust and dirt of the Mallee and her outfit was steadily reduced to cleaning rags by her champagne-fuelled adventures later in the day.

When Cath Bryant found Bowker on his own, her wrath had not subsided.

'If you don't do something about that little bitch, I'll finish up doing something I'll regret. I can't take it any longer. She has to go!'

'A guest appearance in your fashion parade is not an offence, Cath. Besides, her general behaviour is improving all the time, so how about you calm down and give the kid a go?' Bowker replied.

'Give her a go? If it wasn't for Perce, I wouldn't have let her in the front door!'

'Because she's Crayfish's daughter. Is that it?' The question had escaped Bowker's mouth before he could stop it.

Cath's disposition darkened and her face contorted. She snarled through gritted teeth. 'Yes, because she's Keith's bastard daughter. I caught him doing it to Lynette in my own bloody bed. I came back early from shopping and there he was, grunting and puffing on top of the poor girl. Bloody old rapist!'

Bowker's words again pushed past his thoughts. 'So you decided to kill him.'

'The slasher fell on him. The dog…'

'That's garbage, Cath! You dropped it on him and then wound the chain around the lever to make it look like an accident.'

She threw her head back in a fake laugh. 'I wouldn't even know how to lower the thing!'

'You've been driving tractors all your life.' Bowker leaned closer to her. 'You knew exactly what you were doing, except you wound the dog chain from the wrong end.'

Her face hardened. 'Good theory, officer, but you can't prove it wasn't an accident. Either way, he got what he deserved. Just a pity the slasher wasn't spinning when it fell. Let sleeping dogs lie, senior constable. I did, until Yvonne turned up.'

'Did you tell Percy why Lynette left?'

'Why make things worse than they already were?' She pointed her finger angrily at Bowker. 'Don't you tell him either. He's suffered enough already. What's done is done.' She walked away, then came back for one last bout of finger-waving. 'Percy's had his chance to rein in that little tart. Now it's my turn. If I lose him in the process, then so be it. Things can't go on the way they are.' She disappeared back into the crowd.

***

The following morning, Bowker telephoned Cath asking her to visit the police station to make a formal statement in connection with the rape of Lynette Bryant. She refused, promising to deny their racetrack conversation if officially questioned on the subject. She avowed to do nothing to further blacken the Harris name that had already received its share of scuttlebutt over the years. And besides, she said, what was the point of digging up the past when both Lynette and her previous husband were long dead.

Bowker could proceed little further than make additions to the Crayfish and Lynette files, documenting his fiery conversation with Cath and his own suspicions concerning Crayfish's death. He smiled to himself. Prong's theory about there being means, motive and opportunity was accurate. But without knowledge of another more powerful motive, Prong had wrongfully concluded that Percy had dropped the slasher on Crayfish so he could reclaim his childhood sweetheart. Of course, there was always the possibility that Percy may have somehow found out about the rape and killed Crayfish as a result, but Bowker couldn't see how he could have known. Crayfish certainly wouldn't have confessed to him. If Lynette had told her father, why would she then have run off to Melbourne and why would her disappearance remain such a mystery? Perhaps Cath confided in Percy, but if that was the case, why was she so adamant that Percy be protected and not be told about his daughter's rape? No, everything pointed to Cath. And her vicious, almost psychotic reaction to Bowker's accusations left the policeman in no doubt.

Bowker dropped the files back in their drawer, knowing he had insufficient evidence to reopen the sixteen year-old Crayfish case, or cause to investigate a rape where both victim and perpetrator were now dead. But at least he now understood the truth about what had occurred at the Harris property all those years ago. He had also come to appreciate what a cold and calculating woman Cath Bryant could be, given the right circumstance.

***

With drenching early spring rains, a bumper harvest was forecast across the Mallee and northern Wimmera. But as so often happens in agriculture, when the season brings such promise, nature conspires to dampen the celebration. Occasionally it is summer thunderstorms flattening crops and making harvest difficult, although with modern combines equipped with crop-lifters, some of the loss can be ameliorated. A worse problem is consistent rain during harvest where the grain absorbs moisture and is downgraded in quality, or where the seed actually germinates while still in the head of the plant. This year, the setback came in the form of mice. Trillions of them. One female mouse can produce up to ten litters a year, with an average litter size of eight young. With plenty of food such as a good cereal crop, and mild weather conditions, the population explosion is unimaginable. In a quintessential example of a geometric progression, a single female mouse can initiate a breeding sequence resulting in over a million descendants in one year.

A mouse plague touches everyone, not just those on the land. The police residence was new but was still overrun by mice. In bed, Bowker and Rachael felt mice chewing their hair. The rodents invaded the kitchen, eating even the inedible. Items on pantry shelves were not safe, as mice knocked them to the floor for easy consumption. Bowker put foodstuffs on the kitchen table and placed each table leg in a bucket of water. But again, to no avail. Mice ate through the ceiling plaster and scurried down the light fitting before dropping onto the table and devouring the food there. Bowker tried traps, but these began filling before he finished setting the last of his twenty. In the mornings, the mess proved setting traps was counterproductive. The mice killed in traps had been consumed by others, leaving blood and fur smeared across benchtops. As a last resort, he built a Mallee mouse trap. Half a forty-four-gallon drum was partially filled with water. A beer bottle, with a piece of bacon dangling on wire from its neck, was suspended horizontally above the water on the edge of the drum. The theory was simple. A mouse would crawl along the bottle seeking the bacon, reach down for the bait and slip into the water, ultimately drowning. Bowker stood back to admire his work and two mice, in plain sight, met their fate. Happy with himself, he retired to bed. By next morning the drum was full and overflowing with dead mice, the bait had been eaten, and live mice devoured the bodies of their dead comrades. The cat from next door was lying close by, indifferent to the mice walking over her body. Bowker reluctantly conceded his efforts in holding back the murine tide were futile and probably encouraged more mice to visit the house than he actually exterminated.

The Wikmans were having worse trouble due to the age of their house and the multiple points for rodent entry. Their two youngest kids slept in meat-safe cots, enclosed on six sides by fly wire. At school, the mice caused mayhem. In the home economics centre, wooden spoons were consumed along with cooking ingredients. In other classrooms, the mice ate chalk and left fluorescent droppings around the floor. In the town's shops, particularly those selling foodstuffs, the situation was critical. At the supermarket, items were stored in sealable drums, but it was still common to find a mouse in the plastic-packaged bread.

Prong strolled into the police station where Bowker was reading the latest police bulletin. 'Got time to take a quick ride, Greg?' he asked. 'Got something to show you. If you don't see it yourself, you won't believe others when they tell you.'

They drove the few miles south to the Cocamba silos at a railway siding that runs parallel to the main Sea Lake Road. Approaching the silos, the council had put temporary speed restriction signs. Bowker suddenly saw it and slowly shook his head. 'You're right, mate. If I hadn't seen it, I wouldn't have believed you.' For several hundred metres, the bitumen was not visible, being covered completely by a thick layer of mouse flesh.

'The road is as slippery as buggery,' Prong explained. 'Like trying to steer a vehicle on ice.'

'And these were just the one's heading across to the silos?'

'About a billionth of them. Most would have made it across, no hassles. The locals poisoned here last week. They took four wheat trucks full of dead mice away. Bucketed them in with a front-end loader. Four bloody wheat trucks, would you believe it?'

Bowker was still shaking his head. 'Is it putting a hole in their numbers?'

'Nah. They've stopped poisoning. They reckon the poisoned grain may be attracting more of the bastards than they're eradicating. I'll show you something else.'

Prong crossed the railway line and drove into the silo area. He pointed to a forty-centimetre split in the far side of the steel grain shed, its concrete floor covered with the remnants of last season's harvest. A sheet of iron had been bent inwards by the wind and moving through the gap was a brown tsunami of mice.

'How the hell do you get rid of them?' Bowker asked.

Prong slowly turned the car around. 'They'll get rid of themselves. Their population will become so enormous they'll run out of food, and with greater numbers, disease spreads quickly. Unbelievably, they'll be gone as fast as they came.' He laughed. 'Then get ready for the snakes!'

Bowker looked across at Prong. 'Plenty of mice, plenty of food, plenty of snakes?'

'You got it. Worse things can happen, though. Kid got electrocuted in Ouyen when he touched a bath tap. Mice stripped the insulation off some wiring in the ceiling and it contacted a water pipe. Bloody tragedy.'

Bowker's brain took in the scene around him. How could these tiny creatures wreak such enormous damage to life and property?

CHAPTER 24

With the close of the school year rapidly approaching, exams were on the horizon. Offsetting these pressures were more enjoyable traditions such as end-of-year activities and the school social. For the farming kids, the only end-of-year activity was harvest, and for many of the older townies, it was paid work at the silos. As a result, for teachers of these pupils, the final term was chaotic. Numerous students were absent with parental permission, making delivery of the set curriculum a nightmare. Teachers of form 6 subjects fought a constant battle providing and encouraging revision when many farming parents saw a few extra HSC marks as secondary to getting the crop off.

The high school social at Manangatang was usually a pretty relaxed affair, the town being sufficiently isolated to deter visits from district yobbos. Even local lads with girlfriends in forms 5 and 6 tended to mark time in the pub until the social was over. To deter any would-be gate crashers, Bowker parked the police car outside the hall and walked home, expecting potential interlopers to assume a policeman lurked inside. Most of the secondary staff were on duty for the night, the exceptions being Rebecca Johns who was a single mother with two pre-schoolers at home, Pixie Linton who'd been ill all day, and Adrian Weston who had a two-day conference in Melbourne. The teachers were rostered for two hours of supervision apiece, although a few staff like Rachael, Secondary Coordinator Peter Hindmarsh, and Principal Malcolm Swindon, volunteered to stay for the length of the evening. Usually, two staff manned the front steps, another kept an eye on the supper room door at the back, and the remainder circulated within the darkened hall. Supper was scheduled for about 9.00 pm and parents were told to collect their kids at 11.30 pm.

The Manangatang Hall is actually two halls, joined one behind the other. The rear hall, or supper room, is accessible either side of the stage in the main hall. A door to the rear gives external access and serves as an emergency exit.

Malcolm Swindon and Peter Hindmarsh manned the front steps, happy to be away from the ear-piercing, often discordant din radiating from inside. A live band from Horsham was playing, its young drummer a cousin of a form 6 girl on the organizing committee. The band was severely limited by talent, and their repertoire comprised no more than three or four songs. But the kids didn't mind as long as they were loud. And they were deafening.

'This band is shit,' Swindon said with hands in pockets, his backside resting against the front steps handrail.

'You rate it far too highly,' Hindmarsh replied dryly.

Swindon pointed across the road. 'Here comes trouble.'

Barry Lowbury and a tall young man with short cropped blond hair crossed the road from the railway camp. They walked up the hall steps in the bright moonlight. 'How much to get in?' Lowbury asked.

'Sorry, mate. School social. Kids only,' Hindmarsh replied quickly.

'Saw some hot chicks walk up the street. Skirts so short you could see their arse. They in there?' Lowbury asked, pointing into the hall.

'If they were our students, they probably are,' Swindon said. 'But this is an official school function, so it's staff and students only. If I were you blokes, I'd head for the pub. Might find people your own age down there.'

Lowbury was becoming agitated. 'Half those form 6 sheilas are screwin' blokes our age on the weekends,' he said.

Hindmarsh had heard enough. 'Just move on, fellas. It's a school show. You're not coming in. End of story.'

Lowbury's mate took him by the arm. 'Let's get goin', Baz,' he said.

Lowbury ripped his arm away. 'Is fuckin' Yvonne in there?'

'Yvonne who?' Swindon asked with a straight face.

'How many fuckin' Yvonnes have you got?' Lowbury screeched. 'Yvonne, the fuckin' little bitch who bit me on the arm.'

'No, she wouldn't be in there,' Swindon said. 'If she bit you, mate, she'd be in hospital on antibiotics.' Hindmarsh turned away, struggling not to laugh.

'What the fuck's that supposed to mean?' Lowbury growled.

'Let's get goin', Baz,' his mate persisted. 'You can't afford to go to court again.'

'If she is in there, then you give her a fuckin' message from me. Tell the smart-arsed little bitch I'll be waitin' for her!' Lowbury turned to his mate. 'Come on. Benny, teachers are all the fuckin' same wherever you fuckin' go.' He climbed the next step to be in the faces of Swindon and Hindmarsh. 'You can both go and get fucked!'

His mate dragged Lowbury down the steps by the arm. 'Don't take any notice of him, he's had a few too many.'

The two gangers traipsed off towards the pub, Lowbury yelling at the top of his voice. 'I know you're in there, bitch! You're gonna get what's comin', you fuckin' little whore.'

There was no possibility that anyone inside heard what Lowbury yelled, what with amplifiers turned up too loud and feeding back, a guitarist who played only three chords, a base guitarist who was out of rhythm with the drums and a drummer who struggled to keep a steady beat. But most of the kids jumped and swivelled, a few couples groped in the corner, and a few younger boys sat on the seats to the side and watched the action. A disparate group, led by Rachael, danced in a circle with Jimmy Cobb in the centre having the time of his life, showing everyone his signature Michael Jackson moves. Yvonne spent the majority of time dancing with Travis and the other form 4 kids. Sophie Weston sat in the corner, staring into the darkness. Despite the sweltering November heat, Yvonne was the fashion queen in purple tights with yellow leg warmers. She matched these with a knitted multi-coloured short-sleeved top and mauve eye shadow. A purple rinse through her hair completed the look. It was fun all around, with a great country supper supplied by the Mother's Club. By 11.30 pm, most kids were exhausted.

Outside, parent cars started arriving to ferry the kids home to all points of the compass. Among the cars were Skeeta Allender's yellow ute and Percy Bryant's white Holden Statesman. As the clock ticked closer to finishing time, Bowker ambled down to retrieve his car, hoping his presence would mitigate the perilous combination of excited kids and dozens of vehicles moving in an erratic manner. Drivers were tired at this time of night, and more than one farmer would have spent his evening at the pub to avoid a second trip to town a few hours later.

As Bowker shook hands with the principal and his deputy, the conversation quickly progressed to their confrontation with Lowbury and his mate.

'Do you know who they were?' Bowker asked.

'The more sensible one called the other bloke "Baz", so I'm guessing his name would be Barry somebody,' Hindmarsh reported.

Bowker put his hands in his pockets. 'That fits. Barry Lowbury. I've run across him a couple of times already. And he was the one making threats about Yvonne Bryant?'

'Yeah. His mate was trying to calm him down,' Swindon said, waving away one of the moths attracted to the lights above the door. 'If he hadn't been with him, I think we'd have called you down to sort him out.'

Bowker waved away his own moth. 'I'll have a chat with him, anyway. Can't go around threatening people.'

Skeeta Allender alighted from his ute, crossed the road and stood on the footpath. Bowker walked down the steps to meet him. 'Evening, Skeeta. Here to pick up Yvonne, I presume?'

'Yep. That's the arrangement. Brought her in and I'm taking her home.'

'Percy might have something to say about that.' Bowker pointed across the street. 'I think that's his white Statesman under the pepper tree.'

Skeeta turned and saw the Bryant car. 'Yvonne never said nothin' about him pickin' her up. He's never worried about that before.'

'If he wants to drive her home, then that's what'll happen. He's her legal guardian.'

'She's sixteen. She can do what she wants.'

Before Bowker could respond, the door of the Statesman opened and Cath Bryant, rather than her husband, got out. She strode urgently across the street.

Skeeta threw up his hands. 'What's that old battle-axe doin' here?'

'I'm betting the same thing as you,' Bowker replied. He instinctively folded his arms in readiness for the inevitable confrontation.

'Right, Skeeta, you can head off home, now,' Cath ordered with a go-away flick of her hand. 'I'll look after Yvonne.'

Skeeta shook his head in defiance. 'No way. I told Yvonne I'd give her a ride.'

Cath waved her finger in his face and said spitefully, 'You're more interested in her giving you a ride, more like it. But that's all over from now on.'

The confrontation was terminated by an explosion of noisy, laughing teenagers surging out through the double glass doors. A few couples left hand-in-hand, but the majority of kids exited in groups, all looking totally exhausted. Skeeta and Cath scanned the departing horde, each hoping to snare Yvonne before the other. Within a couple of minutes, the hall had disgorged its patrons, the surrounds now flooded with the lights of vehicles turning, reversing and departing in a ballet of controlled chaos. Last to exit the hall was Rachael with Jimmy in tow. Jimmy's mother met him on the footpath. 'Have a good time, Jim?' she asked.

'Yef,' Jimmy said. 'Dancered all night. Now I'm rooted.'

'I think you mean "tired",' his mum said with a wink towards Rachael.

'Yef. Tied.' Jimmy replied, dropping his shoulders and exhaling theatrically.

'Good boy, Jim. Jump in our car.' Jimmy trotted a few metres up the street and climbed into a dusty old Land Rover. 'Thanks, Rachael. You've been a godsend for that little boy.'

'He's a great kid,' Rachael replied.

Jimmy's mother smiled and walked to her vehicle.

Cath grabbed Rachael's wrist. 'Where's Yvonne?'

'She must have gone with the others,' Rachael said quietly, staring at her arm until Cath released her grip. 'There was nobody inside when Jimmy and I came out. I locked the supper room door and turned off the lights.'

'Well, she didn't come out,' Skeeta said.

'You must have missed her,' Rachael replied.

Cath was having none of it. 'I looked at every child. Yvonne wasn't there. God only knows what she's up to this time.'

'I saw her dancing with Travis during the night,' Rachael said. 'Just before supper I checked the ladies' toilets and she was sitting on the floor talking to Sophie Weston.'

'Dancin' with fuckin' Travis! That'd be right,' Skeeta said angrily.

'Watch your language, Skeeta,' Bowker warned. 'Okay, did anyone see Travis Urdevic leave?' Nobody had.

By now the street had cleared and the only vehicles remaining belonged to Bowker, Cath and Skeeta. Half a dozen kids stood on the steps still waiting for parents, so Peter Hindmarsh volunteered to stay at the hall until the last of the kids were collected. And to wait around in case Yvonne or Travis turned up.

But they didn't turn up. Cath and Skeeta separately drove the streets looking for them, but to no avail. Eventually they went home, hoping that the morning would bring a logical explanation for the kids' disappearance. Bowker and Rachael searched the hall again in case Yvonne and Travis were playing tricks. They checked all the cupboards in the supper room, the toilets, under the stage and even up in the unused movie projection room. They found no clue as to where the kids had vanished.

Bowker was now sweating profusely, the stress of the couple's disappearance compounding the stifling temperature. 'Is there any way they could leave the hall unnoticed, Rach?'

'Only if they snuck out through the supper room. But there was a staff member rostered in that area all night. Apparently kids have stashed alcohol outside the hall in years past, so Malcolm was adamant we keep that exit monitored.'

Bowker wiped his brow with a folded handkerchief. 'So, there would have been a teacher on that door all evening?'

'Theoretically, yes.'

'Theoretically?'

'Things come up at shows like this. Maybe a scuffle between kids, or a misunderstanding about the supervision roster. Earlier tonight one of the little kids vomited on the hall floor and that caused a bit of mayhem. The back door was opened at supper time to let in a bit of fresh air, but I saw Donna Cavanagh covering that exit.'

Bowker dropped Rachael back at the station in case a phone call came through regarding the kids' whereabouts. He continued his search around the town and drove out as far as Piccadilly Corner in the unlikely event that Yvonne and Travis had decided to make the long walk back to Winnambool. But his efforts were to no avail. Cath would undoubtedly inform Perce that Yvonne was missing, but Bowker decided notifying Wendy Blake could wait until the morning, given the lateness of the hour and her likely condition at this time of night. If the kids were still missing in the morning, he would also need to contact surrounding police and visit the school to interview any staff or students who had seen them the night before.

CHAPTER 25

After an early morning phone call from a distressed Percy Bryant, Bowker knew he had a full-blown missing persons case on his hands. At 8.30 am, half of the mystery was solved when Travis arrived at school on the bus, but there was still no sign of Yvonne.

Bowker contacted the police in surrounding towns, providing a description of Yvonne, when she was last seen, and what she was wearing when she disappeared. A school photo would follow. He emphasized that if Yvonne was a passenger in a vehicle, it should not be assumed she was there against her will, or that she would seek police assistance. In short, they should be on the lookout for what he termed a wild child, a girl who wouldn't think twice about grabbing a lift with a stranger.

Bowker arrived at the principal's office fifteen minutes after making the calls, the wind whipping up dust and sand in the school ground. He requested copies of Yvonne's school photos before catching sight of Travis seated in the interview room across the passage.

'Doesn't know where Yvonne is,' the principal said. 'And he reckons he left with the other kids at the end of the night.'

'That's bullshit,' Bowker replied quickly.

'I'll leave you to it, Greg. You might get more out of him than me.'

Swindon returned to his paperwork and Bowker entered the interview room, closed the door, and sat in an easy chair opposite Travis. He hesitated for effect, resting his elbows on the arms of the chair with his hands folded on his lap. 'Where's Yvonne, Travis?'

The boy stared at the floor. 'Dunno.'

'You were dancing with her last night.'

He looked up at Bowker. 'Yeah, so what? I didn't see her after supper.'

'So when did you leave the hall?'

'At the end of the night. With the other kids.'

Bowker shook his head. 'I was out the front, mate. I didn't see you go.'

'There were over a hundred kids. You must have missed me.' Travis looked away and stared out the window.

'I don't think so.'

'You ask Leigh Davidson. I walked out with him.'

'Your dope smoking mate?'

He looked back at Bowker. 'Yeah.'

'How'd you get back to Winnambool?'

'Mum.'

Bowker raised his eyebrows. 'What, she brought you in for the social then came all the way back to pick you up?'

'I didn't go home after school, did I? I had my casual clothes in my bag and hung around town until the social started. Ask Hackle. I bought a hamburger there for tea.'

Bowker folded his arms across his chest. 'I didn't see your mum's car after the social.'

'That's because she parked it down in Pioneer Street so you wouldn't see her. She was half pissed.'

'Was Yvonne upset when you were last talking to her?'

'No. She seemed really happy.' He turned his eyes back to the window. 'We even had a pash in the corner.'

Bowker smiled. 'She two-timing Skeeta?'

Travis sprang to his feet. 'Fuck Skeeta. She only hangs around with him now because she's scared of him. He hits her sometimes and threatens to hurt her if she talks to other blokes. Or threatens to dob him in.'

Bowker stood up beside him. 'Dob him in for what? Drug dealing?'

Travis looked away. 'Dunno. She doesn't talk about that.'

'Well, that's bullshit too, Travis.'

'I don't know nothin' about that stuff.' He turned and looked Bowker in the eye. 'All I know is that she used to really like Skeeta, but now she's just scared of him.'

Bowker asked Travis to wait in the empty classroom next door while he had Leigh Davidson called to the general office. As Leigh approached, he hesitated a little as he caught sight of Travis through a corridor window. Bowker hurried him into the interview room and closed the door. 'Take a seat, Leigh.' The boy sat down quickly, anxiety etched on his pimply face. 'You at the social last night, Leigh?'

'Yes, sir.'

'Who'd you leave with at the end of the night?'

'Dad.'

'No, I mean who did you walk out of the hall with?'

The boy shifted in his seat. 'Heaps of kids?'

'Travis Urdevic?'

Leigh hesitated just long enough. 'Yeah, he was there.'

Bowker shook his head. 'I think that's rubbish, Leigh. You just saw Travis in the classroom next door and now you're covering for him.'

'No. I remember him walking down the steps, then he went straight across the road and got in with his parents. Then they drove off.' He looked away from Bowker.

Bowker came the heavy. 'That's a load of bullshit, Leigh. Now, if I remember correctly, you were caught smoking weed at school earlier in the year, weren't you?'

Leigh nodded his head as he started to cry.

'Well, I let that go through to the keeper. Thought I'd give a good kid a break.' He leaned forward so he was only inches from the boy's face. 'But you're not acting like a good kid right now, Leigh. I can still bring a possession of marijuana charge against you. You understand that, don't you?'

Leigh nodded again as he sobbed into his hanky.

Bowker spoke more softly. 'You're covering for Travis, aren't you, son?'

Leigh nodded.

Bowker leant back. 'Okay. Let's start again. Did Travis leave the social with you last night?'

Leigh shook his head and blew his nose. 'No. No, he didn't.'

'Where was he?'

Leigh shook his head again. 'I don't know. One of the girls said he snuck out the back door before the social finished. After we had supper.'

'Why would he do that?'

'Something to do with Yvonne Bryant and Skeeta Allender. But I don't know any more than that.' He looked up at Bowker. 'Honestly, I don't.'

Bowker was inclined to believe him. 'Okay. Did you see him again for the rest of the night?'

He shook his head. 'No.'

'Did you see Yvonne at the social?'

The boy nodded. 'Yes. She was dancing with Travis. And they were snogging in the corner.'

'Did you see Yvonne after Travis left?'

Leigh shrugged his shoulders. 'I think she left with Travis. Well, that's what a couple of kids were saying.'

'Thanks, Leigh. I might need to talk to you again, but for now you can go back to class.'

Bowker saw Leigh out, then called Travis back. The pair remained standing.

'Okay, Travis, cut the crap and tell me what really happened. You and Yvonne snuck out the back door after supper. So where is she?'

Travis became emotional. 'I don't know, Bowker. I really don't know.'

'You and Yvonne were having a good time, dancing and kissing. Then something happened.'

Travis hesitated, assessing his options. 'Okay. Martine Molloy said Skeeta Allender was at the back door and wanted to talk to Yvonne.'

'How could that have happened? There was a teacher on duty there. You're feeding me more bullshit.'

'No, it's true,' Travis said quickly. 'One of the form 1 boys had a gut full of spirits before the social and spewed up everywhere on the dance floor. The teachers were all trying to clean up. I think Miss Cavanagh was on the back door, and she went somewhere to ring up the kid's parents to come and get him.'

Bowker scratched his neck. 'So Yvonne just strolled out the back door to meet Skeeta?'

'That's about it.'

'Leigh said you went outside as well.'

Travis fired up. 'Yeah, okay. I was shitty. I really like Yvonne, and just when I was getting it on with her, that paedophile turns up.'

'So what happened outside the hall?'

'Skeeta and me just pushed and shoved. Then Yvonne says she's going with Skeeta to have a rum and Coke. She says she'll be back before the end of the social and she'll see me then.'

'And she didn't come back?'

The boy shrugged his shoulders. 'Dunno. I was really angry and didn't go back into the hall. I walked around town for a while, then rang Mum from the phone box to come in early and get me. Didn't know Yvonne was missing until I got to school this morning.'

'Anything else you need to tell me?' Bowker pointed a finger at him. 'Better now than if I find it out later.'

Travis looked out the window. 'I've told you everything.'

Travis left the room and Bowker used the school phone to ring the Allender property. Dawn answered and went to fetch Skeeta who she said was still in bed. Eventually, Skeeta came on the line. 'So did you find the little bitch and her pencil-dick friend, or have they fucked off into the sunset together?'

'I've warned you before about the language, Skeeta. Travis is at school this morning, but we still can't find Yvonne.'

'Why are you ringing me? I was as surprised as anybody when she wasn't there after the social. I was supposed to be taking her home.'

'But you took her away during the night though, didn't you? Travis Urdevic said he saw you.'

Skeeta didn't answer for a moment. 'Yeah, alright. We drove out to the Cocamba silos with a few rum and Cokes.'

'So where is she now?'

'No fuckin' idea, Bowker. I brought her back into town and dropped her off at the social. She was worried about getting into trouble because she's doin' some dance shit where she's Queen Victoria or something to do with Rome.'

'Anybody see you drop her off?'

'Fucked if I know. I stopped around in Pioneer Street so she could sneak in the back door when the teachers weren't looking.'

Bowker hesitated a moment or two. 'What if I said that you didn't bring her back?'

'Well why would I fuckin' go back and wait at the fuckin' hall? Why would I get into a fuckin' argument with silly old Cath?'

Bowker ignored the swearing and kept the conversation rolling. 'Maybe to cover your own backside?'

'Cover my arse for what? It wasn't just Travis who saw me with Yvonne at the back of the hall. There were a couple of girls looking out the window as well. If you reckon I was the last person to see her, then I'm up shit creek already. It doesn't help my case to turn up at the end of the night and pretend I'm picking her up, does it?'

Bowker was inclined to agree with his logic.

'Why are you still in bed this morning when your girlfriend couldn't be found last night? I thought you'd be worried sick.'

'Because I thought she was with Travis and I decided they could both go and get fucked.'

'You'll need to come into town this afternoon and make a formal statement.'

'So, I'm wastin' more petrol on the bitch!'

***

Bowker spent the next hour interviewing the half dozen students who witnessed Yvonne's movements the previous night. Those who had observed Yvonne leave with Skeeta were initially reluctant to say anything they thought might get her into trouble, but sensing the seriousness in Bowker's manner, they eventually recounted what they'd seen. It all matched with Travis's account. Yes, he and Yvonne were kissing in the dark; yes, Skeeta wanted to see Yvonne; yes, Travis went outside with her; and yes, they'd seen a scuffle between Skeeta and Travis. The witnesses also agreed they'd never seen Travis so angry. Most of the kids thought him a harmless dipstick, but his anger on this occasion took them by surprise, just as his uncontrolled fury with his father had surprised Bowker.

Bowker spoke briefly to a hastily convened assembly of teachers, but none were able to add anything new to his investigation. They all verified Travis's account of the form 1 boy throwing up. Donna Cavanagh confirmed she was on duty in the supper room and had left the hall to phone the boy's parents, assuming someone would replace her while she was making the call. She'd only discovered this morning that this had not happened. Bowker thus confirmed that a window of opportunity had existed for Yvonne and Travis to leave the building unnoticed by teachers.

A casual aside from one of the form 4 girls played on Bowker's mind. Yvonne had apparently complained about the stifling heat inside the hall and commented how she'd die for a swim. In response, Bowker returned to the station via the town swimming pool. The gates were locked, so he clambered over the six-foot cyclone wire fence. It was a long shot that Yvonne would leave the social for a swim, but sillier things had happened. The water was blue and inviting, the sun sparkling off the little ripples that skated across the surface in the blustery wind. To Bowker's relief there was no body on the bottom. Other than the pool, the town reservoir was the only swimmable body of water within easy walking distance of the hall. It would need to be dragged if Yvonne didn't turn up in the next few days.

Dragging any sort of dam would probably bring back tragic memories for the district's older residents. Some decades ago, five Chinky kids drowned in a farm dam after getting off the school bus. The day was a scorcher, the surface of the dam hot, but below lurked ice-cold water. Their little graves sit in the Chinkapook cemetery alongside the resting places of other small children who succumbed to the epidemics that ravaged the district in the early days of settlement. Perhaps the saddest Bowker had seen was a grave beside the Sea Lake Road. A mother, with three children suffering from diphtheria, left Robinvale in horse and cart for the long journey to the nearest doctor in Sea Lake. She made it a little over halfway before the last of her children died. She buried the three little ones together by the side of the road. Thank God for vaccinations, Bowker thought.

On his return to the station, Bowker phoned Cath and Percy Bryant requesting they attend the station for an interview. He also needed to interview Barry Lowbury at the railway camp and visit the pub to ascertain who else may have been in town last night. At some stage, he needed to ring Wendy Blake to confirm Travis's story about being picked up early.

As he scanned his written notes, the obvious hit him. Travis couldn't have rung his mother because she didn't have a phone. That's why the school had to send notes home. So Travis was lying again. And if he went home with his half-drunk mother at the end of the night as he originally claimed, what did he get up to until then? They needed another chat.

Bowker was back at the school within ten minutes and talking with Travis within fifteen. 'I'm sick of the bullshit, Travis.'

Travis was defensive. 'It wasn't bullshit. I didn't see Yvonne after she left with Skeeta.'

'You said you rang your mother, and she came in early to get you.'

'Yeah. So what?'

Bowker poked him in the chest. 'She hasn't got the phone on, Travis. You think I'm an idiot or something?'

Travis looked away. 'Okay. So, I didn't ring her. She picked me up at eleven-thirty like we planned.'

'Then why lie to me?'

'Because I was shit-scared you'd think I got up to something between when I left the social and when I was picked up by Mum. I just walked around. Didn't see Skeeta or Yvonne again. Promise.'

'Where did you go when you were walking around?'

Travis shrugged his shoulders. 'Nowhere really. Walked up and down the streets. Shops were all closed, except the pub. In the end, I just sat outside Hackle's and waited for Mum to come in. At half-past eleven I met her in Pioneer Street opposite the hospital.'

'Was she really half pissed?'

He shrugged again. 'She'd had a few, I think. There was an empty brandy bottle on the front seat.'

Bowker wasn't convinced. 'If I drive out and ask her, do you think she'd remember picking you up?'

Travis shrugged. 'Probably not. Her memory's gone to shit.'

Bowker raised his eyebrows. 'But she remembered to come in and get you?'

'Yeah, cos I tied the car keys around her wrist with a bit of cord off the blind. Pretty sad, eh? Bottle of piss means more to her than her own son.'

'Don't be too hard on her, mate. She's had a terrible life. You're all she's got.' Tears welled up in Travis's eyes and he looked away, wiping his cheeks with the back of his hands. Now to Bowker's real question. 'You didn't drive yourself in and out, did you?'

Travis shook his head vigorously. 'No. I've told you that before.'

The chat with Travis yielded nothing extra and Bowker returned to the station to follow up his other lines of enquiry. On the way, he visited the railway workers' camp, but as he expected, the crew was out on the job somewhere between Waitchie and Robinvale. He'd need to undertake these enquiries outside their work hours.

CHAPTER 26

While awaiting the arrival of Skeeta and the Bryants, Bowker began a written timeline detailing who was where, and when. So far, he had little. Yvonne and Travis left the hall to meet Skeeta sometime after supper. Skeeta claimed he and Yvonne took a drive to Cocamba before he returned her to the hall before the end of the social. She hadn't been seen since. Travis didn't reenter the hall and asserts he walked around town on his own until travelling home with his mother at 11.30 pm. Just before then, Cath Bryant arrived unexpectedly to pick up Yvonne, as did Skeeta who claimed an understanding with Yvonne that he was taking her home.

With still no sign of Skeeta or the Bryants, Bowker slipped out to Cocamba hoping to discover something that would help prove or disprove Skeeta's account. At the silos it was windy and dusty, so any tyre tracks from the night before were long gone. Bowker walked the perimeter of the area and saw nothing that piqued his interest except that the mouse population had diminished dramatically. The gap in the grain shed wall where the mice had gained entry had been repaired, and out on the road, the constant traffic and hot sun had disintegrated any evidence of the rodent pulp. Satisfied that there was little to see, he drove back into Manang and stopped at the town's reservoir opposite the railway camp. He bush-bashed on foot around the perimeter of the reserve, following a high netting fence with barbed wire strung along the top. Heavy steel padlocked gates served as the only entrance to the compound. To Bowker, it seemed implausible that Yvonne could scale the fence, and he was now convinced the swimming theory was a dead end. But he was happy he'd followed it through. Occasionally, the most off-hand comment turned an investigation on its head and helped point an arrow to the truth. But not this time. He returned to his car and continued along the road past the recreation reserve and the racecourse.

Half a mile on, he spotted Tub Keller and his dog walking their well-worn path. He pulled over near the car graveyard and wound down his window. 'Doing the afternoon shift today, Tub?'

'Yeah. Felt a bit off this morning, but I'm starting to come good.'

'You didn't have that green apple, did you?'

Tub laughed. 'Nuh. Or the good root, unfortunately. I'd have to push it in with an icy pole stick these days anyway.'

Bowker chuckled. 'Any crime up your end of town, partner? Or have you scared them all off?' The dog peed on Bowker's front wheel.

Tub dragged the Jack Russell away by the leash. 'Every now and then I take the dog through the dumped vehicles here in the bush. Today I noticed that somebody's knocked one off.'

'May be looking for parts.'

Tub nodded. 'Probably. This one was a bit better than the others, so maybe somebody thought they could get it going again. Don't like their chances, though. Once those old Falcons die, they die.'

Bowker was suddenly interested. 'Sedan or wagon?'

'Old model station wagon. Grey, with a maroon front mudguard. Obviously had a bingle at some stage.'

Bowker got out of his car. 'Show me where it was, please, mate.'

The old man took Bowker into a nest of old car bodies. Out of sight from the road and accessed via a small gap through which you could drive a car, was an empty gravesite in the heart of this automobile cemetery. The grass was worn in two strips indicating a car had been driven in and out on numerous occasions. 'When did you first notice it dumped here, Tub?' Bowker asked.

'Few months ago. Only been through here a couple of times since, but it was always here. Here for good, I thought.'

'Ever see any kids walking down this road?'

'Occasionally see this young buck in school uniform. Skinny kid. More meat on a butcher's pencil.'

Hide something in plain sight, Bowker thought. The little bastard is smarter than I've given him credit for.

***

It was time to visit Travis for the third time today, but when he crossed the railway line on the northern edge of Manang and stopped at the Robinvale Road, Bowker gave way to the Bryants' Statesman heading into town. He followed the car until it pulled in beside the police station. Travis would have to wait.

'Obviously no sign of Yvonne?' Bowker asked after inviting Percy and Cath inside.

Percy was visibly upset as he sat down. 'Just hope she hasn't followed in her mother's footsteps and shot through to Melbourne. That'd be two girls I've failed.'

'I don't think she's gone to Melbourne,' Bowker replied. 'She was having a good time at the social and gave no indication she planned to go anywhere. Look, I'll tell you what I know so far.' Bowker sat down behind his desk and outlined what he had been able to establish.

'So she took off with Skeeta during the evening?' Cath said, taking a seat beside her husband.

'That's what Travis told me. Skeeta confirmed it.'

'Well, there's your mystery solved. The little tart spent the night with him somewhere.' Cath threw her hands in the air. 'Why am I not surprised?'

'Better that than running away somewhere, never to be seen again,' Percy said sadly.

Cath rolled her eyes, her preference obvious.

'Skeeta said he brought her back, Cath. And he was there with us both at the end of the social, remember. He seemed just as annoyed as you that Yvonne wasn't there to be picked up.'

'Could have been an act,' Cath said. 'Probably up to no good and planned to spend the night together.'

'Well, where is she now? Skeeta was home when I rang the Allenders.'

Cath shrugged her shoulders.

Bowker eyed Percy. 'How come you didn't drive in to pick her up last night?'

'Because Yvonne said Skeeta was bringing her home. I went to bed and didn't even know Cath had been into town until she woke me up and told me that Yvonne was missing.'

Bowker looked back at Cath. 'So why'd you come in when you knew Skeeta was bringing her home?'

Cath leaned closer to Bowker and waved her finger. 'Because I'm sick of her running the show. I told you at the races, I'm not putting up with her alley cat lifestyle anymore. Perce and I have had it out. He knows where I stand.'

Percy muttered without looking up. 'So she becomes another Lynette?'

Cath snapped back. 'Yvonne was gone before I even got to Manang, so don't try to put that one on me.'

'What time did you arrive in town?' Bowker asked.

'About eleven. Wanted to be there in case the dance finished early.'

'Pass anybody on the way in?'

'The only car I passed was that grey and maroon Falcon belonging to the woman who rents Percy's old farmhouse,' she said. 'She'd be taking her useless son home would be my guess.'

'It was dark,' Bowker said. 'How did you know it was Wendy Blake's car?'

'There was a full moon, and besides, the low beam on the driver side doesn't work. Seen the same car go up her drive a couple of times at night. Always had the dud light.'

Percy looked up. 'I've passed it too, Greg. At dusk. You should talk to her about it. Bloody dangerous. In the dark, you think you're approaching a motor bike, then all of a sudden you're squeezed for room.'

'What time did you pass the old Falcon?' Bowker asked.

Cath looked up at the ceiling. 'I dunno, probably around quarter to eleven. Maybe five or six miles out of Manang. This side of Piccadilly Corner anyway.'

So if Travis headed home around 10.30 pm, what was he up to between supper and then? Bowker pondered briefly. 'Did you see Skeeta's car in town when you arrived?'

'Only when he pulled in opposite the hall.'

'See any strangers around the area?'

She frowned. 'Strangers? What strangers would be around at that time of night?'

'Railway workers, perhaps.'

'Saw a few town parents walking to pick up their kids. But no boogeymen hiding in the shadows, if that's what you mean.'

***

Within a few minutes of the Bryants' departure, Bowker heard the burble of Skeeta's V8. 'Why did I need to come to town?' an irritated Allender demanded as he pushed through the station door. 'I told you everything I know over the bloody phone.'

'You need to make a formal statement and sign it. You were the last person seen with Yvonne.'

Skeeta put both hands on Bowker's desk and leant across towards him. 'I dropped her back at the hall. Don't you bloody listen?'

'Take a seat and cool down a bit, mate. I want to go over what you told me on the phone and then I'll probably have a few other things I need cleared up.'

Skeeta slumped down onto a chair, and with Bowker taking copious notes, recounted his movements with Yvonne the previous night. Bowker found no inconsistencies between Skeeta's first and second narratives.

'What sort of mood was Yvonne in when you picked her up?'

Skeeta threw his head back and exhaled loudly through his lips. 'She was in an absolute shit. Something had stirred her up and she wanted to stay at the social.'

'Then why did she go with you to Cocamba?'

'Travis and I were having a push and shove and I grabbed him by the throat and pushed him against the side of the hall. Yvonne said if I left him alone, she'd come for a ride in the car.' Skeeta dropped his voice and looked at the floor. 'I think she's got the hots for him, the little bitch.'

'So the two of you travelled to Cocamba and drank a few cans of UDL?'

Skeeta pointed at his chest. '*I* drank a couple. She wouldn't touch any because she didn't want alcohol on her breath when she got back.'

'So you just talked.'

'Yeah. We just talked,' Skeeta said with a fake laugh. 'She wasn't interested in a drink and she wasn't interested in a root. In the end, I just cracked it and took her back to the hall. I hoped she'd be in a better mood when I picked her up to take her home.'

'But she wasn't there.'

'No. She wasn't fuckin' there. So obviously she was in no mood to come home with me either.'

Bowker was becoming increasingly convinced that Skeeta was telling the truth. Why admit that Yvonne was an unwilling participant in the Cocamba sojourn if he was involved in her disappearance?

'Anybody see you at Cocamba?'

Skeeta shrugged. 'Doubt it. A couple of semis went past, and a car followed me into Manang, but otherwise it was quiet, as you'd expect for that time of night. We were only out there for twenty minutes before I got sick of the bitch and brought her back to Manang.'

'What'd you do between dropping her off and then going back to pick her up at eleven-thirty?'

'Pub most of the time. Sat in the corner and talked to Jacko Powell.'

'And you haven't heard from her since you dropped her back at the social?'

He looked straight at Bowker. 'Don't you think I would have told you if I had? Shit, if she doesn't turn up, who do you think people will point the finger at?'

Bowker stood up. 'Let me know if you remember anything else, anything she might have said. And, of course, if she contacts you, I'm the first one you tell, right?

'Can I go now?'

'Yeah, after you read and sign this. But I wouldn't go too far away.'

***

Bowker looked at his watch. It was just after 3.15 pm and he hadn't had dinner. But if he was going to talk to Travis again today, he would need to catch him at the bus stop before he headed home. Dinner would have to wait.

CHAPTER 27

The seven school buses were all lined up, students wandering across from the new buildings when Bowker arrived at the school. He climbed aboard the Winnambool bus. 'Yvonne not on this morning, Don?'

'No, mate. Waited five minutes in case she was running late, but no show.'

'Did Travis say anything when Yvonne wasn't aboard?'

The driver shook his head. 'Not that I heard.'

'I might grab him when he comes over. We need to have a chat, so you head off without him. I'll take him home. I need to talk to his mother anyway.'

When Travis arrived and saw Bowker, he knew instinctively who the policeman was chasing. 'Yvonne turned up, yet?' he asked nervously.

'Nope. You've had all day to think about it, Travis. Any bright ideas on where she might be?'

He dropped his schoolbag to the ground. 'All I know is that she went with Skeeta. That's the last time I saw her. None of the other kids have heard of her since then either.'

'You said you walked around town and sat in front of Hackle's for a while.'

'Yeah.'

'Did you see anyone else wandering about?'

'A few blokes went in and out of the pub. Weren't wandering

around really. Just got in and out of their cars. The only other people I saw were two blokes crossing the railway line to the camp. One of them was swearing at the top of his voice. Must have had a fight with his girlfriend or something. He was pretty angry.'

'Did you see them actually enter the camp?'

Travis shrugged his shoulders. 'It's dark over there under the trees, but that's where they were heading.'

'See any cars just driving around the streets without stopping anywhere?'

Travis shook his head. 'Nuh. A few cars were parked outside the pub and some outside people's houses or in their driveways. But nobody chucking laps, if that's what you mean.'

'You didn't see a parked car with a person sitting inside.'

'Nuh. There was a big semi parked up near the swimming pool. One of those ones that carry cars. Trucky having a snooze, most probably.'

The bus driver yelled to Bowker that he was about to leave. Travis picked up his bag and moved to climb aboard, but Bowker put his hand on the boy's shoulder. 'I'll give you a lift home, mate. I want to show you something on the way. Besides, I need to talk to your mum.'

Rather than following the bus over the railway line and up the main street, Bowker drove down past the recreation reserve. When he arrived at the auto graveyard, he bounced the police car through the table drain and followed the flattened grass into the old Falcon's hiding place. He saw Travis's mouth drop. 'Great place to hide a car, eh?'

'Dunno what you're talking about?' Travis said unconvincingly. 'I've never seen this place before.'

'Travis, I've got witnesses who saw your mum's old Falcon wagon parked in this very spot.'

Travis played his last card. 'Then I guess Mum parked it here because she'd be half pissed and scared of getting picked up if she went properly into town.'

'Cut the crap, Travis,' Bowker said wearily. 'You've been driving the old Falcon into Manang when you need to do shopping. And you drove it home last night from the social. Cath Bryant passed you out near Piccadilly Corner at about quarter to eleven.'

'Could have been any car she passed.'

'You're missing a low beam on the driver side. It was your car, and you were driving.'

Travis was quiet for a moment as he stared ahead. 'So, are you going to book me?'

'Most likely. In reality, you're probably a lot safer on the road than your mother, and I can see you needed to get groceries. But it's still against the law. I prefer you to get a lunch pass and take stuff home on the bus.'

Travis breathed deeply. 'So what happens to me now?'

'Nothing happens to you now. The driving charge can wait. I'm more interested in what you did between the time Skeeta left with Yvonne, and when you came over here to get the car. It has to have been well over an hour. An hour and a half maybe.'

Travis turned in his seat and looked at Bowker. 'I told you. I just walked around. I was having a great time with Yvonne and then within five minutes the best night of my life turned to total shit. Why go straight home and see Mum flaked out on the floor as usual?'

Bowker felt a tinge of sympathy for the lad as he drove out through the car bodies, over the railway line and onto Winnambool Road. Nothing was said until they were in the Blake's yard. The old Falcon was under a tree and Bowker could see that the driver's side headlight had a crack. 'Give something a nudge with the driver-side front?'

'Bloody roos up near Allender's gate. Saw the first two, didn't see the third one until I nicked the big prick.'

They walked inside, and as Travis had suggested, his mother lay comatose on the couch. Several empty brandy bottles were beside her, along with tin-foil tablet wrapping. 'I wanted to talk to your mum about the car, mate. But that'll have to wait until she's sober.'

He choked back tears. 'She's never sober.'

'Well perhaps when she's at least conscious. You be alright here?'

He wiped his eyes with thumb and forefinger. 'No different to any other day.'

'Got anything for tea?'

'Yeah, there's some baked beans I can heat up if the stove works.'

Bowker patted him on the shoulder. As he left through the kitchen, he switched on all four hotplates. Two worked, so at least they'd have something hot to eat. Travis would anyway.

***

Back in town, Bowker made a quick visit to the pub. The main bar was deserted except for two old barflies perched on stools staring into alcoholic oblivion. Rick Brennan was wiping tables near the back of the room.

'Yeah, Greg, there were a dozen or so in last night. A few cockies who live further out came in for a chat while they were waiting for the kids' shebang to finish at the hall.'

'Skeeta Allender here?' Bowker asked.

Rick thought for a moment. 'Yeah. Came in about, I dunno, quarter past, half past ten. Left about an hour later when we were closing up. Sat over there near the window with Jacko Powell.'

'Who else can you remember?'

Rick stopped wiping and stood up straight. 'Butch, Wiffy, Pizzle, Bullpup. Usual crew. Jingles, Stretch. Piddles and Chomp came in a bit later. Yabby Harris was in here for a while with Prong. Haven't seen Yabby in Manang for months. He and his missus tend to socialise in Tooleybuc where her family come from.'

'How long was Yabby here for?'

Rick screwed up his face as he tried his best to recall. 'Nine thirty to ten-ish, at a guess. Had a pot of light and one of heavy. Said g'day to a few locals he'd played footy with, then shot through with Prong. From what I could gather, they'd been down south buying ewes somewhere.'

'No strangers?'

Rick walked back behind the bar and threw his cloth into an empty bucket on the floor. 'The railway blokes had a counter tea then went home about eight. They start pretty early.'

Bowker ambled across and sat on a stool. 'Any railway boys stay later?'

'A couple. That dickhead who had the run in with Skeeta was here with this short haired blond bloke. Finished up asking them to leave.'

'How come?'

'Shootin' his mouth off about some little bitch he was going to teach a lesson. Angry bastard, he is. His mate was trying to calm him down. But in the end the locals were getting annoyed, so I told them to piss off or I'd ring you to come down. Luckily the blond bloke was able to drag him out. Went back to the camp, I guess.' Rick filled a pot glass with Coke and handed it to Bowker. 'On the house.'

Bowker took a long swig, emptying the glass. 'Thanks, mate.' He placed the pot back on the bar. 'Just out of interest. Was Skeeta here when the ganger was mouthing off?'

Rick dropped the empty glass in a sink of soapy water. 'Nah. He was well gone before Skeeta arrived.'

'Were Skeeta and Yabby here at the same time?'

'Woulda just missed each other, I'd say. Skeeta walked in a couple of minutes after Yabby and Prong left.'

Bowker left the pub having confirmed Skeeta's story but reminding himself that all this legwork could be a waste of his time. It was just as likely that Yvonne would walk through his door and say she'd heard people had been looking for her. That she'd hitched a ride to Swan Hill with some good-looking trucky last night and had come home on the VicRail bus this afternoon. But for the moment, she was a missing person, and it was his job to determine her whereabouts, irrespective of whether foul-play was involved.

Prong's car was parked outside his shop opposite the hotel. Bowker strolled over for a chat.

'Percy's granddaughter turned up?' Prong asked as he unpacked boxes of sheep drench from a large carton and placed them on a set of steel shelves.

'Not yet, unfortunately,' Bowker replied.

'She'll show up. Over the years, we've had the odd teenage kid go missing, but they always turn up somewhere. Eventually they ring their families from Melbourne saying they're not coming back, or they've moved in with the boyfriend in Swan Hill that their folks didn't even know about. There was this effeminate boy who just didn't fit in up here and took off to the city. Eventually he let his mum know he was okay.'

'I hope you're right,' Bowker replied.

'She's as wild as Ned Kelly, that one, so she could be anywhere. But she'll turn up.'

Bowker nodded then began passing the drench to Prong. 'I hear you and Yabby Harris went buying sheep yesterday.'

'Yeah, all the way down to Skipton in the Western District. Bought six hundred first-cross merino ewe-weaners. Beautiful sheep, trucks will be here tomorrow.'

'Rick said you went to the pub when you got home.'

'Yabby wanted to buy me a beer to celebrate the purchase. Right sheep. Right price.'

He passed over the last pack of drench. 'Take your car to Skipton?'

'Yeah. Agent always takes his car. Got to do something to earn your commission.'

'So Yabby drove into Manang and left his car in town.'

Prong picked up the empty carton and began removing the tape that held it together. 'We headed off at sparrow-fart, so he met me at my place in Pioneer Street. Left his car in my drive and picked it up after we left the pub last night. He only had a pot of heavy and one pot of light, if that's what you're worried about.'

That wasn't what Bowker was worried about.

***

When Bowker arrived home, Rachael was already in the kitchen preparing tea. Bowker kissed her lightly on the cheek, sat at the kitchen table and confessed how he was no closer to solving Yvonne's disappearance. 'I'm hoping she's just had a brain snap and that we're all worried for nothing.'

Rachael wiped her hands with a tea towel and sat down at the table. 'I've got a bad feeling about this, Greg. Yvonne has been really settled lately, and her behaviour has improved in leaps and bounds. She's doing well at school and lives for the dance classes. I just can't see her wandering off without telling anyone. Something awful has happened.'

Bowker put his hand on hers. 'I hope you're wrong, Rach.'

'Yeah. So do I,' Rachael replied.

***

After tea, Bowker drove to the gangers' camp. He spoke to the boss who had only heard about a girl's disappearance over his counter-tea. 'Those twin cabs parked under the trees over there,' Bowker said pointing, 'you blokes use them to get back and forwards between here and work, right?'

Cockatoos screeched in the branches overhead. 'Yeah. Four of them. Five of us in each.'

'Are they used for anything else?'

'Sometimes the blokes will ask to use one on the weekend if they want to go into Swan Hill, or perhaps up to Mildura.'

'Where are the keys kept?'

'Inside the portable office when the vehicles are not out on the job.'

'Is the office always locked?'

'Only if we're all away. When we're in camp I leave it unlocked.

It's got the phone in there if one of the men wants to ring their family or something.'

Bowker thought for a moment. 'And if someone wants to use one of the twin cabs?'

'They ask me. I usually say it's okay and they grab a set of keys and go. Why?'

'Anyone use one last night?'

The foreman put his hands on his hips. 'You think one of my blokes had something to do with that girl disappearing?'

'Just covering all bases. That's my job. So, anyone use one last night?'

'Nobody asked to use one. We were all in bed pretty early. The weather's heating up again and by the end of the day everyone's pretty knackered. Go to the pub, have tea and a few beers, then hit the sack.'

Bowker looked at the layout of the camp. The office was separated from the sleeping units, and the twin cabs were a hundred yards further away under a line of sugar gums.

'Where would I find Barry Lowbury?'

'You thinking that fuckin' idiot had something to do with the lost girl?'

'Like I said. Just covering all bases. I'd just like a quick word with him.'

The foreman walked to the third portable unit and after a moment Lowbury stormed towards Bowker.

'What do you want?' he asked aggressively.

'You tell me.'

'Dunno what you're talking about?'

'Yvonne Bryant has gone missing.'

'So I heard at the pub.' Lowbury cleared his throat and spat on the ground. 'What's that got to do with me?'

'I heard you were making threats about what you'd do if you found her.' Bowker leaned closer and stared into Lowbury's eyes. 'Did you find her, Barry?'

Lowbury broke the eye contact and looked away. 'Who told you I was making threats? Bloody liars if they said that.'

'School Principal, a senior teacher, couple of blokes in the pub. And you know what, Barry? I'd believe them before you, any day of the week. So let's cut the bullshit.'

Lowbury looked back at Bowker, but the aggressive attitude had gone. 'I was a bit pissed. Alright? I thought there was a dance on at the hall. Don't see many women in this job.'

'You went looking for Yvonne, and when you didn't get into the social you went off your head. Given your record around females, I'd be worried about what might happen to the girl if you ran into her later in the night.'

Lowbury looked away again. 'Well, I didn't run into her. I went to the pub for a while. That bearded shit behind the bar will vouch for that.'

'He has. He kicked you out. What'd you do after that?'

Lowbury threw his hands up. 'What the fuck is there to do in this town if you can't go to the pub? Jack shit. Dunno how anybody lives in this hole.'

'So where'd you go after you left the pub?'

'Back here? Where else do you think I'd go?' He cleared his throat again and spat on the ground, just missing Bowker's foot.

Bowker kicked dirt over the spittle. 'See anyone about when you left the pub?'

'Just some kid sitting outside the milk bar. Ask Benny where we went. He was with me all the time.'

'I will.'

Bowker got little else out of Lowbury, and his mate confirmed his story. They both said they were in bed by ten o'clock, although Bowker noted the two men slept in different units.

***

On his return to the station, Bowker rang Yabby Harris, even though it was now evening. He'd quickly learnt that the best time to contact a cocky was after tea. During the day, farmers were usually down the paddock somewhere, and ringing their house was a waste of time. Using the CB radio meant everyone in the district knew your business, as one farmer found out when his wife called him home for conjugal duties. Bowker quizzed Yabby about his movements after he picked up his car from Prong's house and was told he went straight home. He didn't see anyone at all in the street, and definitely hadn't see Yvonne.

The next day, Bowker sent the photos of Yvonne to the neighbouring police stations, to the Missing Persons Bureau in Melbourne, and to passenger services in the area. He also contacted 3SH in Swan Hill and ABC radio asking that Yvonne's disappearance be publicised in their police bulletins. If Yvonne's disappearance was not solved in the next week or two, her photo would be printed on milk cartons as a further means of putting her face before the public.

Two weeks later, the first of the milk cartons with Yvonne's photo were distributed across Victoria.

CHAPTER 28

November faded into December and, with still no breakthrough in solving Yvonne's disappearance, Bowker was at a loss on where next to take the investigation. Despite his exhaustive inquiries and meticulous pursuit of possible scenarios, in practical terms, the sixteen year-old schoolgirl had vanished without a trace.

Life went on in the small community. Red Cameron had his unraced three year-old colt entered at Nyah and planned to work two other youngsters under the lights as part of their education. He asked Bowker to drive one of the pair and the policeman jumped at the chance, grasping the opportunity as a rare night out for he and Rachael.

The Nyah trotting track was set in beautiful surrounds amongst river red gums adjacent to the Murray. Under lights, with the drivers' colours and the flashy horseflesh, the night had a magical feel to it, with the horses close enough to touch as they raced up the front straight. To Bowker, this was what harness racing was about, up close and personal, something lost with the newer circuits built inside thoroughbred racetracks. Attendance at Nyah was huge, and Bowker continually scanned the crowd for a teenage face he knew would not be there.

Red's colt unexpectedly ran down the hot favourite in race three and Rachael collected a few dollars at handy odds. The highlight for Bowker, however, was driving fast work after the last race. As they sprinted for two laps under the lights, the smooth track made the sulky wheels hum, and he could only imagine the thrill of driving in a race.

***

With harvest getting underway, the Manangatang silos were first to open for early crops. Bolton, Chinkapook, Cocamba and Annuello would follow over the next few days. Bowker watched with interest as the first trucks began to arrive opposite the police station. Grain delivery was a simple process. A truck would cross a weighbridge to have its gross weight recorded, samples were taken from the load to assess quality, and the load was tipped over a grated pit. The truck would then be reweighed to determine the weight of the grain disgorged. Grain tonnage was equivalent to hard cash, so the aim was to maximize this weight. It didn't take Bowker long to see how the system could be gamed, albeit on a trivial scale. At the initial weigh-in, any dogs or kids brought along for the ride stayed in the cabin with the driver. On the weigh-out, they stretched their legs outside. Bowker even saw one farmer discard his spare tyre before the weigh off. Given the enormous weight of each load, the rorts were of miniscule percentage value but, totalled over the full harvest period, probably made the exercise worthwhile.

Ferret Igoe was in charge of the Cocamba silo and his first job each season was to ready the facility for the receival of grain. The morning after the Nyah trots, Ferret burst into the police station screaming for Bowker. By the time they departed for the silos, Bowker knew what to expect and thought he was prepared. But he wasn't. The gap in the wall of the grain shed had reopened and inside was a human body, or what was left of it. Partly consumed by foxes or wild dogs, badly decomposed and smothered in flies, the sight and smell of the remains caused Bowker to retch and gag. He turned away and pulled a handkerchief from his trouser pocket and covered his nose and mouth. Around the rotting corpse were the torn remnants of a brightly multi-coloured top, purple leggings and yellow leg warmers.

There was no doubt in Bowker's mind that the remains belonged to Yvonne Bryant.

Bowker walked unsteadily to his vehicle and radioed for assistance from Robinvale. He then reported the finding to the CID in Mildura. Both stations immediately had officers on their way. Ferret walked across and leant over the bonnet. Bowker steadied himself against the car door. 'How long were you here before you found her, mate?'

Ferret was still trembling. 'Half an hour. Turned on the power getting ready to test the grain elevators. Then caught the smell. Thought there must have been a dead roo beside the road or something. Wanted to dispose of it before the cockies arrived on Monday and gave me flak for not havin' the place ship-shape. Took me ages to find where the smell was coming from. My dog was making a racket at the grain shed and I saw where the wind had blown-in a sheet of iron. I went to investigate and…' He started to cry, his rodent shaped head half disappearing into the top of his overalls as his chest heaved.

Bowker placed his hand on Ferret's shoulder. 'Hell of a shock, I know, mate. I don't want you driving until you're a bit more composed. I'll take a statement while we're waiting for the other coppers. We can take our time. I can't touch anything here until the forensic people have finished.'

Within forty-five minutes, a four-wheel drive police vehicle from Robinvale arrived with Senior Sergeant Webster and three officers on board. While Bowker briefed Webster, the three Robinvale officers secured the area with police tape.

'And it's definitely the missing girl?' Webster asked.

'Almost certainly, I'd say. The clothes match, the dyed hair matches, and the stature is about right. But the body's very decomposed. Hot weather, heat off the iron, animals, birds, insects. Not a pretty sight.'

Webster exhaled loudly. 'Better show me.'

Bowker sent Ferret home with instructions to communicate with no-one except his wife. The silo manager slowly drove off down the Miralie road, no doubt still in shock.

Bowker took Webster to the hole in the grain shed.

'Fuck me!' Webster blurted out. 'I've seen a lot of things in my twenty-five years with the force, but this stuff still gets me in the guts.'

Bowker waved a cloud of flies from his face. 'Will Mildura CID handle things, or will homicide run the show?'

'Depends on what the forensics tell us. By the position of the body and the circumstances of her disappearance, I think we can assume it's a homicide. So Mildura will most likely withdraw and the Homicide Squad will run the show. You'll be their local lackey. That's the way they normally like to play it. You know, big city boys sorting it out for us flatfoots in the bush.'

The five policemen conducted a preliminary search of the surrounding area and located a few items such as bottles, cans and a cigarette box, all of which they left *in situ* awaiting forensic examination.

Two detectives from the criminal investigation division at Mildura arrived ninety minutes later, with three forensic specialists on site with their crime scene van thirty minutes after. Hundreds of photographs were taken of the body, its location, the surrounds of the shed and silos, and each of the articles the officers had found earlier. Items were bagged and labelled, soil specimens taken, samples of the surrounding vegetation collected and tagged. Measurements of every possible distance relating to the body's location were recorded, and any flat surfaces were dusted for fingerprints, particularly those around the area where the body was discovered. Several prints were found on the shed but were too smeared to be useful.

The final task for the forensic team was to bag Yvonne's body and transport it to a morgue ready for examination by a forensic pathologist. A report would then be sent to the coroner.

Bowker left the others to complete their tasks, anxious to convey the grim news to the family before word circulated about police activities at Cocamba. Considering his close relationship with

Yvonne, Bowker felt Skeeta also needed to be informed personally.

Bowker drove into the police station carport and sat for a couple of minutes with his hands on the steering wheel. It was one of Rachael's afternoons off and he felt a strong need to tell her about Yvonne's death, to feed off her strength and wisdom before he took the wretched drive to Winnambool.

From the moment he walked into the kitchen, Rachael knew something dreadful had occurred. When he described Yvonne's demise, she walked towards him and dropped her forehead against his chest. Bowker put his arms around her shoulders, and they stood in silence for an extended moment. Bowker spoke first. 'This has really shaken me up, Rach.'

Rachael had tears in her eyes when she looked up. 'Greg, the poor girl. She didn't deserve this. Nobody deserves this.' She hugged him for a moment, then took a step back. 'Anything out there explain what happened?'

'Just the body. Looks like someone killed her and left her to decompose in the heat of the grain shed. Once the sheet of iron blew in again, the body was ravaged by birds and animals and insects. Whoever did this is a very callous individual, Rach. Least they could have done was bury her.'

Rachael took a tea towel from the bench and wiped her eyes. 'What happens from here?'

Bowker sat down at the kitchen table. 'The Mildura CID will call in the Homicide Squad, and they'll take over the investigation. There'll be an autopsy and Forensics will prepare a report for the coroner. It'll cover a lot of areas. Toxicology, blood, fingerprints, soil and seeds in her clothes, animal contact, maybe skin under her fingernails, who knows what else. That will form a big part of the investigation given the amount of time since she died. Most of the normal lines of inquiry went cold weeks ago.'

Rachael sat down beside him. 'What'll be your role in all this?'

'The case is out of my hands, but I get the fun bits like going out to Winnambool and breaking the news to the Bryants, and then to Skeeta. Before I do, I'll ring your boss and let him know Yvonne's body has been found. Better the kids hear the bad news factually and upfront, rather than the bullshit that will fester on the grapevine. I'll ask Malcolm to give me an hour before he says anything to the kids. My advice will be to speak to Travis first. He'll know how to handle these things better than me anyway.'

'Usually, the regional office sends their people when tragedies happen. They did that after the car smash.'

Bowker closed his eyes. 'Shit year all round for the kids, eh?'

'Yeah. Shit year all round.'

***

Bowker found Percy and Cath at home sharing afternoon tea with Yabby. Percy was distraught, sobbing uncontrollably as Bowker relayed the awful news. Cath and Yabby were shocked and struggled to speak, although Bowker caught them exchange the briefest of glances as he stood up to leave.

At the Allender's rundown property, Skeeta's ute was in the workshop with the bonnet up when Bowker arrived. Skeeta looked up from the engine cavity, threw a spanner on the bench, and wiped his hands on the backsides of his overalls. 'What have I done this time?'

Bowker was po-faced. 'We found Yvonne.'

'Well good for you, Bowker,' Skeeta said cheerily. 'Melbourne? Adelaide? Mildura? I s'pose it depends on how many miles to the root she got?'

'Found her at Cocamba.'

Skeeta seemed genuinely mystified. 'What was she doing out there?'

Bowker stared straight into his eyes. 'She's dead. Body shoved through a split in the grain shed wall. Half-eaten by foxes.'

Skeeta's face went white. 'What?'

'Ferret Igoe found her when he was preparing the silos for next week.'

'Shit. You're not jokin', are you?' Skeeta put his hands on his head, his breathing irregular.

'Of course I'm not bloody joking,' Bowker snapped back. 'It's as much as I can do not to spew up just thinking about what I saw and what I smelt.'

'Fuck.'

'Yeah. Fuck.'

Skeeta put his forearms on the tray of the ute and dropped his head down onto his hands. When he looked up at Bowker again, he had tears in his eyes. 'I really liked her, Bowker. I really did. She could be a real bitch at times, but I really liked her.'

Bowker put a hand on the tray. 'I did too, Skeeta. But somebody else didn't.'

Skeeta stood up straight and looked directly into the policeman's eyes. 'I didn't touch her Bowker, I swear.'

Bowker folded his arms across his chest. 'Didn't you? How do I know that?' He pointed a finger. 'You were the last person seen with her.'

Skeeta's eyes never left Bowker's. 'Would I tell you I took her to Cocamba if I'd killed her and left her there?'

'People have done stranger things, mate. On the night of the social, did you tell anybody you planned to take Yvonne to Cocamba?'

'Who would I bloody tell? I'd just driven in from home. Besides, I didn't plan to stop at Cocamba. We just drove out the Sea Lake Road and I pulled over into the silo reserve when Yvonne was making noises about going back to the hall. Probably would have gone down to Chinky otherwise.'

'What about afterwards? Maybe at the pub? Tell somebody you'd been out at the silos, or that you'd had a blue with Yvonne down there?'

'The only person I spoke to was Jacko, and we talked about what a shit place the Mallee is. We're both countin' down the days until our oldies snuff it and we can sell up and escape this hellhole. Last thing

I needed was a deep and meaningful about Yvonne.'

Dawn and Peter Allender walked down from the house.

'Everything okay, Greg?' Dawn asked.

'No, it's not, Dawn. We found Yvonne Bryant's body today. Just letting Skeeta know. Best keep an eye on him. He can expect a visit from the homicide detectives.'

Bowker drove slowly back into Manang, wondering how the idyllic life of a small-town cop could suddenly become so complicated. It was about to get a lot worse.

CHAPTER 29

It was a hot, windy day when two members of the Homicide Squad – Detective Inspector Jack Moloney and Detective Sergeant Trevor Flynn – drove into Manangatang after flying to Mildura the night before. Moloney was a man in his mid-fifties with a ruddy complexion, receding ginger hair, a wiry build, and nicotine stains on his fingers. Standing around six-foot-tall, and dressed in a dark suit, he had the stereotypical timeworn face of the veteran detective. Flynn on the other hand was the picture of sartorial splendour. In his early thirties, he was three inches taller than Moloney and in better physical condition. He sported a new grey suit, slicked-back hair and a handlebar moustache. He was handsome in a store dummy sense, but his eyes betrayed a disarming hostility. Moloney parked outside the hotel room he'd booked by phone the night before.

Flynn dragged his suitcase from the boot of the unmarked vehicle. 'Fuckin' hot already,' he said.

'The forecast is for high thirties, so we've been lucky. Can get up to forty-six, forty-seven up here,' Moloney replied.

'Shit, Jack. How could you live in heat like that? And look at the place. Fuck me.' He placed his case on the concrete path outside the motel-style room.

Moloney pulled his own case from the car. 'Came from a small town myself. But up in the Australian Alps, so being too cold was a bigger problem than being too hot. It was a great place for a kid to grow up. Fishing, shooting, riding horses, wandering around in the bush.'

'You're a different bloke to me, then, Jack. City boy, born and bred.'

'With any luck, we'll solve this thing quickly and be back in town by the end of the week.'

'Bloody hope so,' Flynn said, looking across the roof of the car. 'I'm taking out that little red-headed constable from Missing Persons on Saturday night. Bangs like a dunny door, apparently.'

'You haven't wasted much time.' Moloney placed his case beside Flynn's. 'It must really attract the ladies when you introduce yourself as the big dick from upstairs.'

Flynn missed the sarcasm. 'One of the perks of being at the top of the heap, eh?'

'Not for me, Trevor. Thirty years of marriage to my girlfriend from Corryong High School. Started going together in form 4.'

'To each his own, Jack. Been there, done that. Now I just pick the ripest fruit from the tree, no strings attached.'

'The ripest fruit is often the quickest to spoil.'

'Doesn't matter if you're not around when it goes rotten.'

Moloney retrieved a hanger of clothes from the back seat and placed it atop his suitcase. 'You're a charmer, Trevor.'

'Pity the Force can't stretch their budget to separate rooms, Jack. I might have to ask you to take a walk if I latch onto a country sheila in need of a bit of city expertise.' Flynn chuckled as he slammed the boot closed.

'This case could be tricky, so I don't want any distractions. People have seen enough mice up here already this year, Trevor, so keep your mouse in the house until we get back to Melbourne.'

'You're the boss, Jack. Listen, how about I walk up to the cop shop and introduce myself to the local yokel while you're getting the keys sorted out? Stretchin' my legs will do me good.'

'I'll only be five minutes, but suit yourself.'

Moloney entered the rear entrance of the pub while Flynn strode off towards the police station.

***

Bowker was flipping through witness statements when Flynn barged through the station door and roared loudly. 'Alright, Bowker, clean off my desk, get me the Bryant file and then piss off.'

Bowker stood up, jaw tightening. 'What are you doing up here, arsehole?'

'It's Detective Sergeant Flynn of homicide to you, constable. From now on you refer to me as *Sir*,' Flynn ordered.

'Not a hope in hell of that happening, Flynn. And I'll hand over the file to the officer in charge.'

'How do you know that's not me, smart arse?'

'Because obviously you've just transferred to homicide. And secondly you haven't got the brains to conduct an Easter egg hunt. I'll deal with the organ grinder, not the monkey.'

Flynn's face reddened and he leant over the desk. 'You may be fucking my wife, Bowker, but I won't let you fuck up my investigation.'

At that moment, Rachael walked through from the house. 'Greg, what the…'

Flynn smirked. 'Here's the little whore, now. Right on cue.'

Bowker lost control, grabbing Flynn by the throat across the desk. 'I can take your gutless letters and pathetic little presents, Flynn, but you say one more thing about Rachael and I'll do what I should have done in Ballarat.'

Flynn grabbed Bowker's wrists. 'Get your hands off me, arsehole! Your career is over.'

As the two men scuffled above the desk, Senior Detective Moloney walked through the door. He stood for a moment in bewilderment, then exploded. 'What the hell is going on here?'

Bowker and Flynn released each other.

'Private matter, Sir,' Bowker said.

'I'm not buying that, senior constable,' Moloney said. 'It's not a private matter when two officers are trying to beat the crap out of each other.'

'He grabbed me around the throat, Jack,' Flynn said.

'Okay, this bullshit stops right now,' Moloney said, thumping his fist onto the top of Bowker's desk. 'We need to work this case together.'

'With all due respects, Jack, Bowker should be placed on immediate suspension awaiting a disciplinary hearing.'

Moloney looked at Flynn, face reddening with annoyance. 'I'll decide where things go from here, Trevor. If you don't like my decision, you can always go over my head when we're back in Melbourne. Right now, my priority is finding who killed this girl and it should be yours as well. The senior constable is vital to this investigation, and we can't move forward without him. He knows the people, the district and the background to all this.'

'I'm not letting it go, Jack. Not after Ballarat,' Flynn fired back quickly, before mellowing a little. 'But I suppose it can wait a few days until we head back to Melbourne.' He paused. 'But it's not going away.'

Moloney exhaled audibly and turned to Bowker. 'Seems a bit late for introductions, but I'm Jack Moloney. Detective Inspector'

'Greg Bowker,' Bowker replied as they shook hands.

'And the young lady? Your other half, I presume, senior constable?'

Before Bowker could answer, Rachael jumped in. 'Rachael Stow. I'm Greg's partner. I used to be married to Trevor.'

'You're still fuckin' married to me,' Flynn growled.

'We've been separated for nearly twelve months, Inspector Moloney. Our divorce will be a formality once the year is up,' Rachael explained.

'You men worked together in Ballarat, I take it?'

'Yes, sir,' Bowker replied. 'But things became impossible for me at Ballarat Central, so I asked for an immediate transfer. There was a vacancy at Manangatang, so here I am.'

'Better than you fuckin' deserve,' Flynn snapped back.

Moloney raised his eyebrows. 'So, you knew the senior constable had been posted up here, Trevor?'

'I'd heard he'd been hidden away in some back-water. If I'd remembered it was here, I would have asked to be assigned a different investigation. Let sleeping dogs lie.'

Rachael was about to call out the lie, but Bowker placed his hand on her arm.

'Okay. This is how it will work from here,' Moloney announced. 'I realise you two are never going to be best mates, but I expect you to act professionally and in the best interests of this investigation. Trevor and I are staying at the hotel, and other than your work-related duties, I don't want to see any interaction between the two of you. Hopefully by the end of the week our work here will be done, and we can all go back to where we were. Agreed?'

'Fine with me,' Bowker said.

'Trevor?' Moloney said.

'Just until we finish up,' Flynn replied. 'Once we're back in the office, I'll be submitting a formal request for disciplinary action.'

'Your prerogative, Trevor,' Moloney said as he turned to Bowker. 'What have you got for us?'

'I'll make some coffee,' Rachael said.

'Black, no sugar for me,' Moloney replied.

'You know how I like it, don't you Rachael?' Flynn said sleazily.

Rachael didn't reply.

***

Bowker laid out Yvonne Bryant's file on his desk and the two detectives flipped through what Bowker had assembled.

Moloney rested his forearms on the desk and clasped his hands together. 'Can you give us an overview before we get into the details, Greg? Perhaps a bit of background on the victim first.'

'The body belongs to Yvonne Bryant, a sixteen year-old orphan who disappeared from the school social about four weeks ago. Her mother was a Melbourne drug addict who died of an overdose and Yvonne moved up here with her grandfather at the start of the year.

Bit wayward, but very smart, and was just starting to settle into country life when she disappeared.'

'Surprised anyone could settle into a dump like this,' Flynn mumbled.

Moloney ignored the comment. 'What do we know about her father?'

'Her mother, Lynette, left town out of the blue and the story is that she'd been knocked up by some loser when she first arrived in the city. But that's not what happened.'

'So what's the real explanation?' Moloney asked.

'She ran away because she was raped by Keith Harris, a bloke from the property next door where the girl did some housework. His widow, Cath, let it slip out while we discussed Yvonne's errant behaviour. She saw it happen, apparently, but told me she'd deny the whole thing if she was asked about it again. All academic anyway. The bastard was killed in a farm accident not long after.'

'Karma, eh?' Moloney said.

'Yeah. Karma,' Bowker replied wistfully.

'And you say Yvonne moved in with her grandparents when her mother died?' Moloney asked.

'This is where it gets a bit complicated. Her grandfather, Percy Bryant, lost his wife to cancer and remarried Cath Harris after her husband was killed in the accident I just mentioned.'

Flynn appeared confused. 'So he married the widow of the bloke who raped his daughter?' he asked.

'Yeah, but Percy doesn't know about the rape and there's not much point in telling him. He and Cath have been friends since they went to school together in the thirties. Percy has no other children, so when Lynette died, he was on his own. The two farms were combined, so the marriage made good business sense as well.'

'Fuck me. Is this banjo country, or what?' Flynn said sarcastically.

'The Harris side of this tangle have any kids of their own?' Moloney asked.

'Two sons, but the eldest suicided years ago. Kevin is the surviving one, and he and his mother hated Yvonne with a passion. Brought nothing but trouble, they reckon. Plus, she was placed to inherit half the property.'

Flynn was still struggling to get his head around the family tree. 'All this would make the victim a half-sister to the Harris boy.'

'Yeah, but he's not aware of that either, to my knowledge. As far as I know, Cath was the only one who knew who fathered Yvonne and why her mother just up and left.'

'I suppose the locals were baffled why anyone would leave this paradise?' Flynn asked sarcastically.

Moloney ignored Flynn's commentary. 'Anyone else tied up in this, Greg?'

'The victim had a boyfriend, Daryl Allender, but everyone calls him Skeeta. Twenty-three years old and lazy as shit. I suspect he's dealing drugs, but haven't been able to nail him yet.'

'Any other male friends?'

'She was pretty close to a boy at school. Travis Urdevic. Mother's a blow-in drug addict who lives in a derelict farmhouse on the Bryant property. Not a bad kid, given his background. Old man's back in jail after breaching parole and arriving up here to bash up the mother. Travis has a juvenile record and I've done him for driving without a licence, although I'd prefer that than his mother behind the wheel, to be perfectly honest. She's in a self-induced coma most of the time.'

Rachael entered the room carrying a tray with three cups of coffee and a plate of store-bought biscuits. 'Got it sorted?' She moved a few papers and set the tray on the desk.

'Yeah, just about ready to pack up and return to Melbourne,' Moloney joked.

'And the sooner we're back to civilisation the better,' Flynn gibed as he grabbed a biscuit.

'Don't worry, Trevor,' Moloney said. 'We've got a few days before you need to cancel with the little red-headed constable.'

Flynn looked down and Rachael gave Bowker a wink as she left the room.

Moloney sipped his coffee and was straight back to business. 'Okay, Greg, what do we know about the girl's disappearance?'

'Well firstly, Yvonne was definitely at the school social that night. We've got a hundred witnesses to that effect. Secondly, she and her school friend Travis snuck out the back door to meet Skeeta Allender at around ten-ish. There was a physical altercation between Travis and Skeeta before Yvonne drove off with Allender. She wasn't seen again until we found her body.'

'Well, it's open and shut. Why the fuck haven't you arrested the prick already? Could have saved us the bloody trip!' Flynn ranted.

'Because it's not that simple, detective,' Bowker said calmly. 'Skeeta claims he dropped her back twenty minutes later.'

Flynn threw up his hands theatrically. 'Well, that puts him in the clear then,' he said with derision.

'Plus, he returned to pick her up after the social and seemed genuinely surprised when she wasn't there,' Bowker added.

'I bet he wasn't too shocked!' Flynn said quickly.

'So you don't think it's as simple as the boyfriend killing her, then covering his tracks by pretending he was there to pick her up after the dance?' Moloney asked.

'Her body was found at Cocamba, just down the road. Skeeta volunteered that he took her there. They'd had a tiff, so he brought her back. Why tell me that if he knew her body would eventually be found there? Makes no sense.'

Moloney nodded. 'Any other possible suspects?'

'Travis Urdevic wasn't seen back at the social, and I later found where he'd hidden his mother's car in town. He admitted to being very angry that Yvonne had gone with Skeeta, and he had the vehicle to take her to Cocamba.'

'Anybody else?'

'Cath Bryant turned up out of the blue to collect Yvonne from the social claiming she wasn't copping anymore of Yvonne's sluttish behavior. Cath's son, Kevin Harris, or Yabby as he's known, was also in town. He'd been to a sheep sale with his agent, and his car was parked near where Skeeta said he dropped off Yvonne. He left the pub about that time, so it's possible the two did cross paths.'

Moloney frowned and scratched the back of his head. 'It's starting to get complicated, Greg,' he said.

'I know. It's been doing my head in. And just to add to the mix, there's a railway camp on the other side of the train line. Two gangers tried to get into the social. One of them threatened revenge on Yvonne because she'd bitten him on the arm in an earlier altercation at the pub.'

Flynn scoffed. 'Sounds like a lovely girl, our Yvonne. Take her home to meet Mum and Dad.'

'Deep down she was a good kid,' Bowker said without looking at Flynn. 'Good kid with a terrible upbringing.'

'Any local perverts?' Moloney asked.

'The bloke who runs the garage on the highway is a total sleaze, but I can't see him being involved, unless there was a chance encounter. You know, Yvonne alone in the street when he came along. But I still don't think he'd do anything like that. Comes across as one of those dirty old men with his dick in one hand and a stick magazine in the other. All talk and getting no action.'

'This has got the boyfriend's prints plastered all over it,' Flynn said.

Moloney looked at Bowker. 'You don't think it's that simple, do you, Greg?'

'To me, Skeeta's movements don't make any sense if he did kill her.'

Moloney took the last biscuit. 'And the others?'

'With Cath, I think she genuinely came to town to show Yvonne she was being put on a tighter rein. The other possibilities, I'm not so sure about. If Yabby did abduct and kill Yvonne, I can't see it as being pre-planned. He went to a sheep sale at Skipton and his car was parked at the agent's house. If Skeeta dropped Yvonne off near there, then Yabby might have encountered her by pure coincidence. He couldn't have known she would even leave the social.'

Moloney sipped his coffee. 'What about her male friend from school?'

'Travis saw her leave the social, was in an angry mood, and had the means of taking Yvonne to Cocamba either alive or already dead. But he was seen driving home before eleven, so if he did kill Yvonne, it must have been before that time and after Skeeta had returned her to town. I don't think that gives him time to take her to Cocamba and murder her. Besides, I'd be astounded if he harmed her. She was his best friend.'

'We're assuming, of course, that she was killed and her body dumped on the same night she disappeared,' Moloney said.

'I think it's a safe assumption, Jack,' Bowker said. 'She just disappeared off the face of the earth that night. Despite an intensive search, there's not one scintilla of evidence that she was anywhere other than dead in the grain shed.'

Flynn leant back in his chair. 'You're pretty good at telling us who didn't kill her, Bowker. How about you tell us who did,' he said smugly.

Bowker didn't take the bait.

'I worry about the railway ganger,' Moloney said.

'So do I,' Bowker replied. 'History of violence against women and he had threatened her at least twice. Initially I dismissed him as a suspect because the body was found at Cocamba, and transport would have been a problem for him. But his foreman said the gangers often borrow the company's twin-cabs for their own use. At ten thirty at night the men are usually bedded down, so this bloke could have easily slipped out unnoticed, picked up her body if he'd already killed her, and disposed of it at the Cocamba silos. The crew had been working down that way, so he'd know the place.'

'Yeah, but we keep coming back to the same problem, Bowker,' Flynn said, tapping the desk. 'Why was the body at Cocamba if

Allender didn't put it there? Why would the ganger just happen to pick that spot? Why would this Yabby bloke take it down there? Why would the Travis kid dump it there?'

'Skeeta possibly met drug customers or associates from further south there, so Travis may have known that through Yvonne. But you're right about the other two. I've got no idea why they'd pick Cocamba out of a thousand other potential places. Why not just bury the body? It's a complete mystery.'

CHAPTER 30

The homicide detectives prioritised the individuals they needed to interview together and divided the other names between themselves. The plan was to meet with Bowker at the police station at eight each morning to coordinate their strategies for the day. With the discussion wound up, Flynn collected the coffee cups and took them into the kitchen where Rachael was unpacking the dishwasher.

'This is not over, Rachael. Not by a long shot,' Flynn said quietly as he put the cups in the sink.

Rachael stood up straight. 'What? Going to hit me again are you, Trev?'

'Nobody makes a fool out of me in front of my mates.'

'You did a pretty good job of that on your own.'

'Watch your back, Rachael. And tell fuckin' Bowker to watch his.'

Moloney walked into the kitchen. 'You ready, Trevor? I think we'll take a run out to the Allender farm and have a yarn to suspect number one.'

'Yep. Coming, Jack.'

'Thanks for the coffee and bickies, Rachael,' Moloney said kindly. 'Might catch up with you in the next day or so to get your read on the victim. Greg said you knew her better than anybody.'

'I don't know if I can add much to what Greg has probably told you, but I'm happy to have a chat if you think I can help.'

'You never know where one tiny piece of extra information can lead in these cases. I'll be in touch.'

The two detectives drove off to Winnambool as Bowker entered the kitchen.

'You okay, Rach? Did the bastard threaten you while I was talking to Jack?'

'Of course he did. That's his go-to strategy. When all else fails, threaten violence.'

'If he's looking for more trouble, Rach, I'm happy to accommodate him. I'll blow my career before I let him hurt you again.'

Rachael put her arms around his neck. 'Let's just wait and see. I think Jack is a decent bloke. Maybe they'll do their investigation, head back to the city and everything'll return to normal around here.'

'The eternal optimist, eh?' Bowker kissed her passionately, then put his hands on her backside and pushed against her.

'Who's the optimist now?' she said with a laugh.

***

For the next two days, the homicide detectives conducted extended and sometimes fiery interviews, but for all their time and expertise, gleaned little that added to Bowker's findings. So thorough were Bowker's inquiries, that Moloney complimented his detective work on more than one occasion, much to Flynn's growing annoyance.

'We're making bugger-all progress at present,' Moloney admitted as they sat round the desk at their eight o'clock meeting. 'But there's one thing we know for sure: the victim didn't get out to Cocamba on her own. She was transported there, so we're looking for a vehicle as well as a killer.'

'It was bloody Allender,' Flynn said, slapping his thighs in exasperation. 'He took her there to knock down a couple of tubes and have a quick root. They had a blue, he kills her, perhaps unintentionally, he panics and stashes her body in the grain shed. He's scared out of his tiny brain, but he's as cunning as a shithouse rat so he turns up at the end of the social to take her home. Let's arrest the prick and get out of this shithole.'

'If he's that cunning, why does he admit he took her to Cocamba?' Bowker shot back.

'I'll get a forensic team up here tomorrow to vet any vehicles we think possibly could have been involved,' Moloney said.

'With all due respects, Jack, that will tell us shit-nothing,' Flynn said. 'There'll be traces of the victim all over Allender's ute. The bastard's been shaggin' her ever since she moved up here.'

'I'm not worried about Allender's ute, Trevor,' Moloney said. 'I'm looking to eliminate the Bryant's Statesman, the Blake woman's old Falcon, Yabby Harris's car, and all of the work vehicles over there at the railway camp. We need to know if the victim has been in one of those cars, or if any of them have been scrubbed out in the last month or so.'

Flynn wasn't convinced. 'There could be bits of her hair or other bodily material in virtually all those vehicles. She lived with the Bryants, her half-brother lives on the same property, and this Travis kid was her best mate at school. Probably porked her in the car for all we know.'

'We're specifically looking for strands of purple hair, Trevor,' Bowker replied.

'Purple?' Flynn asked impatiently. 'What the fuck are you talking about?'

'She tinted her hair especially for the social,' Bowker replied.

'He's right, Trev. Purple tint. It's in the file. I read it,' Moloney said.

'Must have missed it,' Flynn said quietly.

'Yeah. You must have,' Moloney muttered.

The conversation was interrupted by the fax springing to life. Bowker collected each sheet as it was expelled. Finally, the device chirped and went back to sleep. 'For you, Jack. Forensic report, judging by the letterhead.'

Moloney scanned the transcript, making comments as he went. 'Body badly decomposed with evidence of major animal and insect interference and mutilation. Difficult to determine precise time of death, but likely to have occurred between four and six weeks prior to the body being examined. Cause of death impossible to establish due to the state of the remains, however no evidence of gunshot wounds or powder residues. Impossible to ascertain if any injuries were inflicted prior to death, however cuts on residual shoulder skin are consistent with the torso being lacerated by the sharp edge of corrugated iron. Impossible to make conclusions relating to sexual activity prior to death. Internal organs were missing, most probably due to animal interference, so no analysis could be conducted of stomach and bowel contents.' Moloney flipped to the next page. 'Soil granules found in clothing remnants all consistent with samples taken at the scene. Grass fragments found in leggings identical to specimens taken at the scene. Soil smudges on the back of lower clothing and shoes indicate the body had been dragged into the position it was found.' He flipped to the last page. 'No evidence of drugs or toxins in the cells, although the length of time since death precludes any conclusive finding in this area. Smears were taken for blood analysis. Blood group is AB negative.' Moloney dropped the fax on the table. 'Okay, what does that tell us?'

'Fuck all. She's too badly decomposed to give us any decent clues,' Flynn said dismissively.

'The soil and vegetable samples tell us she was probably killed in the silo area, and the dirt smudges on her clothes indicate she'd been dragged to where we found her,' Bowker said. 'Cuts on her body were probably caused by the body being forced through the narrow gap in the grain shed wall.'

Flynn tapped his temple with an index finger. 'We knew that already, smart arse.'

Moloney quickly corrected him. 'No, we didn't Trevor. We assumed that was the case, now we're pretty sure.'

Flynn decided to change tack. 'Well, if she was killed out there, we can eliminate the railway ganger,' he said. 'Can't see him grabbing a twin cab and trolling the town looking for her in the hope he might be able to drag her into the vehicle.'

'You're probably right, Trevor,' Moloney said. 'But let's get the forensics done before we put a line through anyone. Okay?'

***

A forensic team arrived early the next morning and followed Bowker to Winnambool, hoping to find Skeeta at home before he left on one of his jaunts around the district. Unfortunately, Skeeta had gone to Robinvale chasing a replacement part for the family's old header that had broken down the evening before. His mother doubted he'd be away very long. Rather than wait around, the group proceeded to the Bryants' next door, where Percy and Yabby were both down the paddock stripping. Cath was home, and so was the white Statesman. Cath was furious when Bowker explained her car was to be examined, totally insulted that she or Perce could be suspected of involvement in Yvonne's death. Leaving the scientific team to inspect the Bryant car, Bowker drove across the paddock to Yabby's house. Marlene too was irate, angry at any suggestion that Yabby could be a suspect. Bowker assured her that the car's inspection was strictly routine, but this did little to quell her outrage. 'The little bitch still makes our life miserable, even when she's dead,' she snarled through gritted teeth.

The forensic team were finalising their examination of Yabby's car when Bowker spotted Skeeta's ute speeding along Winnambool Road. The timing was perfect. Bowker left the team to pack up, followed Skeeta home and secured his vehicle. Following the ute's forensic scan, Bowker led the group to Wendy Blake's house where they inspected the interior of the old grey Falcon.

***

Meanwhile back in town, on the suggestion of Moloney, Flynn visited the school and questioned the staff about Yvonne and Travis and the social in general. The majority of his time was spent with Donna Cavanagh, the attractive first-year teacher who had left the supper room door unsupervised while she phoned a parent. The discussion was casual and breezy, culminating in Flynn taking Donna's particulars, including her address and phone number, even though she stressed that Bowker already had those details. The rest of Flynn's interviews were cursory, even half-hearted, the detective showing interest only when Skeeta Allender's name was mentioned. Skeeta was in Flynn's frame, and he wasn't allowing him out.

While Flynn visited the school, Moloney dropped in on Rachael at the police residence. They sat at a wrought iron garden table on the back veranda, each with a cup of coffee. 'So, what was Yvonne like?' Moloney said as he blew on his hot drink.

'A free spirit. Wild, out of control when she first arrived. Sixteen going on forty. Intelligent, talented in a lot of areas, particularly dance. Had a softer side and could show empathy for others with problems. Very supportive of the intellectually disabled boy in her class.'

'Friends?'

'Very close to Travis Urdevic, a new boy with his own horrendous background. She was well accepted by the other students and didn't clash with local kids like some city kids do when they move to the country and think they know it all.' She picked up her cup.

'Could Travis have killed her?'

Rachael placed her cup back on the table without drinking and thought for a moment. 'I seriously doubt it. He had a thing for Yvonne and could become a bit jealous at times. He has a bad temper when pushed to the limit, but I'd be shocked if he hurt her. She was all he had, really.'

'Maybe he thought he might lose her.'

'Possibly.' She picked up her cup and took a sip.

'You had a soft spot for her?'

'Yeah, I did. Deep down she was a good kid. She was just looking for some stability in her life. I nearly cried at dance class when she turned up wearing the same outfit that I always wear. And she really liked Greg, even though she tried desperately to pretend she didn't.'

Rachael took another sip of coffee, then smiled. 'So, what do you really want to talk to me about?'

Moloney smiled back. 'I'm that transparent, am I?' He paused. 'So, what happened in Ballarat?'

'Is that relevant?'

'It is when I'm trying to conduct a murder investigation alongside two blokes who obviously detest each other.'

Rachael rested her cup in both hands. 'Off the record?'

'Off the record.'

'As you gathered, Greg and Trevor worked together at Ballarat Central. In fact, they were quite good friends, played squash together, and a bit of tennis and golf. Greg would come to our place occasionally for tea.'

Moloney nodded and sipped his drink. 'Okay.'

'Look, Jack, my marriage to Trevor was a rocky one before we even moved to Ballarat. One night when Greg came for tea, he noticed I had a bruise on the side of my face. I'd done my best to cover it with makeup, but there was a fair bit of swelling.'

'Trevor hit you?'

She put down her cup. 'He hit me a lot.'

'Okay.'

'Greg rang me the next day and confided his suspicions. He wanted to charge Trevor with assault. I pleaded with him not to, but he still confronted Trevor about it. Of course, that infuriated Trevor and he took it out on me. So I moved out.'

'You moved in with Greg?' He took another sip.

'Hell no. We were just friends then. But Greg looked out for me and eventually we began a relationship and here we are. As soon as my divorce comes through, we plan to marry.'

'Why Manangatang?'

'Trevor painted Greg as the home wrecker, so staying in Ballarat was untenable for both of us. He applied for a quick transfer, this position was vacant, so here we are.' She paused and looked across the back lawn. 'Best thing that has happened to us. We love the Mallee.'

'You were about to say something the other day and Greg cut you short.'

'Trevor made that bullshit comment about not knowing where Greg had been transferred. We've been getting hate mail ever since we arrived. Wait here.' Rachael went inside to the linen closet and removed a cardboard box which she emptied on the table in front of Moloney. 'Off the record?'

'Off the record.'

***

With only the railway vehicles to examine at the end of the day, the police officers and the forensic technicians assembled at the police station for a preliminary report. The Bryants' Statesman and the cars belonging to Wendy Blake and Yabby Harris raised no immediate flags, although hair and fibre samples, plus fingerprints, needed further analysis in the laboratory. Skeeta's ute was a different matter. 'We found that the seats have been scrubbed with heavy duty detergent in recent weeks,' the lead forensic scientist reported. 'More interesting though, in the crevice between the seat and the back rest we found several strands of purple-dyed hair.'

'Not surprised. We knew she was in the car on the night in question,' Bowker said.

'There were also traces of blood,' said the scientist.

'Bingo!' Flynn said, punching the air.

'Could be anyone's, or anything's, and from any time in the past,' Moloney warned.

'We'll need to do more sophisticated tests of course,' the forensic tech continued, 'but even under a magnifying glass you can see that the blood is adhered to some of the purple strands. This indicates the blood was deposited either at the same time as the purple hair, or some time since. Certainly not before. First, we'll need to establish if the blood is of human origin. If it is, once we group it, we'll get a better handle on whether it belongs to the victim or is extraneous to this investigation. If it's AB Negative, then we can be pretty certain it came from the victim. AB Negative blood type occurs in less than one percent of people in this country.'

The forensic team departed for a well-earned sandwich down the street.

'We need to speak to Allender again,' Moloney said. 'Trevor, can you zip out and bring him in for questioning.'

Flynn rubbed his hands together. 'Be my pleasure, Jack,' he said. 'Be my bloody pleasure.'

'Don't mention what forensics found in his car. I want to be present when we confront him with it,' Moloney said.

'Understood, Jack.' Flynn departed with a wide smile and a spring in his step.

Once Flynn had gone, Moloney turned to Bowker. 'He's a bash merchant, isn't he?'

Bowker played dumb. 'Allender?'

'You know who I mean. Flynn.'

'You been talking to Rachael?'

'She didn't volunteer anything. I asked her a couple of direct questions and she gave me the answers. Off the record.'

Bowker hesitated. 'Yeah, he's a shit of a bloke. Not much of a copper either. Can't see how he made detective.'

Moloney scratched his cheek. 'Get the right boss at your station who either loves you, or wants to move you on, and strong recommendations for promotion can follow pretty quickly. Surely you don't think every bloke working in homicide is of perfect character?'

Bowker shrugged. 'Always assumed the cream floats to the top, I guess.'

'Sometimes the scum finds itself up there as well.' Moloney hesitated a moment, unsure how far to take the conversation without crossing the line professionally. 'Look, I'm not saying Flynn doesn't deserve to be where he is, but just between you and me and the gatepost, I don't reckon he'll last very long. It's not just his temper. From the little I've seen, he jumps to conclusions way too early, and his mind doesn't naturally question the evidence. But we'll see. It's early days. He may prove me wrong.'

'Yeah.'

'But I'll tell you one thing. If I catch him belting people, especially women, his career is over. You've already given him a second chance by not reporting him in Ballarat.'

CHAPTER 31

An hour later, Flynn arrived with a handcuffed Skeeta Allender, roughly pushing him through the door of the station. Moloney motioned for Skeeta to sit down, stared at Flynn and pointed to the door.

Outside the station, Moloney spoke sternly. 'Why'd you cuff him, Trevor? He's not under arrest.'

'Didn't want him to do a runner, Jack. Or have a go at me while I was driving in.'

'Take 'em off,' Moloney ordered, turning his back and walking back inside.

Once in the station, Flynn removed the hand cuffs and Skeeta resumed his seat, rubbing his wrists and holding his side.

'What's wrong with your ribs, Daryl?' Moloney asked.

'He caught his side on the door as I was putting him into the car,' Flynn replied quickly.

'So that's how it went down, Daryl?' Moloney asked.

Flynn glared at Skeeta, who after a moment, motioned towards Flynn. 'Yeah, like he said. I banged my side on the door.'

'All sorted now, Jack?' Flynn asked smugly as he sat down.

Moloney ignored his question and sat on the edge of Bowker's desk, arms folded. 'Okay, Daryl, I'm going to put all the cards on the table. Our forensic people found blood on the passenger seat of your vehicle.'

'That's bullshit!' Skeeta replied quickly. 'I clean it every Saturday morning and nobody's been in that seat since then.'

'They found it in the crack between the seat and the backrest,' Moloney added.

'Could be from anything. The dogs often get in the front with me,' Skeeta replied.

'That's bullshit, Skeeta,' Bowker said. 'There's no way you'd put an animal inside that precious car of yours. Plus, there's a dog chain attached to the rail behind the cabin.'

Skeeta thought for a moment. 'Dad and I marked lambs a fortnight ago. I must have thrown a knife on the front seat. Probably still had a lamb's blood on it.'

'The blood's been tested already. It's human blood, Daryl,' Moloney lied.

'Probably mine,' Skeeta said after a moment. 'Working on a farm you often cut yourself on barbed wire or nails sticking out of posts in the shed. Happens all the time. That's why I carry Band Aids in the ute.'

Moloney shook his head. 'The blood's been tested as AB Negative,' Moloney lied again. 'It's extremely rare. Less than one person in a hundred has that sort of blood. But do you know who had that type of blood, Daryl? Yvonne Bryant.'

Bowker leaned forward across his desk. 'You're not going to tell us you have that type of blood too, are you, Skeeta? The forensic team will take a sample for comparison, anyway.'

'I know what my blood group is,' Skeeta said dejectedly, eyes on the floor. 'It's O positive. The old girl used to force me to go to Robinvale with her to donate blood.'

Moloney rubbed his chin. 'Well, that leaves you with a problem, doesn't it, Daryl?'

Skeeta stared into space for a few long moments then looked at Moloney. 'Alright, it was Yvonne's blood. But I didn't kill her!'

'How'd it get there?' Moloney asked, arms folded. 'And don't feed us any bullshit about cutting herself on a farm knife or a bottle top. The blood has dried on strands of purple hair, so the bleeding occurred on the night of the social.'

Skeeta looked back at the floor and spoke softly. 'I hit her. I hit her in the face and her lip started bleeding.'

'Why'd you do that, Skeeta?' Bowker asked.

Skeeta looked up at Bowker. 'She was being an absolute bitch, alright? She was in a bad mood and wanted to go straight back to the hall.'

Moloney put his hands on his knees and leant closer to Skeeta. 'How many times did you hit her?'

'At Cocamba that night? Two, maybe three times.'

'Only really weak pricks belt up women, Skeeta,' Bowker said staring straight at Flynn who looked away.

Skeeta shook his head slowly. 'Well, I didn't kill her if that's what you're thinking.'

'I'll tell you the way it all stacks up for us, Daryl,' Moloney said. 'You were seen by several witnesses driving the victim away from the social and she was never seen alive again. You admit to taking her to the Cocamba silos where her remains were found. Now you admit to losing your temper and punching her severely enough for her to bleed on your car seat.'

'Doesn't mean I killed her,' Skeeta shot back.

'I think you hit her so hard that she died,' Flynn said, standing up and towering above him. 'You panicked and stashed her body where she wouldn't be found, at least in the short term. Then you drove back to town, acted as if nothing had happened, and pretended you were collecting her to take her home.'

Skeeta pointed towards Bowker. 'Then why would I tell Bowker I'd taken her to Cocamba? Why would I tell him that?'

'Because you're as dumb as dog shit,' Flynn replied. 'Or maybe you were covering your arse in case someone saw your lairy vehicle at the murder scene. In your statement, you said you saw two semis go past and a car followed you into town. Pretty hard to mistake that ute of yours.'

'How would anyone see my car?' Skeeta asked angrily. 'It was ten o'clock at night, for fuck's sake.'

'Sorry, Skeeta, but it was a full moon with a crystal-clear sky,' Bowker said. 'Your ute would have been visible from two hundred metres away.'

Skeeta put his elbows on his knees and dropped his head into his hands. 'This is all bullshit! I didn't bloody kill her!'

Moloney knelt down beside him. 'I don't think you took Yvonne to Cocamba to murder her, Daryl. When you hit her, you probably didn't mean for her to die. If you come clean with us now, we could recommend a charge of manslaughter.'

Skeeta raised his head and looked straight at Moloney. 'I didn't bloody kill her!' He dropped his head back into his hands.

'Are you sure, Daryl?' Moloney continued. 'Are you sure your temper didn't get the best of you and you hit her once too often or a bit too hard? I've seen it a hundred times during my career. Things just spiral out of control. So best you tell us the whole story, and I promise we'll put in a good word for you.'

Skeeta sat up straight in his chair and lifted his head in defiance. 'I'm not admitting to something I didn't do, so you can all fuck off.'

Bowker was surprised when Moloney replied. 'Daryl Allender, it is my intention to charge you with the murder of Yvonne Bryant. You have the right to remain silent. If you do say anything, what you say can be used against you in a court of law. You have the right to consult with a lawyer and have that lawyer present during any questioning. If you cannot afford a lawyer, one will be appointed for you if you so desire.'

Skeeta slid off the chair and dropped to his knees. 'Fuck, fuck fuck,' he muttered before starting to cry.

'You're going into the lockup here, Daryl,' Moloney said. 'In the morning we'll transport you to Swan Hill, where a Magistrate will remand you into custody.'

Skeeta slowly recovered his equilibrium, climbed to his feet and looked at Moloney. 'How can I get bail? The old man's virtually broke.'

'Bail is not awarded in murder cases, son,' Moloney explained. 'You'll be taken to Melbourne and kept in custody awaiting a committal hearing.'

'But I didn't do it,' Skeeta said quietly. 'You believe me don't you, Bowker?'

Bowker was deliberately noncommittal. 'You've been charged by Detective Inspector Moloney, and now it's up to the courts to decide. Better get yourself a lawyer.'

Flynn took Skeeta to the holding cell, while Jack sat at the desk filling out a charge sheet. Moloney looked up from his work. 'You're still not convinced, are you, Greg?'

Bowker shook his head. 'Admitting he took Yvonne to Cocamba still worries me, Jack.'

'Nearly all cases have a little gap somewhere,' Moloney replied. 'Everything else in this case fits like a glove. The reason he admitted going there will eventually come out. We'll wrap this up this evening after the railway vehicles have been tested. Trevor and I will take Allender to Swan Hill tomorrow and we'll go back to Melbourne from there.'

Rachael appeared at the door. 'Would you like to stay for tea, Jack? I've made a casserole and there's plenty.'

As she spoke, Flynn arrived back from the cells. Bowker glared at Rachael. The last thing he needed was Flynn making himself at home.

Moloney sensed that too. 'Love to, Rachael, but Trevor and I have some things to tidy up at the pub, so we'll have to settle for a counter tea, unfortunately.'

'You can have tea here, Jack, I can handle things at the pub,' Flynn said, to everyone's surprise. 'Better for all concerned if I give this cosy domestic scene a miss. Besides, I'm not big on Rachael's cooking. The kitchen's not where she does her best work, eh Bowker?'

Bowker was about to react angrily, when Moloney quickly jumped in. 'Well in that case, thanks, Rachael. A home cooked meal would be terrific.'

'My share won't go to waste anyway. Allender will need to be fed,' Flynn said as he walked towards the door.

Rachael looked quizzically at Bowker.

'Skeeta's in the cells, Rach. He's been charged with Yvonne's murder.'

Rachael's eyes widened. 'Hell. Never thought of him as a killer.'

'That's the most common reaction we get in this job,' Moloney said. 'Nobody likes to think their next-door neighbour is capable of acts like this.'

CHAPTER 32

Moloney thought Rachael's casserole was delicious, the meal enjoyed in a spirit of bonhomie. Bowker got on well with Moloney, and liked his no-nonsense approach to upholding the law.

'I spoke to the forensic team before they headed back to Bendigo,' Moloney said as they relaxed in the lounge room with a cup of coffee. 'As expected, the railway vehicles came up negative. So that's another loose end tied up.'

'But I guess we'll need to wait for the fingerprint analysis before we can put a permanent line through Lowbury's name,' Bowker replied.

'Agreed,' Moloney said, sipping his drink. 'I've been impressed by the way you've handled this case, Greg. Your preliminary investigations saved Trevor and I a week's work. The only fresh evidence has come via forensics. I reckon you've got a future working in a plain clothes squad. If not homicide, then at least armed robbery or something similar. You've got a detective's brain and a detective's instinct. I've seen some with it, but plenty more without it.'

'Pretty happy up here at the moment,' Bowker replied. 'But I appreciate the vote of confidence.'

'Well, keep in mind what I said if you start to get itchy feet.'

Rachael was about to join the conversation when the phone rang. Bowker took the call then quickly hung up. 'That was Donna Cavanagh. She's hysterical. Lives around the corner in Pioneer Street. Want to come for a two-minute walk, Jack? I think you'll be interested in this.'

Bowker and Moloney quickly strode the two or three hundred metres to the young teacher's house. The porch light was on and Bowker knocked on the door.

An emotional voice came from inside. 'Who is it?'

'It's Greg Bowker, Donna.'

The door opened quickly, and Donna Cavanagh flew out, throwing her arms around Bowker. 'Oh, Greg. It was horrible. I'm so scared.'

Donna was short, of slight build with cropped auburn hair cut in a fringe across the front. It was a warm night, and she was wearing shorts, a singlet top and no shoes. Bowker allowed her a few moments to gain a level of composure before he put his hands on her shoulders and moved her away a little so he could see her face. Her eyes were red and bloodshot from crying, tears still running down her cheeks. There was a bruise starting to form on the bridge of her nose, and a cut on her right ear that was dribbling blood down the side of her neck.

'Donna, this is Detective Inspector Moloney from the Homicide Squad. Let's go inside and you can tell us what happened.'

Donna led them up the passage to the kitchen, passing her bedroom on one side and the lounge room on the other. They sat down at the kitchen table strewn with the remnants of fish and chips in white paper, two wine glasses, a half-full bottle of white wine, and a scrunched-up pink hanky. A folder of schoolwork was pushed to the side. Bowker noticed a dirty plate and cutlery on the sink.

'What happened here, lass?' Moloney asked gently.

Donna sniffed back the tears as she spoke. 'That policeman, Trevor. The one who interviewed me at school about Yvonne's disappearance, he punched me in the face and on the side of the head when I refused to have sex with him.'

Even though Bowker had explained the substance of Donna's call on their short walk over, the fury in Moloney's eyes was palpable. 'Better start at the beginning, I think.'

'I'd just finished tea and was settling down to correct my form

6 history essays, when he knocked on the door. He said the other policeman had been invited out, so he was left to eat on his own. He thought I might like some company, so he bought fish and chips and a bottle of wine then wandered around here.'

'How'd he know where you live?' Bowker asked.

'He took my address and phone number as part of the statement I gave at school.' The tears again welled in her eyes.

'So you invited him in?' Moloney asked.

'I wouldn't normally do that with someone I'd just met, but if you can't trust a police officer, who can you trust?'

The two policemen exchanged glances before Bowker spoke. 'What happened next?'

'He ate his fish and chips. I had a few chips and drank a glass of wine. I think he might have had two, or maybe three. He was good company, and I guess I felt a bit flattered by a big handsome bloke like him coming around unannounced.' She lifted the hanky and blew her nose. 'After about half an hour, he came around to my side of the table and started trying to kiss and grope me. At that point I told him he should go.'

'Is that when he hit you?' Moloney asked.

'Not right then. I followed him towards the front door, but as we passed the bedroom, he grabbed me and tried to force me onto the bed. When I resisted, he called me a stuck-up bitch and belted me across the nose.'

'Did he rape you?' Moloney enquired gently.

'No. He just whacked me on the side of the head when I curled up around my knees on the bed. I was so scared.' She started to cry.

'Then he left?' Bowker asked.

'He called me a fuckin' little cock teaser, then walked out and slammed the front door. That's when I rang you, Greg.'

Bowker walked a few doors to Bob and Judi Wikman's house and arranged for Donna to spend the night in the spare room. Moloney inspected Donna's wound and recommended she be checked out by the doctor the next day before coming to the police station to provide a formal statement.

With the young teacher safely relocated, Bowker and Moloney returned to the police station where they had a brief chat with Rachael before making their way to the pub. Moloney opened the door to Room 3 and walked inside. Flynn was laying on the bed in a pair of satin boxers reading a copy of *Penthouse*.

'Didn't expect you back this early, Jack. Rachael's casserole playing havoc with your guts?'

Bowker walked in and closed the door.

'What's going on? Don't tell me Allender's done a runner.'

'Donna Cavanagh phoned me,' Bowker said, hands on hips. 'Jack and I have just come from her house.'

Flynn sat up on the edge of his bed. 'What's her grief? I forget to clean up my fish and chip paper?'

'Not funny, Trevor,' Moloney said intensely. 'You physically assaulted her.'

'Bullshit, Jack. Just a bit of slap and tickle. Thought she'd like it rough. A lot of women do you know.'

'Most women don't, arsehole,' Bowker said, his temper rising.

Flynn spread his arms with palms up. 'Look. I arrived on her doorstep with food and a bottle of wine. She invited me in. What does she think I'm there for, a cosy chat on the history of the Mallee? She gave her okay for sex the moment she invited me in.'

Moloney was trying desperately to control his anger. 'Donna claims she explicitly said no to sex,' he said. 'It doesn't get more clear-cut than that, Trevor.'

'You've spent too many years with your missus from up Woop Woop, Jack. It's the way the game works nowadays. You ask to have sex, they refuse, you slap them around a bit, and then you fuck them. The girls love the tough guy treatment.'

'Is that right, Trevor?' Moloney said.

Flynn laid back on the bed and picked up his magazine. 'Storm in a teacup. Nothing to see. End of story.'

'Well here's the start of a new story, Detective.' Moloney said. 'Trevor Flynn, I intend to charge you with the violent assault of Donna Cavanagh of Pioneer Street Manangatang.'

Flynn quickly found his feet. 'You've got to be bloody joking, Jack! Fuck me! Coppers are supposed to look after each other. There's a code.'

'I also intend to charge you with a series of assaults against your former wife Rachael Flynn, then of James Street Ballarat. I also intend to charge you with threatening behaviour and have collected the items you sent through the mail as evidence.' Moloney read Flynn his rights.

Flynn dropped back onto his bed speechless, knowing his career was over.

CHAPTER 33

Christmas was almost upon the small country town with the weather again turning brutal. Temperatures were in the mid-forties with gusty northerly winds funnelling hot air down from the Red Centre. Sport had one round left before the summer break, and the swimming pool became the most popular spot in town. For Bowker, things had slowed after Skeeta Allender was placed on remand, but the arrest still worried him deeply. All the evidence pointed to him, but Bowker's instincts screamed they had the wrong man.

Yvonne Bryant's body was finally released to the family, and ten days before Christmas, her remains were interred in the Manangatang cemetery. Lines of marble gravestones shimmered in the December inferno as the wind howled through the Mallee trees that lined the broken-down perimeter fence. Small bushes, doggedly clinging to life between the outlying graves of long forgotten denizens, bowed in the face of the northerly onslaught. A brown snake slivered into a breach in an old grave where erosion had undermined the stone and where sand had since appropriated the void. The lonely cemetery that evoked a Mallee Garden of Eden in the peaceful verdancy of autumn and spring, today conjured the gateway to hell.

Most of the town was in attendance to pay their respects, to support one of the oldest families in the district. Yvonne's classmates formed a guard of honour as the coffin was carried from the hearse to the grave. Many of the kids were in tears, particularly Travis Urdevic who sobbed quietly throughout. Jimmy Cobb found the whole event unbearable and sat away from the others on a neighbouring grave. A family of kookaburras silently bore witness to the ceremony from a nearby eucalypt.

After a brief eulogy by the Anglican priest, the casket was lowered into its sandy resting place in the shadow of a temporary canvas awning that flapped and distorted in the strengthening gale. Mourners were invited to take a flower from a cane basket and release it into the grave as a last salute to a girl most of them knew, but very few understood. As they queued with their red geranium, Rachael turned sadly to Bowker. 'She won the twenty-dollar bet, Greg. She died before you.'

Bowker nodded sombrely, opening his hand to reveal a rolled-up twenty-dollar note. 'You win, Yvonne,' he muttered quietly as he released it with his red flower into the grave.

As the crowd stood around chatting, Rachael spotted Jimmy Cobb still sitting alone. 'He'll be right,' his mother said. 'This is all a bit overwhelming. He really liked Yvonne. She was very good to him.'

'She was going to ask him to be her deb partner,' Rachael said quietly.

Jimmy's mother burst into tears, touched Rachael on the shoulder, then sat on a white plastic chair to compose herself.

Rachael strolled over to Jimmy and sat down beside him. He had tears rolling down his cheeks and Rachael put a comforting arm around his shoulder. 'Pretty sad isn't it, mate? But things will get better after a few days,' she said.

'It's mine fault that she's deaded,' Jimmy said.

'It's not your fault, Jimmy. The man who hurt Yvonne is in jail.'

'I seed her getted into a car at the social and I didded tell anybody.'

She patted his shoulder. 'You don't have to worry about that, because the police already knew she got into Skeeta's big yellow ute.'

Jimmy shook his head. 'No no no. I seed her getted into Mr Weston's car.'

Rachael was taken aback. 'Are you sure? Mr Weston wasn't at the social.'

Jimmy nodded vigorously. 'He wassed out the back in the lane. I seed him through the window when I getted a drink from the back room.'

Rachael scanned the crowd and noticed Weston was one of the few teachers not at the cemetery. 'You wait here, Jimmy. I'll go and get Greg.'

Jimmy stood up quickly. 'No no no. I don't want to goed to jail!'

Rachael sat him down gently and patted his hand. 'You're not in trouble, Jimmy. I just want you to tell Greg what you've just told me.'

Rachael found Greg chatting to Prong and physically dragged him away. 'Greg, Jimmy says he saw Yvonne get into a car with Adrian Weston at the social.'

Bowker shook his head. 'No, that's bullshit, Rach. Weston wasn't at the social.'

'Well, you have a chat to him. See what you think.'

Bowker walked over and sat down beside the boy. 'Did you see Yvonne get into a car with someone at the social, mate?'

'Yes yes. Out the backed of the hall in the lane.'

'Do you mean Skeeta in his yellow ute?'

He shook his head. 'No no no. It wassed Mr Weston.'

Bowker looked him in the eye. 'Are you really really sure, Jimmy?'

'Yes yes. It wassed his car. A Redded Charger.'

Bowker looked at Rachael and she nodded confirmation that Adrian Weston had such a vehicle. He sometimes drove the pillarbox red Valiant Charger to school and parked it in the shade of a tree beside the car park. At other times he drove his wife's Nissan Sunbird but was happy to leave that car baking all day in the carpark.

'Why didn't you tell us about Mr Weston before, Jimmy?' Bowker asked gently, not wanting him to clam up again.

Jimmy looked at the ground. 'Because I wassed scared.'

Rachael knelt beside him. 'Scared of what, Jimmy?' she asked quietly.

Jimmy looked up. 'I was scared he would punched me again, liked he didded at school.'

'When did he punch you at school, mate?' Rachael asked.

'Whenned I tolded you that I runned into the tanked stand. Whenned my face wassed all swollened.'

'Why did he punch you, Jimmy?' Bowker asked.

'Becaused I looked through a crack in the agged science shed and he tolded me he would hitted me again if I tolded anybody.'

Bowker looked at Rachael and took a deep breath. 'What did you see when you looked through the crack in the shed, Jimmy?'

'I sawed Yvonne and Mr Weston with their pantsed down doing naughty things.'

CHAPTER 34

Following the afternoon tea, ironically served at the venue where Yvonne was last seen alive, Bowker drove to the school. The students had been dismissed early due to the funeral and most of the staff had already departed, including Bowker's new person of interest. But at this stage, it was information he was chasing, not Weston. Bowker sat down with the principal in his office, hoping his cover story would pass muster, and that his questions didn't suggest an undue interest in his Ag Science teacher. Certain facts needed to be established, but given these enquiries were predicated solely on the word of Jimmy Cobb, Bowker was anxious to keep his cards close to his chest.

Following a short discussion regarding the funeral, Bowker casually moved to the real purpose of his visit. 'Malcolm, the legal team are just tidying up the paperwork surrounding Skeeta Allender's murder prosecution,' he lied. 'They've asked me to grab a copy of the supervision roster for the night of the social and the detailed whereabouts of any staff who didn't attend.'

Swinton raised his eyebrows. 'I thought the case was closed.'

'It is closed, but the prosecutors want to be prepared in case Skeeta's defence team throw up an alternative scenario. One relating to someone whose whereabouts hasn't been officially confirmed.'

'Just a minute.' Swindon rustled through some papers pinned on a noticeboard. He finally located the sheet he was after and handed it to Bowker. 'This is the supervision roster we used.'

Bowker perused the sheet. 'According to your records, were any staff unavailable that night?'

'From memory, only Adrian Weston who was at a science conference in Melbourne, and Rebecca Johns who we cut a bit of slack with evening functions because she's on her own with two little kids.'

Bowker nodded. 'What about Steve Linton? I don't think he was there.' he asked, maintaining the pretence of a general enquiry.

'He was rostered on but called in sick that morning. Sick for a few days actually. Submitted a medical certificate when he returned to work.'

Bowker retrieved a notebook from his trouser pocket. 'Addresses of the three non-attendees?'

Swindon scratched his head. 'Shit. Pixie and Rebecca both live in Pioneer Street and Adrian rents a house in Chinky. I'll have to pull the personnel file.'

Swindon found the addresses and Bowker wrote them down dutifully, even though he had them in a file back at the station. Then followed the question that all this had been leading to. 'Have you got the details of Adrian Weston's conference?'

'Melbourne somewhere, but it'll be in the file.' Swindon pulled a folder from the steel cabinet and leafed through it until he found the relevant paperwork.

'Can I take a copy for the suits in Melbourne?'

'Take what you want. Bloody paperwork! The world's gone mad. Soon you'll need department permission to send a kid to the dunny!'

Bowker stood to leave, then asked a seemingly unrelated question. 'How many teachers in Manang have previously taught at another school?'

Swindon shrugged his shoulders. 'Not too many. Hard to get people to apply up here in the sand. Mostly get First Years who are sent here regardless of their preferences. Same as Murrayville and Werrimul and other isolated places. Swift's Creek is another one.'

'But Peter Hindmarsh must have applied for Manang.'

'Yeah, to become a Senior Teacher. Promotion position. The Wikmans are a bit the same. Dwayne Jones as well in the primary. Karly McColl came from Ouyen to marry Prickles and Alan Henderson moved back to help on his parent's farm. Other than that, they're mostly kids on their first appointment.'

'Adrian Weston?'

'Yeah, forgot about him. Came from Broadmeadows West in Melbourne. Just looking for a change of lifestyle, I think.' Swindon chuckled. 'City science teacher showing farm kids how to farm. But somebody has the do it. The locals think it's important to teach the kids what most of them already know.'

'How long's he been up here?'

'Adrian?' Swindon thought for a moment. 'Came at the beginning of last year, from memory.'

Bowker now had the information he needed and returned to the police station to plan his next move. He read the material concerning the two-day science conference, establishing it was run by the Science Teachers Association of Victoria and hosted at a conference centre in Carlton. Bowker rang the contact phone number and explained he was a policeman seeking information relating to a missing person. He quickly received confirmation that Weston was definitely a participant at the conference on the two days, having collected his personal name tag on arrival and having signed a travel reimbursement form at lunchtime on the second day. Bowker thanked the contact for her efficiency and was about to hang up when she joked that Weston didn't stay around after lunch on the second day to participate in the time management session. Better use of his time to start the long trip back to the Mallee, she surmised.

'Are you sure of that?' Bowker asked.

'Absolutely,' she replied. 'Most participants felt the same way about the session. Only three or four stayed around for it. I can name them all, if you want.'

The trip from Melbourne to Manangatang takes approximately

five hours. Had Weston left at lunchtime, he would have been home in plenty of time to be at the social at around ten o'clock even if he stopped along the way for something to eat. Had he stayed until the end of the conference, being in Manang by ten was still possible, but not without everything going right.

Bowker's next call was to Broadmeadows West High School. He was put straight through to the principal and delivered a similar spiel about missing persons. When he mentioned Adrian Weston, the principal's reaction was immediate. 'If Weston's the one missing, I wouldn't try too hard to find him,' she said.

'Why so?' Bowker asked.

'He was basically run out of this place. Couldn't keep his hands off our female students. I reported his behaviour to the department and they transferred him up your way.'

'How many years was he at Broadmeadows West?' Bowker asked, taking notes.

'Nine years too many. I recognised his fetish as soon as I took this job three years ago. My predecessor must have either been blind, or thought it was just too hard to do anything.'

'Where did he teach before he came to you?'

'Geelong Heights. I rang the long-time boss there before I reported Weston to the department. Said he'd had parents of middle-school girls complaining about how Weston was behaving around their daughters. Didn't have enough evidence to officially discipline him, so he pressured Weston to apply for a transfer. Lucky us, we got him at Broadmeadows West.'

'How long was he teaching in Geelong, do you know?'

'Four or five years, I think.'

For Bowker, it was all starting to fit together. 'Was that his first school?'

'No. He started at Kilmore High. By sheer coincidence, my present English Coordinator was a first-year teacher there at the same time. According to her, Weston started a relationship with a fifth form girl who fell pregnant when she was doing her Matriculation. HSC we call it now. They both left at the end of that year when he transferred to Geelong Heights. That relationship went belly-up not long after, apparently. He was married to Belinda, I think her name was, when he came here. They had a couple of young daughters.'

Bowker tapped his pencil on his notepad. 'Surely his relationship with a student would have rung alarm bells all over the place in Kilmore?'

The principal chuckled. 'Happened all the time with the older girls. First year teachers are usually only three or four years older than the kids they teach. I'd know at least a dozen teachers whose spouse is a former student of theirs. In country areas, the older schoolgirls are often the only single females in the district.' She sniggered. 'Haven't heard of any female teachers marrying their ex-students, though. Probably would have made the maturity gap even worse.'

'It's still hard to believe.'

'Remember, we're talking fifteen years ago. Girls got married earlier then. Very few went on to higher education or followed a career. Most peers of older students were in the work force, and some were already married.'

'So, you're saying Weston having an intimate relationship with a student would not have been judged inappropriate at that time?'

'Not with a form five or six girl, no. Some parents even thought a young teacher was a good catch for their daughter. But what spooked me, and the boss at Geelong Heights, was that Weston was consorting with younger girls. We're talking fifteen- and sixteen year-olds. Particularly the ones who were a bit wild and from troubled backgrounds.'

Bowker heard Rachael come through the back door and met her in the kitchen. They hugged and Bowker kissed her lightly on the lips. 'I've made a few telephone calls Rach, and your colleague Mr Weston has a long history of inappropriate relationships with schoolgirls. He's taught at three schools prior to Manang and he's effectively been moved on each time. He knocked up a sixth form girl when he started teaching at Kilmore High.'

Rachael frowned in annoyance. 'Why aren't schools told these things before staff are appointed. If you believe the rumours surrounding the catholic church, the same thing happens there. They just move priests from parish to parish after they get caught abusing kids. Why the hell is nobody ever accountable when they repeat their behaviour further down the track?' Rachael exhaled audibly. 'Okay. I'm down off my soapbox. So, you reckon Adrian is definitely a player in all this?'

'The more I dig, the more neatly Weston fits into what happened that night.'

Rachael pushed Bowker down into a kitchen chair and kissed him on the forehead. 'All you need to do now, senior constable, is explain how Adrian could have been in two places at the same time. Easy-peasy.' She laughed, then took a jug of cold water from the fridge and filled two glasses. She sat down so they faced each other across the kitchen table.

Bowker drank half his glass. 'Weston's confirmed as being at the science conference, but only until lunchtime on the second day. That gives him plenty of time to drive back to Manang in the arvo.'

Rachael rotated her glass on the tabletop. 'But you'd hardly go to a teacher conference, then leave early so you could get back to murder somebody. It doesn't make any sense.'

'Maybe something happened that day that changed his plans.' He shrugged his shoulders. 'Dunno.'

'Why would he want to kill Yvonne anyway? He had a history with girls at other schools, why suddenly pick Yvonne to do this to?'

Bowker shook his head. 'Buggered if I know that either.'

'Are you getting homicide back?'

'Not yet. All I have is the word of an intellectually disabled kid with a reputation for making up stories, and a bloke with a history of non-violent relationships with schoolgirls.'

'So, now what?'

'I'll take a drive down to Chinky and have a chat with Weston and his missus.'

***

The Westons' rented home was old and in need of major maintenance, but it didn't look out of place in the decaying township of Chinkapook. The guttering was loose in places, with stalks of wheat ready to harvest in others. Worn, faded and torn blinds shielded the veranda from the setting sun, and the garden comprised two overgrown clumps of agapanthus and three old kerosene drums encasing straggly pelargoniums. Bowker dodged gaps in the boards as he picked his way along the veranda, at times trusting only the floor joists to take his weight. He banged on the front door, and after a moment it was answered by twelve year-old Bernadette who led him through the house to the kitchen. As he passed the lounge room, Bowker spotted the older sister, Sophie, lying on a bean bag watching *The Curiosity Show* on an old Pye 15-inch black and white TV. She didn't look up.

'The Manang policeman's here, Dad,' Bernadette said cheerily before retreating to the television. Weston's wife looked up smiling from where she was peeling potatoes at the sink.

Weston forced a smile. 'G'day, Greg. What brings you to the hustle and bustle of Chinkapook?'

'Just tying up a few loose ends around the Skeeta Allender homicide case. Can I talk to you outside for a couple of minutes? Don't want to distract Belinda while she's got that knife in her hand,' Bowker joked.

Belinda Weston grinned and light-heartedly waved the knife in Bowker's direction. Adrian remained poker-faced. Once outside, Bowker began his questioning as though just filling inconsequential gaps in the Yvonne Bryant case. 'The day of the school social, Malcolm tells me you were in Melbourne at a teachers' conference?'

'Yeah, for science teachers. I was there the day before as well. Why is this relevant?'

Bowker leant a shoulder against a veranda post and crossed his arms. 'Just dotting the i's and crossing the t's at the behest of the prosecution in Skeeta's case.' He then delivered the same cover story as he did with Malcolm Swindon. 'So, I can put you down as being at the conference for the full two days?'

Weston's face relaxed. 'That's right.'

'All day, both days?'

'Yep. You can check with the organisers.'

Bowker stood up straight and put his hands in his pockets. 'I have. You didn't attend the afternoon session on the second day.'

'Oh, that?' Weston said, feigning surprise. 'I don't think anyone went to that. The topic was time management. Most people thought the best use of their time was to head home.' Weston faked a chuckle.

Bowker wasn't letting him off the hook. 'So, you were back in Manang at seven o'clock-ish, then?'

Weston's face again tightened. 'I didn't go back to Manang. I came here. Why would I go on to Manang?'

'Okay, so you arrived back here at around about that time. About seven, or a bit before?'

'No. In the afternoon I went into the city to do some Christmas shopping. Spent a couple of hours in there, then got stuck in peak hour traffic and the roadworks between Charlton and Wycheproof. Didn't get home here until nearly eleven. You can ask Belinda. I was here when she brought Sophie home from the social. That must have been about quarter to twelve.'

'When do you estimate you left the city?'

Bowker had Weston off balance. 'Why is that important?'

'I've explained that already. The silks want their case against Skeeta water-tight.'

Weston shook his head. 'I left at four or five o'clock. There was a parking ticket under my windscreen wiper when I returned to the car. If you don't believe me, I can show it to you. It's got the date, the time, the lot.'

'Can I see it?'

Weston was incensed. 'Don't see why you can't take my bloody word for it.' He strode aggressively to his red Charger. He fished around on the floor and in the glovebox but came up empty. 'Can't find the damn thing right now, but I swear I was given a ticket.' Bowker said nothing, letting him dangle at the end of his own rope. 'The bottom line is that I didn't arrive back here until after eleven and I didn't go to Manang. Why would I when Belinda was picking up Sophie?'

Bowker took a deep breath and went in for the kill. 'You see, Adrian, I have a problem with all of this because Jimmy Cobb said he saw Yvonne Bryant get into your car behind the hall that night.'

Weston went white, and was speechless for a few moments, before quickly mounting a counterattack. 'You know as well as I do, Greg, that Jimmy Cobb is intellectually backward, and he has a tenuous grasp on reality. He's a compulsive liar and a known fabricator of tall stories.' He shook his head vigorously. 'I can't believe you'd attach the slightest credence to any crap emanating from his mouth.'

Bowker brushed a fly from his cheek. 'So, Jimmy's just making it all up?'

'Absolutely. No doubt.' Weston said aggressively. 'Ask Belinda when I arrived back from Melbourne. She'll tell you exactly the same story that I have.'

'I will,' Bowker said quickly, keen to keep him off balance.

'Bloody Jimmy and his imagination. He's incapable of distinguishing between what's real and what he's just imagined. What else did he tell you? Some really outlandish stuff I bet.'

Bowker smiled knowingly. 'Interesting you should say that, Adrian. He said he saw you and Yvonne having sex in the Ag Science shed. And that you belted him to shut him up.'

Weston gulped a deep breath but reacted calmly. 'Come on, Greg. Surely you don't believe that bullshit. I'm a highly respected schoolteacher. We don't do that stuff.'

Bowker stared straight into his eyes. 'So highly respected that three schools have moved you on because of your unprofessional interest in young girls?'

The aggressive Weston returned. 'Well, that was all bullshit too. I've had one relationship with a schoolgirl in my life, which you've no doubt discovered if you've been digging around at my previous schools. I was still basically a kid myself. There was only three years between us, so it was hardly cradle snatching.' Weston paused for effect. 'Once you get tarred with that brush, it stays with you wherever you go.'

Weston turned and went back inside. Bowker followed, but before he could speak, Weston beat him to his question. 'Belinda, can you please confirm to the senior constable that I arrived home from the science conference at around quarter past eleven. You'd gone to Manang to pick up Sophie, remember?'

Belinda hesitated just long enough to give Bowker the answer he was after. 'That's right, Greg. He wasn't here when I left for Manang, but he was home when I got back with Sophie.' She frowned. 'Why, what's all this about?'

Bowker smiled. 'Just nailing down where all the school staff were on that night. Just tidying up loose ends for the legal eagles in Melbourne.'

Belinda was worried. 'I thought the murder investigation had been finalised.'

Bowker turned to leave. 'Like I said, Belinda. Just tidying up loose ends.'

CHAPTER 35

On his return to the station, Bowker rang the Melbourne City Council confirming that a parking ticket had been issued on the said date at 4.15 pm for a red Chrysler Valiant Charger with the registration number he quoted. A photocopy would follow in the mail. After ending the call, Bowker perused the list of items retrieved from the environs of the crime scene at Cocamba, hoping the parking ticket would be listed there and had somehow been overlooked in the investigation. But after scanning the list twice, Bowker confirmed it was not there. He knew he would have noticed it before anyway.

Over tea, Bowker and Rachael discussed his visit to the Westons'. 'I'm at a bit of a loss here, Rach. I reckon Weston is up to his armpits in Yvonne's death, but where's the motive?'

She shrugged. 'Maybe he was scared their relationship would become public.'

'If that was the case, Jimmy was a greater threat than Yvonne. She was a willing participant, apparently.'

Rachael took a sip from her wine glass. 'Maybe she wanted to break it off.'

'He wouldn't kill her for that, surely. Even if he had that in mind, why drive into Manang in the hope he might find her somewhere on her own?'

'And there was no mention of violence when you spoke to his former principal?'

'No. Appears Weston was just this scumbag who moved schools when he was caught out.' Bowker took a bite of bread and thought for a moment. 'What if Jimmy did just make it all up?'

Rachael shook her head. 'I'm sure he was telling the truth, Greg. He was so upset about Yvonne, and he blamed himself for not speaking up. Usually when he fabricates stories, it's to make himself look good, not bad.'

'The night Yvonne went missing, you said you'd seen her talking to Sophie Weston in the ladies' toilet. Did you catch what they were talking about?'

'They clammed up as soon as I came through the door. Besides, the music was so loud you couldn't hear yourself think.'

'Belinda said she brought her daughter home from the social. I didn't see her collected. Did you?'

Rachael dabbed her mouth with a paper serviette. 'She was waiting with Peter Hindmarsh and a couple of other kids when we left the hall to search for Yvonne.'

'I'll give Pete a ring later, just to confirm it was Belinda who picked her up.'

***

Bowker made the call after *Four Corners* on the ABC and asked Hindmarsh about the kids whose parents were late collecting them from the social.

'All up there were four of them if I remember correctly. Graham and Louise Lloyd, Sophie Weston, and little Matthew Knight. The Lloyd kids were picked up within five minutes of you leaving the hall, and Mumbles Knight arrived from the pub a minute or so later and collected Matthew. It was ages before Belinda Weston arrived for Soph. I thought I'd have to run her down to Chinky myself. You send notices home, and the parents still get the times ballsed-up. Took Sophie two calls from the public phone to get one simple message through to her mother.'

Bowker grabbed his pen. 'Do you remember when she made those calls?'

'The first one was about nine-ish, maybe a smidge later. She asked permission to walk down to the phone box to ring her mother about getting picked up. I was only half listening because there was chaos inside the hall. One-Ball McIver's kid spewed up everywhere. Been on the turps, the little bugger.'

'You're sure Sophie actually made that call?'

'Yeah. I went back outside when the boss started organising the clean-up. I watched Sophie walk all the way down to the phone and back. *In Loco Parentus.*'

Bowker scribbled the time on a note pad. 'When did she make the second call?'

'After the social. She left with the other kids but came back ten minutes later. Said she'd walked up the street and rung her mum about picking her up. Her mother must have a memory like a sieve because obviously she was still in Chinky when Soph rang. She didn't arrive for another fifteen, maybe twenty minutes.'

'Belinda have the younger daughter with her?'

'I think so. I don't reckon she'd leave Bernadette on her own in Chinky. Adrian was away at a conference and he'd struggle to be home by that stage.'

Bowker walked back into the lounge room where Rachael had switched to the commercial channel and was now watching *Magnum P.I..* 'One hunk of a lawman not enough for you, Rach?'

Rachael patted the couch. 'You'll do me fine.'

Bowker laid down on the couch, his head on her lap. 'Things are getting stranger by the minute, Rach. Sophie Weston made two phone calls to her mother on the night of the social. Pete assumes they were to clarify the pick-up time. The first one was part-way through the social, the next was after eleven-thirty and prompted her mother to come in and collect her twenty minutes later.'

Rachael stroked his hair gently. 'Belinda must have forgotten.'

'I don't buy that. Especially if Sophie had rung less than two hours earlier. My guess is that Belinda didn't think she needed to collect her daughter. That second call came as a surprise, I reckon.'

'You think that maybe Adrian arrived home earlier than he claims, volunteered to pick up Sophie, and Belinda thought she wasn't required?'

'That would make sense if he had left Chinky around eleven o'clock to collect her. But Jimmy saw him in Manang just after supper. That's over an hour before Sophie needed to be collected. Something brought Adrian into town early, and something prevented him picking up his daughter.'

'Do you think Belinda would know?'

'She was home in Chinky, so logically she must have some idea about it. Unless, of course, Adrian came to Manang straight from Melbourne. But if that was the case, how would Belinda know she didn't need to pick up Sophie? Plus, it makes no sense for him to bypass home on the chance he'd encounter Yvonne on her own somewhere.'

Rachael stopped stroking his hair. 'Maybe they had a prearranged rendezvous.'

'But why would they? They'd see each other at school the next morning, and unless he had some compelling reason, Weston wouldn't take the risk of going near that hall with all the teachers and kids there.' Bowker patted his head in a silent request for a resumption of relaxation therapy. 'And let's think about the logistics for a moment. There was no way he could be certain what time he'd arrive back from Melbourne, and there's no way Yvonne could predict if, or when, she'd be able to sneak out of the social.'

'So he definitely went home first, you reckon?'

'Yep. He went home first, and something happened there that brought him into Manang. Up until then, I bet it didn't cross his mind. Who takes the afternoon off at a conference to go Christmas shopping and then travels four hundred kilometres to kill a sixteen year-old schoolgirl?'

'So what changed his plans?'

'My gut tells me that first telephone call had nothing to do with the finishing time of the social.'

'Maybe she didn't talk to Belinda. Maybe Adrian was home by then.'

'Too early, I think. The parking ticket was written at four-fifteen. He returned to his car some time after that. There's no way he could be back in Chinky in time to take a call around nine o'clock. Not with peak hour traffic and the roadworks on the Calder Highway.'

'Would you like me to have a quiet word with Sophie? I need to catch up with her, anyway. I'd like her to dance Yvonne's part at presentation evening.'

Bowker sat up. 'She hasn't been to your class for yonks and the show is on next week.'

'She'll pick it up in ten minutes. She's a super talent.'

'Won't your other kids be shitty?'

'They've been practising their butts off, but they all reckon the Cleopatra part is too hard for any of them. I think they're worried I'll cancel the whole thing. I reckon they'd welcome Soph back with open arms.'

'Okay. Have a talk to her. If the social comes up, keep it pretty low key and see if she volunteers anything. Don't push too hard. I'd like to keep our powder dry.'

***

The next morning's temperature had already climbed into the low forties when Rachael found Sophie and her sister eating their lunch in the patchy shade of a flowering gum. A couple of pink galahs screeched loudly in the branches overhead. She wandered across to the girls and sat down on the rough-sawn timber seat. 'How are we today, ladies?' she said breezily.

'Good,' Bernadette said with a wide smile.

'Okay, I guess,' Sophie replied without a hint of cheer.

'How's life in the big city of Chinky?'

'Great,' Bernadette said. 'We've got a possum in our back yard. He runs around on the roof every night.'

'Keep you awake?'

'Sometimes,' Bernadette said.

Sophie didn't respond.

'Hey, Soph, I've got a proposition for you,' Rachael said. 'I'd like you to dance the Cleopatra part at speech night next week.'

'Don't know the steps,' Sophie said, staring into infinity.

'I could teach you in the next couple of lunchtimes,' Rachael said. 'You'll pick it up easily. You're the best dancer in the school.'

'Now Yvonne's gone,' Sophie replied without emotion.

'You were both outstanding. I had plans for the two of you to perform something special together.'

There was a flicker of a smile in Sophie's eyes, but it was shut down almost immediately.

'You can do it, Soph,' Bernadette said enthusiastically. 'Easy peasy.'

'I don't feel like dancing again. Ever,' Sophie said sadly.

'Have a think about it, okay? If you decide to do it, bring your shoes and we'll run through the routine at lunchtime tomorrow. Just you and me.'

Sophie didn't answer, just maintained her gaze at the distant horizon.

'Do it for Yvonne,' Rachael said.

'I've done enough for Yvonne already. And now she's dead.' Sophie's eyes filled with tears as she stood and walked away quickly.

Rachael was in two minds whether to follow and offer some comfort, or to leave the girl to work her own way through whatever was tormenting her. She opted to remain with Bernadette who returned a half-eaten Vegemite sandwich to her lunch box, all the while watching her sister walk off into the distance.

'How have you been going, Bernadette?' Rachael said, trying to lift the mood.

'Pretty good,' she said, but Rachael knew she was worried by her sister's funk.

There was silence for a few moments.

'Did you go along for the ride when Mum collected Sophie from the social?'

'Yeah, Mum had to wake me up because she didn't want to leave me at home on my own.' She giggled. 'I was so tired I kept falling asleep in the car.'

Rachael took a deep breath. 'Was Dad late getting home from Melbourne?' she asked with a pang of guilt.

'No, Dad was already home, then he went off somewhere else. Mum got a big surprise when Soph rang to pick her up.'

Rachael remained matter of fact. 'I guess she thought your dad was going to collect her.'

'No, she didn't think that, because Sophie wasn't supposed to be coming home after the social. When I was getting ready for bed, Sophie rang up Mum to tell her that she really, really loved her, and not to worry about picking her up because she was going to Yvonne's house for a sleep-over.'

Rachael's head was spinning, but she continued as casually as she could. 'So Mum told you Sophie was going to Yvonne's house?'

'No. Later, when Dad got home, I heard Mum tell him what Sophie said.'

'Was Dad okay with that?'

'I guess so. Soph and Yvonne are good friends. Mum and Dad went out the back door, so I didn't hear anything else. When nobody could find Yvonne after the social, Soph had to ring up to get a lift home.'

'And you got a beautiful moonlit ride to Manang, eh?' Rachael said, trying not to appear pushy.

'It was my favourite night because I'm allowed to stay up till nine o'clock to watch *A Country Practice*.'

'That's one of my favourites too.'

After another few moments of silence, Bernadette picked up her sandwich and took a bite. 'I'm glad nothing happened to Sophie like happened to Yvonne. She's been pretty sad lately,' the little girl said. 'That's probably my fault. I get all the attention because of this stupid heart.'

'Don't be silly, Bernadette,' Rachael said, patting the little girl on the forearm. 'Your sister knows why you need special treatment. And look at today, of all the kids to have lunch with, she was over here eating with you. So I'm sure her sadness has nothing to do with you.' She gave the girl's arm an affectionate squeeze.

'Last time Mum took me to the Childrens Hospital, we stayed a couple of nights in Melbourne with Nana and Pa. They took me to the zoo, and we went into the city to Myers and to the pictures to see *ET*. When we got home, I was telling Soph all the neat things we had done, but she was very sad. I think she might have been a bit jealous.'

Rachael wanted to be clear. 'So, Mum took you to Melbourne for a few days and Sophie stayed at home with Dad?'

'Yeah, I had all the fun in Melbourne and poor old Soph had to go to school. Raw deal, eh Miss Stow?'

But Rachael didn't hear. Her mind was being sucked into a vortex of unspeakable darkness.

CHAPTER 36

Rachael hurried home and found Bowker working in his office. His face lit up when he saw her. 'Have you slipped home for a matinee?'

'I wish it was that simple, Greg.' She sat down and recounted her conversation with the Weston sisters. Bowker's expression became more pained as her narrative unfolded.

'You know what you're implying, don't you, Rach? It doesn't get more reprobate than that.'

'Sophie was alone in the house with her father for two nights, Greg. And since that time, she acts as though her soul has been torn out. She's become uncommunicative and totally morose. You know as well as I do that these are the classic symptoms of sexual abuse.'

Bowker closed his eyes and felt his jaw tighten. 'Poor kid.'

'And her suddenly dropping out of dance now makes sense. Her father was there every day looking at her. And Yvonne as well, if we believe what Jimmy told us.'

There was silence for a few moments as the gravity of their suspicions took hold.

'We're talking incest, Rach,' Bowker said cautiously.

'I know,' Rachael agreed quietly.

'If we're wrong, the fallout will be catastrophic for everyone involved, us included. Joining all the dots is one thing, creating an accurate picture is another.' Bowker thought for a moment. 'When are you due back at school?'

'I'm not on period five, so I don't have to be back until two-thirty.'

Bowker checked his watch. 'Okay, we've got an hour. For the sake of the exercise, let's assume everything Bernadette Weston told you is factual and the accounts of Skeeta and Jimmy are also accurate.'

'Okay.'

'Skeeta admits he took Yvonne to Cocamba, she was in a foul mood, he physically assaulted her, then dropped her back in Pioneer Street near the hospital. She never made it back to the social. Agreed?'

'Agreed.'

'Bernadette says Sophie phoned to tell her mother that she was going to stay at Yvonne's house after the social and therefore didn't need a lift home.'

Rachael raised a finger. 'And that call must have come shortly after nine pm because Bernadette was getting ready for bed subsequent to watching *A Country Practice*.'

'Then Weston arrives home sometime after, and his wife tells him there's been a change of plans and Sophie is sleeping over at Yvonne's place. He immediately drives off for some unknown reason, and according to Jimmy Cobb, turns up in the lane behind the hall. There he collects Yvonne, who is presumably returning from Pioneer Street where she was dropped off by Skeeta.'

'So, Adrian just happened to be in the right place at the right time for when Skeeta dropped her off.' Rachael screwed up her face. 'We're attributing a lot to chance here, Greg.'

Bowker leaned back in his chair. 'Yeah, I know.' He thought for a minute then slapped his desk as it dawned on him. 'Weston was the driver of that car Skeeta said followed him in from Cocamba. Weston saw her dropped off!'

Rachael was still skeptical. 'So Skeeta turns out of the Cocamba siding and onto the main road just ahead of Adrian Weston who is on his way into Manang from Chinky? It's a total coincidence that he follows Skeeta into town? The chance event occurs out at Cocamba, not in Manang?'

'I'll put my career on it!' Bowker was now on a roll. 'At this stage, we can only guess at whether Weston was coming to Manang to get his daughter or to find Yvonne. But I bet he saw Skeeta drop off Yvonne and I bet he picked her up behind the hall, just as Jimmy said. And if he did kill her, then he knew exactly where to dump the body to put Skeeta Allender in the frame.'

Rachael was shaking her head. 'But what's the motive, Greg? I can't see it. If the abuse of Sophie is real, it was not new. Neither was his dalliance with Yvonne. Why the urgency that night?'

Bowker tapped a pencil on his desk. 'The key has to lie in what happened when he arrived home from Melbourne. He went Christmas shopping before he left the city, so we have to assume there was nothing too urgent playing on his mind at that stage. He gets home, and all of a sudden takes off into Manang and doesn't arrive home until nearly midnight. Somehow his landscape had changed.'

Rachael thought out loud. 'According to Bernadette, he drove off immediately after her mother told him about Sophie staying at Yvonne's place. But why would that spook him? There'd been a thousand opportunities at school for Yvonne to tell Sophie about herself and Adrian, or for Sophie to confide in Yvonne about her father's abuse. Why would he stress out about a sleepover?'

The couple looked at each other for inspiration. 'When Bernadette mentioned she'd overheard her mother telling her dad about the sleepover, did she say she'd heard anything else?' Bowker asked.

Rachael shook her head and shrugged her shoulders. 'Only that Belinda was really happy because during the phone call, Sophie told her how much she loved her.' Rachael stared at Bowker as it dawned on her. 'She was saying goodbye to her mother!'

Bowker slapped his hands together. 'And I bet when he heard that, Weston knew it wasn't a sleepover, he knew his daughter wasn't coming back. And for a quiet home girl like Sophie to take that action meant Yvonne was complicit, and that meant Sophie had shared her secret.'

Rachael's eyes widened as the truth unfolded in front of them. 'And if Yvonne knew, things would be impossible to control.'

Bowker nodded. 'I think Weston's assumptions were probably spot on. I think Sophie did tell Yvonne about her father and Yvonne advised her not to go home. You probably walked in on that conversation in the ladies' toilet. It would also explain why Yvonne didn't want to leave the hall and go with Skeeta, and it accounts for her non-cooperative mood at Cocamba and her wish to be taken straight back to the social.'

Rachael nodded. 'Makes sense, logic-wise.'

Bowker frowned. 'But why tell another kid rather than her mother or another teacher? Or why not come and see me?'

'Most sexual abuse victims don't speak up because they don't think they'll be believed. Her father is a respected teacher, and she wouldn't know his sordid history. Nobody around here does. Who'd believe he'd interfere with his own daughter? A week ago, I would have found it preposterous myself.'

Bowker wasn't convinced. 'So, she picks the most unreliable and maligned kid in the district to open up to? A kid with a diabolical public image whose support would garner bugger-all credibility?'

Rachael spread her arms out wide. 'She's the perfect choice, Greg. Yvonne's been through the wringer, and most probably was abused as a kid herself when she lived in the city. To her, sex is as everyday as eating and sleeping. If Sophie was to tell anybody, then Yvonne would be the one, I'm sure. For a start, Yvonne would believe her, and she's street-smart so she'd give Sophie an escape plan. And most importantly, she'd have the guts to try and stop it from happening again. With Yvonne, there'd be no stuffing around. She'd tell Adrian straight out that he'd crossed the line and she was going to the cops. Remember what she said when we drove her home to Winnambool that time? People who root their kids should get the electric chair.'

Bowker was sure they were close. 'If Weston believed she'd go to the police, then there's his motive for murder. The bastard's survived a series of schoolgirl scandals, but he's looking at major jail-time if he sexually abused his own daughter.'

They stared at each other again.

'We could be wrong you know, Rach. We're making a shit load of assumptions about thoughts and actions, without much hard evidence to back any of them up.'

Rachael stood up, leant over the desk and took Bowker's hands in her own. 'Call it women's intuition, call it what you like, Greg. But he got at Sophie, I'm certain of it. And for that alone, I want you to nail the bastard to the wall.'

Bowker stood. 'Is Weston at school today?'

'Yeah, he's there. Since we spoke to Jimmy, I can't bear to look at him. After talking to Bernadette, I'll probably vomit next time I see him.'

'I'll take a drive out to Chinky and see if I can catch Belinda on her own.'

***

The full heat of the mid-afternoon had descended upon the Mallee as Bowker parked in front of the Weston residence. The wind was freshening from the west, the veranda blinds whacking back and forward on their leather straps. A refrigerated air conditioner groaned in its battle with mother nature, a signal that Belinda was probably home.

Bowker knocked on the door and a worried Belinda invited him through to the kitchen. They chatted about the weather as Belinda filled two large tumblers with water from the fridge.

'I know why you're here, Greg,' Belinda said as they sat down opposite each other at the kitchen table. 'You've got this bee in your bonnet about Adrian's whereabouts on the night the Bryant girl was killed. Despite what the retarded kid said, Adrian didn't go to Manang that night.'

Bowker sipped his water. 'So he told you about Jimmy?'

'Of course he told me,' she said tersely. 'I wanted to know why you were out here asking questions.'

'So, what did he tell you?'

'That Jimmy Cobb said he'd seen Adrian's car near the Manang hall. But if he really did see a red car, it could have been anybody. Doug Peterson has a red car and so does Jeannie Clark. Could have been someone passing through. Besides, it was night-time. He probably made a mistake. I really can't see why you'd take any notice of what that kid says.'

The lying prick, Bowker thought. 'Well, just so we can clear it all up, you tell me Adrian's movements that night.'

'Movements? You make it sound like he's some sort of criminal,' Belinda said, becoming increasingly agitated. 'He arrived back from Melbourne sometime just before midnight. I went into Manang around eleven-thirty to pick up Sophie and when I got home, Adrian was hiding Christmas presents in the wardrobe in our bedroom. The whole family was asleep by quarter past twelve. Satisfied?'

Bowker took another sip, but his eyes stayed focussed on Belinda's face. 'The teachers said Sophie rang you twice on the night of the social. What were those calls all about?'

She put both palms on the table. 'Do I have to answer all these questions? I feel like I'm under cross-examination?'

'You don't have to answer any of my questions. But it'll help clear things up if you do.'

Belinda inhaled and rolled her eyes melodramatically. 'Okay. In the first call, Sophie said she had been invited to stay the night at Yvonne Bryant's place so there was no need for me to pick her up after the social. When she rang the second time, she told me that Yvonne had gone missing so I would need to come and get her after all.'

'Did you tell Adrian about the calls?'

Belinda looked away. 'Not sure. It was a while ago.' She looked back at Bowker. 'But in the end, I picked up Sophie as per the original plan, so I probably didn't give the phone calls a second thought.'

Bowker knew she was lying, and if he was going to crack open her protection of Adrian, he needed to sow a few seeds of suspicion. But it was a delicate exercise. At this stage he didn't want to reveal the details of Bernadette's chat with Rachael, and he needed to be cautious about how much of Jimmy's conversation he was willing to recount.

'Thanks for answering my questions, Belinda.'

'Then you're finished?' she replied with a sigh of relief.

Bowker drained his glass and set it down loudly on the table. 'To be honest with you, Belinda, I think you're covering for your husband. So, to be fair, I'll let you in on a few things you should know.' Bowker counted on his fingers. 'Number one: Jimmy Cobb didn't just see a red car, he saw Adrian putting Yvonne Bryant into a red Charger. Number two: I know that Adrian has a history of illicit relationships with pubescent schoolgirls and this has triggered his exit from previous teaching positions.'

Belinda stood up angrily. 'This is all bullshit and you know it. Why don't you let sleeping dogs lie?'

Bowker was silent for a moment, assessing the prudence of his next move. She needed to know. 'And number three: Adrian was in a sexual relationship with Yvonne Bryant.'

Belinda slumped down into her chair seemingly gutted before somehow summoning strength and sitting up straight. 'Well, be that as it may, Adrian arrived home just before midnight. So, on the night of the social, he was never in Manangatang. End of story.'

Bowker stood up. 'Thanks for the cool drink. If you think of anything else, you know where to find me. Or just give me a ring.'

As he started to leave he stopped and turned back to Belinda. 'Rachael asked Sophie if she'd dance the main part in the performance next week. To take Yvonne's place and play Cleopatra. But she's not interested apparently. Pity. She's a special talent, according to Rachael. Maybe you can convince her to give it a shot.'

'She's lost interest in dancing, unfortunately,' Belinda said sadly.

'Lost interest in most things.'

Bowker feigned ignorance. 'Any ideas, why?'

'I put it down to puberty blues. When I was that age, I was a bit the same.'

'Bernadette was having lunch with Sophie when Rachael discussed speech night. After her sister wandered off, Bernadette said that Sophie became really sad after you went to Melbourne for Bernadette's cardio tests. Poor girl thinks Sophie may be unhappy because she didn't get to do fun things in Melbourne like she did. Had to spend the whole time at home with just boring old Dad.' Bowker shook his head. 'The burden kids take on themselves, eh?'

Belinda didn't reply and Bowker could see her standing frozen in the doorway as he drove out through the front gate.

***

The final round of tennis before the Christmas break gave Bowker some welcome respite from the tensions of his inquiries. Renegades travelled to the fourth-placed Eureka's home courts, located within a patch of bush on a remote crossroad to the south-east of Manangatang. The directions to get there were simple but still caused newcomers to become hopelessly lost. Turn left off the Sea Lake Road at the Cocamba silos, right at Meridian Road and keep driving until you see two tennis courts in the scrub.

The day was hot, but with little wind. As Bowker drove Rachael further into the never-never, he dodged three enormous brown snakes, with two others not so lucky. The tennis went to form with Renegades winning the early sets, but not without a battle. Bowker slumped into his folding chair after a hard-fought 8–3 victory, swiping away the swarm of flies targeting his sweaty face. As he picked up his towel and reached for the scoresheet, a deep-throated roar echoed through the scrub. The willy-willy twisted across the courts, sending players running for cover and spiralling leaves, fragments of bark, and grains of gypsum into the air. The whirlwind passed directly over Bowker, picking up the score sheet in a haze of dry grass and sand. He watched as the sheet of paper climbed, was flung from the maelstrom and gently floated down into the bush a hundred metres away. Bowker warily picked his way through the scrub, finally locating the score sheet nestled in a pyramid of roly-polies. He started back towards the courts then paused momentarily and stared at the sheet. After recording his scores, he spoke briefly to Rachael and went to his car.

He retraced his route to the courts, but only as far back as Cocamba. The immediate area of the silo reserve had been scoured by teams of experts, so Bowker started his search further from the crime scene, accepting that he was looking for a hypothetical needle in an undefined haystack. After forty minutes, he found it. Three hundred metres from where the body was found and impaled on the flaking bark of a mallee tree, was Weston's parking ticket. Bowker smiled, but it was a bitter-sweet moment. He was systematically assembling evidence against Adrian Weston, but this same evidence would further devastate a small tight-knit community that had already been shaken by the murder and arrest of two of their own. How much worse if one of their most senior teachers had callously killed his schoolgirl lover to conceal heinous acts of depravity against his own teenage daughter? It was time to call Jack Moloney of homicide.

***

Moloney arrived by light plane on Monday morning in the company of Detective Sergeant Linda Hoskins. Bowker collected the pair from the rudimentary airstrip on Claytons Road and transported them to the Manang hotel-motel where Moloney had booked two rooms. Linda was of average height with an athletic build. She had brown eyes and a stern face framed with short curly dark hair. She was an excellent choice for this investigation. She'd previously worked in the sexual crimes area before moving to homicide and her experience would be invaluable when the time came to formally interview Sophie Weston. Bowker unloaded their luggage, leaving them to set up their digs and register their details with Rick in the pub. He knew it wouldn't be long before the whole district knew that the Homicide Squad was back in town. Theories and questions would quickly morph into facts and direct quotes via an endless chain of Chinese whispers.

CHAPTER 37

Belinda Weston was sitting in her Nissan Sunbird, parked crookedly against the curb, when Bowker returned to the station. He drove in behind her and walked to the driver's side of her vehicle. Belinda was sobbing uncontrollably as he opened her door and ushered her into his office. 'Can I get you a coffee, Belinda?'

She shook her head, still sobbing as she sat down. 'I've protected him for fifteen years for the sake of the kids, but not anymore.' She opened her handbag and removed a small diary with a picture of Michael Jackson on the cover. She slowly opened it and leafed through the pages until she found the right spot. She passed it across the desk to Bowker. He read with trepidation, his stomach twisting and his anger rising with the turning of each page. He looked up. 'Oh, Belinda, I'm so sorry.'

'I know the experts say you shouldn't read your kid's diary, but I had to be sure.'

'You did the right thing. All this has to stop.'

'I should have realised this was happening. I knew something was wrong with Soph, but she just brushed it off as nothing. I know Adrian has this thing for schoolgirls, but never in my wildest dreams did I think he'd target his own daughter.' Her sobbing intensified.

'Well, it's all finished. From now on it's about repairing the damage.'

She swallowed before she could talk. 'I just feel like collecting the girls from school, driving to mum and dad's and never coming back to this God forsaken place.'

'It's got nothing to do with the location, Belinda; this would have eventually played out wherever you lived.'

She wiped her eyes with the back of her hand. 'So, what happens now?'

'Things have moved quickly over the weekend. On Saturday, I found a parking ticket belonging to Adrian in the bush close to where Yvonne Bryant's body was discovered.' Belinda burst into tears again. Bowker breathed heavily and continued. 'That puts Adrian at the crime scene sometime after he arrived back from Melbourne. My gut tells me he was there on the night of the social, but he'll probably claim he was just having a sticky-beak in the days or weeks that followed.'

'Or buying weed off Skeeta,' she sniffled.

Bowker was caught by surprise. 'He bought marijuana from Skeeta? How long's that been going on?'

She shrugged her shoulders. 'Since we moved up here, I guess. Skeeta did a run down to Sea Lake with the drugs he got from Mildura. Adrian sometimes met him at Cocamba. Didn't want him coming to our place in Chinky.'

Bowker did the chronology. Skeeta wasn't arrested for some weeks after Yvonne's body was found, so there was certainly a window of time when Weston could claim he bought weed off Skeeta at Cocamba and thus explain how the parking ticket got there. But Bowker couldn't buy that one. If Skeeta had killed Yvonne, there was no way he would have met anyone at Cocamba after that. No, Weston was guilty, Bowker was sure. He surmised the parking ticket was probably on the Charger's dash or passenger seat when Yvonne got into the car. When she got out, or when her body was dragged out, the parking ticket came out with her.

Bowker leant forward, folding his arms on his desk. 'Last week you told me that Adrian got home from Melbourne close to midnight. That wasn't true, was it?'

Belinda shook her head, the tears welling up again. 'No. He arrived home at about nine-thirty or nine-forty-five.' She was now looking Bowker in the eye, the necessity for deceit totally evaporated.

'Did you tell him about Sophie's plan to stay at Yvonne's house?'

She nodded.

'What was his reaction?'

'He was angry. Very angry. All he said was, "the fucking little bitch".'

'Was he referring to Yvonne or Sophie?'

'I don't know.' She started to cry. 'He just jumped in his car and drove off at a million miles an hour.'

'When did he arrive home again?'

She blew her nose. 'Not before I went in to pick up Soph. But he was home when I got back. He was swearing and throwing Christmas presents into our bedroom wardrobe. I sent the kids straight to bed.'

'Did you ask him where he'd been?'

'Yes. He said he was just driving around. Said he'd had a long day, didn't want to talk and just needed a decent sleep.' She re-blew her nose.

'Did you ask him why he was so upset about Sophie going to Yvonne's?'

'He mumbled something about Yvonne being a little slut from Melbourne and there was no way the bitch was going to put ideas into the head of any daughter of his.'

'Did you get a surprise when Sophie rang you at around eleven-thirty?'

She nodded. 'Yes. I thought she'd either be going to Winnambool with Yvonne, or Adrian would refuse permission and bring her home himself.'

Bowker shrugged. 'Didn't you think it a bit strange when Adrian claimed he'd just been driving around for two hours?'

She shook her head, lips pursed. 'When you've been through what I've been through, you don't try and figure anything out. It'll do your head in. I've already had one breakdown, and I'm on half a dozen tablets a day for depression and anxiety.' She wiped her eyes with the back of her hands. 'My life's been shit since my first husband was killed in Vietnam, and I thought I'd hit rock bottom a long time ago. But when I read Soph's diary, I fell straight through into hell itself.' She was weeping audibly, her shoulders heaving with each laboured breath.

'You've been married before?' Bowker asked with surprise.

'To the only man I've ever really loved,' Belinda said between sobs. 'He didn't make it home to see Sophie born.' She began to weep uncontrollably, then choked out something that shook Bowker's equilibrium. 'I only married Adrian so Sophie would have a father,' she said.

Belinda dropped her head into her hands and sobbed loudly. Bowker moved to her side of the desk and squatted down beside her with his arm across her shoulders. 'I'm so sorry, Belinda. I'm so sorry.'

***

When the detectives arrived at the station, Bowker introduced Belinda and précised their conversation. 'Detective Moloney and I will leave you ladies to have a chat,' Bowker said. 'Linda will be the one who talks with Sophie. She has great experience in these cases and your daughter will be in the very best hands.' Belinda nodded and blew her nose into a white lace hanky – the third one Bowker had seen her use in the time they'd been talking. The two men adjourned to the kitchen.

Moloney pulled out a kitchen chair and sat down. 'The wife's obviously devastated. Missed seeing what stared her in the face.'

'Didn't want to see, perhaps. She knew she married a piece of shit with a fetish for schoolgirls, but now she's read her daughter's diary, things have plunged to new depths.'

Moloney brought his fist down heavily on the tabletop. 'Fuck, I hate it when kids are abused. And leopards don't change their spots, from what the experts tell us. All we achieve by locking up these bastards is taking them out of circulation for a few years. An old homicide colleague of mine told his grandson to let him know if anybody interfered with his kids and he'd solve the problem permanently. Maybe that's the simplest solution.'

Bowker sat down opposite. 'Not if you believe in the rule of law.'

'Yeah, I know,' Moloney said, shaking his head. 'I just get so upset when I see what adults are capable of doing to innocent kids. And being her father, or stepfather as it turns out, makes this ten-times worse.'

'And another kid is dead just so he can cover his tracks. It's a nightmare chain of events, Jack.'

'Clear cut you reckon? The abused daughter tells the victim, and Weston commits murder to shut her up.'

'That's my read on it, Jack. The idea that Sophie was staying at Yvonne's, combined with the parting words to her mother would have scared the shit out of Weston. His wife's statement puts him in Manang at the same time a witness saw Yvonne climb into his red Charger. And I'll bet a thousand dollars that Yvonne told him she was going to the police. She was rough around the edges, Jack, but she feared nobody and she called a spade a bloody spade.'

Moloney frowned. 'Your eye-witness is that intellectually disabled kid, right?'

Bowker read his face. 'Yeah, I know that could create problems in a court of law.'

Moloney nodded. 'A barrister would tear his evidence to shreds. Create a mountain of doubt, anyway.'

'That's why I'd like to corroborate his story about her getting into Weston's car. This whole case swings on proving she was in that vehicle.'

'I've got another forensic team coming from Bendigo tomorrow. I'll tell them to go over that Charger with a bloody electron microscope. I also want him fingerprinted so we can run a match for anything found on the grain shed.'

Bowker shook his head. 'The prints on the shed were unusable, Jack.'

Moloney smiled. 'Yeah, but *he* doesn't know that.'

The two men discussed the case for twenty minutes before the fate of detective Trevor Flynn was finally raised. 'Bailed on multiple counts of assault and other charges,' Moloney said. 'Also facing an internal enquiry relating to the misuse of his position as a police officer. He'll get the arse from the force and be extremely lucky to stay out of Pentridge.'

Bowker threw up his hands. 'Hallelujah! I don't want the bastard back here again.'

Detective Hoskins poked her head through the kitchen door. 'Belinda and I have finished our chat.'

'Good. We need to coordinate our moves from here on in,' Moloney said. 'Now, Greg. Other than here or the school, is there a place where we could run a quiet interview?'

'The Infant Welfare Centre is not used today. I could grab a key from the hospital.'

'Sounds good. As soon as school finishes, I'd like Mum to collect her daughters and take the eldest one to the Welfare Centre for a chat with Linda. Greg, you pick up Weston and bring him back here for questioning. At the very least he will be charged with offences against his daughter, so he won't be going home tonight.'

Bowker returned to his office and explained their strategy to Belinda. Any loyalty she once felt to her husband had totally dissipated and she just yearned for the whole nightmare to end. Her chat with Linda Hoskins revealed little she had not already told Bowker, but it helped detail Weston's sordid history at previous schools. The policewoman's chat with Sophie would be the most crucial.

CHAPTER 38

At the end of the school day, Belinda collected her daughters from the bus stop and delivered Sophie into the care of Detective Hoskins at the Infant Welfare Centre. She then returned to Chinkapook with Bernadette, the policewoman to run Sophie home at the conclusion of their discussion. Weston was detained by Bowker as he walked to his car and was taken to the police station for interview.

Weston was immediately on the offensive. 'What's wrong with you, Bowker? You call homicide detectives all the way up here because of some cock-and-bull story a retarded kid tells you to big-note himself? You've got your murderer, so why harass me?'

'You were the last person seen with the victim on the night she disappeared, Mr Weston,' Moloney said coolly.

Weston feigned an indignant chortle. 'According to the most unreliable witness in the Mallee!' he countered.

Bowker opened his desk drawer and removed a transparent plastic evidence bag with the parking ticket clearly displayed. 'Found this at Cocamba, Adrian. We'd be interested in how you think it got there.'

Weston was stunned for a moment. 'It must have blown out of my car when I was driving into work.'

Bowker laughed out loud. 'And landed at the murder scene? That's bullshit. What do you take us for? Complete idiots?'

'Okay. I'll admit I was having a sticky beak at where the girl's body was found. Two, maybe three weeks ago. Must have blown out of the car then.'

'Or maybe when you were buying dope off Skeeta Allender?' Bowker suggested.

Weston was taken aback and Bowker could sense him weighing up his options. Was it better to admit to a drug charge and so provide a plausible explanation for where the parking ticket was found, or should he continue to deny wrongdoing on all fronts? He chose the former. 'Okay. I bought a few grams of weed off Skeeta on a weekly basis, so that's when the parking ticket must have blown out of the car.'

Moloney's brow wrinkled. 'You expect us to believe that Allender would return to the murder scene just to sell drugs? Return to where the victim's decomposing body still lies a few metres away?'

Weston sniggered. 'He's not all that bright.'

'Lots of people aren't,' Moloney said unemotionally. 'Even when they think they are.'

'Why the hell would I kill Yvonne Bryant, anyway? Even if I *was* banging her, a transfer would be the likely outcome. Or at the worst I'd lose my job. Nothing worth risking a murder charge over.'

'Would you risk a murder charge to hide having sex with your own daughter?' Moloney suddenly dropped on him.

Weston went white and was speechless for a moment. 'What the fuck are you talking about?'

'I'm talking about incest, and according to the 1958 Crimes Act that carries a sentence of up to twenty-five years imprisonment,' Moloney said. 'The fact that Sophie's not your biological daughter doesn't change that.'

Weston fumbled for words. 'This is trumped-up bullshit.'

'You've been sexually abusing your daughter. We've got evidence to prove it,' Bowker said.

'Bullshit! What do you think I am?'

'That's an easy question to answer, Mr Weston,' Moloney said coldly. 'I think you are a piss-weak arsehole who is so screwed up in the head that you not only fuck schoolgirls, but you can't keep your dick away from your own kid.' Moloney leant back in his chair. 'So now that I've got that off my chest, don't plan to go home any time soon. You're going to spend the next few nights in a guest room that Greg keeps vacant for shitheads.'

Weston's bravado was waning. 'I wouldn't do that to my daughter. She's like my own flesh and blood, for God's sake.'

'You did do that, Adrian,' Bowker said. 'And when Belinda told you Sophie was staying at Yvonne's house, you shat yourself. You knew she'd probably spilled the beans to Yvonne, and you knew Yvonne would go straight to the police. I think Yvonne confirmed those plans when you bailed her up outside the social. So you killed her to save your own arse.'

Weston looked from one officer to the other. 'What would be the point of killing the Bryant girl when Sophie could go to the police if I'd done what you said I did. It makes no sense.'

'Most kids abused by a family member don't say anything about it for years. Maybe never. They just live a life in hell and withdraw into themselves, like Sophie's been doing since that first weekend you molested her. You were counting on her never putting you in.'

'Twenty-five years for Sophie and twenty-five years for Yvonne. I hope the judge makes you serve them end-to-end. If it was me, I'd give you life without parole.' Moloney then angrily poked a finger in Weston's face. 'I've never believed in capital punishment, but I'd happily pull the lever for a sicko like you.'

Weston wasn't going down without a fight. 'You can't prove I touched Sophie and you can't prove I murdered Yvonne Bryant.'

'We've already got enough to charge you with both,' Moloney replied. 'But I have a forensic team coming tomorrow who will take that Charger apart bolt by bolt.'

Weston looked out the window and said defiantly. 'Save your time. They won't find anything,'

'Get out your ink pad, Greg,' Moloney said. 'We'll get his prints and fax them to Melbourne.'

They fingerprinted Weston before Bowker led him to the cells and locked him down. When Bowker returned, Moloney was writing notes.

'Don't know what sort of fax machines you have in the city, Jack, but with this machine, a fingerprint will come out like a black smudge.'

'I know that,' Moloney replied with a smile, 'but it won't hurt if Weston believes otherwise.'

***

Detective Hoskins returned from Chinkapook after driving Sophie Weston home and apprising Belinda of their interview.

'How'd it go?' Moloney asked.

'Gut wrenching, as you'd expect. Took a while to convince her that I'd believe all she had to tell me. Once she opened up, I got the full story. Awful stuff.'

Moloney frowned. 'And you're completely satisfied she's not making things up?'

'Absolutely. Some of the stuff she described couldn't be fabricated by a kid her age, especially one who's lived a pretty sheltered life. It's all there in my notes. Intercourse, dance costume, intimidation, the lot. It's sickening stuff, Jack. I was hoping to leave all that behind when I transferred to homicide. Dead bodies are easier to deal with than living people with dead eyes.'

'Was the Children's Hospital weekend the only time he got at her?' Bowker asked sadly.

'Been a few times since. The mother took the younger sister to Swan Hill to the dentist on one occasion, and a couple of Saturday mornings she came into town for groceries and brought Bernadette with her. Sophie was desperate to go with her mother, but her father insisted he needed her help with odd jobs at home. She was very scared of him.'

'What were her recollections of the night the victim disappeared?' Moloney asked.

'Said she was depressed seeing all the other kids having a great time when all she wanted was to lay down and die. Yvonne Bryant noticed her sitting on her own in the corner and asked her straight out why she'd become so sad. Sophie decided she'd tell Yvonne because she needed to talk to someone. Said Yvonne knew all about sex and could tell her what she should do about her father. The two adjourned to the ladies' toilets where Sophie recounted the abuse. Yvonne told Sophie that it was very, very wrong. Said it was against the law for parents to have sex with their own kids, and her father deserved to get the electric chair.'

'Did Yvonne give her advice on what she should do?' Bowker asked.

'Not to go home while her father lived in the same house. She invited Sophie to stay at her place for the night and she was'—Hoskins made air quotes—'going to let Bowker know when he came back to get his car after the social, and he would have the fucker in jail by the end of the night.'

'And I bet that's what Yvonne told Weston when he turned up at the social,' Bowker said. 'We need to have another chat with the prick, I reckon.'

'Let's wait until we see what forensics turn up. I'd like to hit him with something he can't fob off as fantasy,' Moloney advised.

***

The forensic team arrived from Bendigo midmorning the next day. With gloved hands and a plastic sheet on the seat and floor, Bowker drove Weston's Charger to the police station and parked it in the carport. After two hours of meticulous inspection, the lead forensic specialist had a verdict. The car was clean, both in a practical sense and in terms of evidence that would link the vehicle to Yvonne Bryant. A disappointed Bowker volunteered to return the Charger to Chinkapook, requesting one of the forensic techs follow him in the police car. Belinda came through the back door when they pulled up in the family's backyard.

'Just returning the car,' Bowker said as he locked the driver's door and threw the keys to Belinda. 'Last thing we need is it sitting around Manang with the locals already speculating about what's going on.'

Belinda nodded towards the police vehicle. 'Who's driving your car?'

'Member of a forensic team from Bendigo. They've gone over the Charger and found nothing that ties Adrian to Yvonne.'

Belinda dragged strands of loose hair off her face and tucked them behind her ear. 'Not surprised. Adrian vacuumed it for half an hour the morning after she disappeared, then washed the interior. He's always kept it in good nick, but looking back, he went a bit overboard that morning.'

'Can we see your vacuum cleaner?'

'Won't be much help. I empty the dust bag into the wood stove when it fills up.'

Bowker raised his eyebrows. 'But you wouldn't run the stove in summer though, surely?'

'Burns all year round because it heats our water.'

'Kitchen must be unbearable this time of year.'

'Yep. But the owner reckons there's no need for an electric hot water service when the stove has done the job for eighty years. Just turn on the air con if it gets too hot, he says. That way we pay for the power and it saves him buying a proper hot water service.'

Bowker swiped away a fly. 'So you reckon anything Adrian vacuumed from his car will have been burnt.'

'Absolutely. With the amount of crap that's blown into this place, the vacuum cleaner would have been emptied three or four times since the night of the social.' She shrugged her shoulders. 'Sorry.'

'I'd like our forensic people to have a look at the vacuum cleaner anyway,' Bowker replied.

***

The forensic team placed plastic sheeting over the kitchen table in the police residence and carefully disassembled the cleaning head, the hose and the dust bag. The dust bag was turned inside out and examined under magnification yielding nothing of value. The cleaning head was taken apart and except for a few pieces of carpet fluff was clear of foreign material. While one of the team held the end of the cleaning hose, another stretched it and shone a torch through, confirming that it was clear. The team's leader smiled at Moloney. 'Hey, Jack. Do you reckon the Force's budget could stretch to a new vacuum cleaner if I mutilate this one?'

Bowker jumped in. 'I'll pay for it myself if you find something useful.'

A team member took a Stanley knife and sliced the puckered hose lengthwise before opening the cut to expose its inner surface. Starting at one end, he carefully examined the inside of the tube. About thirty centimeters from the other end he stopped, grabbed a pair of tweezers and removed a strand of human hair that had caught on a tiny staple that was embedded in one of the crinkles. Bowker and Moloney looked at each other and announced in unison, 'Purple.'

CHAPTER 39

Following the departure of the forensic team, Weston was brought from the police cell. 'Sit down, Mr Weston,' Moloney said. 'Time to tell us the truth.'

'I've told you the bloody truth,' Weston replied aggressively as he dropped into a chair.

Moloney went straight for his throat. 'We found a strand of hair in your vacuum cleaner. Our forensic people have matched it to Yvonne Bryant.'

Weston stared at the floor, his mind desperate to assemble a believable explanation. He raised his head and glared back at Moloney. 'Alright, I admit I was sexually involved with Yvonne. Used to charge me ten dollars a pop, the mercenary bitch. We'd have the odd quickie in the car if I worked late and she was in town. That would explain how the hair got there.' He leaned back in his chair hoping he'd dodged a bullet.

He hadn't. Bowker tapped an index finger on his desk. 'The strand of hair was purple, Adrian. Yvonne dyed her hair before the social,' he said coolly. 'She was in your car the night of the murder, absolutely no doubt.'

Weston shifted uncomfortably in his seat. 'Okay, I did pick her up outside the social, but she was in a shit mood so I dropped her off in Pioneer Street.'

'Where abouts in Pioneer Street?' Moloney asked.

'Up the bottom end where it meets the highway. Opposite the swimming pool.'

'Anybody see you drop her off?'

'Nobody that I noticed.'

Moloney leaned back and crossed his arms. 'That's unfortunate, Mr Weston, because we've got the victim in your car and only your word that you didn't take her out to Cocamba.'

'Well, I dropped her off in Pioneer Street and you can't prove otherwise. What happened to her after that, I can't help you with.'

Moloney flashed the briefest of glances towards Bowker. 'I think you can, Mr Weston. Overnight the lab in Melbourne matched one of your fingerprints to one that was lifted from the grain shed the day the body was found.'

Weston's eyes darted between Moloney and Bowker looking for a way out. The fact that he didn't vehemently deny the possibility of his prints being there gave the officers the answer they were looking for. Weston crossed his legs, then quickly uncrossed them again. He stared out the window without seeing anything, and after a moment finally spoke very quietly. 'I only meant to scare her, alright? I grabbed her around the throat, but when I let go, she wasn't breathing. I panicked.' He looked at the two officers, but they remained silent. 'I saw a split in the grain shed wall and I shoved her in there and pulled the sheet of iron back into place. In a few weeks, she'd be buried in wheat and the loose wall sheet would be held in place by tons of grain. I wanted to hide her where I thought she wouldn't be found until the evidence surrounding her disappearance had gone cold.'

Bowker leaned forward and shook his head. 'Don't you mean you left her where you'd seen her with Skeeta earlier that night? He'd get the blame when her body was eventually discovered. That was the real plan, wasn't it?'

Weston stood, looked up at the ceiling and clamped his hands together behind his neck. 'I just panicked, that's all. I didn't mean to kill her.' He looked back at Bowker. 'You believe me, don't you, Greg?'

Bowker stared at him, his revulsion palpable. 'No, I don't, Adrian.

You killed Yvonne in cold blood to cover up the molestation of your own daughter. And I'm sure if you hadn't been caught, a few years down the track, perhaps Bernadette may have been next on your list.'

Weston slumped down into his chair, dropped his head into his hands and began sobbing. 'I can't see why bad things always happen to me,' he mumbled.

Moloney read Weston his rights and formally charged him with the murder of Yvonne Bryant and with multiple counts of incest against his eldest daughter.

CHAPTER 40

With the news of Adrian Weston's arrest and the subsequent release of Skeeta Bryant, the town as awash with anecdotes. About how this or that resident was long convinced of Skeeta's innocence or had suspected Weston was up to no good from the moment he arrived in town. Bowker became the local hero for solving the crime the city boys had got wrong, and for being a ripper bloke into the bargain. For the good citizens of Manangatang, he was a keeper.

A day after his release, Skeeta arrived at the Manang police station and casually took a seat. 'Just come to say thank you for saving my arse, Bowker. Would have been easy to just slam the book closed and be happy you had a conviction.'

Bowker leaned back in his chair. 'That's not the way the police force works, Skeeta.'

'It's the way that Flynn arsehole worked. He gave me a thumping when he brought me in from Winnambool. Wantin' me to confess to somethin' I didn't do.'

'Flynn is not in the police force anymore, Skeeta. And there's a chance he'll end up in prison for beating up other people.'

Skeeta stood up. 'Well, that's good news all round.' He leant over the desk and shook hands with Bowker. 'I better be off – the old man's been struggling without me on the farm.' He walked to the door. 'Thanks again. For a copper, you're alright.'

Bowker grinned. 'I hope you feel that way after I tell you I'm charging you with trafficking marijuana as well as the assault of

Yvonne Bryant on the night she was killed.'

Skeeta stormed back to the desk. 'Give me a fuckin' break. I've just come out of bloody prison.'

'The law's the law, Skeeta. You'll be charged by summons.'

'Fuck off, Bowker. I come in here to do the right thing and what thanks do I get for it? Zilch!' He stormed out the door, the glass rattling as he slammed it behind him.

Bowker ticked Skeeta's name off a list in front of him. He also put a tick beside Belinda Weston's name. By evening on the day her husband was charged, Belinda and the girls had headed for her parents' house in Melbourne where they planned to stay until Belinda made sense of their lives. Detective Hoskins had already arranged counselling for Sophie in the city, so hopefully over time she could put the nightmare behind her.

After the trauma of his granddaughter's murder, Percy Bryant gradually settled back into a farming routine. Without the turbulence that Yvonne created in his blended family's life, relationships with Cath and Yabby gradually returned to pre-Yvonne norms.

With the Westons vacating the Chinkapook residence, Bowker arranged for Travis and his mother to move in there. The rent was higher, but the amenities were infinitely better. Wendy Blake was a lost cause, but without the constant worry of his father returning, Travis at least had a chance at something approaching a normal life.

Within months, the railway camp was vacated and the gangers moved west to begin work on the Mildura line. Except for Barry Lowbury, the workers had been a positive for the town, injecting badly needed funds into the local economy.

In the end, Rachael danced the part of Cleopatra at speech night, determined to give her group the experience they had worked so hard for. Bowker watched from the wings and fantasised about playing Mark Antony when they got home. Among the cheering audience, Rachael spotted a beaming Marilyn Cobb, Jimmy's mother, and a little further along, Travis Urdevic wiping tears from his eyes.

Bowker leaned back in his chair and thought about his journey over the last year and a bit. He was happy in his job and comfortable in this Mallee lifestyle. His reverie was interrupted by Rachael returning from the doctors. She hadn't been well lately and with po-face she dumped a stack of mail in front of him. 'Guess what's amongst that pile,' she said.

Bowker's shoulders slumped. 'Don't tell me.'

Rachael's face lit up as she grabbed a formally printed envelope from the pile. 'It's my *Decree Absolute*. The divorce is final!'

Bowker sprung to his feet, grabbed Rachael around the waist and spun her in a series of circles while humming the bridal waltz.

'Better be careful, Greg,' she said with a huge grin, 'pregnant women need to be treated with kid gloves.'

The smile on Bowker's face said it all.

EPILOGUE

The previous month's release of Adrian Weston on completion of his thirty-one year jail term brought back memories for Detective Inspector Bowker. Memories of the days before he joined the Homicide Squad and of his twelve years in a one-copper town in the middle of nowhere. Purgatory, Terry the chemist had described it, but Manang had given him the best years of his life. He married Rachael there, and it was where they brought three children into the world. Life was fun, the community tight and supportive, every resident a surrogate parent for their kids. The weather was always warm, but so was the hospitality. In spite of his rapid promotion through the police ranks and the kids' eventual need for tertiary education, part of Bowker wished he had put ambition on hold and stayed where life ran to a slower clock. Where bullshit flowed like a river but where real bullshit was not tolerated. He smiled to himself as he looked out the window of police headquarters in Flinders Street. What did Banjo Paterson say in that poem about the bloke trapped in his city office? *And I somehow fancy that I'd like to change with Clancy, like to take a turn at droving where the seasons come and go.*

'Are you still with us, Bowker,' asked a petite red-headed colleague in her fifties as she tapped him on the shoulder. 'Your phone was ringing, so I answered it.'

'Sorry, Louise. I was a thousand miles away.'

'So's this. Swan Hill.' She handed him the phone and walked back to her desk.

'Bowker, homicide. How's life in God's country?'

'Not too flash for one bloke,' an officer replied. 'A body has been found mutilated and decomposing between two silos at a railway siding at Cocamba, ten k south of Manangatang. Found his wallet on him. Been ID'd as an Adrian John Weston.'

***

The dusty hot wind howled across the Manangatang cemetery as a solitary figure, silhouetted against the setting sun, scraped away the built-up sand on Yvonne Bryant's grave and placed a glass bottle of tattered red flowering gum blossoms against the headstone. As the sun slipped beyond the horizon, a pair of kookaburras laughed joyously, celebrating the day's denouement.